ELK GROVE VILLAGE PUBLIC LIBRARY
3 1250 01099 1788

P9-CRL-280

THE NUMBER 7

Jessica Lidh

MeritPress | fw

Published by
Merit Press
an imprint of F+W Media, Inc.
10151 Carver Road, Suite 200
Blue Ash, OH 45242. U.S.A.
www.meritpressbooks.com

ISBN 10: 1-4405-8306-4
ISBN 13: 978-1-4405-8306-3
eISBN 10: 1-4405-8307-2
eISBN 13: 978-1-4405-8307-0

Printed in the United States of America.

10 9 8 7 6 5 4 3 2 1

Library of Congress Cataloging-in-Publication Data

Lidh, Jessica.
The number 7 / Jessica Lidh.
pages cm
ISBN 978-1-4405-8306-3 (hc) -- ISBN 1-4405-8306-4 (hc) -- ISBN 978-1-4405-8307-0 (ebook) -- ISBN 1-4405-8307-2 (ebook)
[1. Families--Fiction. 2. Secrets--Fiction. 3. Swedish Americans--Fiction.] I. Title. II. Title: Number seven.
PZ7.1.L53Nu 2014
[Fic]--dc23

2014026764

Cover design by Frank Rivera.
Cover images © Igor Stevanovic/Victor Zastolskiy/123RF.

This book is available at quantity discounts for bulk purchases.
For information, please call 1-800-289-0963.

DEDICATION

To Nonnie and Poppop, who taught me how their stories are my story.

ACKNOWLEDGMENTS

This book would never have happened if not for a handful of invaluable people in my life. Mom, Dad, and April, thank you for believing in and encouraging me from the time I first learned to pick up a pencil. Todd, thank you for convincing me I could *actually* write this story, for being my constant sounding board for ideas, and for loving me endlessly. The Nilssons (young and old) and the Wilhelmssons, thank you for showing me *your* Sweden and welcoming me into your families. My wonderful agent, Kimiko Nakamura with Dee Mura Literary, there aren't enough thank yous to fit on this page to adequately express my appreciation for all you've done with this novel. To the good people at Merit Press, thank you for wanting to share my story with the world. I hope I've made you all proud.

Det som göms i snö, kommer fram vid tö.
What is frozen in snow is revealed at thaw.

—Swedish Proverb

I.

This is what I've learned: family secrets are never buried with their dead. They can't fit in the coffins; they don't ignite in the crematoriums. They linger and drift like the smoke of an abandoned cigarette. And I've learned that the living can sense them. We can't see the secrets; we can't even articulate what it is we feel when we're close to them. But they're there. They remain long after the rigor mortis has set in. Maybe it's then that they escape. They get squeezed out of long, taut fingertips and burst into the wide open, gasping for air. And there they hang, waiting for someone like me to come and pluck them down.

Trust me.

Nothing stays hidden forever.

I didn't want to go to Pennsylvania. Dad had requested my help, had *enlisted* my help, but Greta didn't have to go. She feigned a cold the night before we left, walking around the house in her rose-colored robe, carrying a box of Kleenex. The kettle sang on the hour as she sniffled and poured herself another cup of Earl Grey tea with two cubes of sugar and some fat-free milk. Greta wanted to be British. Dad called it a phase, but I called it a con. She spelled her words with misplaced vowels: *colour, theatre, humour.* Her favorite channel was BBC, she obsessed over UK fashion, and she had pictures of Princess Diana and Duchess Kate framed in her bedroom. Dad and I drank coffee. No sugar, no cream, no fuss.

"Louisa, be sure to take some Sharpies and packing tape." Greta sniffled the next morning as she climbed back into bed. "And take some biscuits for the road." *They're cookies, not biscuits,* I glared back at her.

"You know she's not sick," I sighed heavily, leaning against the side of our blue Subaru as I watched Dad struggle to fit his duffel into the back. The engine was already running. Exhaust coughed heavy gray clouds into the damp early morning air.

"Yep."

"So why doesn't she have to come?" I fingered the green fringe on my scarf. I always loved green. Not pink. Not red. And certainly not purple. Green was the color of our front door, and so green always reminded me of home.

"Greta's about to turn eighteen. She needs to learn to make her own decisions. Do you have the thermos?" Dad pulled out my backpack and retrieved the carafe of freshly brewed coffee.

"I'm getting older, too. I'm sixteen now. Why do I have to go? I didn't even know her."

"To be honest, Lou, I don't want to go alone, okay?" Dad sucked wind between his chattering teeth. "Get your mittens and let's go." Conversation over.

The North Carolina morning seemed to be getting darker; it was unusually cool for October. A hiccup in space and time. And I knew it was going to be colder where we were headed. He zipped up his bright orange fleece—the one Mom had given him for his birthday. It was a running joke in our family and memory 32 on my list of memories: *Always gave Dad winter clothes in July.*

As we pulled out of the driveway, Dad waved goodbye to Greta, who stood haughtily in the doorway. Her tall, dark silhouette waved back as I folded my arms in defeat.

II.

At the very least, I thought, Dad saved me from another week of mindless homecoming banter. For two months, I'd endured school hallways canvased with colorful posters about dresses and dates and how "enchanted" the evening would be. There were never any posters for the girls without dates.

I stared at my face in the visor mirror and pulled it close, preferring to look at my image in enlarged, exaggerated frames. Snapshots of pieces of me. I wasn't afraid of seeing the oil, the blemishes, the freckles. It wasn't so bad. But when I scaled back, that's when my features felt out of place. In full-length mirrors I always turned to one side so I could only see my profile. There were my wide, brown eyes that sat far apart from one another, outlined in thin, black pencil. My two thick brows in need of shaping. A pink bottom lip that protruded just so. Greta said I gave the impression I was always pouting, but what did she know?

"It's weird that you're going back *now*—now that she's not even there," I said, sticking my tongue out at myself before flipping the mirror back up, not really knowing how to ask Dad what I was *really* thinking: how he was feeling. We all tended to avoid those types of questions.

"The irony is not lost on me," Dad sighed.

"Well, it's not like either she or Grandpa made that much of an effort to see *us*. And you never talked about either of them. Nothing's going to change now that she's *actually* dead." I bit a hangnail and let my words fall. I could sense the flashing red lights, the blaring alarms; I was getting perilously close to the Magnusson "Do Not Enter" zone, the place we weren't allowed to go, that place where we talked openly about the past.

"Thanks for coming, kiddo," Dad sighed, steering the conversation away from where I was trying to take it. He was so good at that; I called it his "sleight of hand communication diversion." Don't-look-up-my-sleeve kind of stuff.

He leaned over and squeezed my knee apologetically. I wanted to erase the nameless space between us, gulp it down so it wasn't outside of us anymore, but I didn't know how. I pulled my scrawny legs beneath my chin, placed my feet up on the dash, and tugged mindlessly on the rubber soles of my Converse sneakers. Greta thought I needed a new pair, but I loved the look of tattered black canvas. They'd been worn out with love. How could I trash something like that?

"Sure," I mumbled. I was used to repeating words that didn't measure true feeling. I called them "the deficients": words like "fine," "good," and "nice." *How are you feeling today, Louisa? I'm* fine, *thank you.* I was a master of the deficients.

It was a long drive and as we entered Pennsylvania's Brandywine Valley, I thought about chances. Dad always said that we had various chances in life, and it was up to us to choose the right ones to follow. To Dad, everything was a choose-your-own-adventure story. A chance to thrive or to suffer. The only chance we didn't have was the chance to start over, the chance to go back. *Being brave,* Dad used to say, *means never looking back.* But there were times I wanted to look back—times I *needed* to.

Our destination was deep in the rolling woods down a winding, isolated road. Dad pointed up the hill to a house glowing in the fading light. Someone had left the porch light on.

The house was an old colonial with dark orange pine siding, but the paint was chipping off in large flakes. Brown, toothless shutters made the face of the house look cold and stiff. The door wasn't green.

"Looks . . . *nice,*" I choked out, but even Dad could tell it was one of the deficients. I'd once studied the Merriam-Webster thesaurus, resolute in finding replacements for them. I thought I'd be able to expand my vocabulary and shed the deficients like an old skin. I thought I'd be able to drop words like *copacetic*, *salubrious*, and *pulchritudinous* into ordinary conversation. Instead, they stuck with me. I couldn't part with them, or they with me. I realized renouncing the deficients would mean forgetting all those times I had needed them—had relied on them.

And my use for them wasn't over. *Greta*. I sighed. *Why wasn't she here?*

Crinkled leaves hedged a slate walkway to a small portico. I purposely walked along the edge of the walkway, letting the leaves crunch beneath my feet. On the front step sat two squatty pumpkins. Their flesh looked soft with decomposition and I tapped one with my foot. My shoe sunk into the pulp and I recoiled in disgust, wiping the excess flesh on the grass. A small, oxidized copper plaque sat next to the front door with one word: *Hemmanet*. I ran my half-painted, half-eaten fingernails over the embossed letters.

"Swedish for 'The Homestead,'" Dad explained, as if I should have known.

Standing in front of the door, Dad took a deep breath.

"I haven't been here for twenty-three years," he said into the fading light where his words hung in the air on a hanger. He stared up at the roof, surveying what had become of his childhood home. He shook his head absentmindedly. *Being brave means never looking back*.

"Sorry." He turned the key and shoved the door open with his shoulder. Instinctively, he reached inside and flipped on an overhead light. He paused, taking it all in. I watched him, feeling as if I were on the other side of some oversized looking glass. He was on the inside, but I could only gaze in. I was separate from him. He knew this place. This house was his house; not ours, not mine. It was as if I wasn't even there.

We stepped into a small mudroom. A single lamp hung from the ceiling. The air was damp and cold and smelled of antiquity.

"C'mon, the thermostat is in the kitchen."

"Just draw me a map, Dad," I muttered, but he didn't notice. He was too absorbed jumping through time, navigating old memories.

I looked around the foyer. A wooden staircase with two thick banisters shone with years of wear. On the wall, a long wire suspended a gilded frame.

"Hey, Mom," Dad greeted the old painting. He sounded young. Like he'd missed curfew, or was late to dinner.

The portrait glanced casually down at us from a stretched canvas. My grandmother's head rested in her curled fist, and her waxy cheek pressed around the bony knuckles of her left hand. She looked dignified, leering over the foyer—guarding the house, guarding its secrets. Who was *I* to be in *her* house? I knew nothing about this woman or her life. I was a stranger and she a ghost.

I peeked into the front parlor, where brass sconces holding half-burned candles hung on outstretched walls. Lines of soot snaked their way up to a plaster ceiling. Crowded bookshelves framed a giant hearth encasing ashes from a fire long cold.

Dad led me down a dark hallway to a black-and-white tiled kitchen where water stains and brown burn rings marred butcher-block countertops. I tried to picture Grandma standing there, placing sweating glasses of iced tea or saucepots full of tomato soup on the smooth wood surface. She hadn't preserved her kitchen; she'd abused it. This was her workshop.

"I'm afraid to open it," Dad gestured toward the avocado Frigidaire in the corner.

"She's only been gone a couple days . . ." I ran my palm over a divot in the butcher block and let my bangs fall over my eyes. "How bad could it be?"

He walked over and pulled the latch. Inside, he found a last bowl's worth of whole milk, a chunk of Swiss cheese, and a jar of strong mustard. He dumped the milk down the sink, where it poured out in small, sour chunks, and then he walked to the far end of the kitchen where the thermostat was mounted on the wall. He turned the dial and the radiator close to me began to warm.

"Dad?" I wanted to tell him that maybe this trip was meant to be and that maybe this was the fresh start he and I needed. I was about to tell him everything I'd been holding back for a long time when a small voice interrupted from down the hall.

"Hello?"

A tall, pale woman with striking copper hair glided down the hall toward us. Long strides and fluid footsteps. I'd seen that type of movement before. She had to be a dancer. The woman's wide eyes grinned.

"I don't mean to intrude, but I'm afraid your phone's disconnected and no one answered the door," the woman purred to Dad. "I came by to drop off my key. I'm Rosemary. I live down the hill. I've been watching over the house."

"Of course. Sure. Nice to meet you. I'm Christian Magnusson." He stuck out his hand and the woman took it tenderly. "We just arrived a minute ago. Can I get you something to drink? I don't know what Mom has around," he glanced toward the cabinets.

"No, thanks," her voice was soothing, like slow-dripping honey. "I really didn't mean to interrupt . . ." There was an extended pause as Rosemary surveyed the room. Her eyes lingered on me—almost *through* me—and she grinned even wider. I had to look away. There was something intense about her. Her eyes? Her teeth?

"It's good to get life back into the place. Be sure to open the windows tomorrow. Release all this enclosed energy," she smiled. "Christian, it was great meeting you. I'll see you around, Louisa," Rosemary pulled on red leather gloves to acknowledge her departure.

"I'll walk you out." Dad followed her to the foyer.

I shivered, despite standing so close to the radiator. Had I told her my name?

Dad's old bedroom had been dusted recently. It looked as if Grandma had been expecting company—as if she'd made up the bed especially for me. It was creepy.

Dad put my bag down on a small vanity in the corner. None of the furniture seemed to quite fit. It was all just a mishmash of oddly sized Shaker antiques. Some Lilliputian, others colossal.

"The bathroom is across the hall. You have to turn the hot-water faucet twice as far as the cold, but it should work." He opened an oversized trunk at the foot of the bed, pulled out two crocheted blankets, one green, one blue, and set them on top of my bag. The whole operation felt like a hotel check-in. Did I need to ask about a wake-up call? Or what time breakfast would be served?

"Okay," I took a seat on the mattress, the springs squeaking even under my little weight.

"Call me if you need anything. I'll be right downstairs." Dad began to leave. "Oh, and kiddo?" He paused in the doorway. "I love you."

"I know. I love you too, Dad. Night."

"Good night." He closed the door, and I heard him descend the stairs. Then everything was still.

I skipped brushing my teeth and went straight to bed. The sooner I fell asleep, the sooner it'd be morning. The room was warm, but the bed sheets cold. I slid between them as carefully as one enters a cool pool of water. Stretching out my legs past the end of the bed, I felt like a doll in a dollhouse. I thought about Greta. *What was she doing?* No doubt sitting in bed with a cup and saucer balanced on one knee, rolling her hair in pink foam curlers. She slept in them, but I wasn't ever allowed to tell people that. With Greta, there was a lot I wasn't allowed to tell. And lately, there was a lot I didn't seem to know. Still, I wished she were here in this big house with me. I breathed heavily into my blanket and listened to the house's creaks and pangs sounding like the popping joints in an old body. An animal screeched outside, and I wondered: if I shouted out into the darkness, would it answer me back?

I woke with the sun the next morning to find Dad already awake, tossing a freshly toasted onion bagel onto a plate.

"I had to swing by the funeral parlor to sign some papers, so I stopped to pick up some breakfast on the way."

"Sounds good," I yawned. "Is everything okay with the . . . arrangements?" I hated having to ask. I loathed funerals.

Dad poured me a tall tumbler of orange juice. I gulped it down in one shot and wiped my mouth with the back of my hand.

"She didn't want a funeral, so we're doing a cremation," he remarked casually.

I wondered if he hoped I wouldn't think about it, but I did.

"Like Mom." I chewed on a piece of bagel.

"Like Mom," he sighed in agreement.

For a moment, I thought about the oak tree against the stone wall near Mom's plot. This late in the year, the cemetery would be ablaze with color. I closed my eyes, visualized Mom's headstone, and envisioned its inscription.

> Dismiss whatever insults your own soul
> And your very flesh shall be a great poem

Walt Whitman, Mom's favorite. Memory 4. I'd already decided that on my eighteenth birthday I'd get it tattooed. I just didn't know where. My wrist? My ankle? Somewhere I could see it every day. I slowly exhaled.

"So what's the game plan for today?" I fingered the cuff of my pajamas, eager to think about anything else.

"I was going to have you start with the attic, and I was going to work on packing up the kitchen."

"And I thought it couldn't get any worse," I moaned.

But Dad was undeterred by my cynicism. He poured himself more coffee from the pot on the counter. "Later, we can take a walk around the property. We own ten acres."

"I didn't realize *we* owned anything."

I watched him as he ran his hand through his salt-and-pepper hair. He was getting grayer by the day, but it looked okay. I wasn't ignorant of the fact that my dad was handsome. I remembered how single moms reapplied red lipstick at the lunch after Mom's memorial. They munched on cucumber sandwiches, drank Sweet'N Low coffee, and talked in hushed whispers, smiling hopefully at my dad. He never noticed them, but I did.

The wind blew outside the kitchen window.

"Despite everything, this is a good house," he said to himself, staring intently into his cup, but I, of course, had no idea what he was talking about. Despite *what*, Dad? "Be sure to take a jacket; I don't think there's any heat up there."

My grandmother's attic was a mausoleum. A lamp with a mosaic shade rested in a corner. An old, foot-powered sewing machine sat to one side. I casually opened the lid of a cardboard box and found it packed to the brim with red-and-gold glass Christmas ornaments. Loose gray puffs of rock wool insulation burst along the walls as if the house were a teddy bear splitting at the seams. I spelled "Louisa" in the dust atop an organ with yellowed keys and then blew it away. Walking to the far end of the attic, I shoved a circular dormer window with my shoulder and it fell open with a deep sigh. This house needed to breathe fresh air just as much as I did. It would be redundant to say everything in the attic was old. In a large rolltop desk stained with inkblots I found stamps from 1957 and a disintegrating typewriter ribbon. Tucked in one of the letter slots was an unstamped postcard.

The picture on the front was an old photo of the Liberty Bell in Philadelphia. I could vaguely make out the handwriting.

> Tänker på dig som alltid. Kan du förlåta mig? Du måste glömma mig.
> —G

The postcard had never been mailed. I snapped a photo of the script with my cell phone, pocketed the card, and tried to open one of the desk drawers, but it stuck. I shook the drawer, struggling to get it to open, but the harder I tugged, the less it seemed to give. I carefully sat on the dusty floor and propped one foot beside the edge of the drawer. I wrapped both hands around the metal ring and pulled violently. The drawer slid out easily, as if it hadn't been stuck at all. A black, vintage telephone tumbled to the ground with a loud thud. It was a beautiful antique with a gold cradle and a white rotary. The frayed cord hung limply to the side. *Too bad it's missing a plug*, I thought, placing it on top of the desk. *It would have been cool to use.*

Dad started playing a new record downstairs; I could faintly make out "La Vie en Rose." Mom used to sing it to us. She was fluent in English and French because she'd grown up in Montreal. Memory 11. She'd trained at L'École supérieure de ballet du Québec. Memory 115. She was a beautiful dancer. Memory 13. When she died, my mother's parents flew in from Canada and told my dad my mother's death was his fault and that *he*—not the cancer—had taken her away from them. They cried when they said goodbye to Greta and me. Dad never talked to them again after that. And I never asked about them, although there were times I had wanted to. We weren't allowed to look back.

I hummed along to the familiar tune remembering the way Mom's tongue used to roll over her Ls and how she'd swallow her Rs. God, I missed that.

I looked around at the memories of people I never knew. I wanted to map out my grandparents' lives; I wanted to catalog these items, to discover my grandparents in every artifact. But it was too late now. Their voices—their stories—were lost forever. Before leaving the attic, I took a seat at the old, wood desk to study the old telephone once more. I inspected its base, searching for a label or logo, and found the name "Ericsson" embossed on the bottom. Twisting my finger through its rotary, I listened to it *tick, tick, tick* its way back into position. In vain, I picked up the receiver and held it to my ear. No dial tone. No ringing. But there was something else, some familiar sound that I couldn't quite make out. The low hush of white noise?

I held the phone closer to my ear, cocked my head to one side, and closed my eyes to focus on the sound. What was it? A buzzing? A hum? No. It was the familiar shallowness. The steady beat. The inhale. The exhale. Someone was breathing into the other end of the phone. I launched myself from the desk in disbelief and the wheels under my chair screamed. There was no mistaking what I'd heard. I dropped and watched the black receiver swing lifelessly in the air like a heavy body from a wire noose. I steadied my shaking hand and gently replaced the telephone onto its base before darting across the room to slam the window shut. It was time to leave.

I sealed the mystery into a wooden catacomb, and tried to convince myself there was some other way to rationalize it. *Certainly,* I thought frantically, *there must be a plethora of explanations for what happened.* Still, I felt safer leaving the phone locked away like the mad woman in the attic.

I didn't tell Dad what I'd heard. I didn't really know how to explain it to him. I didn't know how to explain it to *myself.* Better to just pretend it never happened, right?

IV.

In an attempt to get some fresh air, Dad took me on a short drive outside the neighborhood. He pointed to homes with well-manicured lawns while relaying simple, one-sentence stories about people he used to know, friends who used to inhabit the old haunts. I just wanted to find dinner.

We finally pulled into Weaver's, the local grocery store, a simple mom-and-pop establishment. Their clientele was pure granola; they asked for local produce and fresh cuts of meat. They demanded organic, fair-trade, and farm-to-table. I was smitten.

Dad veered for the butcher counter. I went for the veggies.

The yams were ugly and lumpy. I turned one over in my hand, inspecting its knots and divots.

"Nice tubers, huh?"

A boy about my age stepped close to me and winked. He carried a watering can in his left hand, and picked up a butternut squash from a pile of autumn vegetables with his right. He smiled broadly at me. He was tall and slender with a round face. Handsome, with short cropped brown hair, long, curled eyelashes, and freckles. He wore a green apron with "Gabe" embroidered in white thread. He tossed the squash in the air before replacing it back in the pile, making his way to a display of hay bales and pumpkins. Blooming mums sprouted from recycled aluminum coffee cans marked $7.50 each. I followed him.

"These are great!" He picked up a coffee can and handed it to me. "Mums bloom while everything else around them dies. They're hardy survivors."

I gave him a wary glance.

"Seriously," the boy continued earnestly. "Take this one for free. Put it out on your front porch and come back next week to tell me it's thriving out there!"

He pointed to the front of the store, his eyes focusing on something behind me. I turned around to see what had caught his attention. Through the store's front window, I watched as snowflakes began to fall in large, wet clumps.

"First snow of the year," the boy smiled. "See you in a week." He winked again, grabbed his watering can, and walked away, leaving me with my arm around a can of amber mums and my heart fluttering.

The drive back to the house was dark. Snowflakes fell onto the windshield with persistence. I breathed heavily into the scarf around my neck.

"I've been thinking, kiddo," Dad began. "This house—" he sighed. "It's a good house. This town is a good town."

Since when?

I looked happily down at the mums in my lap. There was something intriguing about the boy in the store. His strange knowledge of flowers? The confidence I'd be back? His imperfect freckles?

"Louisa?" Dad repeated, interrupting my thoughts. His eyes focused on the road ahead. "Turn on the defroster for me, can ya?"

"Sorry," I fumbled to turn the dial before the heat began to hum in vibrations off the dash.

"What do you think about moving here?" The words came rushing out with such speed I barely understood them. When I finally grasped what he'd asked, I didn't know what to say.

Leave North Carolina? Where was this coming from? Until yesterday, Dad wanted nothing to do with this place. And what about me? I had just started my sophomore year. And what about Greta and her entire social network? I couldn't imagine her moving. She'd throw a fit.

"Greta's going to throw a fit," I answered without really answering.

He looked down at me, and I could see he'd already made up his mind. I wasn't being asked if I thought it was a good idea. Of course not. I was being asked to support him.

"You let me worry about Greta," he uttered. And that was that.

Dad was on the phone with Greta in the other room to let her know his plans as I sat by the fireplace watching the flames dance a shadow-puppet cabaret. I heard him quietly reassure her that moving during senior year wasn't the end of the world. He whispered as if he knew I was listening; he whispered as if I was judging the strength of his argument.

"Greta—the mortgage is already paid for up here. Greta, I—"

I silently wondered if she'd recoil more into the shell she'd recently created for herself. The truth is, we'd all become hermit crabs. Our shells were made of the same substance: vivid memories of Mom, lost memories of Mom, fleeting memories of Mom. We shed our shells just enough in the mornings, sloughing them off and hiding them under the covers of our beds or in between the tiles and the grout in the shower, but when we returned in the evenings, we'd find them—and desperately retreat back into them. My shell was thin. I had my list of tangible, numerical, itemized memories I'd never lose—but Greta's armor seemed thick. She'd crawl into it at night, into the darkness. None of her friends knew. Sometimes I wondered if even Dad saw how she seemed to disappear after dinner. It was one more thing neither of us acknowledged.

Dad entered the living room, his hands behind his head. He looked distressed and came to sit next to me.

"Your sister—"

"I know."

The fire cracked loudly and sent embers floating up the chimney.

"She just seems so . . ." We sat quietly for a while. "What about you, Lou? How are things with you? Things aren't so bad, are they? We're making it okay, aren't we?" He scrubbed a hand down his face, pulling his mouth into a frown. Was he really asking me this time? Did he really want to know what I thought? Or was I just supposed to agree this time, too?

"Dad, it's just as you always said it would be. No going back. One new page. One new chance." I looked up at him encouragingly; it was as close to the truth as I could get. I couldn't tell him how I really felt. He didn't really want to know.

"Everything's going to be okay. I just wish your mom were here."

I pulled out my list of memories—six yellow pages of legal paper stapled together. Staring at the worn paper, he paused. "You started that list the day after Mom died . . . "

"And I haven't been able to add to it for five years. I have 522 memories documented. I can't remember any more."

"You will. She's not gone. Not yet. Memories have a funny way of popping up unexpectedly," he gestured toward the papers.

I rested my head on Dad's shoulder, blinking sleepily, and folded my remembrances back into my pocket.

That night I dreamed of Mom. She was with us in Grandma's house, standing at the kitchen sink and looking out the window. She had her back to me but I recognized her posture, the way she stood with her feet together, pointed out. A ballerina's stance. She was standing tall and healthy. As I approached her from behind, I fumbled in my pockets to find my list of memories. I wanted to show her. I wanted her to know I hadn't forgotten anything. But my pockets were very deep—unbelievably deep—so endless that I couldn't reach the bottom. I couldn't reach my list. I started to panic. I couldn't let her think I'd lost them—the most important pages I'd ever owned . . .

"I know memory 523, Lou," Mom said to me, still facing away.

Suddenly, there it was—my list, six pages, unfolded in my hands on its normal yellow legal notepaper. I leafed through them following the sequential numbers . . . 127 . . . 345 . . . 461 . . . 522. And that's where the list ended. I'd only written 522 memories. I couldn't remember any more. Frustrated, my eyes filled with tears. What was memory 523? What had I forgotten?

That's when the ringing began.

It started as a low hum, but it gradually grew louder and increasingly shrill. It wasn't like a telephone's usual smooth electrical tone; these rings were sharp, like a bell. Like a steel alarm bell. One long vibration followed closely by a short one. I jerked awake, my dream dissolving like sugar into water.

I sat up in bed straining to hear. The rest of the house was dark and still. I glanced at the clock on my bedside table—3:13 A.M. I crept to the hall and followed the noise to the base of the attic steps. Whatever the sound was, it compelled me to move forward. Slowly, I climbed the old staircase one step at a time, my feet falling hard against the bare, dusty floors. An invisible force drew me reluctantly to the desk. The phone's receiver trembled in its cradle, and the attic walls seemed to shake with its electrifying ring. *Was the floor moving or was I?* Fingering the black wire, thick like licorice, I followed the cord to its full length, down to its frayed ends, and remembered with a start that the phone wasn't plugged in.

The old relic was ringing! I desperately wanted it to be Mom calling. But when I reached—quivering—out toward the phone, I hesitated. I was scared to think what Mom would say to me, what she thought of me. Was she angry we'd be leaving North Carolina? Was she sad we'd have to abandon her in that overcrowded cemetery? Would she cry? Would I?

When I answered, though, the caller on the other end wasn't my mom. It was the same hoarse breathing I'd heard before. It sounded like it was issuing from a pair of croaky lungs, their hollows filled with dust and cobwebs. There was a pause, a clearing of the throat, and then a woman's voice began.

"Gerhard once asked me if I'd ever watched someone die," spoke a woman, breathing a long sigh. Her enunciations were old; very 1940s, like Katharine Hepburn. Long, drawn-out syllables and soft Rs, like "dahling" and "cab drivah." The voice belonged to a born New Englander with cheeky inflections.

"'I have,' he continued. 'In another life. Long ago.' When he said it, I remember his eyes were like beautifully etched, dark obsidian glass. They looked so fragile that at any moment I was afraid they'd shatter into a million tiny pieces right in front of me." The woman took a deep breath, as if lamenting the memory. "That was the night he first told me he was a murderer."

Then the line went dead. No dial tone, no operator. Just *click*.

V.

Back in North Carolina, I found myself sitting quietly, trying to forget the phantom phone call. This was the second time I needed to ignore my curiosity. How long could I avoid acknowledging what was happening to me?

But I had to focus on my most immediate concern: leaving behind my home. It was eerily cold for the South, and the strong wind nearly knocked our "FOR SALE!" sign off its chain.

I was sad to leave, but I'd come to terms with it. Greta was miserable. As it happened, we were moving on her eighteenth birthday. Dad bought her a conciliatory dozen donuts and shoved an unlit candle in one before we sang her a half-hearted "Happy Birthday." She looked at us both like she wished we hadn't bothered. Now she sat in the backseat, her chin in her palm, completely shut off in an iPod world. The Smiths. *Of course,* I scoffed. *She's starring in her own John Hughes movie.* Dad ignored her. I wished I could. Since our return home, I'd watched Greta experience four of the five stages of grief. The first day, she went around the house telling Dad she wasn't leaving. No way, no how. He couldn't make her. The second and third day, Greta was awful to be around. She yelled and cried. Swore to Dad that he was ruining her life, and threatened to run away. The fourth day, she begged Dad to let her finish out her senior year. She promised straight As, saying she'd live under house arrest. On day five, Greta took a vow of silence.

The roads in the Brandywine Valley were different from those in North Carolina. They curved dangerously and sloped without warning. They had blind spots and bends and one-lane bridges. As we passed old stone houses with smoking chimneys, I tried to imagine what this area looked like long ago: a huddled group of soldiers drinking mulled wine on a front stoop. Redcoats, maybe. Women walking down the road in long skirts with muddy hems, carrying large baskets of bread or apples or laundry. My mind saw them all.

At five-thirty on Saturday night we turned onto October Hill Road. The woods, now layered with a fresh blanket of November snow, were still as mysterious as they had been only weeks before, and the house was still as alluring as we'd left it. Even Greta, despite her tantrum, seemed enchanted. She stepped out of the car and stared at the house while Dad and I unloaded.

A white piece of paper jutted out of the black metal mailbox next to the door. I ran to retrieve it, smiling to myself as I skipped past a lone coffee can of radiant chrysanthemums.

"It's a letter from Rosemary inviting us to dinner tomorrow night," I read aloud as my eyes scanned the page.

Dad set Greta's bag down at her feet.

"Do we have to go?" I asked apprehensively.

"Why wouldn't we go?"

"I don't know. She's . . . strange."

"Well, she's the closest thing you have to a home-cooked meal. Tonight, we're ordering in," Dad shouldered past me to open the door, and Greta and I exchanged knowing glances. *Since when did Dad ever cook?*

"Happy birthday to me," Greta muttered under her breath.

Once inside, I ushered Greta through the house, pointing out the bathrooms and kitchen. She gave little feedback except for a couple grunted acknowledgments. In a way, this house was already more mine than hers.

I showed her my room and tried to be encouraging, but my sister refused to share my excitement. She glanced around the space with distaste.

"Come on, Greta. I'll show you your room," Dad mumbled, leading the way.

Her bedroom was noticeably larger than mine, and Greta seemed silently pleased. She had a small writing desk and a window seat on the back wall. She walked to the window and pulled back the heavy velour curtains. The moving van was pulling into our driveway and it was already dark outside.

"So what's there to do around here?"

At long last, Greta offered a small smile. It wasn't much, but it was enough. Dad crossed the room and put his arms around her, relieved to be free of the guilt she'd put upon him. I stayed in the doorway. Had Greta finally reached stage five? Acceptance? Dad seemed eager to believe she had, but I wasn't convinced.

Dad and Greta retreated downstairs to help the movers, but I held back. Tiptoeing down the hall, I opened the door to the attic stairs and glanced up into the dark shadows. Within seconds, I found myself standing in front of the telephone. I didn't even remember climbing the stairs. Staring down at the small antique phone, I held the receiver to my ear. It was dead.

What was happening to me?

On Sunday night, the three of us followed the instructions on Rosemary's note to "venture down the hill to the red cottage." Traveling the road by flashlight in four inches of snowy slush was an escapade. Dad and Greta both slipped, but I was the only one who fell. About half a mile down the hill lay a quaint stone wall. It lined the road and looked so natural to the landscape it was as if God fully intended this road and this wall to run parallel to each other forever. At the end of the wall perched a lit lantern. The candle flickered in the night. A squat, little red cabin with white trim and a wood-shingled roof greeted us warmly.

Dad patted down his leather jacket in embarrassment. "We probably should have brought flowers or something . . ."

"Like what? We've been unpacking all day," Greta replied unforgivingly as we reached the wooden door. She lifted the heavy brass doorknocker, and we stomped the snow off our shoes.

Wiping her hands on her apron, our hostess beckoned us inside and took our coats. "Nice to see you again, Christian." She shook his hand. "Hi, Louisa."

Her smile was flawless. She stood tall and casually in flat leather moccasins, khaki pants, and a red wool sweater with a Peter Pan collar. For a middle-aged woman, I had to admit she was quite attractive.

"Rosemary, this is my older daughter, Greta."

"Pleasure to meet you, Greta. I hope all of you like pork chops and cinnamon apples?" Rosemary raised her eyebrows hopefully, and Dad nodded on behalf of the three of us.

"To new neighbors," our hostess motioned for us to take our seats at her dining room table around heaping platters of steaming food.

I glanced around at the rustic furnishings. The dark, unpolished support beams that ran along the walls exposed the old architecture of the house. One half of the open-concept room looked like a newer addition to the former structure. This house—or at least half of it—had to be as old as ours. Against the far wall stood a stone chimney that stretched to the ceiling. A stout wood-burning stove jutted out from the hearth and heated the room. A cast-iron steamer sat atop the smooth, black surface and I watched a thin line of white steam escape into the air.

It had been a long time since my family shared a meal like this one. I glanced at Greta, who looked like she was thinking the same thing. We hadn't had a meal like this one since Mom was alive.

I couldn't figure out Rosemary's angle. What did she want in having us over for dinner? There had to be more to her than the friendly neighborhood welcoming committee. I didn't trust her.

"So, Rosemary, what is it you do?" Dad asked, handing me a bowl of garlic mashed potatoes.

"I'm a dental hygienist," she smiled.

I should have known. Those teeth.

"And I do a bit of astrology on the side."

"What, like horoscopes and stuff?" Greta asked skeptically.

Rosemary pursed her lips and shrugged. "More like charting planets and interpreting their movements."

"Huh?"

"Oh, you know, a little bit of this, a little bit of that. It's nothing, really. Just a hobby." Rosemary wasn't offering too many details.

"So can you, like, tell my fortune?" Greta's question sounded like a challenge. She locked eyes with Rosemary, and I admired her tenacity to hold the wide-eyed woman's gaze. I still had difficulty looking straight at her.

"Well, I'm not really a fortune teller, per se," Rosemary corrected.

"I was born November first."

"Okay," Rosemary said, resigned, and I wondered if she was about to make up a terrific lie. "You're a Scorpio with a very strong will. You're independent. You set goals for yourself and then you strive to achieve them. You can be moody, sensitive, and compassionate. Should I keep going?"

"You left out dramatic," Dad chimed in.

"Happy belated birthday, by the way." Rosemary winked at Greta and began buttering her bread before changing the subject. "You know, I moved in here eight years ago. I got to know your parents pretty well. They were truly lovely people. I was so sad to hear about Eloise's passing."

"Thank you. It was nice to hear she had neighbors like you looking after her toward the end." Dad gave an appreciative glance across the table. They were the only two people at the table who ever knew my grandparents.

"These pork chops are delish," I said while forking another bite into my mouth. "Thanks again for having us over." I didn't mean to sound cynical, but I did.

I studied the artwork on Rosemary's walls. No photographs, I noted. It was as if her family had never existed, as if she'd sprouted from the earth as routinely as a daffodil or spring tulip. There must have been fifteen or so framed paintings of various sizes and subjects hanging in organized chaos. Mostly still lifes in oils and acrylics. But there was one painting that I took a particular interest in. It was unassuming and hung in a dark corner, far from the dining table. I only saw it as we got up to leave, and I walked closer to get a better look. An oil portrait of the back of a girl's head. Her hair was dark gold, the color of straw at harvest, and she was surrounded by darkness. On top of her head sat a crown of wildflowers—daisies, mostly, and some blue cornflowers. *An odd portrait*, I thought, *why gaze at the back of someone*?

"Do you like it?" Rosemary asked, gliding over next to me.

"It's strange." But I couldn't take my eyes off of it.

"Your grandmother gave it to me. Apparently, your grandfather painted it and wanted me to have it," Rosemary informed me.

"Mom gave it to you?" Dad came closer to inspect the painting himself.

Greta stayed by the door, a silent plea for us to leave.

"She said it reminded him of his sister." Rosemary folded her arms and smiled encouragingly at the two of us.

"I didn't know Dad had a sister." Dad leaned in close, squinting at the canvas, as if waiting for the girl to turn around. What *was* she looking at?

"And a brother, apparently. Though your mom requested that I never ask him about them," Rosemary gently rubbed her right earlobe. "I've always wondered what it is she sees," she sighed looking deeply into the painting. "Isn't it strange it spoke to you, too, Louisa? Of all the paintings up here, you picked that one."

"Lou's always been one for the macabre," Dad smiled, turning around to tousle my hair. I moved away from his beneath his hand.

"Oh, would you call it macabre? I've always found it rather peaceful," Rosemary said with reassurance. "Louisa, what do you think?"

I didn't know how to answer. There was something dreadful there. Yes, I agreed with Dad. But what was it?

"Dad, it's getting late—" Greta called over to us, literally tapping her foot.

Rosemary grinned as if waiting for me to answer, but I couldn't. Or, I wouldn't. I shrugged my shoulders and went to join Greta at the door. Dad and Greta were already outside while I still struggled with a mitten. I turned around to tell Rosemary good night, but I stopped when I saw her face had turned dark and serious. Her eyes narrowed and looked desperate as they focused on me. I was suddenly frightened of her.

"Louisa," she spoke in a voice so low only I could hear her. "You're a Pisces—I could spot you from a mile away. There's something about you coming here. Something about that house." She pointed a long finger up the hill. "I don't know what it is. All I can tell you is that you need to be patient. You're going to need to do something; I don't know what. But it's important you're here. You need to be patient and you need to *listen*." She paused, and I didn't know whether I should run or ask her more. Before I had the chance to do either, her gaze softened and a friendlier expression returned. "Let me know if you need anything, okay? I really adored your grandmother. She'd want me to look after you."

I mumbled "G'night" and ran into the darkness to catch up with the rest of my party, wondering what, exactly, she knew that I didn't.

VI.

In the dim light of the dark evening, Grandma's portrait looked longer than before. I stared up at her through the doorframe as we took off our jackets in the mudroom. We were intruding in her space.

"What was that about, Dad? About me being macabre?" I questioned, offended, still staring up at Grandma's countenance. Her eyes leered down at me with condemnation.

"Oh, I don't know," he sounded a bit apologetic. "Maybe that was the wrong word. What I meant was perceptive."

"But you said 'macabre,'" I challenged.

"A slip of the tongue," he explained.

"From the English professor?" I scowled.

Greta walked straight through the foyer. Had she ever noticed the painting before? How could she miss it? The portrait of the mistress of the house? The eyes that seemed to follow my every move?

"That wasn't there when I was growing up," Dad gestured, following my gaze. "But it doesn't surprise me she had one commissioned. She was always a bit traditional in that way. And proud."

"Was that why you stopped talking? Her pride?" I turned and faced him head on wanting so badly for him to tell me the story. "Or yours?"

"Maybe," he murmured retreating into the parlor. He wasn't ready.

Greta and I hadn't expected Dad to make us start school so soon, much less on the Monday before Thanksgiving. Dad reassured us that this school year would be the beginning of something great. He tried to convince us that this was a better school than our old one, but Greta just gnawed hopelessly on her toast smothered in brown beans, an English staple in her otherwise American diet. I stared out the window into the darkness. Even the sun was still sleeping.

Greta had her college applications in their manila envelopes, signed and sealed. She placed them carefully in our metal mailbox as we headed out the door, but there was something wrong with the way she handled them. She held the envelopes loosely with both hands, cradling them as she lifted the mailbox lid clumsily with her elbow. It was unnatural to see her fumble. Greta saw my concern but answered me only by tugging her sleeves further over her gloves. She didn't want to talk about it, and she left me on the front step to start Dad's Subaru in silence.

The air was cold. Really cold. The hairs in my nostrils froze, prickling. I wore an oversized, flowy sweater that fell off my shoulder and a new pair of boots Greta encouraged me to buy last Christmas. Truthfully, I felt ridiculous. I'd have felt more comfortable in a pair of plain jeans and Chucks, but I decided to do something totally different: listen to my sister's fashion advice. I pulled a loose-fitting knit cap over my chestnut bob and inhaled slowly, ready to start the first day of my new life. I wanted to get this first part over.

In the car, Greta looked over at me. "You look really pretty, Louisa."

Usually, I was content just knowing my hair was brushed and my clothes wrinkle-free. Rarely did I feel beautiful—or even pretty—with my boyishly long limbs and stubby little nose. But now that Greta said I looked pretty, I felt validated. Because Greta said it, I believed it.

"Welcome to Andrew Wyeth High! We're so happy for you to be here," the principal's secretary said as she handed us two folders.

I smiled as I opened the packet and leafed through the inserts: my class schedule, a map of the school, a list of contact numbers, e-mail addresses, my locker number, my lock combination, and fliers from each afterschool sports team and club. I was mostly interested in my schedule:

7:20 A.M. – 8:10 A.M. Speech Mr. Duncan, Rm. 222

8:15 A.M. – 9:05 A.M. Algebra II Ms. Nestles, Rm. 145

10:10 A.M. – 11:00 A.M. English Mrs. Proctor, Rm. 215

11:05 A.M. – 11:55 A.M. Lunch Cafeteria

12:00 P.M. – 12:50 P.M. Film Photography Mr. Franz, Studio I

12:55 P.M. – 1:45 P.M. History Mrs. Laughlin, Rm. 100

1:50 P.M. – 2:40 P.M. Earth Science Mr. Topes, Lab IV

Dad had signed me up for Film Photography. Art wasn't my best subject, but it was something I was excited to learn. I'd attempted a couple self-portraits in the past—one in smudgy charcoal and one in Crayola blue violet. The latter I had titled "Louisa in Lavender." Neither had been very good.

The secretary looked up at the clock on the wall. "Let me know if you need anything. The first bell's going to ring in fifteen minutes."

Greta and I exchanged schedules while we walked together. She had Tennis first period. I dropped her off at the gymnasium. We agreed to meet back at the front of the school at the end of the day. And then I was on my own—to venture into the vast wilderness of Wyeth High. Survival was not guaranteed. Room 222 was tucked at the end of a long hallway upstairs. Mr. Duncan greeted me at the front of the class and showed me to a seat in the back of the room.

As one of the first students in class, I had the opportunity to study my peers as they entered the room. Most girls entered in pairs or flocks. High school girls always reminded me of geese, waddling in groups and squawking as they strutted from one spot to another. None came to sit with me.

I suddenly missed the comfort of North Carolina. I missed familiar faces and names. Here, everyone knew each other. They already had their places and social circles. Even if they were geese, at least they had their gaggles.

At long last, a back-row companion came to join me. He had tan skin and long, half-hearted curly brown locks. He wore a tie-dyed shirt, frayed jeans, and a pair of leather flip-flops. *Seriously*, I thought, *flip-flops in November?*

"You new?" His voice was deep. Really deep. His backpack fell off his shoulder and to the floor.

"Yeah."

It was all I could think to say.

"I was new here last year," he said indifferently looking to the front of the class. I couldn't really tell if he was speaking to me or just thinking out loud. Every word he said was monotone. *Stoner*, I assumed dismissively. Then he turned to me and smiled.

"So where you from?" It was a nice smile. A smile, I thought, he probably didn't flash often enough. And his eyes were large and lovely beneath his big eyebrows. His skin looked sun-kissed for so late in the year.

"North Carolina."

"I backpacked the Trail through Damascus once," he leaned over to me—close enough for me to smell his cheap, musky body spray, close enough to feel a surge of unexpected intimacy—and whispered, "Got poison ivy in places I didn't know could itch." He then sat back up, grinning, as the opening bell rang.

"Chris." He extended his hand. He had dirt underneath his fingernails, but not in a grimy way. It was more of an "I spend my weekends rappelling from rocks and spelunking water caves" dirt-under-my-fingernails.

"Louisa." We shook and then turned to the front as Mr. Duncan wrote "PROPOGANDA" in large, block letters on the blackboard.

"Today we're going to watch *Triumph of the Will*, one of Adolf Hitler's most famous examples of propaganda," Mr. Duncan announced as he turned off the lights and began the film. "Think about our recent conversations about propaganda and how this film fits into that genre. We'll discuss the images and film tomorrow."

In English, I sat in the front row and met a girl named Allison. She had deep-set dimples and wore a stiff-collared blouse under a pink argyle cardigan. I didn't recognize the insignia on the sweater, but I knew Greta would.

"We're reading *1984,*" she said, handing me her copy at the beginning of class. "It's kind of weird."

"Wait 'til you get to the end." I glanced at the cover and returned the paperback. "I read it a couple years back." I didn't disclose how much the book had affected me. I didn't tell her how it was one of the most important books in my life. Dad had given me the book to keep my mind off of Mom's cancer. As if it were that easy. In the hospital waiting room, sometimes in that god-awful armchair at the foot of her bed, I read because I didn't want to watch the drip, drip, drip. As Mom nonchalantly leafed through her *People* magazine, I read.

I sped through *1984* angrily. I wanted to throw the book and shout at her. At Dad. At everyone. *This isn't a normal thing, Mom! Normal people don't have to sit here and watch their moms hooked up to that! Normal people don't have to sit here and pretend like this is fine!* That's what I wanted to shout. But I didn't. I couldn't. Instead I sat there, furious at everyone for acting like everything was okay. For me, things were not okay.

"There are occasions when a human being will stand out against pain, even to the point of death."

Orwell made me realize my mom might die. And then she did.

"Yeah," Allison jerked me back to the present. "Well, we're supposed to be almost done, and I'm only on chapter five." Allison took her pencil, twirled it around her hair and pinned it up in place. "Are you sisters with that new tall blond?"

"She's my older sister."

"She and I have Gym together. She's gorgeous!" Allison sighed. "It's too bad about her injury. She looked like she'd be a good doubles player."

"Her what?"

Allison popped her chewing gum and turned to face the teacher beginning her lesson on misplaced modifiers. By the end of class, I was surprised to find that I actually knew the difference between a misplaced and dangling modifier. Maybe grammar wasn't so bad after all.

"So what do you think of Pennsylvania?" Allison asked as we walked to lunch together.

"It's all right."

I was still getting adjusted and finding my niche, but I was adapting quickly. Greta still considered the move social torment, but I quietly wondered if even *she* was beginning to come around.

"Where do you live?"

"October Hill Road. The orange house."

"Oh man, that place is ancient. Any spooks?" Allison grinned.

I shook my head and hoped she wouldn't see my uncertainty. Allison invited me to sit with her friends. It was a godsend. I would have rather sat alone in a bathroom stall than face sitting alone at lunch. But after spending ten minutes at their table, I wondered if the bathroom stall was a better fit for me. Sure, I blended in well—my Greta-inspired outfit matched Allison's J. Crew table—but I felt like an imposter. I excused myself from the group and made my way to the lunch line. I was glad not to be sitting alone, but I wished I could find another table of girls who were more like me.

What would those girls be like? What would we do together? Picnics with our favorite books? Brontë sister tea parties? Thoreau-inspired walks through the woods? Would we live deliberately? Would we suck the marrow out of life? Or am I the only teenager who thinks of stuff like that?

As I took in the panoramic view of my new cafeteria, I saw Chris sitting at a table with other kids that looked like him: hippies, Dead Heads, nouveau-Rastafarians. Chris whispered something in the ear of an attractive girl with dyed black hair and pale skin. From the look on her face, he wasn't delivering Whitman lines. She grabbed his shoulders and fell against him, laughing. *Take note, Louisa*, I thought. *Try to avoid seductive voice and deep brown eyes.*

In Photography, I was lucky to be sitting in on the first day of a new lesson and a new assignment. I was half-listening to Mr. Franz explain the criteria of the project, staring at my 35mm camera, and wondering why Dad couldn't have signed me up for Digital Photography, when something Mr. Franz said perked my ears.

"You'll want to investigate old family photographs. Ask relatives about the context of the photos, who's in them, how the pictures came to be."

As he paced back and forth at the front of the room, all the girls in class followed him in dreamy doe-eyed stupors. He was young with a lean build, and he dressed smart. A Ramones T-shirt under a corduroy blazer. Occasionally, he'd wink at the class, making us feel like we were close, personal friends rather than students. I could see how he'd captured the fancy of some of my classmates.

"This project is about digging deep into your family history, looking at grandparents, aunts, and uncles differently." He paused, giving us time to process the assignment. "The photos need to be a timeline of the person's life. Think of it as a retroactive Facebook timeline, but I don't want anything electronic. This is *Film* Photography. We're going old school, so ideally, the oldest picture should be more than twenty years old.

"Assemble the photographs in chronological order and display them in an album. This is a photographic *essay.* I want to see art, creativity, thought. I don't want to see misspellings or Scotch tape. These essays need to look professional; we'll be showcasing them at the Wyeth Spring Art Show. And guys? Make sure you don't use any priceless family heirloom photographs. I don't want any angry phone calls from Mom, chewing me out about how you retouched Aunt Mildred with watercolor."

Someone raised her hand. Mr. Franz acknowledged it by lifting his eyebrows.

"When's it due?"

Franz rubbed his hands together. "In a month. End of December, due the week before holiday break. That's why I'm giving it to you now. Spend Thanksgiving talking to your family and searching through albums. Now, take the rest of class to start brainstorming." Mr. Franz retreated back to his desk in the front corner of the room.

Who could I showcase? I didn't have an extensive family; I didn't really know either set of grandparents. Not even those in whose house I was now living. God knows I couldn't ask Dad about them. He was a regular Fort Knox. So while other students sat constructing lofty branches on family trees, I spent the remaining ten minutes doodling sketches of the old, black telephone.

Greta had had a fantastic day. People had flocked to meet her, and she'd already received two invitations to the next football game. *So much for worrying about being a social pariah*, I thought. I listened to her relay the day's activities on the car ride back to the house, watching as she drove with the same gracelessness with which she'd handled the mail that morning. Hadn't Allison said something about an injury? What'd happened? Something was wrong, but I was too afraid to ask. She'd angrily accuse me of prying—as she had done countless times before—and then I'd feel even further isolated from her. This was the fortress Greta had built around herself. She was on one side of the moat, and I on the other. So I did what she'd trained me to do: I looked away.

That evening, after answering all of Dad's incessant questions about our day and the school—Did we learn anything new? Did the teachers seem qualified? Were there healthy lunch options?—we sat down to a salmon dinner. Dad was usually a lousy cook, when he cooked at all, but he did have one or two good signature dishes and this was one of them. He said he'd learned the recipe from his father, who would drive the hour or so to Philadelphia to buy fresh salmon from the fish market. It was one of the few stories Dad had ever told us about the man, so I had committed the details of the story to memory. Grandpa would bake the fish whole: skin on, head intact, and the body stuffed with dill and garlic butter. And then he'd fillet it tableside: delicately removing the head and tail, carefully slicing the large fish in two, and removing the bones as he made his way from top to bottom. Dad talked about the process as if it were an art form and Grandpa, the artist. Grandpa served his salmon with new potatoes and homemade crème fraîche, dyed orange with red caviar. The ritual had been passed down to my father, one of the few family traditions bestowed. It seemed that any others had worn down with time.

So salmon dinner is what Dad prepared in celebration of our new school. He'd cooked it perfectly.

"I have news," Dad began, nervously clearing his throat. "The house in North Carolina sold."

Neither Greta nor I spoke. What was there to say? There was no turning back now.

"I guess that's that," Greta finally whispered before taking a sip of water.

"Let's toast this new beginning!" Dad held up his glass encouragingly. "To Chadds Ford Community College for creating an English position for me midsemester, to Andrew Wyeth High School for making a home for you both on such short notice, and to Gerhard Magnusson's salmon dinner for being the one meal I can do justice!"

My jaw froze in place. My mouth went dry.

"What?" I choked.

Dad gave me a blank stare and blinked twice. Greta looked at me as if my entire existence made her life more difficult.

"*Gerhard* Magnusson?" I repeated, disoriented.

"My dad's name was Gerhard Gustav Magnusson. I've told you that before."

Of course. Eloise and Gerhard Magnusson. How had I missed it? For weeks, I'd thought about the call. And now I knew. It wasn't a dream—it was my grandmother. My *dead* grandmother had called me.

Dad held up his glass, but Greta only raised her eyebrows acrimoniously. She folded her arms as I sat in agony, unable to talk about my discovery. I was onto something.

"Tell us something about him," I said finally. I was tired of being in the dark, tired of the secrecy.

Dad paused and stared across the table at both Greta and me and realized he couldn't deflect. We were waiting for him to answer.

"He used to, uh, keep model trains." He scratched his brow with a bony knuckle. He looked a bit uneasy, but did he also look relieved? I couldn't tell. Maybe it was good to exorcise these stories slowly. After all, we couldn't live in this house without knowing them. Dad would have to confess sooner or later.

"He ran them all through the house. There are a couple little cutouts in the bookshelves in the parlor. You might have seen them." He gestured with his fork. "That's where he ran the tracks. Ran them through the walls, down to the cellar. Sometimes when he was working, he'd put a smooth stone or pinecone on one of the cars and send it up. Little deliveries just for me. I felt special when he did that. I kept them all, but I'm sure they're lost now."

Something Dad said reminded me of my Photography project.

"Dad, we kept all those picture albums from the attic, right?" I flaked off a piece of the pink flesh and held it to my mouth.

"I think so." He wiped his mouth with a cloth napkin. (Memory 11: she only used cloth napkins. She said they were better for the environment and "très chic.")

"I have this photography project . . . I need to find four photos of the same person from different stages in his or her life. I was thinking about using Mom, but I just wanted to look at all our old photos to be sure."

Dad smiled thoughtfully at the mention of Mom. It was a knee-jerk reaction for all of us.

"Do you think you could identify old photographs of Grandma and Grandpa?" I coyly took another dollop of crème fraîche and plopped it on my potatoes. I didn't want to give anything away by showing too much interest in the old photographs. I didn't want anyone to suspect anything abnormal, like my sudden dying interest to know more information about Grandpa.

"Mmm," Dad stalled, obviously distressed by my request. "I could try," he sighed with resignation.

At ten-thirty, I retired to my room. I hadn't yet unpacked all my stuff, so I put off the night's homework and decided it was time to truly move in. I spilled the first box's contents onto the bed: hairbrushes, barrettes, a stack of old magazines I planned to one day read, past honor roll certificates, and a few cards my grandmother had sent me when I was younger. I had kept them hidden in a shoebox in my bedroom with other mementos from childhood: ribbons from swim team, notes from teachers, and pictures of Mom. When Dad got the call Grandma had died, I pulled the cards out to reread them. There were only five. All birthday cards, but I never received them on my birthday. Always at Christmas. They were plain—nothing overly sentimental or too personal. She'd never written anything inside, just a scribbled "Grandma and Grandpa M." A $10 bill accompanied the cards twice, and once I discovered a pressed clover. I don't know why I kept the cards. It would probably bother Dad to know I had. I was unloading the second box when I heard a trembling sound above me. The sharp shrill noise sent a shock through my nervous system.

This time there was no denying the legitimacy of the ringing. Since the last call, my rational brain fought to believe that it had all been a dream; I earnestly wanted to think that I had imagined the entire endeavor. But deep down I knew that the ringing, the voice, and the message had happened.

I rose from my place at my bed and quickly stepped out into the hallway. I looked to the right where shadows pranced along the walls like waves of tall grasses. They moved erratically, a tempest of light. Greta's bedroom door was closed. *Where was everyone? Could they hear the phone too?* I walked against the shadows toward the attic stairs, but the darkness seemed to pull me back. The shadows weren't grasses at all; they'd transformed into wild brambles, and I had to fight my way through them. Inside the attic stairwell, the strain ebbed and I suddenly felt propelled forward. A gust of damp air pushed me up the stairs to where the telephone rested on the desk. I carefully placed the receiver next to my ear and waited for my grandmother's voice.

VII.

When I turned seventeen in 1950, Mother decided to ship me off to live with her sister, Aunt Joan. No young daughter of hers was going to marry an old angler like she had, oh no. So, seemingly overnight, she uprooted me from Marblehead, Massachusetts, to Philadelphia.

I remember waiting in the central station for Aunt Joanie to come fetch me. I had never seen so many people! Flocks of single girls boarding trains together; young city slickers in pressed pinstriped suits and polished two-toned Oxfords; old, tired-looking men with cigarettes dangling from bottom lips and creased newspapers folded gently under their arms. Everyone was in a hurry to get somewhere.

A young black porter whistled to me. "Hey, girl, you comin' or you goin'?"

"I'm looking for my aunt, thank you very much." I was searching for her, glancing over the heads of people walking around me.

"'Cause it looks like you lost." His smile was wide and white.

At that moment, the steam engine's whistle screamed, and I turned to watch the train slowly leave the station. When I went to answer the porter again, he was gone. His smile was my first welcome to the big city, and he was right. I was lost.

Aunt Joanie hadn't been entirely honest with Mother when she told her there were loads of young GIs looking to get married in Philadelphia and why didn't she send me down for the summer? Aunt Joan didn't mention Uncle Buck had drunk himself straight out of a job again and they needed someone to help pay the rent. So the first thing Aunt Joan did after she met me at the station was take me to Sears Roebuck and buy me a clean dress and high heel shoes on store credit. The day after, she marched me back into Sears in their dress, on their credit, and she demanded they give me a job. They did. I was soon the new face of their Estée Lauder counter right in the middle of the store. I had never worn makeup a day in my life.

Aunt Joan couldn't find work as easily as I could, but eventually she got a job working the late shift at Old Blockley, Philadelphia's General Hospital. Mainly, her job involved fetching coffee and cigarettes for the doctors, and magazines and cigarettes for the patients. Every once in a while she would complain of an acute nervous condition, and would send me in her stead. The hospital didn't seem to mind very much as long as someone showed up. I'd sometimes take samples of nail lacquer from the makeup counter to the geriatric ward and paint the old ladies' fingernails. They seemed to like me all right.

One late night, when the hospital wing was dark and silent, I found Mrs. Maudelle, an eccentric old woman with a mane of wild, white hair, pacing the halls looking for her prized mare. The doctors used to say Mrs. Maudelle was 50 percent insane, 50 percent ornery, and 100 percent Southern, but I liked her. She was from Lexington, Kentucky, and she'd walk around telling everyone about the days when she was best in show. She said when she'd crossed the Mason-Dixon Line to marry her husband her life went to hell. She was probably right.

This night, her eyes spanned the walls and floor anxiously. She asked me who I was even though we had met countless times before. I tried quietly coaxing her back into her room, promising to bring her samples of her favorite rouge the next time I saw her, but the harder I pleaded, the wilder she got. She started scratching me and pulling at her hair and her robe. Then she screamed after the doctor in the white suit at the end of the hall. I saw him turn slowly toward us, but as he approached I saw he wasn't the doctor at all. He was the custodian.

"Good evening, ladies. How can I assist you?" He approached us warmly, but his smile was sad.

"Please, doctor," said Maudelle. "I can't find my beautiful mare; the one with the gold-stitched bridle."

"Madam, you can't expect a horse to be out on a night like this. It's storming outside. Please, allow me to escort you back to your room and we will look for her in the morning when there's better light." He smiled tenderly at me, hoping I would keep up the ruse.

"Room 480," I whispered, locking eyes with him.

He held out his arm, and the old woman took it fearlessly. He gently led her back down the hall to her room. By the time she was back in bed and settled the morning shift had arrived. The young man and I found ourselves punching out together, and then standing in the cold morning rain. We trotted across the street to Gary's Diner and poured into a booth.

I fumbled with the buttons on my jacket and tried rubbing out a couple brown stains on my cuff.

"I've got blood on me," I pointed to where Mrs. Maudelle had scratched me. That old Southern gal had some fight left in her after all.

"Haven't we all?" the young man said. His tired eyes penetrated mine deeper than any others had ever before.

"Gerhard Magnusson," he introduced himself, his soft, Swedish tongue incapable of producing the hard "G." Holding out his hand, he smiled tenderly, and in that moment I fell in love for the first time in my life.

VIII.

Dad and I pulled into Weaver's parking lot Wednesday night, and I was eager to see Gabe and share the good news. Two and half weeks later, my mums were looking better than ever. Even with all that snow.

The shop was understandably busy. Customers bustled about trying free samples of fresh goat cheese and chestnuts while getting lectured on the benefits of buying farm-fresh, never frozen, hormone-free turkeys. Dad and I navigated the crowds in search of our basic Thanksgiving fare. We liked to keep things simple on Thanksgiving; at least that's what happened after Mom passed away. As we turned down the dairy aisle, my eyes caught sight of a familiar head of copper hair.

"Hey there, neighbor," Dad beamed as he walked up next to Rosemary. She lifted her eyes and gave her big, dental-hygienist smile. I envied her ability to pull off red lipstick.

"Hi Christian, Louisa," she nodded to me. I waved while peering behind her, trying to get a glimpse of the produce corner. "Doing your Thanksgiving shopping?"

"A bit late, I'm afraid. This week's gotten away from me," Dad explained.

"You and me both," she laughed.

Truth be told, I hadn't really seen my dad interact all that much with women other than my mom. Dad hated chitchat. Sure, he'd been forced to make small talk with women at school functions before, but when given the chance, he almost always sat by himself. And people pick up on that kind of thing. But with Rosemary, Dad seemed genuinely interested in talking with her. I processed all of this as I stood there smiling dumbly, my attention focused at the back of the store. I was looking for someone.

Before I knew it, Dad asked something awful. Truly awful.

"Are you spending Thanksgiving alone?"

After that, I walked around glumly gathering nearly everything on our list. I still hadn't seen Gabe. *Not that he would remember you anyway,* I told myself. And now Rosemary was coming over for Thanksgiving. Didn't she have her own family?

I grabbed a cooking magazine near the checkout while waiting for Dad and began reading an article on "Turkey Gastronomics."

As I neared the end of the article, a familiar voice casually asked, "So was I right?"

I tried to conceal my excitement behind the waxy pages.

"I mean, I wouldn't promise something and then not deliver, would I?" Gabe grinned, and I was sure he could tell I was a nervous wreck.

Would you?

"They're perfect," I smiled and could feel my cheeks grow hot. "Alive and well."

He was better looking than I remembered. He was taller, and his eyelashes seemed to curl forever. Girls would kill for lashes like his. He rolled up the sleeves on his mustard button-down shirt. "I'm just glad you liked them. Happy Thanksgiving!"

He took a roll of stickers from his green apron and peeled a big, colorful turkey from the parchment paper, sticking it on my fleece just beneath my collar. It seemed like his thumb lingered a second longer than necessary. My guts seized up inside me and I couldn't breathe. And then, putting an end to our moment, an older woman wearing a homespun sweater with cartoon Pilgrims came up and asked Gabe where the turkey basters were. *Really? A turkey baster was ruining my moment?* I wanted to say something to the woman to let her know where I thought she could put the turkey baster once she'd found it. Instead, I just smiled and walked away. Gabe might have just saved this from being a disappointing Thanksgiving after all.

It was 6:45 when I heard Dad rap at my bedroom door on Thanksgiving morning. The sun was just peeking its nose over the horizon, but the house was, for the most part, still dark.

"Dress warmly" was all the instruction I received. I could hear Greta's loud protest from across the hall.

He had coffee and tea in thermal mugs waiting for us in the kitchen. We each grabbed a piece of raisin toast and followed him out the back door.

We trailed him to the heavy cellar doors leading to the underbelly of the house. Dad and I descended the stairs while Greta waited above. The room smelled damp. A naked light bulb dangled above a workbench covered in sawdust and small scraps of metal. A few stray model train cars lay in a lifeless pileup.

Dad gestured to the table. "I guess Mom never came down here after he died."

He walked to a wall where a variety of tools hung from hooks and nails and grabbed a long bow saw, ancient by the looks of it.

"Just you wait," Dad said in response to my doubtful expression. "They don't make tools like this anymore. And Swedes," he added, lifting the saw for me to see, "use the best tools. My father brought this with him when he came over in '46 right after the war. Don't ask me how it got past customs." Dad examined it with awe, as if it were a glistening saber instead of a rusty farm tool. He then handed it to me. "Now, let's go find our Christmas tree," he said with enthusiasm.

The three of us headed deep into the woods. The snow had melted, and the leaves on the forest floor were a foot deep. I turned the saw over in my hands inspecting its wooden nails and sharp teeth and wondered about its owner. I couldn't tell Dad what I was thinking. What would I say? How would the conversation begin?

Dad, what happened between you and Grandma and Grandpa?

Hey, Dad, our new house is kind of haunted.

So, Dad, Grandma says "hi."

Yeah right. The entire situation was ludicrous. No. I couldn't tell him.

We came to a small clearing in the trees about fifty yards long and thirty yards wide. A foundation of an old stone chimney sat in one of the corners, and on the opposite side was a cluster of small, crooked headstones—mangled teeth jutting out of the earth. Many were split in half, lying in two pieces on the hard ground. Some were simple with a single initial, and others looked relatively new, having survived the elements well. The most recent date I could make out was 1802.

"Your grandpa used to bring me to this spot when I was little," Dad rested his right foot on a fallen log, "before everything got so complicated. He used to tell me I needed to learn how to listen to my own heartbeat. He said that people didn't know how to sit quietly, to breathe, and to listen. I didn't get it back then, but I think I finally understand what he was trying to say . . ."

"What is this place?" I whispered.

Greta silently read the epitaph on one of the stones. She bent down and ran her index finger over the chiseled indents.

"This one was only seven months old," she exhaled.

"Dad did some research and found out this plot of land had been the residence of the Ashe family for three generations. They'd been slaves early on, and after the Civil War they moved on to someplace else. Naturally, there were no records of their leaving. For a long time, Dad came out here to think or read or blow off steam. It was his place of solitude."

"It's kind of a morbid place to do your thinking." Greta turned toward Dad, who was sipping coffee with his free hand on his hip.

"My father identified most with working people. He admired more the man who built the house than the one who lived in it. I brought you here to show you a little more of our new place because this isn't just my land and my house anymore. You're both part of it. You're part of the story." He paused to clear his throat. "Now that I'm living here again, I'm getting sentimental. You girls deserve to know the truth." Dad grabbed Greta's hand, and I saw her wince. Dad didn't seem to notice. Or, at least, he pretended not to.

"What do you guys think about that one?" Greta's eyes lit up as she subtly pulled her hand away and pointed across the cemetery toward a squat Fraser fir. It was perfect.

The smell of turkey seeped throughout the house like thick gravy as we decorated the house for Christmas. Dad insisted on basting the bird every thirty minutes even though I told him basting dried it out. Two pumpkin pies were already baked and cooling rather pleasantly on the windowsill above the kitchen sink. They each had large cracks in their centers, which to me symbolized perfection.

"I wonder why the can of Libby's always makes *two* pumpkin pies. Seems like it's not very accommodating to the smaller, nuclear families of America," I commented, wrapping a garland around the tree.

"Thanksgiving isn't a three-person holiday for most families," Greta replied, pouring herself a glass of diet cola. No ice. That's how they drink it in England.

"The *average* American family is 3.14 people," added Dad from the corner where he crouched, untangling strands of Christmas lights.

"Three-point-one-four? A family-*pi* eating pumpkin pie? How splendid!" I exclaimed, smug with cleverness.

"Not to mention—" Dad added as he joined us near the tree. For a moment, I thought he looked like the Sundance kid, sans mustache. "—there are going to be four of us dining today. Half a pie each."

Rosemary arrived with a cast-iron teakettle in one hand—white steam rising out of its spout—and a basketful of yeast rolls in the other.

"I come a 'wassailing'!" She smiled cheerfully, holding up her kettle in greeting.

The sweet smell of mulled cider drifted to our noses. She set everything down on the bench in the mudroom and untied a green handkerchief to release her auburn hair. She'd painted her lips red, like *Kamikaze cherry*. She was lovely.

I looked to Dad. His eyes shone with a brightness I didn't recognize, and unexpected jealousy washed over me. Dad had secret looks reserved for women other than his daughters? I stared at Rosemary with a sense of panic. What was she doing here interrupting our Thanksgiving? I was finally at peace with our 3.14 family Thanksgiving; we didn't have room for one more. But before I could slam the door, before I could plead with Dad that all he needed to be happy were Greta and me, before I could gain control of these foreign feelings, Rosemary was in the house, unbuttoning her coat and hanging it up. Unaware of my alarm, Greta went to take the kettle but then looked as if she didn't think she could lift it and grabbed the breadbasket instead. Dad gave me a head tilt toward the kettle. I grudgingly fetched it, and we retreated back into the living room with our half-decorated fir sitting in the corner.

Rosemary leaned over and whispered quietly in my ear so no one else could hear, "Don't worry, Louisa. It's only turkey and green bean casserole."

It was a statement of truce, an olive branch. Rosemary wasn't here to pillage. She was here because, like us, the can of Libby's was too big. After two servings of turkey and stuffing, one very large helping of sweet potatoes, and three rounds of cards, Rosemary announced her exit. If there was one wonderful, redeeming thing about a four-person nuclear family, it was having enough hands for a game of Spades. For that, and I suppose for a number of other things—Dad's new bright eyes, for one—I was glad Rosemary had joined us. She'd kept her end of the day's bargain by not trying to steal Dad away from me.

IX.

I was sitting in the parlor gazing out the front window at my coffee can of blooming chrysanthemums and daydreaming about Gabe, the boy with long lashes, when the lights in the house went out.

"Dad! I think I blew a fuse!" Greta called down from the top of the stairs.

"Give me a sec," Dad called from where he sat grading papers at the kitchen table. "The fuse box is in the cellar."

"Only *Greta's* hair dryer would blow the whole house," I heard him mutter as he grabbed the flashlight and walked out the back door.

A draft whistled through the creases in between windowpanes. The sugar maples across the street swayed with the wind. Their boughs looked heavy, and I spied several galvanized buckets clinging to their trunks waiting patiently for sap. How long had they been there? Who'd hung them? Had it been Grandpa?

Suddenly, the room ignited with a yellow burst like a mistimed camera flash. The lights were back on. The buzz penetrated the room and was followed by a high-pitched whistle. *What was that sound?* Out of a hole in the bookshelf near the fireplace chugged a miniature locomotive. One of Grandpa's old model trains. It ran the length of the mantel before slowing to a halt. There it sat, as if waiting for me to approach it. Another whistle called me closer, but I was too afraid.

I glanced around the room wanting to share the strange occurrence with someone other than myself. The hairs on my arms stood up, and I felt someone watching me from behind, urging me on. I couldn't sit still any longer. I got up from my spot near the window and walked carefully toward the mantel.

"Louisa," Dad interrupted my step and I yelped with a start.

"Dad!" I yelled.

"Sorry. Didn't mean to scare you. Hey," he took his gaze off me and stared at the mantel, "where did *that* come from?"

I silently answered him by pointing to the hole in the shelf.

"Weird. Must have been trapped in the wall. All these years . . ." As he walked closer to inspect the small toy, a slight breeze blew through the room drawing his attention away. "Hey, when I was outside, I noticed the attic window was open. You must have left it open when you were up there." He rubbed his hands over his upper arms.

"No," I thought back to that first day in the house. "I'm sure I closed it." And I was sure. I'd been in a hurry to escape the attic after listening to the breathing in the phone. But I'd definitely walked back across the room to close the window. Anyway, I would have noticed it was open by now. I had since been back up there.

"I was just outside and saw it open. The house is freezing. Just go take a look and close it," he sighed falling onto the sofa and removing his glasses. "And clean up that stuff while you're at it," he gestured eagerly toward the train as if he couldn't stand the sight of it. One more riddle I had to figure out on my own.

I approached the attic door tentatively, the tin model train resting quietly in my palm. I climbed the stairs of my own free will, but I had a sinking feeling that I was being summoned. And Dad was right. The stairs were much colder than the rest of the house. The window had to be open, but I wasn't the one who had opened it. Before I reached the top of the stairs, the telephone jumped to life.

Gerhard and his twin brother, Lars, were different in as many ways as they were alike. In appearance, one was a carbon copy of the other. In mind and disposition, however, they were as different as could be. People said they were separate sides of the same coin, made of the same metal, but looking out at the world from opposite angles.

No sooner were Lars and Gerhard born that the family bestowed them nicknames: *Lyckliga Lasse och Gamla Gerhard. Lucky Lasse and Old Gerhard.* One twin arrived in the world smaller than the other, close to death with a weak little chest; the other twin was big, red-faced, and healthy. Eventually, Lasse's lungs developed into great, loud noisemakers, and Gerhard's eyes, even as an infant, were pensive—the eyes of an old soul. Both survived to live up to their names.

Lasse was never temperate; he either loved without abandon or got so angry the ground seemed to shake beneath him. There was no limit to how much Lasse could feel. Because of this, people didn't know what to make of him. Some shook their heads at him disapprovingly, others sought him out just to hear him laugh. And Gerhard? Well, Gerhard was happy to stand back and watch.

But one afternoon in their fifteenth year, Gerhard was mistaken for his brother.

"Come on, Lasse!" a crowd of boys chanted as they flailed their arms wildly beckoning for him to join. "We're going down to the beach!" There was something in the way the boys hollered and jumped, something in their youthful grins that made Gerhard incapable of telling them the truth. He didn't want to disappoint them, so he spent the rest of the day as Lyckliga Lasse Magnusson.

He'd never anticipated such an adventure. All afternoon he said and did things he'd never dare do as himself. But as Lasse, he was fearless. He skinny-dipped on the shore before winning an impromptu boxing match with another boy from the adjacent town; he stole a neighbor's horse for a sunset ride and took off, bareback, through golden fields of rapeseed. It was one of the greatest days of his life.

That evening, he walked home with a new sense of confidence and wonder.

Things are going to be different after today, he'd told himself. *I am going to be different.*

But as soon as he spied his house in the distance something changed. In the front yard, Lasse sat whittling a small, wooden horse.

Gerhard stood and watched his brother meticulously shave away pieces of the body and sand down the rough edges. And in that moment, everything that had happened to Gerhard that day, all of his newfound tenacity, collapsed within him.

"Hej, Gerhard!" Lasse welcomed his brother a little too boisterously.

Everything about Lasse was too much: too loud, too rambunctious. It's why people loved him. But Gerhard's world was quiet, his soul gentle. He couldn't compete with Lasse in that way.

He returned to the house just as he always had; no one in the family called attention to his swollen left hand that had delivered the day's victorious blow or noticed his sun-kissed cheeks from smiling under the high noon sun. Everything was just as it had always been. And Gerhard couldn't help but feel like he'd lost an opportunity for something wondrous.

X.

When I walked into Photography Monday afternoon, I found Gabe sitting at my table just two stools away from mine.

"Hey, Mums." He smiled warmly.

What is he doing here? I wondered, trying to keep my cool.

"Hi," I smiled, confused and elated at the same time.

We stared at each other while I tried to figure him *and* myself out. He kept grinning smugly like he knew a secret about me.

"I didn't know you were in this class," I said at last.

"I didn't know you went to this school," he leaned in closer to me.

"I started here last week," I explained.

"You have a lot to catch up on, Gabe," Mr. Franz interrupted, approaching our table with a stack of papers. "Feeling better?"

"You know how it is, Mr. Franz," Gabe smiled, shrugging.

"I know how you conveniently get the stomach flu before every Thanksgiving holiday," Franz answered sternly, but his eyes revealed a genuine fondness. "Ask Louisa if you have any questions about this." He pointed to the packet explaining the photo essay project. "Welcome back."

Throughout class, I kept feeling Gabe's gaze. I didn't want to look and check to see if I was right. I was too afraid I'd be wrong. But I could feel him. I was certain he was staring. My problem was that I liked Gabe. I liked him a lot. I liked the way he looked at me. I liked how confident he was. But I didn't like how vulnerable I felt around him. With Gabe, I risked betraying myself. With Gabe, I risked heartbreak.

"So you had the flu when I saw you last Wednesday at Weaver's?" I asked at the end of class, standing up and tossing my backpack over one shoulder. He'd looked fine to me. I flushed as I remembered the way his thumb lingered on the turkey sticker.

"It's an illness of necessity." Gabe started walking with me to the door. "Thanksgiving is our busiest time of year. My parents need me at the shop."

So that's why he was always there, and how he was able to give out free flowers. His parents owned Weaver's. I bit my lip, waiting for him to say something more, but he didn't.

"Do you have any—" I blurted clumsily, yearning for the conversation to continue, "—cookie cutters? At the shop, I mean."

"Hmm," he twisted his mouth in thought. He really was beautiful. Flawless skin, flawless eyes. "I think so. You'll just have to come by and check for sure," he smiled.

I let out a quick, nervous chuckle before Allison came up in the hall behind me and grabbed my arm to walk with her.

"I'll see you later," Gabe hollered after me, waving.

"I wouldn't say this normally, but because you're new I feel obligated," Allison leaned over and whispered. "Gabriel Weaver is off limits."

I thought about Allison's warning as I walked down October Hill Road to Rosemary's cottage after school, but I shook off her words of caution. Whatever her reason was for trying to dissuade me from getting to know Gabe didn't matter. And, anyway, I had homework I needed to focus on. I'd been assigned a new project in history class, and I needed Rosemary's expertise.

My neighbor opened her door right as I lifted my hand to knock, letting a wave of warm air greet me from inside. Not only was it warm, but her place smelled wonderful, like peppermint and vanilla.

"Hi, Lou!" Rosemary's copper-toned hair was banded together in a loose ponytail.

We sat on the couch, and I took out a spiral notebook and pen distractedly.

"What's up?" Rosemary leaned back on the couch, pulled up a knee onto the seat cushion, and rested her face on her hand with curiosity.

"I need help recreating a *Poor Richard's Almanac* based on Benjamin Franklin's." I explained. "I'm in charge of the astronomy and astrology portions. Naturally, I thought of you. Could you help?"

"Of course! But first let's talk about the differences between astrology and astronomy," Rosemary began. "The two branches are often confused. Astro*nomers* study what, where, and how the stars and planets are, whereas astro*logers* study the effects of those movements."

"Right. So I thought it would be fun to chart my group's horoscopes for the astrology portion of the project." I pulled out the piece of paper on which I'd noted every group member's birthday.

She picked up a thick book filled with columns of numbers and symbols from a stack on the coffee table, then looked over the birth dates of my peers. I purposely didn't write the names next to the dates, especially my own. I was interested to know what she'd blindly say about me. She flipped to the page for August.

"This guy—I'm assuming the gender, so correct me if I'm wrong—this guy born on August tenth is interesting."

My ears perked up as she began to describe Chris, my beguiling neighbor in History, who'd joined my group after I'd hoped he wouldn't. This was a big project, and he certainly didn't appear to be the workhorse type. "He's very sensual and passionate, and he finds people doing things for him—women, especially—because they're just naturally drawn to him. He knows this and he uses it to his advantage. He's a sly one." Rosemary eyed me and I wondered if she knew I was fond of him. I couldn't deny he was a bit of an enigma. What was he like under all that tousled hair and bronze skin? "He's incredibly creative, and his passion goes beyond romance. He's smart, and he likes to learn new things, but he doesn't know what he wants. He's a heartbreaker, that one." She stopped. "Are you going to write this down?"

"Oh, right."

Embarrassed, I picked up my notebook and began jotting down what she'd just told me. I'd been so focused on what she was saying, absorbed in her ability to read the secret meanings of birthdays, I had completely forgotten this was for school and not just for fun. A small part of me felt guilty for believing what she was telling me. Still, something supernatural had taken over my life since the move to October Hill Road. I couldn't deny—or explain—the magic behind my grandmother's phone calls. Perhaps now was as good a time as any to start keeping an open mind.

Rosemary continued describing my classmates as I recorded the data. Though my birthday was sandwiched in the middle of the dates on the paper, she'd waited to read that one last.

"So, Louisa, we come to you." Rosemary folded her hands and looked softly at me. "You share the same birthday as your mother, don't you?"

My words caught in my throat, and suddenly I couldn't speak. It was true. I'd been born on my mother's twenty-eighth birthday, March first. *How did she know?*

"You and your mom are extremely closely connected, even if you don't sometimes feel it," Rosemary said soothingly.

I could sense the tears crawling from the back of my throat up to my eyes. I fought them. Part of me didn't really want to listen to anything more Rosemary had to say, but like a listener to the siren's song, I felt bound to hear her out. She kept looking at me with tender eyes, waiting for me to give the okay for her to continue.

"Go on," I swallowed.

"You have an inner strength, Louisa. You're incredibly intuitive. In all things that you do, you search for truth and purpose. You have the capacity to *feel* life more than others do. In that way, you are lucky. The dichotomy to that, though, is you can sense others' pain and trouble when everyone else seems oblivious. There are aspects to this sensitivity you probably aren't even aware of yet. But you're smart, and you have your mother's vitality. She had this gift, too."

"My mom," I cleared my throat, "she always knew when something was upsetting me. I suppose a six-year-old can't hide her feelings too well, but even when I was trying to keep something from her, Mom would ask if there was anything I wanted to talk about. And I always felt so relieved after confiding in her. My dad is great at so many things, but there are times I wish I didn't need to spell things out for him. I know he wrestles with trying to be Dad *and* Mom, but there are times I struggle trying to be strong for everyone. I get tired of pretending. Does that make sense?" I don't know what made me confess everything to her in that moment. I wasn't even aware how long I'd been crying.

"Louisa," Rosemary smiled and placed her hand on my knee, "you're a very special girl. As soon as we met, I knew there was something different about you. You're on the cusp of something really wonderful. I, for one, can't wait to see how it all plays out."

"What do you mean?" I wiped away the tears.

"I don't quite know—only that you're supposed to be here. I don't know how else to describe it."

It felt good to talk about things I usually didn't. Greta and Dad rarely spoke of Mom. Not because it was too painful, but because we'd exhausted ourselves retelling stories and memories in the years after her death. Now, Mom was only mentioned as a side note. We all thought about her on Christmas and Thanksgiving. We grew nostalgic when we smelled lilacs—Mom's favorite flower, memory 111—but these moments didn't compel us to *mention* her anymore. The three of us had our personal remembrances when those moments arose, but we cherished them quietly.

Before I left, I wanted Rosemary to answer one last thing for me. I didn't know how to broach the subject without sounding crazy; I didn't want Rosemary to grow suspicious of me. So as I was putting my winter coat back on, as nonchalantly as I could manage, I coolly asked the thing that had been on my mind almost ever since we moved here: "Rosemary, what do you know about ghosts?"

XI.

Standing in Rosemary's front hall, my inquiry paused in the air before flying out her open door. I wanted to run after it, take it back, and stuff it back down my throat. Rosemary would for sure think I was crazy, if she didn't already. But I stayed, and Rosemary motioned for me to close the door.

"Well . . . here's the thing." I ran my hand through my hair nervously, trying to find the right words, trying to sound as elusive as possible. "I think my Grandma Eloise is trying to *contact* me . . . "

My voice trailed off and I recoiled, guarding myself against the possibility that Rosemary would call me deranged. Instead, she ushered me into her kitchen and began scooping heaping teaspoons of ground coffee into her drip coffeepot. She nodded supportively for me to continue and plugged the little machine into the wall. It gurgled loudly awake.

"Go on."

"I keep getting these *messages*," I chose the word carefully, fearing "phone calls" might sound more delirious. "It seems that she wants to tell me a story about my grandfather."

"Uh-huh."

I waited for her to explain it to me. I waited for her to tell me she already knew, that she was in on the secret. Instead, she leaned back on the kitchen counter as if she was waiting for *me* to explain it to *her*. I threw up my hands.

"Well, what does it mean? You're the psychic!"

"Louisa, it could mean many things. I can't tell you why you're receiving these messages," Rosemary replied sympathetically. I could tell she wanted to help more but couldn't. But at least it seemed as if she believed me.

"Could you maybe give me the top three possibilities?"

Rosemary smiled, but she looked powerless. She hopped up and sat on the laminate ledge, bouncing her heels on the cabinet doors.

"Well," she sighed, "do you think you're the only one in the house receiving the messages? If so, maybe you should wonder why your Grandmother Eloise picked *you*."

"I'd bet anything I'm the only one," I sighed to Rosemary, jumping up and sitting next to her. She paused and took a deep breath.

"It's like the stars," she began. "After they die—many from collapsing under their own weight—they explode, sending fragments of their fiery cosmic bodies out into space." Rosemary's eyes opened wide with excitement. When she could tell I wasn't following her, her face grew serious and she continued. "By the time we see the bright explosion, the supernova, here," she pointed toward the floor, "the star's already been dead for weeks, months, or, sometimes even millions of years. We get these shockwaves of a life that *once* existed, but doesn't exist anymore.

"So maybe that's what you're getting. These messages from Eloise are the vibrations—the echoes—of her life. You're getting a glimpse of what used to be. You're seeing her light."

"She wants someone to remember," I whispered to myself.

The realization caught me off guard. I thought about Dad and his relationship with his parents, specifically his father. There was so much I didn't know. And what about Dad? Did he even know his own father? All of Dad's history had been waiting here for him. It waited, knowing he'd one day return. But there had to be more to it. Where did I fit in?

I stared at the knobs on the stove. Dad wouldn't want me interfering with his past. He'd made that clear in just about everything he'd said, everything he'd done. Even if he did admit to getting more sentimental, he certainly wasn't waxing poetic with memory after memory. He's the one, after all, who taught me how to wrap up my feelings beneath layers of brown paper and twine. He kept his emotions buried away—boxes within boxes within boxes. Like endless Russian nesting dolls. I couldn't tell him about the phone or about Grandma. He'd freak. God, why did he make it so hard?

"And one more thing, Lou," Rosemary reached over and squeezed my hand as the coffee drips sputtered quietly to a halt. "Supernova shockwaves can often form their own, new stars. Light created by light."

If only she knew how impossible that seemed.

Later that night, Dad reluctantly cleared boxes and chests, searching for photographs. Searching for evidence of people and lives I never knew. For an hour, we'd been in the cold attic rummaging through stacks of old newspaper and photo albums filled with nothing but pictures of deserts, mountains, and open sky—the latter of which I bewilderingly held up for Dad to see. I'd kept my eye on the desk the entire time, but it stayed quiet. The phone sat dead.

"Sorry, kiddo. I know you're frustrated," he said, blowing some dust off an old picture frame. "Here's a picture of me!" He held up an eight-by-ten of a baby boy in a red wagon.

"At last! A picture of a real human being!" I made my way over to him. "Dad, you're adorable, but I wanted to find pictures of Grandma and Grandpa. How is it that you've never shown us *any*? That painting down in the foyer is the first I've ever seen of Grandma. Do you realize how weird that is?"

It was a low blow, even I'll admit it. Out of the corner of my eye, I saw Dad drop his shoulders in shame. I attempted some damage control.

"I just want to know what my grandparents looked like. That's all. Living in this house, I kind of sense them around. And I feel bad not knowing more about them—and what happened to them." I shouldn't have asked for his help. He didn't want to help. He didn't want to dig up old memories. I was infringing on Pandora's territory, I could tell.

"What do you mean what happened to them? They died."

"Forget it," I shrugged. The old reliable shrug. Just like the deficients, I could rely on the shrug to get me out of a lot of unpleasant conversations.

And then Dad did something unexpected. He shut the box, sat back against part of the scaffolding, and relaxed his shoulders.

"Okay," he whispered. He was finally ready. "Your grandfather was stoic, almost somber. It was his way. It was the Swede's way. He was a man of few words. He always tried to teach me to be like him, but I wasn't. I was loud and energetic, and I liked to express my opinion and debate. I think he saw my outspoken nature as a personal failure. He couldn't ever rein me in. He and I didn't have the relationship the three of *us* do . . . " Dad's voice trailed off. He was struggling with the story. How much to tell? Where to start? "He died after we'd grown apart. You were eight—too young for a funeral."

The irony! Three years later and I'd be sitting in a cold church staring down an urn of ashes. Staring at what was left of my mom.

"You've got some of his best qualities, I think," Dad said, shifting the conversation, looking over at me. "You're a good listener, and you think before you act, Louisa. I've always admired that about you. Look at me? I'm a spontaneous, impulsive wreck. That's why we're here and not in North Carolina, right?"

"I always thought I was like you," I whispered. How much did he know about Grandpa? Did he know he was a murderer?

"When I left for Lehigh, I saw it as an escape from my life here. Not that my life here was that bad, but I just always felt . . . contained. I never felt I was able to be a kid. Dad wanted me to grow up. He tried harnessing my energy with long walks through the forest. He'd write me letters warning me about the danger of zeal and leave them for me in my room. He'd reiterate the virtues of patience and solitude. It was as if he didn't know how to talk to me. 'The day we fear hastens toward us, the day we long for creeps,' he'd write. But he'd never tell me about those things he feared or those he longed for. It didn't seem like he had any passions; there was just always this very serious man who never smiled, never laughed. I didn't want that life. I asked Mom about it, but she'd just shrug her shoulders and tell me that one day I'd maybe understand. 'You remind him of a different life,' she'd say. But I didn't get it, and her answers were good enough for me. So after I left, I was hesitant to come back. I didn't want to get trapped back here. Maybe you'll know what I mean in a couple years. Those first couple years of freedom are irreplaceable."

"But I don't feel trapped," I protested.

"I know, and I'm glad. But at some point you're going to take off . . . see the world, spread your wings, all that Dr. Seuss stuff. Greta's about to do it. Hopefully you'll come back more often than I did. But you're both different than I was." He gazed at the boxes in front of him. I could tell this conversation was difficult for him. But he knew he needed to tell it. He knew I needed to know.

Dad took a deep breath before continuing. "One weekend I came home to visit. Dad and I took one of our walks through the woods; he was quiet, as usual, but this time, I could tell something weighed on him. He almost seemed incapable of speaking. Many times he'd inhale deeply, as if about to say something, but then he'd just let it go. Finally, he stopped walking, turned to me, and asked, 'Christian, what's the difference between the coward and the hero?' The question shocked me—it was as if this was some ideological test he'd been meaning to administer for a long time. I studied his face, searching for the answer. But there was nothing. What did he want me to say? His face was blank. It just stared back at me, and it almost felt as if his eyes were studying me, or looking at me for the first time. I don't know. I can't explain it the right way. It was as if he was surprised to see *me* standing there in front of him and not someone else."

"What did you say?" I asked, eager for Dad to continue.

"We stood in silence for minutes—five, maybe ten?—until finally I realized what I wanted to say. All of my resentment and anger I felt toward him for never accepting me for who I was and for always making me feel like I was a disappointment, all of it came boiling to the surface. And I allowed myself to tell him what I really thought."

"What did you say?" I repeated.

"I told him that he was the coward and I the hero," Dad swallowed hard, closed his eyes, and tilted his face back toward the ceiling.

"What did he do?" My impatience betrayed me. The words came rushing out, interrupting Dad's memory.

"That's the thing. He hugged me and told me I was right. He said I'd always been right, asked me to forgive him, and then he turned and walked away. One week later he had his stroke. God intervened and took away my dad forever."

"But I thought you said he died when I was eight?"

"He had his stroke when he was sixty, but it took sixteen years before he actually died. That's when you were eight. After the stroke, his body and mind buckled like a paper fan. Looking at him, you'd think he was closer to eighty. Mom said his mind was still there, but you'd never know it. He couldn't speak, couldn't walk, couldn't communicate in any way. I just thought it was her way of reassuring herself that not all of him was gone.

"It's the most selfish decision I ever made, but after the stroke I decided to leave. I was scared and young and stupid. But I was also mad. I never had the dad I thought I deserved, the dad who loved me for me. So I moved to North Carolina, married your mother in a courthouse, rented a nice little apartment, and then she got pregnant with Greta. I finished grad school, accepted a job teaching, and the rest is history.

"I finally reached out and invited them to come and visit when Greta was born, and then again when you were born, but Mom never forgave me for leaving. She accused me of abandoning Dad and said there was much I didn't understand. Needless to say, they didn't come. Eventually, I gave up trying to make amends for leaving. It was too hard. I felt too ashamed. My last phone call home was on the night your mother died, but I got the machine. And for whatever reason, I couldn't bring myself to say anything. And I vowed at that moment to stop trying to bridge my new life with my old. Because here's the thing: when given the opportunity, *I* ran. I ran away from home at twenty-one years of age. But I've often thought about what would have happened if Mom had been there to answer that last call . . ."

Dad closed his eyes and pinched the bridge of his nose. Finally, after years of mystery, years of my guessing about my grandparents, he'd revealed to me the truth. The story of how he'd originally learned to plow through, to just keep moving forward. Somewhere along the way, he'd lost the ability to know when to look back. He did that with his parents and he did that with Mom.

"That's why you never met them. It's eerie that we're now combing through this stuff looking for them." Dad sat up to get back to work. He opened a lid to a box and started digging through it. "It feels good, though. I need this."

I watched him methodically pull out small items and place them in neat little piles.

Suddenly, I didn't just feel like I was looking for my grandparents—I was chasing them.

XII.

Gerhard never forgot the exact moment he rewrote his fate. Later, after it was all over, he'd often wonder if things would have been different had he simply turned down the old man's offer. He said it all began with a girl.

Agnes Landquist needed her bicycle repaired, and no one knew bicycle mechanics better than Gerhard. He fiddled with any bike he could get his hands on. He'd disassemble and then reassemble the spokes, the forks, and the chain. He saw each part in his mind, and he watched how the pieces fit together.

One day outside his school, Gerhard and Agnes sat in silence as he worked diligently greasing her bicycle gears. Agnes studied him with awe. Occasionally, he'd ask her to hand him his wrench or his pliers, and she'd slowly lean over and delicately place the tool in his hand. Their fingers touched once or twice, and Gerhard's stomach ached with adolescent love. He wanted to kiss her, but he didn't dare. She wanted him to kiss her, too, but isn't that the way of first love?

Before long, an old man with silver hair came searching for his delayed daughter. The man stood back, quietly watching Gerhard's hands. Gerhard knew him immediately. Kjell Landquist, Agnes's father and Trelleborg's station manager.

When Gerhard had finished, the man leaned in and asked, "Can you fix anything else, son?"

"Sir?" Gerhard shielded his eyes from the sun, staring up from where he crouched next to the bicycle.

"We're down a man at the station, and I could use someone whom I don't need to explain something to twice. Come see me this afternoon."

Gerhard stood up slowly, closed the lid of the grease can, wiped his hand on an old rag, and wheeled the bicycle to the girl waiting next to her father.

"Thanks, Gerhard," she whispered as her father started walking away.

The man turned and chuckled. "Come see me this afternoon and I'll give you some bigger toys to play with."

Later that day, Kjell hired Gerhard as a train mechanic. It was Gerhard's sixteenth birthday. Gerhard had been working for Kjell exactly one month when he arrived at the station one day to find his father waiting for him. The tremendous man sat awkwardly on the small platform bench, smoking his bent pipe. Leif Magnusson was a ferryboat captain. He was used to the rock and sway of a choppy sea. The railroad, with its grounded station and defined tracks, was a world away from his own.

Gerhard took a seat next to his father and waited for him to speak. Leif was a man of few words, and Gerhard had learned to listen.

"Lasse has decided to join me on the ferry," he began. Gerhard nodded; he'd always suspected his brother would follow in their father's footsteps.

"It's good for him to start work like me."

"*Ja, javisst.* Of course." Leif paused and puffed repeatedly on his pipe. "*Lyckliga Lasse och Gamla Gerhard,*" he chuckled remembering the nicknames. Gerhard frowned at his epithet, wishing he'd been the one they called lucky. He wanted to be the one with the fighting spirit.

"It's been hard for him . . . watching you come here every day. He wants so badly to be like you," Leif coughed and crossed his arms.

Gerhard stared at his own feet, doubting his father's observation. *Had he come all the way to the station just to talk about Lasse?*

"My boys are no longer boys," the old man reached into his pocket and nonchalantly pulled out a small leather pouch.

"I'll give him something, too, don't worry. But I wanted to give this to you alone." Leif slowly produced a gold chain as long as Gerhard's forearm. At the chain's end hung a worn, but polished, pocket watch. "Your grandfather's."

It's magnificent, Gerhard thought as he reached out and accepted the gift, letting his palm feel its weight. He popped open the case and inspected its round face. A small, loopy, antiquated inscription read, *Till min son*. "To my son." Gerhard held it to his ear. Nothing.

"Here," Leif took the chain and showed him how to lift the winding crown and spin it clockwise.

Gerhard inspected the watch with scrutiny. He shut his eyes, held the device to his ear, and visualized its gears. He imagined what its insides would look like once he stripped away its exterior. What were its inner workings? How did it run? He imagined tiny wheels, tight springs, and flattened screws. He envisioned how all the pieces fit together, how one wheel turned another, which turned another. All parts performing their proper functions. Everything in synchronicity.

"You have to wind it every day. But if you do, it will never fail you," Leif advised, stroking his beard and taking a long puff on his black pipe.

Gerhard snapped the watch shut, securing the memory of the moment within the gold case forever. That's when Gerhard began measuring his life in minutes.

XIII.

Dad and I took armfuls of albums and boxes of photographs downstairs to the kitchen. He continued searching through the photos for people while I fixed us some coffee and split pea soup.

"My father used to make us pea soup on the first Thursday of every month. It's how his mother, Åsa, made it," Dad smiled as he thought back on the memory. I prodded him further trying to dig up older recollections.

"Dad, there's so much you seem to know that you've never told us. What else did Grandpa say about Sweden?"

"Oh, not much. He didn't really talk about his family. Mom told me not to ask him, so I didn't."

"And you never asked her why he didn't want to talk about it?" *What would you think about him if you knew the truth*? I silently asked. *I could tell you, Dad. I could tell you everything I know, but would you want to know?*

"I guess I didn't think about it. *You* never really asked about Grandma and Grandpa before coming here. I was like that, I suppose."

Ugh. He could be so frustrating when he was right.

We sat down to our warm, savory dinner. Greta said she wasn't hungry and stayed in her room. The wind whooshed against the windows at the back of the house, and we could hear a draft infiltrate the house somewhere along the frame of the kitchen door. I shook with a December chill.

Dad laid a meager spread of photos on the table as he sipped his soup. I watched him study the pictures carefully. Occasionally, he'd pick one up and then set it back down again. A couple times he smiled wistfully. I wanted so badly to ask him, to urge him to tell me what he was thinking, but I let him take his time. No good would come of me interrupting and rushing him. At last, he looked up at me. He seemed startled to see me, as if he'd forgotten I was sitting there.

"Here she is. This is my mom," he pointed to a photo of a woman sitting at a typewriter.

I picked up the worn photograph and studied it intently. The picture was taken from the side; she was sitting and staring at her typing. Her ankles were crossed beneath her seat. She wore a button-down blouse and a kerchief tied tightly around her neck. Her hair was curled and pinned back. She looked lovely. In the background of the picture, an old Bavarian cuckoo clock hung on the wall.

"She liked writing poetry," Dad continued. "She had elegant handwriting, but she was an amazing typist. She was beautiful, wasn't she?

"And this one," Dad picked up a square, scalloped-edged photograph and handed it to me. He swiveled his chair so we could stare at the picture side by side. "*This* is your grandpa."

The man in the photo had a furrowed brow and a long, clean-shaven face. He wore his light hair swept to the side. He had thick-rimmed glasses and a striped sweater. He was watching something intently off-camera, but he wasn't smiling.

Gerhard Gustav Magnusson. My grandfather, the murderer. At last, we meet.

I recalled all the questions I didn't have answers to, the anecdotes Grandmother relayed to me during my time in her house, and the mystery that surrounded this young man with the sad eyes.

"Good-looking guy, wasn't he?" Dad held the picture next to his own face. "Any resemblance?"

I looked fondly at the features of my grandfather and compared them to my dad's. Their chins were exactly the same square shape. Their noses were long, not short and upturned like mine. Their foreheads were also similar, wider than most. Dad's hair was graying and receding but lay in the same position as Grandpa's. The only distinct difference was in the eyes. Noticeably, Dad's eyes were full of life. In Dad's eyes there was light, whereas Grandpa's eyes looked lackluster. I discovered a lump in my throat that hadn't been there when we first sat down.

"He was very handsome," I said matter-of-factly, clearing my throat. "Just like you, Dad."

"I was thinking about going to Weaver's later," Dad said, wiping up the last of his pea soup with a hunk of sourdough and taking a bite. "I thought you might . . . want to tag along?"

I couldn't tell if Dad was insinuating anything about Weaver's tall, handsome shelf-stocker, but I didn't care. The thought of a chance encounter with my attractive schoolmate enthralled me. Even if I'd already seen him in class that day.

"Would love to."

Looking down at my meal, I realized I was carefully picking my slice of sourdough to little pieces, crumbling them into my empty bowl. Dad eyed me suspiciously while I laughed nervously and quickly got up from the table to clean up.

Dad and I walked to Weaver's even though the winter cold was biting. It wasn't far from the house, and Dad and I were getting used to walking downtown. There was something magical about the woods at night. I stole Greta's turquoise pashmina for the evening. Wrapping it tightly around my neck, I inhaled her perfume. *She even smells good*, I thought with slight jealousy. I thought briefly about asking Dad about her. Had he also noticed how she incessantly tugged at her long sleeves these days? Was he worried, too? But I couldn't bring myself to ask. In some stupid way, I felt as if talking to Dad about her would betray her trust. No, I couldn't ask him. I'd have to question her about it myself. So while Dad carried our folded canvas bags under his arm, we walked in silence. The two of us chose to conserve our energy; the thought of talking only made me colder. I shone the flashlight ahead of us.

Our journey took us off-pavement, and I couldn't help but notice the crunch of the frozen earth under our feet. I wondered if Sweden felt this cold all the time.

I thought more about Grandma and her decision to contact me. Why me? I wasn't special. I was a skeptical teenager, sometimes cynical, and constantly second-guessing myself. I did well in school and helped Dad around the house—though definitely not as much as I should. All in all, I considered myself pretty short of extraordinary.

Did Grandma want me to expose my grandfather for who he really was? Could I do that? What would that do to Dad?

Supernatural oddities like this usually fell upon weird people in movies: psychics, ghost hunters, outcasts. It was strange how Grandma never fully addressed me. If she *had* singled me out, decided *I* was the one she wanted to relate the story to, why didn't she ever speak directly to me? Maybe she couldn't. Maybe those were the rules of the ghostworld, or afterworld, or wherever she was calling me from. Suppose I had to prompt her? After all, I had my own questions regarding Grandpa.

I didn't immediately go to the garden section of Weaver's. That would have been too desperate. If Greta had taught me anything regarding the opposite sex, it was to act completely indifferent. *It drives them crazy*, she had explained as if we were talking about a pack of feral dogs.

It happened when I was standing over the yams again. I was placing one of the big, lumpy vegetables in my basket when he came up beside me, pretending to restack the pile of produce. He pushed himself so close to me our arms touched. I didn't jump. I just continued to inspect the produce as if he hadn't startled me. Even though, at that moment, something inside me dissolved.

"We've got to stop meeting like this, Mums." He smiled, piling the yams into a pyramid.

"Do we?" I whispered.

He looked so pleased, and I wanted so badly for him to kiss me.

"You need a Christmas cactus? We've got the best cacti this side of Chester County."

I turned to face him. "Seriously, what is it with you and your plants?"

"I dunno," he shrugged. "I've got a green thumb. Everything I touch comes to life. See?" He reached out and grabbed my hand. Spinning around with our hands enclosed, I stared into his faultless eyes. This was a test. A battle of wits. How was I going to react? How did he want me to act?

I held on tightly and replied, "Your hand is freezing."

A momentary glimmer of disappointment swept through his eyes. Whatever the test, I'd failed it. I didn't know what I was supposed to say. But before another second could pass, his familiar smile returned.

"You wanna hang out this Friday?"

Wait, what?

"Sure," I dropped his hand.

Did that really just happen?

"I get off at six."

Our eyes locked. Neither of us looked away, and I'm pretty sure we were standing closer than what was typical of friendly classmates.

"I was going to make cookies . . . " I heard my voice trailing off, but I couldn't remember what else I was going to say.

"Could you use a hand? I mean, even if it is 'freezing'?"

Finally, Gabe broke the eye contact to inspect the hand I'd just held. He turned it over, playfully offended.

"Are you as good in the kitchen as you are in the garden?" I teased.

"Lousy, actually."

How could you be lousy at anything?

"Five October Hill Road. Do you know it?"

"I'll be there Friday at seven," he held up both his hands and wiggled his fingers. "With . . . *gloves*—not bells—on."

Then he winked and walked away. He was still on the clock, even though it seemed like he'd just spent an hour with me. I took a deep breath, smiled gleefully to myself, and ventured off to go find Dad.

Friday night, Dad had initially insisted on answering the door until Greta came to my defense. This was the first time I'd ever had a boy over to the house, and Dad was unsure how to handle his younger daughter dating. *So much for Greta paving the way for me,* I mused. Apparently there was a whole new set of worries Dad succumbed to when he realized I wasn't the boyish, ten-year-old daughter he thought I'd be forever. The transformation had even come upon *me* suddenly. I was learning as I went, like a paint-by-numbers for dating. I wanted to be cool like Greta, but more importantly I wanted to be cool like me.

"Isn't that sweater a little tight on you?" Dad had asked when I told him I was having a guy come over.

"Dad, it's not the sweater that's tight!" Greta laughed from where she lay reading a tabloid magazine on the couch in front of the fireplace. "She has boobs and a waist, you know."

Dad eyed me anxiously. I held up my arms and shrugged. Greta had helped me pick out something to wear. It was her sweater.

"Maybe you could wear that soccer jersey I bought you? That's fun," Dad said encouragingly, but I caught him gulping with trepidation. "Boys like soccer . . . "

"That grungy thing from London?" Greta sat up and glared from her spot on the couch. *Was she really insulting something British?* "Dad, she looks fine! Louisa, you're perfect." Her head fell back on the couch and I saw the magazine lift back into the air.

Dad stomped off into the kitchen while I stood in the hallway confused. When he returned, he held a piece of blue cloth bunched in his hands.

"You're making cookies, right?" He stuffed the bundle into my hand. "Wear this."

I held up an oversized apron he usually wore when he grilled in the summer. I looked at Greta for some kind of defense, but I was on my own.

Dad was tinkering with Grandpa's toy train when there was a knock at the door. He must have found it upstairs. I'd left it on the hallway table, but did I leave it there intentionally, for him to find? Didn't I secretly want him to talk to me about it? If only he provided me the right opportunity to tell him the truth about Grandpa. If only I were brave enough to just come out and ask, "Dad, do you know who your dad *really* was? Let me tell you."

Dad had spent the afternoon flipping every switch in the cellar, had followed wires through the walls, and had changed whatever batteries needed changing, trying to bring the train back to life. But it wouldn't run. It stayed dead. He'd at last resorted to taking the entire train apart and spreading its pieces out on the living room floor. I wanted to tell him I thought it was useless—that the train had already delivered its message—but Dad seemed intent on bringing it back to life. Why? How could it help?

When the knock sounded, I noticed he gripped the screwdriver a little too tightly. Was he more focused on my visitor or the train? Walking through the living room to the front door, I saw his eye arch to make sure I was keeping my end of the deal. The bulky blue apron hung around my neck and was tied at the waist. Dad chuckled, satisfied, as I passed him. I mockingly stopped in front of him to curtsy.

"Okay, okay," Dad shooed me on to the door.

It was dark outside and the large fir wreath Dad had hung on the front door blocked the window. Out on the front step stood Gabe, his arms wrapped around a very large, and very red, poinsettia plant. But someone else stood there, too: Rosemary. Both faces greeted me eagerly.

"He accidently knocked on my house first," Rosemary explained, thumbing toward Gabe. "And I just thought," she shrugged, "I'd see if your dad wanted to come by for a cup of coffee?"

I ushered my guests into the mudroom, quickly shutting the door behind them. Rosemary unwrapped her black cashmere kerchief and let her red locks fall into place around her face. She shook her scarf free of stray snowflakes and stomped her rubber galoshes on our braided area rug. Gabe danced a balancing act while holding the large, potted plant and stepping out of his own soaked boots. He didn't seem nervous, only eager, but I was quivering inside. *Gabe Weaver was inside my house.*

I graciously accepted the plant from Gabe so he could remove his coat. "It's gorgeous!"

"I love your portico! I haven't seen one like it in all of Brandywine," Gabe replied enthusiastically, staring wide-eyed at the mudroom around him. I had no idea what he was talking about.

"Your doorway," he motioned to the place he'd just stood. "I helped my dad restore our house a couple years ago. I've got a whole glossary of architectural jargon up here." He tapped his temple with his index finger. He walked over to a wall and lightly rapped on it with his knuckle, "Horse hair plaster?"

I stared at him dumbfounded while he grinned. We entered the foyer, and Gabe's eyes moved delicately over the crown molding and the staircase: its banister, the decorative brackets, and the worn walnut steps.

Dad stood in the entry to the living room. He'd removed his reading glasses and was casually holding a model train car in his left hand, but I could tell he was nervous. As far as I knew, this was the first time he'd seen Rosemary since Thanksgiving.

"Hey there, Rosemary." Then Dad noticed Gabe crouching next to the stairway running his hand over the wood. Dad cocked his head, unsure what to make of him.

Gabe stood and walked across the foyer, hand extended. "Hi, I'm Gabe Weaver. My parents own the grocery store in town." Gabe motioned to the stairwell. "Walnut floors. You don't really see those around here anymore. They're in great condition!"

Dad took Gabe's hand.

"Christian Magnusson, Lou's father."

I let out a slow breath of relief as Dad relaxed his stance. He wasn't acting like a maniac; he wasn't even mildly embarrassing. And then it was over. After the introductions, Dad turned back to face Rosemary.

"Do you want to come in?" he gestured.

"I thought maybe *you'd* like to come down to my place for a cup of coffee?" Rosemary glanced at me for approval. I nodded hopefully at them both.

"Ah, but I just put a pot on here! Come on in!" While the two retreated into the warmth of the living room, Rosemary glanced back at me and mouthed a silent "Sorry."

In that moment, I wanted to throw my arms around my redheaded neighbor and thank her. How did she know I'd need a dad diversion? Maybe she really was psychic.

I led Gabe through the hallway to the kitchen, his gaze studying the architectural detail in every room.

"Thanks for the flowers," I blushed. Gabe was the only guy who had ever given me flowers except for my dad.

"My pleasure," he answered.

I handed him two eggs and nodded toward a bowl on the countertop.

"Have you got one of these for me?" He fingered the strap of my apron and the small motion made me weak.

If I knew nothing else about Gabe, it was that he didn't follow the normal rules of personal space. He stood where he shouldn't stand, but I loved the closeness. I welcomed his innocent intimacy. He made me feel nervous and excited, and I loved that feeling.

"You can have mine," I said, eager to pawn the blue bulk onto someone else. I began untying the apron from behind me.

"But your sweater . . . " He didn't look interested in going forward with the handoff. "Is that what you're planning to bake in?" He looked me over, seemingly unimpressed with Greta's "baking clothes."

"I'll be right back. Crack that egg in there. The recipe's on that card on the table, and the trash can's under the sink." I was already out of the kitchen, shouting down the hallway as I went to my room.

Back in skinny jeans and an oversized plain cotton shirt, I rolled up my sleeves to prepare for work. I smiled knowing that Greta's outfit now lay rolled in a heap at the foot of her bed. Gabe gave me an approving nod as he slowly beat the egg with a whisk.

"So about that photography project," Gabe began. "Who are you going to feature?"

"My mom," I answered hesitantly. Did I really want to go into it? Wouldn't it just spoil the mood?

"Are your parents divorced?"

"She died when I was eleven. Breast cancer."

It wasn't hard to say anymore because it was so frequent a question that it didn't really bother me, but I looked at Gabe to see if *he* was uncomfortable. But he just continued whipping the eggs, and I was thankful. Most people felt uncomfortable when I told them my mom was dead; they looked away, sighed really loudly, or looked at me full of pity. I always felt the urge to apologize. And I didn't want to apologize for my mom dying. But Gabe just kept whisking. I had never felt so good after telling someone about my mom. How did he do that?

"It's really special that you picked her for your project, then. I just picked my weird Great-Uncle Bob," he grinned.

"If he's weird, why did you pick him?" I opened a cupboard to take out the flour and sugar. Measuring three-quarters cup of sugar, I added it to Gabe's bowl and cut in two whole sticks of softened butter.

"Uncle Bob's missing his nose." He said it so matter-of-factly that I let out a nervous laugh.

"What?"

"He's missing his nose," Gabe smirked mischievously. He certainly loved to shock and awe. "Lost it to frostbite in Korea, in 1950. He refused to get a nose job even though the Army offered to pay for it."

With Gabe, I never knew what to expect. Whether he was standing too close, grabbing my hand next to a stack of yams, making me smile after telling him my mother was dead, or telling me stories about his noseless great-uncle, I was constantly on alert. There was something very special about this long-lashed boy.

The evening continued with storytelling from us both. He told me how he grew up in Brandywine Valley, how he had hopes of going to Penn State, and how he wanted to own his own nursery one day. The last part I found especially endearing. How many teenage boys would admit to wanting to grow flowers for a living? Gabe was different. He was sure of himself, and his passions were honest.

At the end of the night, Gabe and I were both covered with flour. I was thankful I'd changed my clothes. I wrapped a dozen of the treats in aluminum foil as payment for Gabe's help. Orange cardamom cookies happened to be his mother's favorite, so he was grateful for the gift. I walked him to the foyer where his poinsettia sat in the corner. The room looked much more inviting with the red leaves. Indeed, it was beginning to look like Christmas.

"That," he pointed to the planter, "don't put it outside. You might even want to put it in there, by the fire." He pointed to the living room. "They don't like to be cold. Be sure to water it when it feels dry."

I opened the door to the mudroom, where he started putting on his boots and overcoat. I stood watching him, wishing he didn't have to go.

"Wait!" he exclaimed, jumping up with one boot on. He hopped carefully on his bootless leg to the entrance of the living room.

"It was great meeting you, sir," he waved to Dad and Rosemary sitting on the couch. "And sorry again about before."

"Come back anytime, Gabe," Dad saluted happily to my friend.

Rosemary waved with a giant smile. They sat with their socked feet propped up on the coffee table with two empty mugs on the table next to the couch. They seemed giddy with each other despite the late hour. For a moment, I felt like I had exchanged roles with my dad. He was acting like the love-struck teenager, and I, the responsible adult.

As Gabe hopped back to the mudroom to put on his other boot, I wondered how this night could have gone any better.

"Thanks again for the cookies." Gabe held up the mound of tin-foil.

"Thanks for helping." And then there was the moment. That uncomfortable moment of new goodbyes. Should I hug him?

Ironically, for once, Gabe didn't come in for the type of personal touch we'd already shared at Weaver's. He stayed in the mudroom while I stayed in the doorway.

"I'll see you on Monday, Louisa," he smiled as he pulled on the gloves he'd promised he'd wear. And then he left, disappearing into the dark winter air.

After Gabe had gone, I cleaned up the kitchen while trying to eavesdrop on the conversation in the living room, but I couldn't hear anything over the clanking of dishes in the dishwasher. Once I'd finished, I went to say good night to Dad before retiring to my bedroom. I caught him and Rosemary sharing an afghan, laughing in unison at something Dad had just said, and I was sad to have missed the joke. If I were a betting woman, I would have bet anything that the two were holding hands under the blanket.

"Night, Rosemary."

"Night," she smiled.

Climbing the stairs, I was consumed with excitement for new beginnings. Dad and Rosemary were a good match. Dad deserved companionship. The type of companionship neither Greta nor I could provide him. He'd been flying solo long enough: over five years. I closed my eyes and quietly hoped the relationship would blossom into something more permanent than chance encounters and late-night chats over coffee.

"It is getting late . . ." I heard Rosemary say as I reached the top of the stairs. To which Dad answered, "Are you free tomorrow?"

I stayed up the rest of the night waiting anxiously to hear a ringing from above. But unlike other teenage girls, the phone call I was waiting for wasn't coming from the boy I'd just spent my evening with. I was waiting to hear more about a man I'd never meet. But the old rotary never rang.

XIV.

"Good night?" I teased Dad at the Saturday morning breakfast table.

Greta rolled her eyes at my badgering; unlike me, she seemed completely indifferent toward Dad's new love life. He reached across the cream-colored vintage tablecloth I'd found in the attic and grabbed one of my cookies from their plate on the kitchen table. Tossing the small morsel into his mouth, he squinted, making a face.

"Gabe was cute!" Greta exclaimed through spoonfuls of cereal. "Taller than I expected."

"I like his eyes," I added.

Greta agreed, lifting her eyebrows as she sipped her tea. "Absolutely!" she dabbed her mouth with a napkin. "Those lashes!"

"He was very *nice*," Dad interrupted, an emblematic plea for us to tone down our girlish musings.

"Rosemary stayed late, Dad," Greta stated matter-of-factly.

"She and I are going into the city today. We can give you girls a ride if you want to check it out. I know we haven't sufficiently explored Philly yet. I'm sorry about that," he said, reaching for another cookie.

"I've got plans," Greta replied. Neither Dad nor I was surprised.

"I'd like to go, but I don't want to cramp your style, Dad," I harassed while smugly taking a bite of breakfast.

"I have no style, Louisa. The offer is on the table." He spread his paper out on the table, smoothing its crease.

"Then I accept."

Dad and Rosemary dropped me off at the Philadelphia Convention and Visitors Bureau while they headed off to Little Italy for lunch. I'd brought along my 35mm, hoping I would be inspired. It hung at my side as I stepped into the reception area of the visitors center.

Colorful displays of brochures and business cards lined the walls. I leafed through the first display, waiting for something to catch my eye. As I began on the second shelf, my index finger landed on a blue-and-yellow brochure for the American Swedish Historical Museum. I slowly lifted the glossy pamphlet from the wood case.

"Excuse me?" I leaned over the Welcome Center desk toward the fragile-looking old lady who sat behind it. I held up the brochure for her to see and pointed, "What can you tell me about this museum?"

The woman's skin hung loose around her cheeks and her pink lipstick looked like it had been applied by a raccoon. She lifted her eyeglasses from the gold chain that hung around her neck.

"The American Swedish Historical Museum," she read aloud, and I wondered if she'd be any help to me at all. "Seems to me you'd want to go there if your family came from Sweden." She really was something. "A third of the Swedish population left during the immigration boom at the end of the nineteenth century, you know."

Each word she said was delicate and spoken with determination. Her voice was soft and high-pitched. "It's open from noon to four today. But it's a ways away, so you'd have to take a cab. It's probably a $10 fare."

"Thanks," I nodded, satisfied.

"Good luck," her voice wavered as I spun around, en route to find a cab.

The museum's exterior was massive and loomed ominously at the bottom of a long, empty parking lot. An embossed sign, drilled into the mortar next to the door, advised me to ring a bell to be let in. A preoccupied middle-aged woman hurried me inside.

"Five dollars for student admission," the woman said while shuffling through a stack of envelopes. Bills, to be sure. I handed her a ten and she gave me a look of disapproval like I was inconveniencing her.

"It's a self-tour." She handed me my change and a map of the museum. "You start over there." She pointed to the back of the lobby before scuttling away.

I folded the map and put it in my back pocket, straining my neck to stare up at the lobby's ceiling. Blue-and-gold painted squares framed a canvas of a newly discovered America: bare-chested natives meeting colonists in pewter helmets on a desolate sandy shore. English? Swedes? I didn't know.

I crossed the empty lobby to an adjoining room where I read about Alfred Nobel and the Nobel Prize. I studied the wall of black-and-white photographs of Nobel Prize winners. All their expressions were somber, serious, and studious. This museum wasn't anything like I thought it would be. Where was my grandfather in this lonely place? Where were the answers to my questions? Where was Gerhard? Trelleborg? Me? I trudged on. Maybe I'd made a mistake in coming. Maybe I wasn't supposed to be here.

Once I was done exploring the main exhibits, I came to the final room of the museum—a simple library with thickly bound books with cracked spines, rows of VHS tapes, and a small selection of DVDs. Across the library, a small, feeble man with white hair sat at a wooden table leafing through a photo album. On the bridge of his nose rested a pair of rimless square spectacles, and he eyed me suspiciously as he turned the page. He wrinkled his lips as he let out a long yawn. Waving it away, he covered his mouth and turned his attention back to the book in front of him. On the back of his chair hung an old herringbone jacket, and I noticed his shoes were untied and positioned next to his socked feet resting on the carpet below. Clearly, this man had settled in for the afternoon.

"*Är du svensk*?" The man grumbled halfheartedly. For a moment I wasn't sure if he was addressing me or not.

"Swedish?" He inquired again sleepily; his voice seeped in a singsong accent. The library was warm, and even I found myself a little drowsy. I looked out the window; the clouds looked dark and heavy.

"No. Well, yes," I answered unsure of the right answer. The man smiled, his eyes bright.

"You look like my granddaughter. Come here, I want to show you something," he reached over to pull a second chair closer. I draped my jacket across the back and took a seat next to his.

"That handsome young man—" he began, pointing to an old photo of men in old sports uniforms with their socks pulled up to their knees and their shorts shorter than modern fashion, "that man is me. I was seventeen."

I leaned in closer to get a better look: some of the men were smiling, though most were not. But the boy the man pointed to was looking straight into the camera with a large grin.

"Soccer?"

"Handball," the man replied. "Not very popular here in America." The man let out a deep sigh and turned another page.

"Me," he pointed to another picture where the smiling boy could be seen again, still grinning. "We had just lost the match."

"Then why are you smiling?"

"Because my girlfriend was taking the picture," the old man winked at me and chuckled. He sat back in his chair and placed his palms on his chest, under his suspenders. "So, we seem to be the only ones here today. What's your excuse?"

"Curiosity," I said as rain began to sound against the window. *Pit, pit, pit, pit.*

"Aha . . . " The man smiled running his hands up and down the elastic straps. His eyes were gray, kind, old. His skin was loose and blotchy: like droplets of brown watercolor had fallen from a suspended paintbrush above. His ears had tufts of white cotton sprouting from inside, and his eyebrows sat low and bushy.

"Can I help you?" He cocked his head to the side, with budding interest.

"I don't know." I bit my lip, uncertain how to proceed. "My grandfather came from Sweden. I need to know more about him."

"Need to, huh? Solving some ancient family mystery?" He chuckled before scratching his nose and becoming serious.

What an odd thing for him to guess, I thought, my mouth slightly ajar.

"Well I happen to be from Sweden, too," he continued, "But first . . . " The man looked down at a brass watch on his wrist. "It's time for *fika*."

"Fika?" I asked, unaware of its meaning.

"Coffee, dear," the man pushed away from the table and I watched him stretch his arms out and flex his toes before placing his shoes back on his feet. "It's a terrible thing, getting old." He stood and I reached for our jackets, but he just waved me on. "Leave them, we'll be back. And you can see," he held out his arm and gestured around the room, "there's no one to take them."

I followed the old man whose name I did not know to an old elevator and stepped inside. He seemed friendly and harmless enough. I watched as he pushed the round "B" button. The light on the button was out, and I wondered how long it had been dark. We rode in silence down two floors to the basement.

We continued into a utility kitchen where the man reached into a cabinet and retrieved a can of coffee and a French press.

"The first thing you should know about us Swedes is that we take coffee breaks," the man said.

"That explains a lot. My dad and I are addicted," I grinned.

He took five heaping scoopfuls from the can and dumped them into the glass container. He walked gingerly to a large coffeemaker and pulled down on a red lever, releasing steaming water into the press. "There are three things you need for a successful *fikapaus*: good coffee, which we have here," the man held up the French press and handed it to me, "don't push it down just yet." He walked farther into the kitchen to a stainless steel refrigerator and struggled to haul open its heavy door. "Cookies . . . or cake," he pulled out a plate of delicacies: pink cookies, round cinnamon rolls, dark chocolate balls, and fat little tubes of something light green. "Come . . . " He gestured for me to follow him into another room, flipped on a dim floor lamp, and slowly lowered himself into an oversized armchair. Next to the chair were a small stool and a table where he set the plate. The cinnamon rolls, dotted with large chunks of sugar, looked especially divine. I placed the coffee beside him.

"Ah, the cups," he began to pull himself from the chair but I ran back to the kitchen where I searched four cabinets before finally finding a pair of chipped teacups.

"And the last thing?" I asked him, entering the room again.

"The last thing is a friend." He smiled, pushing down the press and enveloping the whole room with the smell of bitter coffee. "So there," he said, taking a cup from me, filling it with the dark brew, and returning it to my hands. I settled onto the stool next to him as thunder clapped from somewhere above.

"You would think I work here, but I don't. I just give them money and they let me come here every week to peruse the library and drink their coffee," the man chuckled and took his first sip. "I've donated half of the library, too. I used to think my children would want my old books, but . . . " the man set his coffee down and shrugged his shoulders, "some people just don't care about the past. Either that, or they're afraid of what they'll find when they look back."

I nodded my head, immediately thinking of Dad. I sipped slowly, careful not to burn my tongue. I reached for the plate of sweets and began to nibble on one of the cinnamon rolls. It tasted as divine as it looked.

"So, *flicka*, let me help you solve your mystery. What part of Sweden was your grandfather from?"

"The south. Trelleborg." I stared at the way the man's hands shook. I tried to act nonchalant but I was studying him intently, secretly wishing it were my Grandpa in front of me. I had so many questions for him. So much left unanswered.

"Skåne," the man nodded his head, "where the fields are painted yellow. I, too, am from a coastal town. Landskrona. Have you been there?"

"No. Unfortunately my grandfather died before I knew him."

"Skåne used to belong to the Danes, did you know that?"

"No."

"In 1658, Sweden took it back. But to this very day, the people of Skåne still sound Danish. We speak deep in the backs of our throats," he tilted his head back and tapped his Adam's apple with his forefinger. "Truthfully, I think we sound a bit like frogs." The man laughed, a phlegmy cough that made him choke.

"You're telling me my grandfather sounded like a frog?"

"He did, indeed," the man smiled. "Is he your *morfar eller din farfar*? Your mother's father, or your father's father?"

"My dad's dad. Gerhard Magnusson."

"And your father? He hasn't told you much about him?"

"It's kind of a long story . . ." I shifted my weight on the stool.

"All the good ones are," the old man winked. "How do you like the coffee?"

"It's strong but good," I said truthfully. "Especially on days like today."

The man sat quietly for a couple moments, sipping his coffee and smiling.

"There are books upstairs that we could research," he pointed to the ceiling. "Find out more about your Gerhard Magnusson."

"I'd like that."

"Why does it take people so long to want to discover more about where they come from? It took me sixty-eight years to begin to wonder. Maybe," the man scratched his chin, "the closer we get to the end, the more interested we are in the beginning."

I took another bite of my cinnamon roll, wishing I had a better idea what I was supposed to do with my discovery, my family secret. Was I supposed to tell Dad or not? When would I know the answer? Or was I supposed to die with the secret like my grandparents did?

"But you," he raised his cup to me, "why the curiosity? You're what? Fifteen?"

"Sixteen."

"My granddaughter's fifteen and she hasn't once asked me about Sweden. So I worry. All of this," he raised a trembling index finger to his aged temple, "all of this will just disappear one day. Gone. Lost forever. And I wonder, are the memories—the stories of my life—worth anything to anyone other than me?"

"I have to believe so. After all, finding lost stories is what brought me here today, right?"

The man let out a short "Mmm," but I didn't know if he was agreeing.

"I've spent countless hours up there in that little room dwelling on the single irony that the legacy I leave will be the collections of other people's stories in *my* donated books. Not one book is about me."

"That's sad," I sighed. "What I wouldn't give to find my grandfather's story in a book somewhere."

"Would you read it?" The man looked at me pleadingly, his eyes hopeful.

"It's a funny thing, you know. I think I'm reading it now. Being here . . . discovering things about him, discovering things about myself," I admitted. What was it about this old man that made me able to speak so openly, so honestly? Maybe it was because we seemed to be looking for the same thing—a bridge between our pasts and our futures. Or maybe it was because he was the only one I *could* talk to. "This mystery, this journey, wouldn't be possible if I knew where to find the answers. This wouldn't be the same if I were just reading it in a book. There's something better in having to look for it, to seek it out."

"So should I leave my memories behind?"

"Of course you *must*! You must leave them behind! I mean, if that's how you want to think about it," I blushed. "But that's the thing . . . your granddaughter? She's not ready for them yet. When she's ready, she'll find them. As long as you leave them for her. You *have* to leave them for her, otherwise, you're right. They'll be lost."

"Thank you," the old man reached over and tenderly patted my hand. "More coffee?"

By the end of the afternoon, the old man and I had consumed an entire press of coffee and leafed through six of his large books filled with old newspaper clippings, photographs, and other descriptive historical texts. He'd shown me a Swedish book with gold lettering and a cracked spine, and opened it to a map of Scandinavia during World War II.

"You see these countries in blue?" He put his thumb on Denmark and then on Norway. "And this one in red?" He crossed over Sweden into Finland. "They were all invaded. Finland by Russia, Norway and Denmark by the Germans."

"Why doesn't Sweden have a color?" I asked with interest, looking over the map. I'd never seen one like it before.

The old man closed the book and took out a cloth handkerchief. He dabbed his nose and sighed heavily. I couldn't tell if the pause was intentional.

"We don't . . . we don't like to talk about that," he folded the cloth and tucked it back into his pocket. "Maybe another time . . . "

I didn't press the issue though I was dying to know more. The old man was visibly uncomfortable, but it seemed unfair of me to ask him to continue. He'd been so helpful already, and stories had to be told at their own pace. I was learning that all too well.

He pulled out another text and his mood seemed to change. He smiled warmly, seemingly amused with himself. With a botanist's guide in one hand and an old map in the other, the old man taught me Sweden's different provinces and their corresponding flowers. He pointed out the city where he grew up and dragged my finger east across the Baltic Sea to the Swedish island Öland.

"Where you can eat the best potato dumplings," the man licked his lips longingly. "My grandmother made the best potato dumplings with salted pork in the middle. I can still taste them, just the way she made them."

At four o'clock I reluctantly gathered my things together and asked the woman at the front desk to call me a cab.

"Thanks for entertaining an old man on a rainy afternoon." He took off his glasses and held out his hand to me. "If you ever need anything, or you desire another *fika*, you know where to find me. I hope you solve your mystery."

"There is one thing," I suddenly remembered the postcard in the attic and scrolled through the pictures on my phone to find the snapshot. I held up the screen for the old man to see. "Can you tell me what it says?"

The old man squinted and held his glasses up to his nose. He read the message aloud and it felt good to finally *hear* the language as it was written. It's not like I knew how to pronounce the foreign words. And when I'd shown the photo to Dad, he'd only shrugged.

"It says, 'I'm thinking of you always. Can you forgive me? You must forget me.'" The old man looked at me quizzically. "What does it mean?"

"I don't know," I sighed, clearing the screen and pocketing my phone. "Thank you for today. And I hope you do leave those memories for your granddaughter. I'm beginning to realize that's exactly what my grandfather did for me in his own way," I shook his pale hand and thanked him again before turning to go.

"*Hej då, flicka.*"

"Goodbye."

In the cab back to the visitors center, I realized how happy I was to have spent the entire day in the Swedish museum. It didn't matter that my camera had stayed in its case. I was meant to spend the afternoon with that old man. He'd taught me more about Sweden than anyone so far. More than even Grandma.

Dad and Rosemary were waiting for me when I returned to the visitors center. They were sitting on the steps, holding hands, excitedly bragging about their day. It involved window-shopping at Rittenhouse Row before discovering what they deemed their "favorite sight of the day": *The Dream Garden*, a 100,000-piece glass mosaic by Maxfield Parrish and Louis Comfort Tiffany.

As we climbed into the car to head back to October Hill Road, Dad and Rosemary presented me with a cannoli packed with sweet ricotta cheese. I didn't have the heart to tell them it wasn't half as good as the Swedish cinnamon roll I'd eaten during my first *fikapaus*. I ate the pastry quietly in the backseat, thinking about how strange it was that both Dad and I had spent the afternoon looking at intricate pieces of two very different mosaics. Would he be as interested in mine as I was? Would he want to know how he might be, in fact, the center of it all?

XV.

The house was empty when we got home.

"Did Greta say where she was going?" Dad asked.

"I can't remember."

"Neither can I." Dad scratched his graying temple with his knuckle. By ten o'clock, Dad was anxious, but I knew Greta would come waltzing through the front door without offering an explanation. She'd always felt entitled to more privacy than the rest of us. Dad had taught her well.

"Could you text her?"

"I already did. Three times." I scanned through my sent messages.

Greta, where are you?

Greta?

Greta, Dad's worried about you.

"Nothing?" He swallowed.

"Nothing."

He spent the entire night sitting at the bottom of the steps staring at the front door. He didn't call the cops; he knew, as I did, that she'd left of her own free will. She'd been smart about it and had bided her time until Dad and I thought she was okay. We'd believed, perhaps naively, that Greta was transitioning as well as the rest of us. Now she was calling our bluff. It was midnight before I resigned myself that she wouldn't be back tonight and went to bed. Dad stayed by the door. We didn't say good night. We didn't say anything.

I made coffee Sunday morning in silence, but I banged the pot around a bit more to remind Dad that *I* was still around. I poured us both mugs of coffee but then tossed his down the drain. I angrily let his mug crash into the sink and didn't bother to see if it'd broken.

What made Greta think it was that *easy* to just leave?

I'd wanted to run plenty of times: run away from home, from North Carolina, from the hospital, from Mom's funeral, from everything and everyone. Right after Mom died I once went so far as to print directions to Kill Devil Hills, believing that if I could just get to the beach and put my feet in the cold water I'd wake up from some terrible dream. I didn't make it past the end of the street before I realized how selfish it seemed. Dad and Greta were just beginning to grieve for Mom; I didn't want to be responsible for more loss. But deep down *I'd* wanted to run away.

I clenched the sink until I thought my fingernails would fall off, and I finally allowed myself to feel the thing that I'd tried to convince myself I wouldn't feel. The emotion of which I was most afraid. *We needed to look back. We were incapable of moving forward.*

Greta came back Sunday night while Dad and I were eating dinner and went straight to her room. Dad didn't go after her like I thought he would. He got up from the table and disappeared. Now it was he who was running. He couldn't face her. He didn't want to hear what she had to say, what made her leave. He left me alone to clean up the dishes.

Was I really the only sane person in the house? The only person who wanted to sit down and actually *talk* about the state of our family? Even if it would be painful? I threw everything in the trash as noisily as I could before going to bed. The plates crashed the loudest. I wanted them both to hear me. I wanted them both to know I wasn't running away.

On Monday morning I was eager for a distraction. But instead of finding a respite, for the first time I found myself in the line of fire of another type of scandal—teenage drama. I became aware of my situation when Allison pulled—or rather, forcefully dragged—me from my locker into the girls' restroom before first period.

"You and Gabe Weaver spent Friday night together?" Her tone demanded an answer.

"Yeah, we made cookies—" I said before she shushed me to silence.

"I thought I told you he was off-limits?"

"You said to stay away from him, but you never explained why—"

"Sssh!" She hushed me again, crouching down to look for feet under the stalls.

"What? Are you interested in him?"

"Are you kidding?" she snapped before growing quiet when a toilet flushed. She turned fearfully to see who would open the stall door. I followed her gaze. But when she saw a freshman emerge, Allison continued her distraught rant.

"Jennifer Adams has been trying to date Gabe since last year! She's already told every girl in school that he's going to prom with her. They're practically together."

"So?" I silently remembered seeing a very pretty brunette sitting next to Gabe in the cafeteria.

"*So*," she sarcastically repeated, "you're dead."

I just stared back at her, unable to wrap my head around the idea that one batch of cookies could cause so much trouble.

"Jenn Adams is one of the most popular girls in school. Maybe you don't know that yet because you're new. So maybe she'll have mercy on you."

I laughed. Allison was obviously hysterical. Before I had to listen to any more of her gross overreaction, I muttered something like, "See you in English," and pushed my way out the door.

I thought that was the end of it. But then, in the middle of History, Chris leaned across the aisle to me and whispered, "So, you and Weaver, huh?"

I felt myself cringe in my seat. I literally must have sunk two inches in my chair.

"What?" I asked back, defensively.

"You and Gabriel Weaver? You're like a thing now?"

I rolled my eyes, already tired of the gossip—the details of which I didn't even fully know.

"Who said?" I zipped up my hoodie and tried to recoil within it.

"He did. Word around school is he's telling everyone he spent Friday night with you."

"He did not!" I blurted a little too loudly.

The entire class, including Mr. Duncan, turned to look at me before continuing the lesson. Chris chuckled to himself.

"He came over my house—" I whispered.

"And made cookies, I know. That's all he's saying, Louisa. I hope you didn't think I was insinuating . . . " Chris grinned at me, the whiskers on his chin a rough contrast to his tan skin.

"So, what's it to you?" I seethed from a clenched jaw.

"It's nothing to me. I just," he paused in reflection, "I would have pegged you as someone who lived more dangerously than Gabriel Weaver. Then again, you are messing with Jenn Adams's property, so maybe you're more daring than I thought."

"Christopher and Louisa," an annoyed Mr. Duncan glowered at us, "is there a problem?"

"No, sir," said Chris as I vigorously shook my head, my cheeks burning with embarrassment.

When the bell rang, the class stood to leave, and I couldn't help but notice my female classmates glancing at me with curiosity. Were they reading me my last rites? Silently humming a farewell taps?

"So, about this almanac project . . . " Chris began as he swung his army-green messenger bag over his shoulder.

Internally, I groaned. Chris hadn't done his end of the group work.

"You haven't started have you? The almanac is due on Friday, and you haven't started," I blurted accusingly. He looked surprised, then scoffed.

"Yeah. I haven't finished. You think maybe you could help me with my part?"

"What? The weather report too difficult for you?" I sneered.

He looked hurt, and I regretted snapping at him. I took a deep breath, brushed my hair aside, and exhaled. I was on edge from being the center of the gossip machine, but that was no excuse to be so mean.

"Sure." I managed a weak smile.

"I work at the coffee shop, Fat Bottoms, in town. I take my break at five-thirty. Do you think you could stop by?"

"Sure."

"Great. See you then." As he left the classroom, I couldn't help but remember what Rosemary had predicted about Chris: *Finds people doing things for him—women, especially—because they're just naturally drawn to him. And he knows this. He's a sly one.* Bemoaning my gullibility and feeling especially chump-worthy, I dragged myself to second period.

Allison didn't talk to me in English. I figured she wanted to distance herself from the dead-girl-walking. I sat alone at the end of a different table at lunch, and no one even attempted being nice to me. Later, Gabe was missing from Photography. Someone said he left school sick. *Worst school day ever.* On the car ride home from school, Greta was quiet behind the wheel. I wasn't in any mood to talk either, so we rode for a while in silence. Not only did I not *want* to talk; I found myself incapable. I was sure if I opened my mouth, I'd start crying. Or yelling. Or both.

I stared out the Subaru window remembering the night before. I'd heard Dad climb the stairs at midnight and enter Greta's room. He didn't knock, and Dad *always* knocked. Whatever limited conversation they'd shared, it had lasted only three minutes before the door slammed shut. I don't know if Dad or Greta slammed it, but whoever it was left an exclamation point echoing down the hallway.

"You know, Louisa, if Gabe wants to hang out with you, he should be able to," Greta eventually said as we turned down our street. So she was just going to ignore her own issues and focus on mine? Fine. Whatever.

I threw my head against the headrest in defeat. "I'm not going to worry about it. If people at school don't like me, it's predestined. I'm used to doing my own thing."

Greta drummed her fingers on the steering wheel. "Well," she began, staring ahead, "I think it's kind of sweet how Gabe bragged to everybody about your date. I mean, *everybody* knew about it."

She was right. He had spent Friday night with me, but was it a date? He'd told everyone about it, but did that make it official? Shelving my anger for the time being, I called a temporary truce with my sister.

"Thanks, Greta."

"Yep," she smirked, nodding her head as we pulled into our driveway.

Fat Bottoms sat on historic Main Street in an old two-story row house. Wrought-iron café tables dotted the veranda. Inside the entry of the house was an ornate, antique wooden bar defaced with multicolored fliers announcing local music concerts, community events, and apartment rentals. Behind the counter stood a girl with dyed black hair. I thought I recognized her as Chris's friend, someone I'd seen him sitting with in the cafeteria at school. A gold nose ring pierced her nostril and rubber sparkly bracelets lined her forearms. She glared at me as I walked in.

Chris stood at the industrial cappuccino machine and steamed milk. His Levis were holey, his shirt tight around his biceps, and his hair pulled back into a rubber-banded ponytail. There was no other way to describe Chris than he looked hot. Smoking, drool-worthy, hot. I was suddenly excited to see him.

"Can I get you something?" the girl greeted me, unsmiling.

I stared at the chalkboards above her head; the menu was scripted in pink. Chris looked up and smiled.

"She's with me, Lacey," his deep, monotone voice actually sounded peppy.

Lacey rolled her eyes and turned around, disappearing behind a beaded curtain. I guessed they weren't as close as they'd appeared at lunch.

"Ex-girlfriend," Chris informed me. "*Recent* ex-girlfriend." He looked up at a clock hanging on the wall and said, "I'm not on break for another ten minutes."

"That's okay, I'll wait," I shifted my backpack to my other shoulder.

"What can I get you to drink? I make a really good hot cocoa," he smiled, and I realized I wasn't mad at him anymore for dragging me into helping him with his assignment last minute.

"Sounds good."

"Help yourself to any table. There are two rooms in the back, too. I'll bring it to you when it's done."

I started to walk away.

"Thanks for coming, Lou," he called after me.

I was caught off guard by his use of my nickname, but it sounded kind of natural coming from him. I was obliged to Chris for getting me out of the house—even if he was just using me for schoolwork.

I found a little two-top table in one of the corners of a back room. A fire of sorts cracked in the fireplace; it was one of those synthetic logs that made green and blue flames. This place was so beatnik, so hipster, so Chris. A white-waxed candle burned from the inside of a Mason jar on top of a mustard-yellow vintage tablecloth. A Spanish guitar streamed soft Christmas songs from a stereo at the front of the shop.

Chris brought me an oversized mug of liquid chocolate before returning to the front. While I waited, I started thinking about the old man from the museum and about how I wanted to talk to Grandma on the phone. I pulled out my notebook and scribbled: *Who was Gerhard Magnusson? Murderer? Father? Grandfather?* I tapped my pencil on my notebook. So many questions unanswered. Would I ever find out the truth?

Chris joined me at my table, interrupting my thoughts. I stuffed my notepad back into my backpack as he dropped a packet of twelve pages in front of me. Curious, I leafed through them. Twelve completed months, January through December, day-by-day weather reports and forecasts. And the workmanship was good. He'd completed his part of the project.

"But I thought you—" I stammered, confused.

"Eh," he shrugged, smiling. "I needed an excuse to see you."

I felt my face grow hot as the blood rushed into my cheeks. Chris's eyes met mine across the table: the same brown eyes I'd cautioned myself to avoid.

"So we're good? To turn in the almanac on Friday?"

I swirled my finger on the rim of my mug, watching the steam slowly escape. Chris nodded and then stretched his arms behind his head. I couldn't help but notice his biceps, and I silently told myself not to stare.

"So when do *I* get invited over to bake cookies?" Chris laughed. I sensed the question was a veiled insult directed at Gabe and furrowed my brow.

"Sorry, Chris, my Christmas baking is done," I lifted my mug and warily took a sip, careful not to burn myself.

He grinned, looking satisfied, and folded his arms. "You aren't like other girls," he said out of the corner of his mouth while keeping his gaze fixed on me.

"Oh, come on," I groaned and rolled my eyes.

"I wanna show you something. I've got an hour." He checked his watch. The impulsiveness in his voice told me this idea was not preplanned.

"Are we leaving?" I asked; he was already holding my coat.

He untied the apron that hung around his waist, and we exited the coffee shop two steps at a time. He walked me around the front of an old diesel-chugging Volvo station wagon and opened the passenger-side door. The chivalrous gesture was unexpected from my holey-jeaned friend, and I felt a bit awkward as I climbed into the Swedish vehicle. The upholstery smelled faintly of citrus and incense, and I scrunched my nose in mild distaste.

Chris got into the front seat next to me and immediately started the engine, put the car into gear, and drove off before I could ask where we were going. Or why.

We drove west on Baltimore Pike, avoiding the Delaware state line. The heat was turned on the highest level at our feet, and Chris cracked the windows. The cold air enveloped my face, and it suddenly felt easier to breathe. The wind felt good blowing through my hair and on my skin, so when Chris looked over at me for unspoken consent, I nodded an "okay" and gripped the door handle a little tighter.

The mix of hot and cool air set my brain on fire. My mind started moving a million thoughts per second. I closed my eyes for clarity, and, like flashes, I caught glimpses of my young grandpa crouching next to an upturned bicycle, and I saw him getting up every morning and winding his prized pocket watch. It was like an old film reel with bursts of color and shadows. One thing was constant, however. My grandfather's eyes were noticeably different. They weren't the forlorn eyes from the photograph Dad had showed me. These eyes were full of adolescent happiness. Something had happened between these scenes I now witnessed and the photograph Dad had shown me. In that photo, something inside him was missing. And I felt in my heart a smoldering of ashes from something that once was bright and alive. I sensed I was close to understanding. But just when I felt I was going to fully grasp what Grandmother was trying to tell me, the car stopped.

I opened my eyes to find us sitting idly on the side of a very dark rural road. Chris cut the engine and turned out the headlights, and we were suddenly engulfed in darkness. Despite the eerie quiet, the strange surroundings, and my uncertain feelings about my companion, I felt safe. It was then that I noticed a large residence far off the road. A single porch light illuminated a three-story brick house framed by four white pillars. It sat down a long dirt driveway lined with hay bales and broken fence posts. The place was very big and very old.

"That house," Chris leaned over me to point out the passenger-side window. His elbow brushed my collar. He seemed to notice and lingered a moment too long, his arm extended over me, our faces close together. "That house was part of the Underground Railroad. Harriet Tubman stopped there while leading seven slaves to freedom." He paused to let me think about what he was saying.

"I'm big on civil liberties. That's why I love living here." He was animated. "This place . . ." he pointed to the ground, "this is where it all happened. Our country's future was mapped here in the eighteenth century and then reshaped in the nineteenth. We're constantly walking among the great ghosts of American history."

Ghosts.

"I guess I never thought about it like that," I admitted, breathless.

"That house, Allen Agnew's place and its history, is so important. Those people were so important. I mean, can you even imagine what it must have been like risking your life, with no guarantee any of it would pay off? It was all so damn self-sacrificing."

I inhaled a breath of cold air. My senses seemed heightened. The hair on my arms stood up, I could smell Chris's aftershave, and I could hear all those familiar noises of the night: crickets, branches, and the wind. Slowly, Chris leaned over and grabbed my hand in both of his. He was even closer now. His breath hung heavily on my neck and the warmth of it made me quiver inside. He stared at me, wanting to say something, but I couldn't tell what.

Chris continued, unaware of the tingling effect his touch had on my skin. "I wonder, you know . . . what is it about someone that enables her to be so noble? Which part of her makeup, her framework, decides to risk living and breathing for someone else? Is it a loose screw or a secure bolt? And if it came down to it . . . which one do I have?" he whispered into my ear.

I hadn't expected Chris to be so passionate. I had always taken him to be mysterious and ambiguous. Maybe it was his defiant wardrobe or his long hair. Either way, I couldn't figure him out. Who was he really? His honesty caught me off guard. And I didn't know the right answers to his questions. In fact, I didn't have *any* answers, right or wrong. I sat speechless even though I wanted to say something meaningful. Leaning back and looking me over, he studied me from head to toe. I could tell he was thinking about kissing me. How far would he take this?

My thoughts were stuck on something he said. There was something familiar about the mention of nuts and bolts. But before I could compose my thoughts, Chris had dropped my hand, restarted the car, and was making a wide U-turn in the middle of the road. Our excursion had come to its end, and I was in need of the reprieve. I had to catch my breath.

Chris dropped me off at my house, even though his break was just ending and he'd be twenty minutes late back to work.

"Thanks for taking me there," I said sincerely.

"I just wanted to properly introduce you to where you live. You're on the other side of the Mason-Dixon Line now, sweetheart." He chuckled more to himself than to me.

I got out of the car and thanked him again, shutting the door behind me. He turned on his radio and increased the volume as he sped down October Hill Road, not waiting to see if I got into my house safely. From the curb, I paused before going inside. I watched Chris's brake lights glow in the distance and waited for the vibration from his radio to fade into silence. I shuddered in the cold night air, missing the heat from his dashboard.

Studying a large spider web in the corner ceiling of my bedroom, I thought about how Chris was more complex than I'd previously believed. Tonight, he'd shown me another layer of his persona. And he'd almost kissed me. I was certain of it. He'd come in so close. We'd been cheek to cheek. I'd felt his breathing and his warmth. He'd wanted to, and so did I. What had stopped him? What had stopped me?

I was pondering this when I heard a shrill ringing above me. My next call.

XVI.

One night in early September 1939, when Gerhard was seventeen, an unwelcome visitor arrived at the Magnusson door. Gerhard was sitting, fingering a letter he'd received earlier in the day. He didn't hear the first knocks, and when his mother, Åsa, barked at him to answer, he couldn't take his eyes off the envelope.

He opened the door and immediately wished he hadn't. The smell of *brännvin*, vodka, hit his nose. There, leaning peculiarly against the doorframe, swayed his uncle Pontus.

"Does my father know you're here?" Gerhard remarked with a sigh.

"Come now, nephew!" Pontus smiled.

Gerhard felt queasy. The stench was overwhelming. Pontus stumbled forward and put his arm out for support, and Gerhard jumped in to keep his uncle from collapsing. *Just wait until Father gets here*, he thought.

"Where's that beautiful mother of yours?"

With her gray, wiry hair and curved, aging chin, Åsa rushed to the door and went after the drunk man with the wood handle of her straw broom. Gerhard stepped back to let her swing. The sight was quite amusing. When Leif returned from work, he spied an angry wife in one corner of his house and his bruised, sobering brother in the other. Åsa sat at the table aggressively rubbing ointment on her hands, glowering at the mound of flesh across the room, a cold cloth covering his right eye.

Gerhard sat distracted at the kitchen table staring again at the cream envelope. He didn't know what to make of it. Were its contents good or bad? He'd read the letter multiple times, but he was still unsure. More than that, he wanted to know what Lasse would think of it.

"Is dinner ready, Åsa?" Leif asked, refusing to yet acknowledge Pontus. He'd lived this scene before. They all had.

Åsa gestured toward the stove where the sausages lay black and crisp from neglect. Leif quietly nodded. Anna, Gerhard's sister and peacemaker, quickly grabbed a bowl from the cupboard and began transferring the little sausages to the dish. In her soft and placating voice, she asked Gerhard to fetch the mustard. He folded the envelope in half and stuck it into his breast pocket. It would have to wait until later.

The family sat for dinner as usual. Pontus sniffed noisily from his bench by the fire.

"Will you be joining us, Pontus?" Leif asked over his shoulder, never taking his eyes off the tabletop.

Pontus found his feet, rubbed his palms together, and took a seat next to Lasse.

"*Tack, Bror*," he thanked his brother. "And *tack så mycket*, Åsa, for this feast!" The man's stomach growled as he spied the food. He looked at his nephew and pointed to the jar of mustard. "*Ursäkta*, nephew, pass the *senap*?"

All watched as Lasse grabbed the jar and handed it to his uncle. Pontus forked a generous six sausages onto his plate as the rest of the family gaped.

"There you are, Gerhard," he smiled, nervously, handing the meager contents of the bowl back to his nephew.

"I'm Lasse," the twin answered, taking the bowl and placing a conservative three sausages onto his plate. "I'm the one with the beard." Lasse scratched his face proudly in Gerhard's direction.

Pontus only grunted, two sausages stuffed into his mouth, as he stared across the table.

Leif folded his hands, placed his elbows softly on the table, and stared suspiciously at his brother. "So what brings you to Trelleborg?"

"I've come looking for work!" Pontus announced loudly. "I thought you could help."

Åsa let out a sarcastic laugh. *Pontus Magnusson, the nomad, came looking for work?* The man traveled from sibling to sibling, overstaying his welcome, picking up odd jobs, and squandering his earnings on aquavit. Gerhard had always thought of Pontus as *blodigelen*, the bloodsucker, the leech.

"But what of Göteborg, Pontus?" Åsa inquired of his former home.

"Göteborg," Pontus began, spitting bits of pork out of his mouth as he spoke, "has no work. Naturally, Leif, I thought you could help."

"Naturally," Leif lamented. "And where do you plan to stay?"

"Why, here with you!" Pontus slapped Lasse on the back, cheerfully. "And what with everyone talking exports—the Soviets in Poland, and Germany demanding more steel—surely, Trelleborg has *something*."

Pontus batted his eyes around the table.

"We don't talk about those things here," Leif informed him calmly.

"Well, Hitler may be the best thing to happen to Sweden since—"

"Pontus, I swear to God, if you're going to sleep under my roof, you are forbidden from speaking that name in my house!" Leif erupted and Pontus nearly fell out of his seat.

Gradually, Leif unclenched the fist he'd pounded on the tabletop.

"Once I earn enough, I'm headed for America." Pontus unbuttoned his shirt and revealed a small satchel hanging around his neck. From the bag he produced a worn red ticket for the White Star Line. A one-way fare from Göteborg to Liverpool to Boston. He held the ticket to his nose and sniffed greedily.

"Where did you get that?" Lasse asked, his eyes wide with excitement.

"A friend of mine gave it to me," Pontus shrugged, tenderly folding the ticket and replacing it around his neck. He winked at Gerhard across the table. Gerhard looked away, remembering the letter in his own pocket.

"And what will you do in America that you can't do here?" Leif inquired.

Pontus waved his brother off. "The details can wait."

The meal continued. No one spoke. Gerhard opened his pocket watch wondering when he could steal away with Lasse. He needed to show him the letter. They needed to talk about its contents. Would he understand its implications?

"Gerhard, Agnes Landquist and I are going to the shore later. She was asking about you. You should come with us." Lasse flashed Gerhard a mischievous, knowing glance before adding, "We're going swimming."

A vision of Agnes Landquist, beautiful curves tightly wrapped in a white cotton swimsuit, flashed quickly in his mind. He hadn't seen Agnes in a long time. He wanted to go, but he was too afraid. He didn't want to compete with Lasse for her affection. He didn't want to lose.

"I have to go to the station," Gerhard lied.

"But it's past the workday, surely—"

"We received a letter today," he cleared his throat, hoping to change the subject. "From Lukas Österberg with the city council." Gerhard reached in his pocket and pulled out the envelope, handing it to Lasse. "Neither of us needs to complete our mandatory military service next year."

Leif wiped his mouth with a napkin. "What?"

"Österberg wrote to say our duties to serve Sweden are more valuable right now in Trelleborg."

"What did I tell you?" Pontus grunted in between chews.

Leif's eyes narrowed. "That's ridiculous." He threw his napkin on his empty plate. "So Sweden will be helpless should the Germans decide to invade? And what of the Soviets?"

"But you heard the German foreign minister in Stockholm," Pontus interrupted, "Hit—I mean, *Germany* will respect our neutrality."

"Don't be naïve, Pontus," Leif snorted angrily. "The English and French have already declared war. Sweden should be prepared!"

For the second time that night, Pontus waved his brother off, unconvinced. Anna's head bowed as she slowly ran her fingernail over the hem of the napkin in her lap. Her shoulders slunk into her body. She reminded Gerhard of an owl caught in the afternoon thunderstorm. He squinted to see her as she seemed to disappear into the shadows of the room. He looked over and waited for his brother's reaction to the letter. He watched as Lasse's eyes scanned the page, but in the end, Lasse handed the letter back without a response. Whatever his thoughts—his feelings, his disappointment, his relief—Lasse kept them locked away. Discouraged, Gerhard excused himself from the rest of the meal, his dinner only half-eaten.

XVII.

I tossed the phone back in its cradle. I'd tried desperately to interrupt my grandmother's storytelling, but her voice carried on without pause. I had questioned, spoken over her, and eventually tried yelling into the receiver, all to no avail. It was as if this story had been orated to tape. But there were no batteries, no power source. How was the phone running? How had my grandmother done it? This wasn't a conversation—it was a dictation.

I began to wonder how many phone calls came when I wasn't around to answer them. Did they come when I was at school? Did the story continue when I couldn't answer? Or did I hear only what Grandma wanted me to hear? What did she want me to do? I tried asking her.

"Grandma, what is it you want me to do?" But she never answered.

The word in the halls Tuesday morning was Jennifer Adams wanted to "have a chat" with me, and I knew most people were hoping for fisticuffs. By late morning, the rumors had reached the powers that be, and Jenn and I were both called to the principal's office before lunch.

We were welcomed to sit in cheap armchairs—she in her designer jeans and I in my ratty sneakers—in the main office and wait for the principal to arrive. Staring ahead into empty space, Jenn applied a thick coat of shiny lip gloss; I bit my lip nervously. For five minutes, she didn't look at me once. I opened my mouth to begin some sort of explanation before thinking better of it. What did I owe her? God, it was stupid.

The principal came in, handed us copies of the student handbook, and referenced us to the pages "Assault, Threat of Force, and Bodily Harm."

"There are rumors," the principal began, taking a seat behind her desk. She seemed tired and far away. "There are rumors that the two of you need some sort of mediation. Let me just say, it would behoove you both to work this out—whatever the issue—amiably. Do you think you need to speak to a counselor?"

"No, ma'am. Louisa and I really have no idea why we're here. I mean, I don't even *know* her," Jenn offered first.

I just sat there. *Funny,* I thought, *she doesn't know me, but she knows my name.*

The principal stared at us, assessing our threat level. She tapped her fingers on her desk and arched an eyebrow. The clock ticked noisily from the wall. Everything dragged.

"So you have nothing to talk about?" She glanced my way. "Louisa?"

"I guess not," I sighed looking at Jenn. She continued to ignore me.

"Fine. Just keep those"—the principal nodded toward the handbooks—"and remember the expectations of you here at WHS. You can go back to lunch now."

Out in the hallway, once we were out of earshot, Jenn at last turned toward me. She stood a small distance away, but her shoulders leaned in as if some invisible force held her, preventing her from clawing my eyes out.

"You're a horrible person," she sneered accusingly. "You should just hear what the school is saying about you!"

"Oh? What are they saying?" I challenged defensively.

"They say your dad is getting it on with the town witch and that the two of you cast spells together," her voice was high-pitched, and she pronounced each syllable succinctly between her front teeth. "It's positively ghastly. No wonder your sister wants to kill herself!" She jeered before storming off.

"Yeah, well, I'll be sure to have the next spell cast on you!" I spit back feeling my knees nearly buckling under me. As I steadied myself against the wall, Jenn's apathy echoed down the hall with her heels. *Greta*, I sighed, slowly unclenching the fist I didn't realize I'd made.

Sitting with Gabe in Photography, I was still fuming with anger. I sat rigidly in my seat, looming over the table like a crow.

"Why did you tell everyone about Friday night?" The words forced their way out through my clamped jaw.

Gabe gazed across the table from me while winding the film in his 35mm. He'd gotten his hair cut. His ears stuck out from his head.

He shrugged.

"You know I'm public enemy number one, right?" I scoffed.

Mr. Franz was making his way around the class, sending tables of students to the darkroom to develop their film.

"Sorry about that," he looked like he really was. "Jenn can be kind of . . . intense."

I stared at him waiting for more of an explanation.

"Jenn and I were never going to happen. You provided a way for me to let her know that." His camera clicked. His roll was done.

"*I provided a way?* So I was just an opportunity?" I was beginning to feel sick.

"What? No." Gabe looked at me like I was crazy.

"Table four," Mr. Franz called.

I took my camera and retreated to the darkroom. Gabe grabbed his camera and followed me, catching up.

"I didn't mean—"

"No, Gabe, it's okay. If you needed a scapegoat, I can be that. It's cool," I shrugged casually, nearly choking on the lump in my throat.

I'd fallen for it. The mums, the eyes, the cookies. I was a fool. *Real smooth, Lou.*

There were three of us in the darkroom: me, Gabe, and a short boy whose name I could never remember. Something about the darkness made us feel like we had to be quiet, like we were in a library or a catacomb. The short boy was practiced at this. Before I could copy his movements, he was spooling the first few inches of film onto a plastic reel, placing it carefully with a developing tank into the double-zippered changing bag, and shoving his hands into the sleeves to process the film. *Jeez, he moved fast.*

"Listen, Louisa," Gabe said, trying to whisper so low he wouldn't disturb the boy.

He fumbled for my elbow but I jerked away, still feeling pretty humiliated. I was thankful we were in the darkroom and could barely see each other's faces. Gabe was standing close to me and I'm sure I looked pathetic. I focused my energy on trying to open the back of my camera. But my fingers kept fumbling and I couldn't figure out how to work it. The harder I tried, the more I struggled. Finally, Gabe reached around my waist and found my hands where they clutched my camera. With his hands on mine, he helped me unfasten the casing of the camera and remove my film. He was so close to me and his hands felt soft on my fingers. The curve of my arm fell in place with his, and hurt as I was, I wanted to lean back and let him hold me. As I slowly turned around to face him, our noses nearly touching, the short kid opened the doors to the classroom, flooding the darkroom with light.

"Hey!" I yelled, squinting my eyes at the blinding light.

Gabe withdrew from behind me and held up a hand to block the brightness. "You could have exposed my film!"

"Jerk," I muttered under my breath.

Gabe and I were left alone in the darkroom. At any moment table five would come barreling into the room.

"Louisa, I really like you. I told everyone in school about Saturday night *because* I really like you. And I knew it would get to Jenn and then she'd back off. I'm sorry if people started talking," Gabe explained, hurriedly. "But you gotta know," he laughed, his hand groping for mine and clasping it earnestly, "Jenn's got nothing on you."

Before I could process his words, Gabe's other hand shyly brushed up the length of my arm and came to rest gently on my neck, under my hair. It was such an intimate place to touch. It felt so foreign but so . . . *oh*. He leaned his face down to mine, and as our lips were about to touch, table five opened the darkroom door. Gabe backed away in surprise. Kiss number two averted. I bit my lip anxiously. No one seemed to notice how tense my posture was or how Gabe hadn't even unloaded his film. I left the darkroom, unprocessed film in hand, feeling rather undeveloped myself.

By the week of Christmas, I hadn't received any more phone calls from my grandmother, and I started obsessing over when the next one would come. I tried to remember every detail of every call to conjure up some clue I'd overlooked. Maybe there was no end to the story. I spent some evenings down at Rosemary's cottage, frustrated. For some reason, I couldn't bring myself to divulge too much of the truth to Rosemary. I didn't want to tell her about the phone or the specifics. But I did want her to explain it all, and I got discouraged when she couldn't. I wasn't being fair. After the second week with no phone call, I realized I needed to leave my neighbor alone.

I set up my own makeshift headquarters in the attic. It didn't surprise me at all that neither Dad nor Greta noticed when I snuck away up the dark back stairway. These days it seemed as if each of us was consumed in our own pursuits. Since Greta ran away, it was as if Dad burrowed into himself deeper than ever. The conversations about Grandma and Grandpa ceased. He'd retreated back into his shell, and I wasn't welcome to snoop around. So I poured over old artifacts by myself searching for further proof of my grandparents' existence.

I lined the attic floor with open books I'd checked out from the local library. Scattered around the old desk were maps of both the Brandywine Valley and of Sweden, pamphlets I'd borrowed from the Chester County Historical Society, and printouts from their microfiche machines. I'd found a scanned copy of the deed to our house with Grandma and Grandpa's signatures and a solitary photograph of Grandma from a local newspaper dated 1977. She'd attended a seminar about some of the older buildings in the county at the Historical Society titled "If Walls Could Talk." When I found the photograph and printed it out, I circled her face with a blue marker and highlighted her name, Eloise Magnusson.

The longer I stared at her young face, the more I discovered similarities in my own features. She parted her hair in the same way I did, her brow furrowed like mine, and our cheekbones had the same distinct pronunciation. There was no mistaking that I was her granddaughter, and she stared out from the photograph with some satisfaction, as if to introduce herself to me. Her eyes were pale and wide as if to say, "You found me, at last!" It was a bittersweet discovery I couldn't share with anyone.

In Photography class, I occupied myself with the photo essay project, bringing in pictures of my mom and my grandparents. I used some class time to study Gerhard's photos: the background, the people, the clothing, the expressions, each and every small and unassuming nuance. I needed something to help me figure out the next chapter of his story.

The photo research also gave me time to revisit old pictures of my mom. I loved cataloging Mom's fashion trends: the perms and high-waisted pants of 1985, the short Princess Diana hairdo of 1987, and the navy-blue frocks she loved to wear during both her pregnancies. One picture in particular, I lovingly and intentionally selected for the essay: Mom in shiny aerobic tights, leotard, and bunched leg warmers doing a Jane Fonda leg lift on the floor, with me in front shadowing her stretch. It was one of my favorites, not only because it represented Mom as a dancer, but because of the expression on her face. She was looking forward, hand on her hip, leg in the air, and her eyes were so bright. She stared beyond the camera at Dad. I could almost hear her comment before the picture was snapped, "Isn't it amazing she's ours?"

I was sad to turn in the completed project. I didn't have my answers yet. Gabe could tell I was preoccupied. He was in competition for my attention, and he seemed hell-bent on being the victor.

"What's up with you, Louisa?" Gabe asked as we entered the lunchroom on Friday before break, but I just kept walking. "Listen," he stopped and grabbed my hand, forcing me to look at him. "My parents are taking me skiing on Monday. It would be awesome if you could come."

I smiled for the first time in a long while. Where had I been for the past weeks? I needed to realize Grandmother's story was a past that I couldn't change. Standing in the school hallway with winter break upon me, and Gabe's hand wrapped around mine, I snapped back into the present. It felt good to feel sixteen again.

Rosemary phoned that evening to say she'd made soup with some rhubarb she'd preserved from her own garden last summer. She asked if we wanted to come down and try it. I told her I'd never had rhubarb soup, but that I'd extend the invitation to Dad.

He'd been spending his free evenings repairing the siding on the house, but his working hours were dwindling as winter's darkness crept earlier each day. He had already nailed some of the loose boards, and he decided come spring he'd start repainting the wood. The house would remain its original orange color, but he'd change the door to moss green. Just like in North Carolina.

"Rhubarb soup, best served warm and mashed with cream," Dad shouted to me as he climbed down the ladder. "How does she know about rhubarb soup? Rosemary—" he smiled, reaching the bottom of the ladder. "She's really something."

"Maybe it's her psychic powers," Greta mocked from the doorway.

Dad ignored her. Would they ever speak to each other like normal people again?

Greta and I both declined the soup. Instead, she offered to take me shopping for ski pants. She'd been skiing before, but I never had. I didn't even know skiing had its own pants, so I was shocked at the variety of ski apparel and accessories. And I was especially stunned at the cost of it all. Greta loaned me $99.00 for the pants—put it on her new debit card—a charitable gesture I was surprised to receive. She was usually pretty selfish when it came to her money. Dad had opened bank accounts for both Greta and me when Mom died. Most of the money we couldn't touch until we graduated high school, but Dad did give us a meager monthly allowance and urged us to try to limit our expenses.

"Thanks for the loan, Greta. I'll get you the money as soon as I can get to the bank," I said. I held the door open for her as we left the store. "Can I buy you a cup of tea as thanks for now?"

As soon as we walked into the dimly lit coffee shop, I spotted Chris behind the front counter. Two young girls giggled as they accepted ceramic mugs from my friend. Somewhere inside me, a thin harp string of jealousy hummed as Chris smiled flirtatiously back at the girls.

We approached the counter and Chris grinned knowingly at me, "Hiya, Lou."

Greta looked at me for an introduction. I was hesitant to give one: not because I thought Chris was her type, with his clumps of waxy curls, his tie-dyed wardrobe, and his unshaven whiskers. Greta liked her boys older, in polo shirts and khakis, with gleaming white smiles. I was hesitant to introduce them because I was afraid Greta would outshine me. She had it all. Tall, blond, beautiful. What was to prevent Chris from falling head over heels for my doe-eyed, buxom sister, leaving me by the wayside?

"Chris, this is my sister, Greta. Greta, this is my friend, Chris. We're in History together," I said cautiously, bracing myself for Chris's ogling.

But it didn't come. In fact, he didn't take his eyes off me. Since our last encounter, I'd begun to notice that when Chris looked at me, he often seemed to be looking into some more intimate part of me, like he could tell my secrets or see my thoughts. With Chris, I always felt vulnerable, and there was something intoxicating about the vulnerability.

"How about two cappuccinos? On the house?"

"Actually, do you have any Earl Grey? Cream and sugar?" Greta interjected.

Chris looked to me for my order.

"Make that two," I smiled.

"I'll bring 'em round back when they're ready." His voice remained its usual, flat range.

I led Greta to an empty table.

"This place is neat," she complimented, looking around the room. She put her coat on the back of her chair and offered to do the same with my shopping bag filled with ski apparel. "And what was up with that guy? He was really staring at you."

Greta eyed me suspiciously like there was something more I wasn't telling her. I shrugged innocently and handed her my bag.

"Just a guy from class."

The two of us sat quietly for a while. It was weird. I realized she and I hadn't really been truly alone since the move. Despite the fact that we drove to school together every day and lived under the same roof, we didn't talk about substantive, life stuff. Once again, I was faced with the quiet truth of just how far we'd grown apart. After all, Greta had her secrets and I had mine. Could I trust her with mine? Would she even care?

"You know," she paused, softly pulling a strand of hair behind her ear. "You never asked where I went." For a moment she looked embarrassed with the admission.

"Yeah, but—I mean, what did you—"

"Or why. You didn't ask *why* I left. You and Dad have both been in your own little worlds since coming up here. This family is so good at running away from our problems. Why is that? Sometimes it feels like I'm not even here in front of you." The words came gushing out, like they'd been dammed up too long. Greta was showing the cracks in her shell.

"Greta, *you* left. And then you just come back and act like nothing happened! Who's the one in denial?" I felt my face growing hot. Were we really going to do this here?

She held up her right wrist and pulled back her sleeve. I saw exactly what I suspected, what I feared: thin, purple lines. Scars. Four of them lined up against her skin. I felt sick, and I looked away.

"Why haven't you asked? Why hasn't Dad? I know you've seen them. You've been suspicious ever since Thanksgiving," she paused. "You want to know where I went? I went to see Mom. I took the Greyhound back to North Carolina to be with her again. I mean, we just *left* her there."

For whatever reason, I wasn't surprised. It was like I knew all along. I knew, and all I felt was a deep, penetrating sadness that she hadn't asked if I would go with her. I would have.

She took a deep breath before continuing. "Dad didn't give us a chance to prepare our goodbyes. *He* made the decision to move up here. *He* made the decision to leave her behind, but you know what? *I* wasn't ready. So I went back to say goodbye for real.

"It just seems like you and Dad both keep trying to move forward without her. You both keep trying to assure each other we're not all screwed up, but we are, Louisa. We're screwed up. We haven't moved on. We can't. We're stuck in this pattern of pretending everything's perfect. I know you and Dad think I'm just a spoiled brat. *What does Greta have to be sad about?* But it's not as easy for me as you think . . . "

"It's not easy for me, either!" I blurted out. "You act like I've just forgotten her. How dare you pretend to know what I'm feeling? You literally have no clue." The words came spilling out, falling like guts in a botched operation. Other café patrons glanced toward our table, so I lowered my voice but stayed firm. "I haven't moved on, Greta. And I haven't forgotten her. I'm still trying to figure it all out just like you. Just like Dad."

Greta looked away when Chris brought us our tea. Before I could stop him, he pulled up a chair to join us. Greta stood up and started buttoning her coat.

"I'm suddenly not in the mood," she said, wrapping her scarf around her neck. Her voice was cold, and Chris gave me a sheepish look realizing he'd interrupted something.

"I can drive Louisa home," he offered.

"That'd be great." She grabbed her keys off the table and didn't bother to say goodbye. Her mug sat untouched.

The darkness outside seemed overwhelming. Brandywine Valley was quiet tonight. Chris was bundled in a bruised leather bomber jacket, his hair pulled back. I wondered if it took effort to find clothes that looked so *used*.

"You—" Chris paused as he blew into his clamped hands, shifted his weight, and looked intently at me. "You want to get outta here?"

"Yes," I said breathlessly.

We walked to his car in uncomfortable silence. I was clearly distracted, and he looked like he was brainstorming ways to apologize for earlier. But the thing was, I was glad he'd interrupted the conversation. I wasn't ready to confront Greta. I didn't want to have that conversation.

"Your sister's hot," Chris said as he turned the ignition and the Volvo growled awake.

I punched him on the arm. He laughed and held his bicep in mock-injury.

"Shut up," I sighed, playing mindlessly with the automatic window toggle.

"There's a place I want to take you," Chris said seriously.

"Yeah, I've heard that one before. From you, actually."

He smiled in response, looking at the road. I studied his silhouette. His brown skin looked even darker in the dimly lit car. There was something so exotic about him. The skin? The hair? The tattoo I'd recently spotted on the inside of his forearm? He ejected a cassette tape from the old car stereo, flipped it over, and inserted it again. Then he adjusted the volume to a loud Roger Daltrey belting out "Teenage Wasteland." He began strumming his fingers on the steering wheel, and I unleashed on an invisible drum kit. For a moment I just let it all out. With Chris, I felt I could be reckless. I never knew how far he'd push me, or how far I'd allow myself to go.

As the music slowed, I decided to question him.

"So what's your deal?" I folded my arms. He furrowed his eyebrows in response. I rephrased my question. "What's with the ponytail and the tie-dye? The flip-flops in winter? You *enjoy* being different," I brazenly declared. It was so easy being daring around Chris. I didn't feel like I needed to impress him. He didn't make me feel nervous, not in the same way I felt around Gabe.

"What do you want to know?" Chris shrugged.

"The tattoo? What does it mean?"

"Which tattoo?"

I reached over and grabbed his wrist, turning his arm upward and exposing the small, black character. I didn't dare ask about possible others.

"It says 'turtle.'"

"Why do you have 'turtle' tattooed on your wrist?"

"What about you, Louisa? What's your deal?" he deflected.

"What do you want to know?" I swept my bangs out of my eyes.

Chris looked over at me, inhaling in contemplation. "Tell me something no one else knows about you."

His eyes went back to the road. I scrunched my mouth to the side. Not a question I willingly wanted to answer. We sat for a minute without saying anything, the music soft and distant, before pulling into the dark parking lot of an industrial block of warehouse buildings. Chris parked the car, and I reached for the door handle. Chris grabbed my arm, holding me back.

"Come on. There must be something."

"I can kind of hear dead people. Well, not people. Just one person. One dead person."

I don't know why I said it. Why the honesty? Maybe I knew Chris wouldn't call me crazy. Maybe I knew he'd believe me. Maybe it was Rosemary's initial assessment: Chris can get people to do things for him—admit things to him. Or, maybe I just needed to tell someone.

He didn't look at me like I was crazy. He didn't scoff, or taunt, or even ask whose voice I was hearing. He just smiled, patted my knee, and looked up at the lit building in front of us.

"Come on."

He opened the door and got out of the car. I followed, dumbstruck and slightly smitten. Chris led me to a heavy-looking, rust-colored metal door on a loading dock. There was a small handwritten "Open" sign stuck next to the doorknob with electrical tape. I had no idea how we got here. I didn't know if we'd been in the car for ten minutes or thirty. I didn't know if we were still in town or somewhere else. Part of me knew I should be nervous—standing in front of this most unwelcoming door in the bitter cold—but part of me felt excited. A new journey with a new friend. A confidant I trusted. Someone who knew my secret, or at least someone whom I'd entrusted with it, whether he believed me or not.

"Ladies first," Chris mused as he heaved the door open, flooding the landing with fluorescent light.

Squinting my eyes and knocking the snow from my snow boots against the building, I took a step inside. I was awestruck. Rows, towers, and carefree piles of books upon books upon books. Chris had brought me to the Mecca of used bookstores. Housed in a vacant warehouse, Skip's Used Books was a Brandywine Valley institution. Genres were written in Sharpie on scraps of white paper haphazardly taped to the end of each aisle. I'd never seen anything like it. I turned to look at my friend, my mouth agape. His turned up in a knowing smile. He grabbed my hand and steered us down the first aisle, letting the books consume us.

"This is awesome!" I giggled excitedly, tugging tightly on Chris's grip.

My friend let me navigate the bookstore. Occasionally he'd pick up a book and read the inner sleeve while I selected books by the armful: an illustrated *Jane Eyre,* a book on photography, a history on Scandinavia, and a collection of Charles Schulz's early works. I even found a Swedish-English dictionary, circa 1948, and picked it up just to have on hand. After I'd explored every aisle twice, handling hundreds of used books that spanned a century (or more) of publication, I took my stack to the front desk.

"Seven dollars," the balding man in glasses held out a greasy hand.

"Seven dollars for ten books? That's less than a dollar a book!" I said in disbelief.

"How much did you want to pay?" the awkward man chuckled, looking to Chris.

I looked at Chris to express my amazement but came up speechless. It was the first time I really looked at him under the fluorescents. He stood there, gazing intently at me with his large brown eyes in his vintage leather jacket, looking absolutely incredible. Under all the unshaven scruff, long curls, holey jeans, and dirt under the fingernails, Chris had a James Dean appeal. I'd seen it before: the first time we met in class when he told me about his backpacking in North Carolina, the time I watched him make advances with Lacey in the cafeteria, and that night in his Volvo when he took me to the Agnew Pennsbury Township and questioned his likelihood of doing the right thing. Everything Chris did was tender; under it all, he had such a gentle soul. And he carried himself with such humility despite being, quite possibly, the most handsome guy in school. He was a rough-cut diamond. Standing there in the bookstore, the balding man's hand still outstretched, I felt privileged to see the real Chris, the one he didn't show most people. And I felt connected to him. As if this bookstore was now *our* hidden secret. As if we both understood one another, even if no one else did. At sixteen, it was rare to find someone else who truly got me.

I handed the man my seven dollars, grabbed my books, and walked over to where Chris stood by the door.

"Ready to go?"

He quietly smiled, putting his hand on my back as he held the door open for me. His hand on my back transcended all of my previous girlish experiences with innocent flirtations. Chris was older and wiser. He had done this before. And *this*? Whatever it was left me breathless.

"With you? Anywhere."

We climbed into his cold, dark car that smelled sweetly of orange rind and sandalwood. The windshield had already developed a thin sheet of ice. Under the pale blue light of a humming street lamp, Chris took my books off my lap and tossed them casually in the backseat. I sat motionless, helpless to do anything but watch as he leaned across his armrest and nuzzled his chin against my neck. He breathed deeply, hot air moistening my skin. *This is too much,* I thought. But when his lips at last met mine, I was already gone.

XVIII.

On Christmas Eve, the streets of Trelleborg were frozen, dark, and quiet. A candle flickered in a lone window here, a shadow brushed against a laced curtain there. Where was the moon?

For the fourth time that night, Gerhard stopped to set his gift down, rest his shoulders, and wrap his scarf tighter around his neck. He clapped his mittened hands together, the sound echoing down the empty street, before lifting his load and traveling on.

The bell tower at *Sankt Nicolai kyrka* loomed tall and great against the black December sky. Beneath it, Gerhard felt incredibly insignificant. He wished Lasse were there to keep him company so he didn't feel so alone.

"*God jul*! Merry Christmas!" Gerhard warmly greeted the church pastor who crouched on a small ladder in front of the church's doors with a hammer in one hand and two wreaths in the other.

"*Oy*!" jumped the frail man, steadying his balance. "Välkommen, Gerhard! You frightened me! Without your brother, I didn't hear you coming. How his laugh can carry."

Gerhard forced a smile. He looked back at his gift and then at his wet boots. Suddenly, it didn't seem sufficient.

"Forgive me," he apologized, trying to block the sight of his gift, a tall and heavy pine, behind him.

He knew he should have selected a different one. This tree was smaller than the ones he'd picked in prior years. But there was something about this one that had called to him earlier that afternoon. *You deserve greatness*, he'd told the tree, and he'd chopped it down with the utmost care. But now, standing in the dark, he wasn't so sure.

The old man carefully descended from his post.

"Here!" He chuckled and handed the wreaths to Gerhard. "I'm just getting ready for the others. They haven't come yet, but they will."

The man quietly smiled, cocking his ear to one side as if expecting to hear footsteps in the snow. He stuffed his pipe with loose tobacco while Gerhard surreptitiously set the tree to the side of the yard. But the pastor followed him, and Gerhard cringed, expecting disappointment.

The pastor patted the exposed trunk approvingly, "It's good."

The two men stopped and looked out at the dark streets, silently sharing the moment. The older man breathed deeply to assure himself he still could, while Gerhard's thoughts took him to the latest news coming out of Finland. Helsinki had recently been bombed, the Soviets officially invading, crossing Finnish borders, on November 30.

"The world seems to be getting colder," Gerhard remarked, not really knowing the proper thing to say.

"Oh, it's never as cold as you think," the pastor smiled, taking Gerhard's arm and leading him back into the church.

Gerhard set the damp tree at the front of the altar, and the pastor handed him two long planks of wood to make a simple stand. Once in its proper place, there was no denying this was the leanest tree Gerhard had ever cut down. It was tall, but it was also thin and the branches spare.

"It's not the best tree, is it?" Gerhard tilted his head to confirm the pine was, in fact, leaning heavily to one side.

"Nonsense," the pastor scoffed and handed Gerhard a crate of paper decorations, the same ones that had adorned the tree every year since Gerhard was a boy. "'In simplicity and godly sincerity . . . do we have our conversation in the world.' 2 Corinthians 1:12."

"It's leaning!" Lasse cried as he entered the church carrying a copper kettle and a basket of warm saffron buns. "Can't you straighten it?"

"*Tack*, Lasse. Are your mother and father far behind?" The white-haired pastor took the pot and beckoned to a table where Lasse could set the buns.

"They're waiting on Pontus. He cut himself shaving and there's blood everywhere," Lasse laughed and scratched his brow. "Idiot," he muttered quietly.

Gerhard started hanging red strips of thin paper on the bare branches and filling paper cones with caramel candy. His brother joined him.

"Have you ever seen such a thin tree?" Lasse dipped his hand into the crate.

"But it smells good," Gerhard inhaled slowly.

Lasse leaned in and sniffed. "Smells like winter."

"Smells like Christmas," Gerhard corrected.

"You're such a romantic."

By eleven, the first families arrived on foot. Fathers on kick sleds pushed young children through snowy streets. Cloaked women with wool kerchiefs clung to lit torches and hummed Christmas melodies. They stepped carefully in wet sled tracks and clasped hands with young daughters. Leif, Åsa, Pontus, and Anna arrived just in time to join the church choir. The small assembly started low, quietly warming up. *Godafton mitt herrskap*. Good evening, gentlemen.

It was nearly two o'clock when the sanctuary finally fell still. Gerhard and Lasse sat in the front pew, teasing a pigtailed girl about the *jultomte,* the Christmas elf.

"You better hurry and put out some porridge on your front step! He'll pass your house if you don't, and then no presents for you!" Lasse grinned wide-eyed as the little girl stared doubtfully at the two older boys. He jabbed Gerhard in the side.

"Everyone knows the *jultomte* isn't real," the girl protested.

"Yes, but why take the chance?" Gerhard asked earnestly.

"*He* still puts out the porridge for the *jultomte*, and he's seventeen!" Lasse laughed, pointing at a blushing Gerhard.

"I do," Gerhard confirmed. "And the *tomte*'s always come. So hurry home and do as we say."

The girl's mother called to her from the back of the church and in an instant she was gone. Lasse and Gerhard gathered their coats and followed sleepily.

"It's not silly," Gerhard defended himself.

"Oh, come on," Lasse groaned.

"It brings good luck."

"It brings mice," Lasse playfully shouldered his brother before jogging ahead.

The crisp night air smelled bitter, like rust or iron. The cold made their bones ache and their limbs numb. Lasse shuddered and hopped twice to help his circulation.

"Ready, *Bror*? We'll race home."

But Gerhard just stared at the sky. It was too wondrous to go back just yet. There was still something magical about these early hours. Christmas morning.

"Can't we take the way by the shore?" he asked hopefully.

"*Helvete*!" Lasse cursed under his frosty breath, and then remembered he was in front of the church. "Oh."

"It's too beautiful to go back now," Gerhard began, but Lasse held up his hand.

"We'll race to the shore, then."

"Let's take our time," Gerhard pleaded.

"Oy, oy, oy, Gerhard. You really are something. I'm freezing like a dog!" Lasse looked annoyed while lighting a hand-rolled cigarette, but his tone softened as he exhaled. "Well, come on."

The two brothers rounded the path by the shipyards and strained to hear a low hum breaking the silence of the evening. Drums? Motors? No.

Stallarna. The stables.

Down near the docks sat a squatty old barn with a rotting wood door. The old horse stables. It'd been sitting there for two hundred years, and in the summer, the seamen could still smell manure when they walked by. Old barn smells had a way of lingering for centuries.

"Should we?" Gerhard asked, but Lasse was already headed in that direction.

A sign in the window read *STÄNGT*, CLOSED, but the penetrating sounds from within alluded to something else. Lasse reached for the latch, and the boys stepped inside.

The room was warm; a fire blazed behind an iron grate. A weary fiddler played sadly in the corner. Twenty shipyard workers, brutish men with biceps the size of ham hocks, leaned heavily on each other. Pontus, with his deep, baritone voice, stood near the fire on a footstool, leading the men in Bellman's "Epistle 72." The twins sighed at the sight of him. One of the men toward the back of the crowd wept somberly as he remembered a woman he once loved. His salty tears mixed with the burning drink he lifted to his lips. *Stallarna*, where the spiritless found spirits to warm their souls. Lasse and Gerhard sipped slowly on mulled wine, listening to the sad song of the sleeping nymph. They waited until the end before pulling Pontus from his pedestal and away from his adoring audience. His hair, his pores, his breath smelled sweetly of *brännvin*, and the barkeep gave his singer a pint for the walk back. The uncle stumbled as his nephews pushed him out into the snow.

The three men walked in silence as they passed the tall grasses on the shore. Glimmering waves crashed quietly on the shadowed sand. Pontus stopped to blow his nose in a dirty rag.

"Nephews, let me tell you this now before I'm too sober. I don't think I'd have the courage to say it without . . . " He lifted his drink—a toast to the night's sky—and gulped loudly. The twins stopped and stared at their red-rimmed, sad-eyed uncle. "Those words you heard tonight? The old man's sermon about miracles and divinity? Don't you believe it."

Pontus rubbed his nose with the back of his hand and sniffed. The twins exchanged unknowing glances. Their breath danced in the air before it disappeared.

"There are no miracles in this world. There is only you and me. There is only this," he reached into the snow and gave a handful to each brother. "Feel it. Is it a miracle?"

Gerhard stared as the snow melted and dripped out of his hands.

"Of course not. We make our own miracles, boys. Don't let them fool you into believing we don't."

XIX.

I woke up to the smell of bacon. Someone clamored in the kitchen. The sound of pots, pans, and lids falling and cascading across linoleum penetrated the house. I pulled my cover to my chin and turned toward the dark corner of the wall. First day of Christmas break and I was awake at seven. Classic.

I blinked my eyes and shifted to my back, staring at the ceiling. At least bacon was one of the best smells to wake to in the morning.

Sighing, I pulled myself up and sat on the side of the bed, shuffling into my sheepskin-lined moccasin slippers. I wasn't used to cold, bare floors. Slippers in North Carolina were for show. Slippers in Pennsylvania were a necessity. They were the first thing I put on in the morning, and the last thing I took off before sliding into bed.

Finding the strength to stand, I pulled on a pair of red pajama pants Dad had found in a box in the attic. I stretched and then bent down to look at myself in my vanity mirror. Smeared mascara under my right eye and a messy ponytail stared back at me.

So this is what late-night make-out hair looks like, I smiled smugly recalling the previous evening.

I wiped away most of the makeup smudge and pulled my arms through an oversized button-up cardigan. I closed my bedroom door behind me as I sleepily made my way down the steps. Passing Greta's bedroom, I gave the door a quick rap. She groaned from behind the door, but she'd be joining me in the kitchen soon enough. I knew her too well. Once awake, Magnussons couldn't go back to sleep. Dad called it "work ethic." I called it "insomnia."

I was happy the phone calls from my grandmother had—presumably—resumed. I marveled at Grandma's storytelling. It was less than a week before Christmas, and this last phone call's wintry setting seemed appropriate for the season. Did Grandma know that? Could she see my calendar, from wherever she was calling? Could she tell the holiday was approaching? Could she see *me*?

"Morning, kiddo!" Dad greeted me from my reminiscent stupor, swinging his spatula and nearly dropping a pancake to the floor.

"Morning." I hitched up a pant leg to scratch an itch on my ankle, yawning.

Dad stared at me, the pancake still on the end of the spatula. "You're getting taller every day. Long legs. Just like your dad." He turned back to the stove. Flipped the flapjack and let it sizzle on the skillet.

I slumped into a chair at the kitchen table with one leg up, resting my chin on my knee. My eyes closed involuntarily.

"Sleepy?"

"Dad, it's Christmas break. This should qualify as child abuse, truly. You're lucky you have bacon," I said, grabbing a slice from a plate on the table and waving it at him accusingly.

"Here." He set a mug of steaming coffee in front of me.

"Ah," I happily inhaled. "The addiction continues."

"Is Greta awake?" he asked, finally acknowledging her existence.

"Yeah, but not voluntarily. You might be able to shut me up with coffee. But Greta—"

"Heads are going to roll!" Greta announced on her entrance into the kitchen.

She and I glanced quickly at each other, but even more quickly we glanced away. Dad didn't even notice the tension between us.

"Greta needs something stronger than caffeine," I sneered.

She ignored me, unwrapping a Lady Grey tea bag and tossing it into an empty mug.

"I don't want to hear it, girls," Dad warned. How did he not see it? "I'm in a good mood. The sun's out. It's going to be a good day!"

I leaned back in my chair to look out the kitchen window. Just as I'd expected: overcast, like the usual Pennsylvania-in-December gray day. Dad was giddy. I eyed Greta suspiciously, but she was consumed with pouring hot water into her mug.

"What's with today?" I plucked a slice of bacon from where it sat on a grease-soaked paper towel.

"Today," Dad waited with a dramatic pause and placed his hands on his hips, sticking out his chest to make a proclamation. "Today, Greta gets a set of wheels!"

My eyes darted to Greta just in time to see her choke on her first sip of black tea. She set the mug on the table, dabbing her mouth with a napkin.

"Excuse me?"

Dad walked over to her, placing his hand on her shoulder. "It's long overdue, Greta. It's something we should have done a long time ago." He placed his other hand on my shoulder.

I rolled my eyes. I crunched my bacon while Dad had his moment of paternal joy. Greta was speechless. So he was just going to buy her forgiveness? Or her love? Or whatever it was he thought he was missing. It all made me a bit sick. What we needed was to talk about us. Not cars. Not Christmas. Us.

"Seriously? I don't have to drive the station wagon anymore?" Greta asked tentatively, as if Dad could take back the offer at any moment. She didn't trust him completely. I didn't either.

"Yes, really. The Outback is a *sports utility* wagon, a four-wheel-drive sports utility wagon that's been good to you. Show a little respect to the old girl." Dad smiled, dishing up a pair of blueberry pancakes and setting them on the table.

"I'll pay whatever respects I have to, as long as I don't have to drive it anymore," Greta said, hardly able to contain her excitement. I guess his strategy worked. They were acting perfectly happy with each other.

"My only restrictions," Dad held up a cautionary finger before turning back to the skillet to pour some more batter. "Used, under fifteen thousand, any color other than red, and you promise to always come home."

"Of course!" Greta exclaimed before adding, "But Dad, red is my favorite color."

"A favorite color of the police, too. Red cars are magnets for speeding tickets. How about gray? It's a nice, sensible, mature color," Dad nodded approvingly.

"Gray," I joked. "To match her hair color?"

Greta kicked me under the table. She wasn't going to let me ruin her chances of getting a car. So I shut up, and ate my blueberry pancakes with extra syrup. Neither of them fooled me. Whatever it was Dad was doing was only masking the truth. It'd all come to a head eventually. I figured I'd just sit back and wait.

After breakfast, we picked Rosemary up on the way down the hill. It seemed like she and Dad couldn't get enough time together. Since the move—since meeting Rosemary—Dad had exhibited a new happiness. It wasn't something I could wholly attribute to one thing: the new surroundings, the new love interest, or something else. And in the end, I didn't mind.

We pulled into the first car lot. Greta's foot tapped anxiously on the Outback floor. I supposed she was nervous about making such an important decision: choosing a fashionable, safe, reliable, affordable car. Fashionable being the highest priority, reliability being the second. We got out of the car and, as she and Dad ventured down a row of sedans, Rosemary and I stayed back, letting the two of them have their room to privately discuss options.

"So, how's it going?" Rosemary asked casually.

It was something I admired about her: her perceptive ability to know when there was something bothering me. She'd come to me, but I never thought of her as meddlesome.

"It's okay," I replied. "I got another message last night. It was a story about Christmas. Kind of appropriate, I guess."

"You're getting closer, Louisa. It's like you're about to collide. Whatever it is, it's going to be big. I can feel it. Just be patient."

"Yeah. I still wish I knew my role. She's set me up for a lot of questions and not a lot of answers."

"They'll come."

"How can you be so sure?" I stopped walking.

Rosemary turned to face me. "Things like this don't happen without a reason," she shrugged.

"I'm not so sure anymore."

"Just wait, Louisa. The answers will come." She started walking and I followed. Up ahead, Dad and Greta were peering into the window of a blue Toyota Camry. "If you don't mind me asking—and let me know if you do—how are things going with you and Gabe? He seems like a nice young man," she leaned over and knocked her shoulder playfully into mine.

"Oh, Rosemary, I'm going skiing with him. As in 'meeting the parents' skiing. I'm kind of nervous," I admitted. "I like Gabe because he's upfront with me, even though I didn't think he was in the beginning. With Gabe, I kind of feel like what you see is what you get. It's refreshing."

"But?" Rosemary raised an eyebrow, hearing the uncertainty in my tone.

"Is there a 'but'?"

"You tell me."

"Well, there's this other guy, Chris—"

"I knew it!" Rosemary clapped her hands animatedly. "The Leo."

"What?"

"That time you came to my house for the almanac report? I didn't tell you, but there was something with the August tenth birthday guy. Like a spark from a piece of flint, but I couldn't get a handle on it.

That's how it works, sometimes. Just a little flicker of light letting me know that there's something more there."

She paused, letting me revisit that moment on her couch when she first described Chris. It seemed like a lifetime ago. I knew so much more now. I knew more, but also less. Everything seemed muddled. Chris and Gabe. Greta and me. Leif and Lasse. Dad and everyone—and everything—else.

"I got that from you the first time I met you, too," Rosemary continued. "When you came to my house for dinner, there was this glow around you. I still see it sometimes."

I could feel blood rushing to my cheeks. I wasn't used to this type of attention. The way Rosemary characterized me, surrounded by the glimmer of the supernatural, made me shiver. Anytime I let my mind wander, or really dig deep into the stories from Grandma—the stories about Grandpa—a knot clenched in my stomach. It wasn't an ill feeling or nervousness. It was just perplexing: something there I couldn't see, something I couldn't hold on to.

"It's unsettling."

"I know. I'm sorry."

Rosemary put her arm around me. The gesture felt natural. I reached up and grabbed her hand and we walked, in mutual appreciation, to join the others. By one-thirty, we'd exhausted four of the five used-car lots in town. Discouraged and hungry, both Greta and Dad were getting punchy with salesmen, with Rosemary and me, and with each other. It was time to take a break.

"So," Rosemary interjected, cutting off one of Dad's protests, energetically clapping her hands together, her elbows sticking out parallel to the ground. "Who's ready for lunch?"

With relief, I eagerly held up my hand.

We drove to Weaver's after Rosemary swore on her life that the Weaver's deli sandwiches were without equal in all of Pennsylvania. Dad and Greta were too hungry to care, and I wasn't about to forego a trip to my favorite neighborhood grocery store.

The four of us sluggishly stood in front of the deli counter. Dad scratched his head in contemplation at the menu on the white board. Greta crossed her arms in frustration, and Rosemary nervously beamed a peace-making smile.

"I'll have the roasted red pepper on focaccia, Ned," she ordered first, pleasantly paving the way for the rest of us.

The stocky man behind the counter pulled a pencil from behind his ear, scratched out the order on a slip of pink paper, winked at Rosemary, and then looked back at the rest of us. Rosemary turned toward me, silently pleading for me to place an order so Dad and Greta could take our friendly lead.

"The avocado and feta, please. In a pita. With sprouts." I smiled at the man.

"Mayo?"

"Absolutely."

The man looked at Greta. "How 'bout you, sweetheart?" Ned asked while adjusting one of his rolled sleeves, exposing more of his beefy left arm. He reminded me so much of Brutus from Popeye. The hefty chin and shaggy black beard. Dad's head immediately jerked up in response to Greta's new nickname.

"I'll have the tuna on rye, *Ned*," Dad remarked, giving Ned the good old fatherly once-over and looking none too impressed. He then put his hand around Rosemary's shoulder as a public declaration of ownership. I scoffed at the blatant testosterone, slightly amused that it was coming from my father.

"Turkey club. No mayo, no bacon, no tomato. On wheat," Greta finally decided. "Toasted."

As Dad paid for the sandwiches, my eyes darted around the store for Gabe.

"Excuse me," I called after Ned, who was slicing turkey on a meat slicer behind the counter. He lifted his head in acknowledgment without turning around. "Is Gabe working today?"

"He's on the register."

Rosemary took a seat with Dad and Greta at one of the three round tables next to the deli. Dad eyed me suspiciously when I told him I'd join them in a moment. Greta began working on a crossword in a newspaper someone had abandoned. It was obvious she was frustrated with Dad but didn't want to come off as ungrateful. Over the morning, she'd found several cars that piqued her interest: a canvas-top Jeep that Dad had deemed "impractical for Pennsylvania winters," a Ford Mustang that Dad labeled "too sexy," and a Kia Sportage, which Dad also refused, declaring it "a tin can." So much for his three limited restrictions. Greta was getting impatient. I was glad to step away from the table for a minute to find Gabe.

At the front of the store, I saw him bagging groceries for a middle-aged man. His blue eyes met mine for a split second before he returned to finish his conversation with the customer. From what I could overhear, he was giving the man advice on compost bins.

"You always want to rinse out the eggshells before adding them to the pile," I heard him say.

The man seemed genuinely grateful to Gabe for the tip, thanking him before leaving the store with groceries in hand.

"Another happy customer?" I said in greeting, finding a lull in the checkout line.

"As always," Gabe folded his arms casually. "What brings you in?"

"Deli sandwiches." I tossed my head toward the back of the store. "My family's exasperated as a result of starvation. The usual." I shrugged playfully.

"Ah, I see."

"We're out shopping for a car for Greta as kind of an early Christmas present, and thought we'd stop in for some lunch. I didn't even know you served lunch."

"Every day. Hey, we still on for Monday?" he asked. "I told my parents you were coming, and they said you could use my sister's old skis. You're about her size."

"Yes, we're on," I replied, relieved. "Thanks for the loaners. I didn't know you had a sister."

"Yeah, she's studying abroad in Belize. She doesn't need *skis* in *Belize*," Gabe chuckled at his own lame rhyme.

Someone got in line behind me.

"So we'll pick you up at seven on Monday?" Gabe straightened back up, unfolding his arms and smiling at the customer. He looked so friendly and adorable in his green apron. *His parents must love him working here*, I thought to myself. He had the perfect face to represent the family business.

"I'll be ready," I answered, retreating back to the deli, fully knowing—meeting the parents, having never skied a day in my life—I would be anything but ready.

Back at the table, the conversation was, unsurprisingly, about cars.

"I still vote for the white Buick," Dad commented to the table while taking a first bite of his sandwich.

"The one with the tan upholstery?" Greta looked up, trying to remember.

"Yeah, it was impeccable."

"It was impeccable because 'Grandma' died before she could drive it anywhere."

"What? Rosemary, back me up here. That car was hip." Even Dad's usage of the word "hip" came out sounding old.

Rosemary, in mid-chew of her roasted pepper on focaccia, held a hand to cover her mouth as she shook her head in disagreement. Dad's choice, the white Buick, was a lost cause.

"What?" Dad looked surprised.

"It really was an old lady's car, Christian," Rosemary said from behind her hand, before swallowing.

"Well, I thought it was hip." There was that word again.

"Maybe, Dad, that's because . . . " Greta started, but stopped herself midsentence. She wasn't willing to risk losing a car she hadn't even been given yet. Dad scrunched his mouth. He knew when he was being insulted.

I sat down to my sandwich in its blue plastic basket, picked up a folded section of discarded newspaper, and willingly immersed myself in anything but car talk. The newspaper was dated yesterday, and my eyes scanned the page absentmindedly.

"What about that cute VW beetle?" Rosemary suggested, a dot of hummus on her bottom lip.

Dad motioned to his own lip and Rosemary embarrassedly wiped her mouth clean. "That was a coupe. What are the girls going to do with a coupe?" Dad prompted.

"Drive around together?" Rosemary answered innocently.

Dad smiled, realizing he was fighting a losing battle. I just batted my eyes and returned to the paper. Greta was noticeably silent.

"Great sandwich," Dad chimed in after a prolonged moment of quiet.

We all nodded our heads in agreement but said nothing. I flipped the paper over and casually looked at the classifieds. My eyes rested on a small for-sale ad. Restored Glam: '67 Mercury Comet. Haul-away only. 812-6776. Ask for Edna.

I was interested. "Dad, what do Mercury Comets look like?"

"Muscle cars." He paused. "Like *American Graffiti* muscle cars."

"Like a Steve McQueen muscle car?"

"Cooler than Steve McQueen," Dad joked, cocking his head to the side in confusion. "How do you know about Steve McQueen?"

"I've seen *Bullitt*," I said defensively.

"What are you talking about, Louisa?" Greta asked, annoyed. She wasn't interested in our banter.

"I don't know," I shrugged. "There's an ad here for a '67 Mercury Comet. Thought Dad might want to go see it and relive some of his youth," I teased.

Rosemary laughed, and Dad held his sandwich out at me, shaking it as he answered, "I'd be surprised if the thing still ran."

"Actually, I am surprised *you're* still running, Dad," Greta chimed in.

Setting down his sandwich, Dad sighed, wiping his hands on his jeans in defeat.

"Call and see if it's still available." He winked at Rosemary. "And how much it costs."

Within thirty minutes, the four of us were standing in Edna's front yard—a littered jungle of scrap metal, spare parts, and dissected automobiles—staring at the most beautiful car I'd ever seen.

XX.

Sitting at the breakfast table early Monday morning, I still couldn't believe it. At any moment, I could walk to the window and look out at the stunning new automobile sitting in our driveway: the fully restored Comet Caliente. With its moss green and chrome exterior, brown leather steering wheel, and $10,000 price tag that was well under Dad's allotted budget, everything about it was perfect.

"It was my boy's car. He loved this thing," Edna had said nostalgically, running her finger over its waxy hood. "He's dead now. Passed away two months ago."

"I'm very sorry to hear that," Dad offered his condolences.

Edna folded her arms and leaned against the car, letting it embrace her. She looked our group up and down guardedly. She was feeling us out. Were we good enough for her son's prized hot rod?

"Yes, well." She stopped to pick at something in her teeth, squinting at us. "I just want to get rid of it now. Can't stand to look at it anymore, t'be honest."

"I understand that completely," Dad gulped, looking at Greta and me. "More than you know."

"How much do you want for it?" Greta chimed in, hesitantly.

Edna turned from Dad to look at my sister. "I could get a lot for it on the In-ter-net," Edna spoke deliberately. "But I only really want what Roy spent restoring the thing."

Twice she referred to the car as "the thing," and I wondered silently if it was some form of disassociation. After Mom died, I remember walking around the house and deeming some of her things illegitimate: her garden shoes (the ones she wore before she got ill, the ones she wore every spring when she planted annuals in the garden, when she grew tomatoes with such tenderness); the reusable 7-Eleven Big Gulp she carried around with her throughout her chemotherapy (she was constantly complaining of thirst, and she refused to drink the water in plastic bottles that Dad bought in bulk because they were "wasteful"); her Rodgers and Hammerstein CD collection (how many times had I joined her for the second verse—the only verse I knew—to sing a mom-and-daughter duet of "The Surrey with the Fringe on Top"?). When Mom died, all those things became alien to me. I *needed* them to be foreign. Their significance and purpose were too painful to confess. And so, I imagined, came to be the Comet for Edna.

"Ten thousand dollars," she finally nodded in declaration. "Cash. Title's in the glove compartment, signed and ready to go."

Instantly, Dad ducked under the hood, inspecting the engine. He circled the car more than once and let out a couple approving grunts while Greta, Rosemary, and I stood on the sideline, speechless.

"Greta, you're sure you want to buy a manual? I thought you wanted automatic, not a stick like the Subaru."

"I'll be fine, Dad," she tried to quickly dismiss whatever doubts he had.

Greta was so nervous I could hear her deep breathing next to me. At one point, she reached over and grabbed my arm just to release some tension. None of us dared speak.

"I've got a check right here." Dad reached into his breast pocket, pulled out his billfold, and began scribbling the price of the car. He held it out to Edna, then hesitated. "I can assume the heat works? It's freezing out here."

"You think my son's a damn fool? 'Course the heat works! This is Pennsylvania!" Edna snapped the check from Dad's grip and handed him a key attached to a fuchsia-dyed rabbit's foot.

"The luck is complimentary," Edna winked at Greta, turned on her heels, and retreated back into her house. The screen door banged loudly.

The deal was done. Dad walked over to his older daughter and held the keys in front of her, smiling. "Merry Christmas, Greta."

"C'mon Louisa!" Greta shrieked.

We climbed onto the front bench seat together, giggling. It smelled like cherries. We drove out of the driveway, waving out the window to Dad and Rosemary, who stood holding hands in our dust.

Monday morning, before sunup, I sat happily at the kitchen table eating a bowl of Frosted Mini-Wheats, knowing that gorgeous green car sat outside. And knowing that most college campuses don't allow freshmen to have cars meant that gorgeous green car would soon belong to me when Greta left for school next fall. I even convinced Greta we should christen it "The Thing." She obliged happily but refused to let me smash a bottle of root beer on its grill in celebration.

I heard footsteps in the hall and looked expectantly at the doorway for Dad. He greeted me with a smile and a yawn, still in his favorite pajamas: a UNC sweatshirt and shorts.

"Morning, kiddo. Are you ready? Want some coffee to go?" He held up a travel mug to me.

"No, that's okay. I'm kind of nervous." It was true. I was crazy-nervous, not sure if winter sports and I mixed well or not.

"Don't be nervous. We're Swedes. We're practically made of snow!" Dad laughed. I gave him a halfhearted chuckle. "Your Grandpa once did the Vasaloppet. Or so the legend goes."

He pulled out a chair and joined me at the table. I glanced up at the kitchen clock. Gabe would be here in five minutes.

"The Vasa what?"

"The Vasaloppet. It's kind of a big deal in Scandinavia. Ninety kilometers of cross-country skiing. In other words, brutal torture," he smiled introspectively.

"How many miles in ninety kilometers?" I hated doing math on the fly, but Dad was good at it. He was good at everything.

"Fifty . . . " He scratched his chin. "Fifty-six? That sounds about right."

"Fifty-six miles of snow? On skis?"

He laughed at my bewilderment. "Well, that's just what my mom told me. When I was a kid, Mom loved bragging about all of Dad's athletic abilities. He could wander aimlessly in the wilderness and always find his way back. When they were newlyweds he once did a triathlon, and he did the Vasaloppet. Before they met, of course, back when he still lived in Sweden."

Jeez, Dad. Why didn't you ever tell us this before? I thought. But I already knew the answer: I wouldn't have cared. Now, I cared with burning intensity.

"What else did Grandma say?" I inquired covertly.

It was good to hear him opening up again. There was still so much I had to figure out. It hurt my head thinking about it. But before he could answer, there was a soft tap on the front door. Gabe had arrived. My questions for Dad would have to wait.

We pulled into the ski resort two hours later. The drive was pleasant: Gabe's mom peppered me with questions about my life in North Carolina, Dad and Greta, and my other interests. I found his mom striking, though completely different from my own mother. She was tall and had wiry, overblown, thick gray hair. She didn't wear a stitch of makeup, and her skin was tough and creased from years of working—and playing—outside. Her eyes were very pale and she looked old, but wise. When she smiled, I felt warm. I imagined she wore Birkenstocks and thick wool socks. She was a grown-up flower child. For the most part, Gabe's dad just drove. Occasionally, he offered a one-liner or made some obscure reference to something I didn't understand, and everyone in the car laughed. They seemed like a very happy family. I was comfortable with them.

"We'll see you kids around four. Gabe, you have the credit card for lunch, right?" Mr. Weaver had just finished unlatching the four pairs of skis from the top of their Subaru—a detail Dad complimented when he shook Gabe's hand in the mudroom before walking out to meet his parents. ("Subaru drivers, huh? Good people.")

"Yeah, I have it."

And then the Weavers were gone, off to mingle with other ski friends in the lodge's lounge. Gabe and I walked through the lodge to pick up our lift tickets, affixed them to our jacket zippers, and then laid our skis in the snow, ready to click our boots into place. Gabe showed me how to do everything. He described the concept of "plowing" by angling the skis into a point in front of me, and he explained that veteran skiers did not have to plow. He told me that sometimes the best way to stop was to just fall over. Then he finished the lesson by saying, "Really, Louisa, when you're at the top of the mountain looking down, there's no better feeling. Knowing you're out here," he stretched out his arms, "on this gorgeous day with good snow . . . there's just no better feeling." He smiled at me, excited on my behalf.

"Let's do it," I committed myself enthusiastically.

The ski lift was the first of my struggles. It all happened so fast. One moment, I was standing casually in line making conversation, and the next moment I was being rushed to a line on a platform while a giant chair rotated madly toward me. As my valiant instructor, Gabe took my arm in his, the ski pole dangling from my wrist, and nearly pulled me to the launch spot. And then we were swept off our feet—literally—and scooped into a ski lift chair rising farther and farther from the ground. The first ride up, Gabe leaned back to adjust the safety bar into place on our laps. But I soon learned that moving the safety bar caused the chair to rock unsteadily each time we lowered and lifted it. This generated more panic in me than riding without a safety bar, and I asked Gabe to just "let it be."

The one thing I liked about the ride up was the complete serenity of being alone. Certainly, we had people in front of us, behind us, and below us, but for the four-minute ride to the top of the mountain, we were able to just enjoy each other and our surroundings. Gabe was right—it was a beautiful day. For the first time in December, it seemed that the sky was without clouds: just a cerulean blue expanse. I looked for its stopping spot on the horizon but couldn't find one. It was endless. And the sun seemed twice as bright with its rays reflecting off the snow. Gabe and I beamed happily at each other through the glare. It was four minutes of complete contentment. And then the chaos began again.

Dismounting the chairlift was probably the action I struggled with the most. Again, everything seemed to happen in three-quarter time. I watched as we approached the top of the mountain, the exit ramp growing closer.

"Okay, now when I count to three," Gabe instructed, "put your skis on the ground and push off from the chair and just go. Okay?" He turned to face me. I'm sure the look on my face was one of pure terror because he let out a sympathetic laugh.

"And if I can't?" My voice seemed smaller than I remembered.

"If you can't, you ride the chairlift back down the mountain alone. And everyone coming up will know you couldn't get off. Okay? Here we go . . . "

"No!"

"One . . . "

"Wait!"

"Two . . . "

"Gabe!"

"Three!"

He grabbed my arm, and I felt my skis touch ground. Gabe pulled me up from the seat and the chair pushed us off as it swiveled back around the lift station to go back down the mountain. We drifted off the ramp to the gathering at the top of the slope. I wouldn't call my movements skiing, per se, but I *was* moving on snow. And that, I thought, should count for something.

"You did great!"

"You pulled me!"

"Well, you still did great." Gabe smiled and my nerves faded. "The hard part is over."

I watched as other skiers exited the lift and immediately flew down the mountain. It was nonstop. Wave after wave and chair after chair, people just kept coming and going. Some, like me, took a moment at the top to analyze the slope, take a breath, and enjoy the moment before taking the plunge.

"Gabe?" I glanced at him sheepishly. "Don't leave me?"

"Are you kidding? I'm staying with you every minute of this thing! You go down, I go down, okay?" His enthusiasm and encouragement made me want to leap out of my skis and kiss him. He was confident in me. I could do this.

"Look." Gabe motioned behind me.

I turned around to see what he was looking at. There, a young girl who couldn't have been older than eight sat back in her boots, bent her knees, adjusted her snow goggles, and kicked off from the top of the slope. Within moments, she disappeared down the hill.

"If she can do it, you can do it. Let's go."

Gabe let me take my time on the slope, but by the time we reached the bottom I seemed to have picked up the basic technique well enough. I didn't fall a single time. My skis crossed only once as I attempted to slow down on one of the bends. But above all else, Gabe amazed me. He descended the mountain easily without ever taking his eyes off me. Those fleeting moments when I felt comfortable enough to lift my eyes from the ground of snow in front of me, I met his gaze. He beamed with excitement for me, and it felt good to know he didn't think I looked like a fool. Rather, he seemed unexpectedly impressed with how quickly I caught on.

As we waited in line for a second time to take the lift back up to the top, Gabe admitted his surprise. "You're better than I thought you'd be, Mums."

I smiled, remembering our first encounter in the flower section of his parents' store, when he had handed me a coffee can filled with blossoming chrysanthemums, so confident I'd return. And I did.

"You know, I thought you were kind of crazy that first night in Weaver's. Practically forcing your flowers on me," I admitted.

We were getting closer to the front of the line. My heart rate picked up as I saw the chairs swing around and pick up the anxious skiers. I spotted the eight-year-old picking up a chair alone, her little legs dangling and swinging from the chair mid-air. I envied her courage.

"You were standing over yams!" Gabe rebutted. "Not much a guy can do with that."

I laughed. Then gulped. One more couple in front of us, and then it was our turn to get picked up.

"Ready?"

"I kind of have to be, don't I?"

"Yep." He hooked arms with me again and I let him lead me to the proper place. Then, with a jerk, the chair buckled our knees and we were rising.

"I could get used to this," I smiled, turning to look at my companion. He looked nervous, and I didn't know why. I looked down at his skis: both intact. His poles: one in each hand. "Something wrong?" I furrowed my brow.

"Are you kidding?" Gabe inhaled and leaned in close to me, his lips touching mine.

Our first kiss: suspended above the blue square slope I'd just conquered, floating between a white earth and a pale blue sky. It lasted long enough that we couldn't deny its existence, but short enough that the next part of the ride was spent in an awkward silence. It didn't help that the chair behind us was occupied by three college-aged boys who sent out encouraging jeers. At the top, as we readied ourselves to dismount, I felt completely confident, and I let it get the best of me.

"And then the ski lift stopped—" Gabe gasped for air during the retelling of my fall to his parents on the way back home. His eyes were watering with tears from laughing. "And the attendant walks out of the station and tells Louisa . . . wait, wait. Louisa, you tell it."

"He says, 'I haven't seen a fall like that since Niagara,'" I said, unimpressed.

But Gabe's parents fell into hysterics, and even I couldn't fight the laughter any longer. I crossed my arms defiantly and fought a chuckle. Gabe reached behind the seat and put his arm around my shoulders, pulling me closer to him. He kissed me on the forehead before laughing some more and turning back to watch the road. It only took a few minutes before I relaxed under his embrace. The newness of the contact was thrilling, but silently I wondered about Chris. What would he have thought about my day?

On Christmas Eve, I nursed a pretty nasty bruise on the left side of my body where I'd landed during my epic fall. Dad and Greta had both been thoroughly entertained by the story; Rosemary was the only one who expressed any form of sympathy. She offered to make me an herbal muscle rub from menthol, but I graciously declined, deciding to wear my wounds with pride and suck it up.

I spent the day, in preparation for our first Christmas morning in our new house, baking brown bread. Since Mom had passed away, we were used to simple Christmases. I learned early on that Dad had a weakness for dark rye bread, and I used Christmas Eve as an excuse to go through the nearly five-hour process of preparing it. This was my fifth year baking it, and so I appropriately deemed it a tradition. But this year's bread was different.

I'd meant it to be a surprise. While combing through Grandma's albums in the attic, I'd stumbled across her old recipe book. It was stuffed with loose recipes—some clipped from magazines, others handwritten—and on a couple of scraps, she'd written some lines of poetry. Dad had mentioned she'd dabbled as a poet. They were beautiful musings, and I felt lucky to have found them. I don't know why the book was in the attic and not in the kitchen. Was it another memento left behind for me to find? Another breadcrumb on my way to finding her? Inside the book, I'd found a yellowed page of handwritten notes for rye bread. It was eerie reading the directions, written in Grandma's stream of consciousness. Grandma recited the recipe with phrases such as "Don't be afraid to knead the dough good now" and "I usually add a couple scoops of flour, if it needs it." I brought the recipe down from the attic intent on baking it for Dad. Maybe he'd remember the taste from his childhood. Maybe this would bring him back to her.

Fingering the recipe, carefully making sure the page didn't get splashed with milk or crusted with sugar, I heard my grandma reading the instructions to me. I heard her voice the same way it streamed through her old phone late at night. And I felt so close to her, baking her recipe, in her kitchen, with her bowls. I pressed the fennel and star anise in *her* mortar and pestle, I formed two round loaves on *her* butcher-block countertops, and I baked the loaves in *her* oven. The same oven she used to bake the same bread for my dad years and years ago.

While baking the rye bread my thoughts took me back to Grandma's storytelling. For two months, I'd been listening to her narratives about Grandpa. Two months and a handful of phone calls, maybe more. I'd lost track of how many times my telephone—*her* telephone—rang. I'd listened enough times that I felt like I knew the family she described to me: Åsa's resolve. Leif's pride. Anna's benevolence. And the twins: Gerhard, Lasse, and their inseparable bond. I knew this family, and yet . . . I didn't feel like I was any closer to the end, no matter what Rosemary said.

As I worked the dough in Grandma's kitchen, I hoped that the next phone call would feature a victory for Lasse. There was so much goodness in him, I could feel it. I needed to hear that he had joy in his life. I needed to know he'd been happy.

That evening, Christmas Eve, I listened to the story I'd been waiting for.

XXI.

After celebrating the New Year, Gerhard and Lasse read the daily news about Finland's seemingly failing attempts to defend against a ravenous Red Army. Sweden stood firmly on "nonbelligerent" ground, sending relief supplies—but not troops—abroad. The Magnusson family needed a distraction from the destruction to their east, and Gerhard decided to provide it for them. What he didn't anticipate, however, was the secret battle that would ensue within him.

"I'm going to enter the Vasaloppet," he announced proudly one morning over breakfast.

"Like hell you are!" Lasse snorted and jabbed Gerhard's stomach with his fork. "Look at that paunch! What have the trains done to you? The ferries have been good to me," Lasse inspected his own impressive bicep, doubled in size since beginning his work with his father. "I should enter the race, if for no other reason than to ensure you don't kill yourself!"

Gerhard smiled. Lasse had taken the bait.

They didn't have much time to train. Sweden's annual cross-country ski race was in three weeks, and Lasse was right. He was in far better physical condition than Gerhard.

Gerhard excelled in all things cerebral; he outwitted his brother with little effort. He excelled in school, and his teachers adored him. He was used to being on top. But he questioned his physical capacity. As the days wore on, he felt the odds stacking up against him, and as much as he had difficulty admitting it, he didn't like it.

The brothers looked at the Vasaloppet as their magnum opus. All of their smaller petty competitions—the intellectual contests, the physical trials—leading to this point seemed juvenile in comparison. Suddenly, the Vasaloppet represented more than just a ski race. Gerhard's attention-grabbing decoy had grown bigger than he expected. He became obsessed. Every waking minute he thought about techniques to quicken his pace, to sustain his endurance, to beat his brother. A week before the race, the church hosted a party for all the Trelleborg skiers; the small coastal city was sending seven of its men to Sälen to compete. Before the party, Gerhard watched as Lasse bent over their washbasin, lathering his thick, blond beard with soap. And Gerhard suddenly realized how much older Lasse looked. He seemed stronger, more handsome. Gerhard reached up to touch his own face and loathed its boyishness.

He was also nervous about the evening's festivities—almost more nervous than he was about the race—because he knew most of Trelleborg's young women would be at the party.

"We'll have fun tonight, yeah, Gerhard?" Lasse asked, buttoning his vest.

"I don't like to dance," Gerhard confessed, lying on his bed, fiddling with his pocket watch.

"Liar! You don't know how." Lasse tossed his hand towel at his brother. "It's not that hard. You just do a little of this," he held one hand to his stomach and the other he suspended in the air, dancing around the room, leading an invisible partner. "And then a little of this," he spun the partner around. "They like it when you hold them close." He winked, dipping the woman to an almost impossible depth. Gerhard smiled. For a fleeting moment he wanted to call off the race.

"Just think of women as if they were that watch," Lasse gestured to the keepsake in Gerhard's palm. "You gotta wind 'em up before they'll work." Lasse laughed deeply, ducking from the pillow Gerhard threw at him.

There was no forgetting—no escaping—the war even for the night. Gerhard and Lasse both noticed the heavy drapes in the church windows as they approached.

"To prevent airstrikes," Lasse jabbed his brother in the ribs with his elbow. "Der Rote Baron. The Red Baron," he said, referencing the famous fighter pilot, in an exaggerated German accent while pointing to the dark sky. "We're in hiding."

Gerhard looked down the main street of the town. Heavy drapes hung in every window of every house in Trelleborg. *When had that happened?* He felt like a stranger in his own town.

Inside the party, Pontus offered Gerhard a snaps glass filled to the brim with aquavit. "Some strength for the race. Flavored with caraway seed; you'll like it." The two stood away from the dance floor.

Gerhard swallowed the liquor down quickly, watching as his brother pressed himself against a pretty dark-haired girl on the dance floor. Pontus laughed.

"It's good when the cheeks turn red," Pontus chuckled.

"It tastes like fire," Gerhard coughed.

Pontus nodded and smiled. "So why aren't you out there?" He gestured to the group of dancing young people.

Gerhard shrugged. "I'm waiting for the right moment."

"Let me tell you about the right moment," Pontus put his heavy, thick hand on Gerhard's shoulder. With his other hand, he reached into the inside pocket of his jacket and produced his prized ticket to America. "One night in Göteborg I was at a boxing match with a friend. We'd both placed bets on the same fellow to win, a big Pole named Kozerski. He had arms like tanks," Pontus patted down his own, flaccid biceps. "Anyway, my friend had this ticket." He waived the red paper in front of Gerhard's face. "He always talked about getting out of Sweden, going to America. Said he was waiting for 'the right moment.' He wasn't just a talker, my friend. He was really going to do it. This was all before the war, of course. It would have been easier for him to get out then," Pontus paused to belch. Gerhard leaned away from his uncle. He suddenly needed another drink.

"The Pole and the other guy fell out of the circle. Kozerski lost his balance and took a blind swing. Hit my friend on the nose. Right here," Pontus pointed to the bridge between his eyes. "My friend fell over. Dead. I couldn't believe it. I reached down to try to save him . . . hell, I didn't know what to do. I could tell he was dead, though. You just know these things. One day you'll see a body and know what I mean."

Gerhard looked to his uncle, waiting for him to continue, but it appeared as if Pontus was done.

"So you stole his ticket?" Gerhard asked in disbelief.

"Right out of his pocket. I didn't know what else to do." Pontus shrugged his shoulders. "All this to say . . . get your ass out there. Lasse is making you look like a goat standing over here by yourself. Or worse, standing here with *me*."

Pontus walked away, and Gerhard realized with a shock that his revolting uncle was right. He felt sorry for himself. He needed to get some fresh air. Outside, he lit a cigarette and looked up to the sky. He thought about Lasse as he reached into his pocket and ran his fingers over his watch. It was comforting to feel its smooth surface. The watch reminded him of his role. At the station, he was important. People respected him there. He didn't have to worry about competing with Lasse; he didn't have to worry about women or dancing.

Exhaling into the night air, he suddenly realized he wasn't alone. In the darkness about twenty meters away stood Agnes Landquist, the same girl whose bicycle he'd repaired so long ago. Tonight was the first time Gerhard had seen her in quite a while, though he saw her father often. She probably didn't remember him, at least not in the same way he remembered her. But there, outside in the bitter winter air, she advanced toward him and coolly laughed.

"You look so much like your brother. I almost thought you were him."

The moon illuminated her figure as she walked closer and Gerhard realized just how much she'd changed since the last time they'd met. Her cheeks were thinner, her curves more pronounced, and she held herself as a confident, beautiful woman.

"May I join you? I needed a break from the party," she said, never taking her eyes off Gerhard.

He nodded.

"May I have one? I've never smoked a cigarette before." Agnes gestured to Gerhard's lit cigarette.

"I'm out of paper. Can we share this one?" He held it out for her.

She took it and wrapped her lips around it, looking like she'd done it before.

"I didn't know girls smoked."

She shrugged and handed the cigarette back. For a while they smoked in silence. Eventually, Agnes reached down and wrapped her hand around Gerhard's. He didn't move. He couldn't breathe.

"Is it true what they're saying?"

"What are they saying?" he asked, already knowing what she really meant. She wanted to know about the rumors circulating town. She wanted to know about Hitler's Army.

"That *they're* coming to Sweden." Her voice fell hard on the unnamed.

"Yes, I think it's true," Gerhard answered, putting out the cigarette but holding onto her. It was the first time he'd touched a woman; he gripped her hand tightly to keep her from noticing his trembling.

"I think so, too," she breathed into the night.

They stood for a long time without exchanging words. She guided his right hand to the small of her back and took his left in hers. Listening to a fading waltz floating out from the party, they drifted in the snow creating beautiful, looping circles wherever they stepped. She placed her head on his shoulder. He smelled her hair's faint traces of rosewater. They danced slowly. At last, she stopped and looked up at him. Her eyes were wet, but Gerhard couldn't tell if it was the cold or something else. He wanted to give her everything—his love, the moon, the world—in that moment. He'd wanted her from their earliest days in school together. He would have surrendered everything to her if she'd asked him.

"I think I'd like to kiss you," she whispered.

She lifted her mouth to his. She tasted of tobacco. It reminded Gerhard of the station. Her lips were soft and wet. It was obvious this wasn't her first kiss, and Gerhard hoped she couldn't tell it was his. He shuffled his feet nervously and steadied his hands on her hips. Agnes breathed heavily and clung passionately to him, as if she wanted him to carry her off, far from the church, far from the party. But something about her desperation made Gerhard feel as if she wasn't clinging to him, but to something greater. She seemed eager to lose herself, but she wasn't giving in to passion or the moment or to him. She was giving up. She was letting go. This isn't how he wanted it to be. She shut her eyes tightly to keep the tears concealed; he kissed her eyelids one at a time, and then he had to go. He couldn't surrender with her; he wasn't willing to give up. Not yet. That would only come later.

In Sälen, on the night before the race, no one in the Magnusson family spoke of the Winter War or of Germany. Each twin quietly prepared for the race in his own way. They took to the trail to analyze the conditions of the snow, the bends in the slope, and the density of the air.

"It's good, Gerhard."

"What is?"

"This," Lasse said, stretching his arm out in front of them. "Today we're boys. Tomorrow, men."

Gerhard walked slowly. He wanted to win; he'd worked so hard.

"I went to Kalmar last week," Lasse lit a cigarette and offered one to his brother, who waved it away. "Walked right into the naval office and said I was ready to enlist."

Lasse waited, but Gerhard said nothing.

"Gerhard, I want so badly to be a part of it. I feel ready."

"It?" Gerhard asked though he already knew the answer.

"Everything," Lasse inhaled. "This war."

"And did you enlist?" Gerhard kept the panic from his voice—the anger and the fear—deep in his belly. *Was this a challenge? Was Lasse testing him?*

"They told me I was out. Not eligible. 'Go back to Trelleborg,' they told me. 'Stay on the ferry. Österberg's orders.' I told them I had come to enlist. I told them to screw Österberg, that I had a right to fight, a right to wear the uniform."

Gerhard's brow narrowed as he stared at his brother. *What did Lasse want from him?* He was glad Lasse had been turned away. He didn't want to lose his brother to a fight that wasn't theirs. But Lasse wouldn't understand that, so he only stared back into his brother's wounded eyes.

"I'm nobody, Gerhard!" Lasse suddenly burst out, running a hand through his hair. "You . . . you have your plan. I know you've been secretly stashing away money to go to college. And you'll get there . . . you'll get there because you're you. Don't you know I know that? But me? What have I got? I'm never getting out of Trelleborg.

"So tomorrow, when we meet back here again," Lasse flicked his cigarette into the snow and began walking away into the darkness before shouting over his shoulder, "don't try to do me any favors. Got it? Tomorrow we level the field. It's just you and me. Racing the same race, fighting the same fight."

The conditions the next morning weren't ideal. The snow was wetter than normal, and it clung to their skis. The air was heavy and saturated; another snowfall was on its way.

Lasse and Gerhard stayed in motion, keeping their muscles warm and their adrenaline going. They knew that the family stood somewhere on the sidelines, but they didn't dare look for them. Neither wanted any distraction from the race ahead. It was possible that one or both brothers would not finish.

"Gerhard, I don't think we should start together," Lasse announced ten minutes before the signal.

"Whatever you want, Lasse," Gerhard replied, masking his disappointment. When he'd suggested the race, this wasn't how he'd imagined it would be.

"So, I'll leave you here. Best of luck," Lasse held out his hand.

"I'll see you at the finish," Gerhard accepted his brother's gesture.

Lasse lifted his ski poles and pushed himself away into the crowd. Gerhard lost sight of him within seconds.

All of Sälen grew silent as the minutes quickly counted down. Everything slowed down: Gerhard took deep, deliberate breaths and lifted his poles, ready to push off. Then the flags at the starting line lifted into the air, letting the skiers pass. The Vasaloppet had officially begun. Sixty-one kilometers into the race, Gerhard stopped to vomit. He pulled his skis to the side of the track and fell onto his side. He retched three times before dragging himself back to the course. Gerhard was tired and cold and wanted desperately to quit, but there was nowhere to go. He had to complete the race. It was dark when Gerhard arrived in Mora. He wanted to collapse; his muscles throbbed and felt like they would seize at any moment. He saw Leif waiting alone by the finish line. *Where were the others?*

"Lasse came in forty minutes ago." Leif took off his fur cap and put his arm around the elder twin. "You did well, son."

Gerhard was still catching his breath.

"Everyone's in the pub celebrating with him."

Gerhard's hands shook as he tried to untie his skis, so Leif bent down to help him.

"Did you plan it?"

Gerhard looked at his father and for a moment neither man spoke. Leif's eyes pleaded something to his son, but Gerhard didn't know what it was. Did his father know the race had been a ruse? A distraction from the suffocating air back in Trelleborg?

"Just don't tell him," Leif sighed as he lifted the skis onto his back before turning toward the town. "God knows how many times he's fallen in your shadow. Just don't tell him you let him win."

It was a lie, but Gerhard couldn't bring himself to confess the truth. He had tried his best to win. He had raced and lost. Lasse had won on his own merit but Leif already believed otherwise, and Gerhard let him.

XXII.

Because Dad had already given Greta "The Thing" for Christmas, she wasn't expecting to open any other gifts except the one from me. But Dad, being wonderfully true to form, presented her with a gift certificate to AutoParts for replacement headlights, floor mats, and other miscellaneous and unanticipated expenses that come with owning a car. Of course, I still had to pinch myself—that car would be mine in a short period of time.

"You don't get it until September when I leave for school!" Greta hissed at me, reading my hungry expression while she opened the gift certificate.

"Jeez," I answered. "Merry Christmas."

I handed her my wrapped gift, a small Mason jar filled with flowers I had collected and then dried from Mom's funeral. I'd wanted to keep the jar for me, but I realized Greta needed it more than I did. She recognized the miniature yellow and white roses immediately.

"Louisa, this is weird," Greta admitted holding the jar up for Dad to see.

I reached out to take the jar back, but Greta snatched it closer to her.

"No. I'll keep it," she smiled and glanced at the clusters inside.

As she turned it over, I spied the insides of her wrists still speckled with slivers of scabs. She saw my gaze, though, and pulled her sleeves to conceal her secret. No one saw them but me.

The rest of the morning continued with a brief opening of gifts, breakfast in the living room with a fire in the fireplace, and the Vince Guaraldi Trio's *A Charlie Brown Christmas* record playing on Grandma's antique hi-fi. Greta lay sprawled on the couch, reading her new subscription to *Vogue.* Dad was absorbed in his gift from me, sitting in his usual armchair, his legs crossed. I'd bought him a random assortment of model train parts I found in an antique shop down the street from Fat Bottoms. Maybe I was inspired by Grandpa's set in the cellar, or maybe I bought them because Dad deserved his own collection to complement his father's. Either way, he appeared to like the gift and immediately began tinkering with the switch box. For a moment, I wished he'd been smoking a pipe, just because it would have completed the nostalgic Christmas family scene.

As for me, I sat near the fire looking over my gift from Dad. He'd collected photos from the attic and pasted them into a shiny, new leather-bound album. He'd labeled everything. I turned page after page of pictures of Eloise and Gerhard. I saw photos of my father as he grew up. And at the back of the book he put snapshots of us. Not just the three of us, not just the family-pi. He'd included pictures of Mom. This album contained the family Dad never had. I couldn't believe he was giving it to me. This was the most special, most thoughtful gift I'd ever received. Most shocking was that my Dad had been able to assemble it. I didn't know he had it in him. Maybe he was braver than I thought.

There was a soft tap at the door. Neither Dad nor Greta stirred from their vegetated states. *Guess that means I'm getting the door.* I picked myself up and walked to foyer, shuddering as I entered the mudroom—it was bitterly cold outside, and even my moccasins couldn't protect my feet from the arctic floorboards.

To my surprise, I found Chris out on the front step, hands in pockets, watching the road with his back turned to me. I opened the door.

"Chris?"

"Hey! Louisa!" He seemed nervous, looking over my shoulder into the house. "You want to hang out?"

"Uh . . . You do know it's Christmas morning, right?"

For a brief moment, Chris looked surprised. "Oh, right. Hmm . . ." He shifted his weight anxiously.

What was wrong with him?

"My dad's not a big Christmas person, so I often forget, you know?" Chris explained.

I noticed how he pointedly didn't mention his mom. He looked cold, and I *knew* I was freezing. The only thing I could think to say was, "You wanna come in?"

"What? On Christmas morning?"

I laughed. "Chris, *you're* the one who came over here."

"Wouldn't that be weird? With all your family and stuff?"

Ah, so there was the source of his anxiety.

"What? It's just me, Greta—whom you've met—and my dad. It's no big deal. Nothing's open for us to go anywhere anyway. And I kind of want to hang out around here, you know?"

It was true. I liked hanging out with my family-pi on Christmas just as much as I liked being with them on Thanksgiving. It was good for us to find each other after weeks of following our own paths in this new place. Of course Chris being here kind of mixed things up, but I was mildly curious to see my rugged friend interact with my family. I was similarly interested to see what Dad would think of Chris.

We walked into the living room and neither Dad nor Greta looked up. Chris cleared his throat. That caught Dad's attention immediately, and he was on his feet in an instant. Greta moved her magazine out of the way to witness the train wreck.

"Dad, this is Chris." *Thank God, he's not wearing holey jeans on Christmas morning.* His hair hung loose, and he tucked the curls nervously behind his ears.

Chris held out his hand, which Dad shook, though he was obviously surprised to meet this stranger on Christmas morning.

"Hey, Chris. Merry Christmas! Do you and Lou go to school together?" Dad's over-enthusiasm came off awkwardly. I silently hoped the weirdness didn't last too much longer.

"Yeah, we're in History together." Chris was doing a good job of keeping eye contact. I knew that was important to my father.

"That's cool," Dad replied, again sounding uncomfortable. Thankfully, another knock at the door interrupted the conversation.

"That must be Rosemary! I invited her over . . . " Dad explained. He seemed grateful to escape the living room.

"Hey, Greta!" Chris smiled over at my sister.

She waved indifferently from behind her magazine. I could tell Chris got some satisfaction from the fact that Greta didn't seem to like him. Perhaps he was more comfortable with the people who disliked him than with the people who did.

Dad soon returned to the living room with his arm around Rosemary. While I wished her a Merry Christmas, Rosemary couldn't take her eyes off Chris and I knew that she immediately recognized him as the Leo from my school project. I realized I didn't even have to introduce him, but I did anyway.

"Rosemary, this is Chris," I smiled guiltily. "Chris, Rosemary."

"Nice to finally meet you," Rosemary said holding out her hand. They shook.

She didn't once look at me, but I watched her assess Chris up and down, analyzing him with the same gaze she'd examined me with that first night in this house. I suddenly remembered those wide eyes and those bright white teeth.

The record on the player had stopped spinning, so Dad went over to put on something else: Tchaikovsky's "Dance of the Sugar Plum Fairy." The opening strings made me shiver. This tune always made me feel creepy. Rosemary went to sit with Greta. The piano concerto was engrossing, and the scent of a new pot of vanilla chai tea drifting in through the kitchen seemed to be the remnant of a dream. I felt compelled to go and sit opposite my sister. She looked happy and sleepy, enveloped in the familiar music. Greta yawned. I wanted to stretch my limbs and lie next to her; I wanted to pretend we were young again. It was Chris, shifting his weight uncomfortably next to me, who snapped me back into reality.

"Wanna go for a walk?" he asked hesitantly. I could tell he was afraid to wear out his welcome.

"Sure," I sighed, looking longingly back at the parlor as I followed Chris to the mudroom to fetch our coats. Outside, the sky looked like rain. I was beginning to learn how to identify snow clouds: They were thick, gray blankets, like gravy or cement. No texture. No billow. And true snow clouds smelled like metal, but I loved the scent because it was electric.

But today, there would only be rain. The clouds were higher in the sky, darker and full figured. Beautiful in their own right, but they weren't going to produce the white Christmas I'd come to expect while living in Pennsylvania these past two months. Had we really only been here two months? North Carolina seemed like a lifetime ago. And in a way, it was.

Chris led me down October Hill Road past Rosemary's cottage. I appreciated Chris's relaxed personality. At one point we walked for five minutes in complete silence and both seemed comfortable and happy that way. When Chris spoke, he always spoke with purpose. Neither of us felt the need for idle chatter. We were both content to enjoy the moment quietly to ourselves.

I started thinking about how different Chris and Gabe were, and how I liked them both. Gabe liked noise, mostly because he had a lot to say. And I didn't mind because Gabe's conversations were always so lively and energetic. At school, he'd talk endlessly about his future plans for his nursery or how he wanted to travel after high school or how much he loved working at the shop. He was exciting to listen to. He was infectious in all the right ways. His capacity to share life's excitements was much greater than anyone I'd ever known. And then there was Chris. Chris, the guy I just couldn't seem to get a hold on, but the one I wanted to.

Chris and I reached a small footpath that led off the main road to an old covered wooden bridge. It was overgrown with ivy and clematis—dead from the winter's bite—and the stream it once forged was gone. Dried up, disappeared forever. The wood was rotting in some places but held firm beneath us. It was once painted red. I was amazed that, in their boredom, local teens hadn't used the bridge as a graffiti canvas.

As if reading my thoughts, Chris answered, "You'll be surprised how much respect Chester County kids have for our old relics. Must be something in the water."

"I can't believe this thing is still standing." I reached up to balance myself as I stepped onto a cinder block and up onto the bridge. It was dark, but light filtered in through holes in the roof and gaps between the planks.

"Kind of cool to think George Washington could have walked this bridge or ridden over it on his horse," Chris remarked as he pulled himself up next to me.

"Or Paul Revere."

"Paul Revere was up in Boston, Louisa," Chris chuckled at my expense. I shoved him playfully, embarrassed.

"Over by the Brandywine Battlefield is the Ring House, which Washington used as his command post before the battle in 1777. I'll take you sometime," Chris took a seat on the end of the bridge facing the road, dangling his feet off the edge.

"I'd like that."

I joined him. The bridge was cold beneath me; I shivered and sat on my mittened hands to keep my bottom warm. Chris put his arm around me, hesitantly. He smelled good like aftershave, but his chin remained rough with patches of scruff. It felt nice to be near Chris. I thought about Gabe. What would he think if he could see me now? But we weren't dating . . . were we?

"I'm sorry about this morning," he apologized. "Like I told you, my dad's not much of a Christmas person. My mom used to be the one to put up all the decorations, hunt for the perfect tree, and plan the dinner. All of that."

"Where is she now?"

"Divorced and remarried. Living in Jacksonville with a new family. New husband. New house. New kids. She doesn't like us much."

Chris stared out to the road. I reached into my back pocket for the folded pages of my memories of Mom. Tentatively, I pulled the packet out and handed it to my friend.

"It's my third copy. I carry it around all the time, so it usually gets pretty beat up."

I watched as Chris opened the pages and read the title, scrawled at the top: "Memories of Mom."

"When I was ten, Greta twelve," I began, "Mom was diagnosed with Stage 3 breast cancer. She died seven months later, after nonstop chemo, a double mastectomy, and radiation treatments. I watched my mom lose weight, her hair, and her breasts. When she finally lost her life, I hated myself for being selfish enough to wish she could have lived through the pain for me. I hated my dad for not stopping it, and I hated the doctors for not discovering the cancer sooner. Sometimes I hated her for giving up. I harbored a lot of hate," I confessed, ashamed. Never had I admitted to the anger before. Not to Dad, not to Greta, not even to the therapist Dad took us to after Mom's death. I didn't know why I confessed it now to Chris.

"I hated my mom too," he responded. "I hated her for destroying my dad. I hated her new husband. Hell, I even hated her new dog." Chris's body was tense. The hand that clutched my papers was balled into a fist, and I could tell he was close to shutting down.

"It's a hard thing to deal with at any age," I said softly. "But especially when you're a child, and especially when it's your mom. I know," I gently took the papers back from my friend, took his hand in mine, and looked over my memories for the millionth time. Chris stayed quiet but didn't let go of me. I wasn't used to being the one comforting.

"This one, memory 212, is one of my favorites." I nervously leaned my head into the curve of Chris's shoulder. I was used to people fussing over me even though it was something I hated. I didn't want to fuss over Chris, but I didn't want to sidestep his emotions, either.

"Memory 212: Mom learned to play the ukulele and especially loved playing 'Across the Universe' on the little stringed instrument."

"We played it at her funeral," I informed Chris. "Oh, and this one, memory 230: *Blamed Yoko Ono for breaking up the Beatles.* She never forgave Lennon for that one." I smiled, conjuring up another memory. "She called my dad 'JoJo' because she loved 'Get Back' so much. It was her favorite Beatles song."

"What memory is that?"

"One hundred."

"What's your last memory?" Chris continued staring at the road, letting me lean against him.

"Five hundred and twenty-two," I shuffled to the last page, embarrassed I couldn't remember. "She called me '*mon petit chou chou.*' She made me promise to never forget it."

"*Mon petit chou chou*?" Chris asked, seeming amused.

"My little cabbage," I translated. "But I don't let anyone else call me that."

"So what about Rosemary?" Chris finally turned to look at me.

"What about her?"

"Are you okay with her? She and your dad acted pretty comfortable in there."

"I've gotten to the point where I want my dad to be happy. Obviously, I don't want him to forget my mom—as if he ever could. But, just because he loved my mom doesn't mean he has to be alone for the rest of his life. And Rosemary's nice. She adds something. I think it's refreshing."

"You know, Lou," he kissed my forehead, the scruff of his beard itching my face; it was an honest kiss and his lips were warm on my cold skin. "You're very wise."

"And you're not as tough as you seem," I added.

He scoffed, but rolled up the cuff of his coat, exposing the black tattoo on his left arm. "After my mom left, I toughened up. I didn't want to be happy because I didn't think I deserved to be happy. So

I kind of fell into a depression, and Dad freaked out because it was too much for him to deal with. So he sent me away. Every summer I went to camp for unstable kids," Chris chuckled sarcastically. "Anyway, last summer Dad sent me to Colorado. One of those tough-love camps he thought would get me 'motivated to do something with my life,'" Chris said, channeling his father. "I spent the summer blazing trails in the Rockies. It was hard work: cutting down trees, digging trenches, sleeping outdoors under the stars, eating red beans and rice every day. But I loved it, Lou. I loved being out in the wild, working with my hands. It got to be a spiritual thing for all of us, working as one tribe in nature. We were the only ones out there for hundreds of miles. The leaders encouraged us to associate ourselves with something natural, like a tree, element, or animal."

"You're a turtle?" I ran my bare thumb over his tattooed wrist and it sent an electric current through my spine. The touch was intimate. This place, the setting. Chris had a way of making every moment close, personal, and sensual.

"I'm a turtle. Quiet. Steady. Unimposing."

I smiled and a clap of thunder boomed above us; lightning illuminated the sky. How did the storm come upon us so quickly? I started to get up, prepared to race back before the storm worsened, but Chris pulled me back onto the bridge. Here, we were covered from the rain. We could sit, listen to the light symphony playing on the roof above us, and wait out the worst of it.

"You're a turtle," I smiled again, my heart skipping a beat as the rain began to fall in buckets: like God had opened the sky and turned on the faucet right above us.

Chris leaned in and kissed me. My stomach slowly untangled itself inside my body, and I silently wondered if my pot of mums would survive the storm.

XXIII.

After the Vasaloppet, the wind in Trelleborg shifted. It took Gerhard by surprise. He'd begun noticing the small changes—tiny nuances of which most people seemed unaware—but it was only after the family returned from the race that he allowed himself to believe his observations were substantive. People lagged behind the hours of the day, and time began to feel expendable and meaningless. He watched as men walked the streets unshaven and saw how women shuffled slowly, their hosiery rolling down at the knees. The heavy, muslin panels in every window made houses feel like prisons. And in the mornings, people came out gasping for air as if on the brink of asphyxiation.

Gerhard watched his mother labor tirelessly. She still had her sharp tongue and was as obstinate with Pontus as ever, but her movements were more purposeful, as if she had to decide which of her actions were absolutely necessary.

Though they didn't discuss the war—Leif continued to forbid anyone mentioning *Der Führer* in his house—Gerhard kept up with the news at the station. The Third Reich was now an inkblot, seamlessly seeping over and under country borders. Still, Gerhard and Lasse discussed the war in hushed whispers late at night.

"Did you read the headline today?" Lasse whispered to the dark ceiling.

"Yes."

"We've denied England and France access to Finland."

"I said I read it, didn't I?" Gerhard turned on his side to face the wall. He didn't really want to talk.

"Well?" Lasse was persistent.

"Well, what?" Gerhard was tired and confused. He didn't know what to think or what to believe.

"They want to help, so what are we doing refusing them? Pontus says we'll remain neutral. He says we haven't been in a war since 1814 and we're not going to enter one now. What do you think, Gerhard?"

"I think you shouldn't let Father hear you talking politics with Pontus."

On April 9, 1940, Germany invaded Norway and Denmark simultaneously. In one fell swoop, the Nazis enclosed Sweden to the north, west, and south. Swedish trade with the Western world instantly halted and rationing began. First meat, then eggs, and when coffee became unavailable, people became despondent.

Åsa kept her ration tickets in a locked drawer in the kitchen. Wartime brought out the worst of suspicions, and Åsa didn't need another excuse to be wary of Pontus. She watched how he stared longingly when she'd thumb through her *snus* supply. Wisely, she kept the small tobacco tin in her skirt, the safest place she knew.

"*Svinet luktar illa.* The pig smells bad," she'd hiss to her husband each night. "Can't you tell him to bathe?"

"I'm not my brother's keeper," Leif would answer stoically.

"Oh, but Leif, aren't we?"

When Anna came home one evening with news that her school was starting a collection of relief supplies to send to Norwegian and Danish households, their mother felt compelled to help. Åsa got that familiar, spirited look in her eye that made the family question what she had up her sleeve.

"I know just who to ask for help," Åsa chuckled, smugly enjoying a private joke with herself. Her smile concealed a secret plan, and no one dared to ask her to reveal it.

Åsa commissioned the help of the neighbor's girl, a cunning five-year-old with blond braids. She had an impish face, a devilish grin, and she never said a word to anyone. The townspeople called her

"Nilsa" after the naughty little boy in Selma Lagerlöf's famous tale, *The Wonderful Adventures of Nils*. She was Åsa's perfect accomplice.

"Nilsa, I have something for you," Åsa informed the little girl the next day when she'd come to play tricks on Åsa's hens.

The small girl stepped warily into Åsa's kitchen and, sensing a trap, cautiously inspected her surroundings. From wax paper, Åsa slowly unwrapped a large loaf of freshly baked cardamom bread for the little girl to see.

"Smell it!" Åsa encouraged.

The girl leaned in and hungrily inhaled. In a blink of an eye, the little girl reached out to snatch the bread away, but Åsa was too quick. She wrapped it up before the girl could protest.

"You may have it, but you must do something for me."

Nilsa nodded, licking her lips and keeping her eyes on the waxy parcel.

"Do you see those boots on the table?"

Nilsa turned and spied a brand new pair of leather boots in her size sitting on the kitchen table. Åsa had recently purchased them with coffee money she wasn't spending.

"Take those boots and wear them all day. Run through town. Bring them back tonight and I will give you this bread."

Trying to find the trick, the little girl cast a doubtful glance at Åsa.

"No tricks today, Nilsa. Wear those boots and you will get the bread. Will you help or won't you?"

At six o'clock there was a small knock at the door. Åsa opened it to see little Nilsa holding up the new pair of boots that now looked worn, scratched, and soaked in melted snow.

"Very good, Nilsa."

The two exchanged payment and off the little girl ran, her sum under her arm, to see what other tomfoolery she could accomplish before bedtime.

Åsa joined Anna in the living room as Leif and Lasse walked in the door. Back from another tiring day on the water. They retreated to their bedrooms to change clothes.

"Did you get them?" Anna asked, looking up hopefully from her stitching. Åsa held up the dirty boots.

"Wonderful!"

"Are you sure it will be all right?" Åsa asked as she plugged her upper lip with snus.

"Just fine. The school specifically said no new articles. The Nazi soldiers won't allow anything new over the border. Once I'm done patching this blanket, the package will be ready." Anna sat threading her needle, her eyes wide with hope.

"How do we know it won't be intercepted?"

"We don't."

"How do you know what they need?"

"I told you. Nothing new. No money. They sent the school a list of addresses and requests. Boots. Dresses. Pants. All *loppis*, all second-hand. Momma, I swear, the world is coming down to lists. I see them every day. Lists of displaced children, lists of supplies, lists of rules, addresses, names, cities. They scare me."

Åsa looked over the care package Anna had put together. An empty journal. A jar of salt. Three used candles. Muddy boots. A patched blanket. All bound for Norway.

How soon before they'd begin receiving packages themselves?

"I received a letter from Kristina in Narvik," Anna's voice trembled as she recalled her best friend from childhood. They'd been separated when Kristina's family moved to Norway, but their friendship survived in letters filled with happy memories and promises of future meetings. "She heard the Nazis were coming, so she buried her family's silver in the backyard. The ground was so frozen she twisted her ankle trying to shovel a hole deep enough. When they arrived in the middle of the night, the Nazis ordered her family to abandon their home."

Lasse joined the women and watched as their hands moved meticulously, bundling the gifts in brown paper and twine. He sat quietly, eagerly listening to Anna's tale. He, too, knew Kristina. At eight, he'd fallen in love with her, but by ten, she'd moved away.

"They only had time to collect their coats," Anna continued. "Kristina took her father's Norwegian flag from his bureau and unfolded the red-and-blue cloth, laying it out on her bedroom floor as the Germans waited downstairs with their guns. Her family ran from the house, Kristina and her mother on horseback and her father on foot. They're hiding with relatives now. She couldn't even tell me where she was. There was no return address.

"Momma, I'm hearing stories like this at school, too. The children come to me with horrifying accounts of what they're hearing at home. I see the fear in their faces. I don't know what to do; I don't know what to tell them."

"You tell your students . . ." Åsa began, placing the last gift, the grimy shoes, in a wooden box with the other wrapped provisions. "You tell them to send boots."

XXIV.

"I've been asked to submit a paper on Poe's 'The Bells' to *The American Poetry Journal*," Dad announced proudly the following afternoon to Greta, Rosemary, and me. He'd been published before, more times than was standard for community college professors, but I knew Dad's intellect begot boredom if he didn't keep busy.

I usually knew when Dad was working on a scholarly submission. He'd go days without shaving and disappear into his study for hours. In North Carolina, I'd take him trays of coffee and cookies to which he'd say "thanks" with a heavy sigh, signaling me to leave. But I knew he was grateful for my encouragement of caffeine and sugar, even if he never said so.

I was saddened that I hadn't noticed the usual symptoms of a forthcoming submission. Was I so wrapped up in my new life that I was blind to the goings-on in my own house? Was Greta right? Were we all invisible to each other?

And then I saw it. Yes, that familiar five o'clock shadow that accompanied Dad's sleepless nights of writing at the computer. There, too, was the silent sparkle of excitement behind his eyes when he was close to finishing. How long had Dad been this way? How long had I been too distracted to notice?

"I didn't know you were working on a submission, Dad." I could hear the hurt in my voice.

"Oh, right. Sorry, kiddo," he scratched the back of his head. "I figured you didn't know when I had to make my own coffee." He chuckled.

"Oh, oh, oh! Do your thing, Christian!" Rosemary suddenly became animated. She shifted her weight on the couch, pulling her legs under her and pointing excitedly at my dad, sitting in his armchair.

Greta perked up her ears. Dad rolled his eyes and shook his head.

"What thing?" Greta asked trying to understand.

"It's nothing," Dad propped his elbows up and folded his hands under his chin. He looked slightly embarrassed.

"Please? You're so good," Rosemary implored.

I wondered if she knew, as both Greta and I knew, Dad could always be won over with flattery.

"Okay, just once." He paused. "Consider this my curtain call," Dad sighed as he pulled himself from his armchair dramatically. He cleared his throat, furrowed his brow, and stroked his thumb and forefinger mischievously over an invisible mustache. He arched his left eyebrow and stared at us intently, one eye twice the size of the other. He was channeling Poe.

I glanced at Rosemary, beaming toward my father. Her eyes shone with adoration. And then Dad introduced the poem, his voice an octave deeper than normal. He spoke low and slow like a bass drum. The attention of the living room was his.

"I now recite for you three ladies 'The Bells,' composed by the misunderstood genius, the madman, the grotesquely Gothic Mr. Edgar Allan Poe."

As Dad began, his voice was high and light.

Hear the sledges with the bells—
Silver bells!
What a world of merriment their melody foretells!

He started happy and cool, but as he recited, his tone became more menacing. His tempo slowed and hastened, erratically, hauntingly. He alternated his rhythm and speech, keeping all of us entranced with the words.

On the human heart a stone—
They are neither man nor woman—
They are neither brute nor human—

They are Ghouls:
And their king it is who tolls;

The sky outside the window was black. Thin slivers of frozen rain beat against the window glass. Dad's charade was eerie as the fire sent shadows like pitchforks on the walls. As he got deeper in the poem, as it grew darker and more sinister, as Rosemary and Greta laughed, delighted with fright, my mind traveled to that heavy block of black metal sitting in the attic. I visualized the phone's smooth base, its shiny gold cradle, and, under Dad's booming recitation, I heard its shrilling. And in it, I heard the ill-boding, bewitched hopelessness of its screaming bell. As Dad neared the end of the poem, I felt the sorrow—and the telephone's weight—in my chest.

My mind went to Lasse. He seemed tortured. It was obvious he felt inferior to Gerhard; at least the way Grandma told it. Lasse was the boy who couldn't be tamed, whereas Gerhard was the son who did everything right. Lasse thought with his heart; Gerhard with his head. I wanted to champion for Lasse. Whatever his endeavor, I wanted him to succeed.

Dad's performance lingered with me for days after the last lines were spoken. The show elicited a slow panic within me. No one else seemed to be affected in the same way, and no one seemed to notice my distress.

I was becoming more and more troubled by Grandma's recent calls. She was building to something; I could hear it in her voice. She sounded reluctant to end her chapters, like she was clinging to the last line, like she was anticipating that I'd visualize the end before she got there. And the connection didn't go dead immediately anymore. It used to be like Grandma was cut off—barely able to speak the finishing sentences. Now, Grandma held on at the other end of the line, waiting for something. I could hear her breathing, hear dread in her silence. And then she'd be gone.

Two days later, walking down October Hill Road, the pathway wet from constant rainfall, my head ached from thinking about my other newfound dilemma: Gabriel Weaver and Christopher Harris. In North Carolina, I was a girl devoid of boyfriends. Greta had more than her fair share of male suitors. I was always fine with my one or two girlfriends. And, truthfully, I was always fine on my own, too.

It wasn't that I didn't want a boyfriend or that I wasn't interested in boys. There were plenty of boys at my old school for whom I carried secret crushes, but they never seemed to notice or care about my existence. Now, I was suddenly thrown into a love triangle for which I wasn't fully prepared. I withheld asking fate why it couldn't have sent me *one* of these boys, why it had sent me both at the same time. Instead, I asked Rosemary.

"Hi, Louisa. Thank you so much for coming to help me. I've got all the decorations put away but the ones on the Christmas tree." She ushered me inside. "Can I get you anything? Hot chocolate? Tea?"

I hung my jacket on her little rustic three-armed coat rack and looked around the room. She was right—the cottage was practically void of all holiday decorations. Rosemary was much more organized than I'd ever realized. I figured most single women in their early forties had a routine, had boxes of their stuff with their labels, and a way of life they didn't have to share with anyone. Of course Rosemary was organized. There was no one else in her life to muddle things up.

"Oh, but you're a coffee drinker, I remember. Let's get the tree taken care of, and then we can share a pot of dark roast," Rosemary winked.

She remembered I liked coffee. Were we really that close? Were we becoming . . . friends? I smiled in agreement, rolling up the sleeves of my sweater. Sizing the stout tree up and down, I figured it would take us twenty, thirty minutes maximum, to get all the ornaments boxed properly.

We worked silently for the first five minutes, carefully wrapping each ornament in crepe paper and piling them gently in a plastic bin labeled "Christmas."

"So, Rosemary . . . " I timidly began. "What's the real reason you wanted me to come over here?"

She peeked out from behind the other side of the tree, looking confused. "What do you mean?"

"Well, I thought you needed to talk to me about something. That's why you asked me to come over," I tried to read her puzzlement. Was it a ruse?

"Oh, honestly, Louisa, I just needed your help," she shrugged, smiling. We continued wrapping quietly. It was warm in her living room and I felt a little sleepy.

"I'm going to go put that pot of coffee on," Rosemary winked as I let out a loud yawn.

I took a seat on her couch and propped my feet on her coffee table, leaning back. It was nice to feel familiar here. I could vividly remember our first get-together, a pork chop dinner, just two months ago.

Rosemary joined me on the couch with a pot of coffee in one hand and two speckled ceramic mugs in the other.

I sighed, suddenly exhausted. "I don't know what to do."

"What do you mean?" Rosemary took a sip, innocently arching one eyebrow with interest.

"Chris and Gabe. Gabe and Chris," I motioned with my hands. Chris in my right, Gabe in my left.

"Hmm, I see," Rosemary smiled to herself. She was so beautiful with her reddish locks hanging loosely around her face. Her heavy bangs swooped to the left, though they kept falling in her eyes and she kept pulling them back. A constant battle with which I could sympathize.

"Well," she opened her eyes widely, staring into her coffee. "What do you like about each one?"

It was a question I'd asked myself a hundred times. And yet, my answer changed each time I thought about it.

"Chris and I have a lot in common," I began. "You know, his mom is out of the picture, too. He's really a very sensitive person despite the hard exterior. And he loves history. He loves it in a way that he makes me love it, too. And he's great with taking adventures. And, God, I love his skin. Tan skin in December. He told me he's part Cherokee and blessed with a darker complexion. Lucky, huh?"

Rosemary laughed, clearly delighted with my happiness.

"But Gabe is so cute!" I whined, exasperated. "And he definitely has less emotional baggage. I like that he's confident in what he wants to do with his life. It's a level of passion you don't often find. He has good parents. Parents, I might add, he doesn't mind hanging out with. And he always makes me feel like I'm the only person in the room. Do you know what that feels like?"

I meant it as a rhetorical question, but Rosemary sighed loudly, leaned back, and let the couch envelop her.

"Yes," she exhaled.

I knew she was sighing about my dad.

"Well, I could go on for the next hour about things I like about them. What I want to know is who I should choose to be with."

"Who says you have to choose at all?" she asked innocently. It was a question I was anticipating.

"What? So I'm going to go around kissing both of them all the time?"

Never would I have admitted this to Dad. Maybe Greta. It was a new feeling for me, to share my emotions so openly. Rosemary had unknowingly introduced me to the world of female allegiance, where we could tell each other things that weren't usually public knowledge. Girl secrets. Greta and I only recently started unlocking our secrets to each other, however cautiously. I knew Rosemary would keep our conversations in confidence. And it was nice to get some of it off my chest. Talking about it aloud made my feelings easier to sort through.

And then the thought came to me: Rosemary could, for all intents and purposes, tell me which boy I should be with.

"Rosemary, can't you like, read people and all that? See their stars and know their futures?" I could hear my tone accelerate. I couldn't hide my excitement.

"What do you mean?" Rosemary suddenly looked uneasy. She rubbed her thumb on the side of her mug nervously.

"Oh, come on! You could tell if Chris or Gabe is better for me. Or, even, tell me which one I should pick. You know, don't you?" I clapped my hands together eagerly. All of her hocus-pocus astrology finally had a purpose.

Rosemary shook her head. "I don't go around constantly looking into people's futures, Lou. Not even mine. It's no way to live, really. It's just a hobby."

She warmed her cup of coffee by pouring herself some more. I could feel she was ready to move off the subject, but I wasn't ready to let it go.

"Rosemary, I'm serious. I need help. I'm so confused," the confession sounded pleading. "Can't you do something? At least look into my chart and tell me? Or look up my birthday to see who I have a stronger connection with?" It seemed too good to be true. Rosemary could provide me with a definite answer.

"I've looked at your chart, Lou. And I don't know whom you should choose," Rosemary admitted, looking frustrated.

I couldn't tell if she was disappointed in my request or her inability to help. I hoped the latter. I felt my shoulders slump. For a fleeting moment, I'd truly thought she could guide me. Or at least point me in the right direction. Now, I was no closer to figuring out which boy I liked better. And I needed to. I couldn't juggle both of them for much longer without one of them growing impatient, and I didn't like being caught in the middle of my own indecision.

"I *can* tell you," Rosemary softly encouraged, placing a hand on my knee, "I see you happy. I see you very happy, Louisa. Feel comforted knowing you'll make the right decision, whatever you decide."

Surprisingly, those few words did make me feel better.

Monday morning, Greta and I drove to our second semester at Wyeth High School in The Thing. Rather than park in our usual, indiscreet section of curb on one of the neighborhood streets a couple blocks from school, the engine growled loudly as we proudly pulled into the WHS parking lot. Heads turned. Jaws dropped. And all Greta could say as she checked the rearview mirror and powdered her nose was, "Isn't it much better this way?"

Allison caught up with me at my locker before classes. She'd cut off all of her pretty curly hair over break and tied a ribbon around it for her first day back: a green headband in a halo of curls.

"Hi, Allison."

Mine was hardly an enthusiastic greeting. Ever since I first learned of Allison's incessant desire to be in-the-know with the goings-on at Wyeth, I grew less inclined to make her a close confidante. And this morning was a perfect example of why that was a wise decision.

"Gabe said you hit the slopes over Christmas."

I turned into my locker, reaching for a book I didn't need to hide an annoyed eye roll.

"Sure did."

Allison blew a purple bubble of rubbery chewing gum. I watched her as it grew too big. *Pop!*

"That's like, a big thing, you know," she informed me as she regained her composure.

"Allison," I sighed, trying to sound tired, not annoyed. "Does it really matter? At the end of the day, do you really care that I went skiing with him?"

For ten seconds, Allison chewed and blinked. Like she couldn't understand what I meant. She looked me up and down, trying to figure me out, analyzing me like Darwin and his Galapagos.

"Yeah," she smacked her gum loudly, her face illuminating with self-realization. "I do."

I let out a surprised snort. I suppose other girls appreciated her skills as an informant; Allison clued other people in when they were this week's hot gossip. I assumed she considered herself a public servant, and that I was a rare breed to her: the indifferent. Somehow, my ski trip with Gabe validated something in Allison. Her place in the teenage high school caste system? I silently wondered if this was how Diane Sawyer or Oprah heard their callings.

Sighing reluctantly, I shut my locker and turned to my classmate.

"What do you want to know?" I surrendered. I decided to give Allison the abbreviated version of events. My official statement. I didn't doubt it would be public knowledge in less than an hour. "I met his parents. He taught me to ski. We like each other. No further questions."

Allison didn't know about Chris. As one of the outsiders, he was completely off her radar. To her, he wouldn't have been important enough to talk about. And I didn't volunteer to introduce him to the public. I figured he liked being where he was, and maybe even made a conscious effort to stay there.

I met up with Gabe in Photography. It was the first time I'd seen him since the ski trip. He winked at me as I sat down at the table. My heart instantly swelled and I felt that same rush I got when he first challenged me with his coffee-canister chrysanthemum. I fought the stupid smile I could feel creeping onto my face. I bit the inside of my lip, losing the fight. And Gabe knew it. He grinned from ear to ear.

It was finals week. All around me, the other students in my Photography class fidgeted, squirmed, and drummed their fingers too loudly on plastic binders. I expected at any moment the entire room could implode.

Gabe and I were the only ones sitting still. Our eyes locked on each other, unaware of the chaos surrounding us. It made Mr. Franz uneasy.

"Louisa, Gabe, heads down, keep your eyes on your own papers," he looked at us suspiciously, handing us our exams as we grinned back at him. He raised an eyebrow, contemplated separating us, then shook his head and continued to the next table.

Ninety-five minutes later, after properly labeling the various components of a 35mm, after defining terms like “ambient light” and identifying the common missteps in ruined photographs (overexposure, dust on the lens, and shutter speed too slow), I turned in my exam. One down, four to go. The bell rang at the exact moment I quietly handed Mr. Franz my paper. As students eagerly grabbed their backpacks and elbowed their way out of the classroom, Mr. Franz came to the table where I stood, gathering my books.

“Hey, Louisa,” Mr. Franz pulled up a stool and took a seat next to me. He folded his hands in his lap casually. “Could you meet me after school? There’s something I want to talk to you about.”

I looked at Gabe waiting by the door. He looked concerned but left me alone in private conversation with our teacher.

“Is everything okay? Is this about my exam? I kept my eyes on my paper—” It was compulsive worry-speak spewing from my mouth.

“Louisa,” Mr. Franz chuckled and held up his hand for me to stop. “Everything’s fine. I just want to talk to you about an opportunity that I’d like to share with you. Listen,” he checked his watch, “I don’t want to get into it now, and you have to get to your next final. Come and see me before you leave for the day.”

Gabe wanted to go back to the photography room with me after school, but he had to get to Weaver’s instead. He was on the schedule until close. “If you need anything, stop by the store.”

I walked out with him to his car, looking around for Greta to let her know I’d be held up for a little while.

At the far end of the parking lot, I spotted Chris sitting on the hood of his Volvo with a group of friends. Without looking, I could feel his eyes following Gabe and me. And the only thing I could do was hope Gabe didn’t kiss me. The whole thing made me feel awful but not as awful as I felt when I saw my sister’s car.

Someone had scrawled "Brandywine Witch" in thick smudges of red lipstick all over the exterior. The crimson words gleamed on the green paint in blaring juxtaposition. It was horrible. Gabe stood speechless.

"Who—?" he began, but he already knew the perpetrator.

"You know who," I replied angrily.

"Jenn," he sighed. "I'll take care of it."

Mr. Franz was sitting on the corner of his desk when I entered and he motioned for me to take a seat at the closest table.

"A friend of mine has a gallery in Philadelphia. He's asked me to prepare a show for the end of the month."

"What do you mean 'prepare'?" It was probably rude of me to interrupt, but I was trying to figure out my role in his story before he got to the end.

"My friend wants me to put together a small portfolio of my work for display. It will run through February. Why do you look confused?"

"I—"

"Believe it or not, Louisa, I'm a photographer, too. Schoolteacher by day, photographer by weekend. Like Spider-Man, but not as cool."

I stared blankly back at him, not sure what he was getting at.

"Anyway," Mr. Franz cleared his throat, recovering from his joke. "I graded your project over the break. You did an excellent job, Louisa. Really, it's one of the best photo essays I've seen. I'd like to ask you if you'd be interested in showing it with my work at the gallery. Occasionally, I like to share my students' work alongside my own. You'd get full ownership of your project, of course. I'm not trying to show it as a piece of mine. I just thought it'd be nice to show some student work at the gallery too, and yours is exceptional."

For a moment, I only stared at my teacher as he leaned back casually with arms crossed, waiting for my answer. And then it finally began sinking in. My photography project would be on display at a real art gallery in Philadelphia. I shook my head and opened my eyes wide with elation.

"Yes! I'd love to!"

"I'd understand if you had some hesitation. Your project was intimate and special . . ."

I immediately thought back to the snapshots I'd included of my mother and smiled.

"Mr. Franz," I said graciously, "I'd be honored to show my work next to yours."

"Great!" He clapped his hands together. "I'll send you the details about when and where as the time gets closer."

I gathered my things and started heading for the door, feeling euphoric.

"Oh, and Louisa?"

I stopped in the doorway and turned back to face my beaming teacher.

"You got an A."

XXV.

Gerhard reported for his day's work earlier than necessary, left his engine clean, and kept a strict adherence to departure and arrival times. He was compulsive with his pocket watch and obsessive about time. The first thing he did before getting out of bed each morning was sit up, swing his legs over the side of his mattress, and wind his watch, cleaning its face with an old cloth and polishing the gold casing.

At the train station, Gerhard performed his usual routine. He signed in. He picked up the key for his train, engine car Number 7. He drank a cup of tea and tried to believe it was coffee. Trelleborg Station had a single office. It was actually a converted broom closet nestled in the back alongside the toilet. On the wall hung a calendar, a telephone, and a thorough chart of the train lines and timetables. Gerhard had visited this office only three times: the first when he was hired as a mechanic at the age of sixteen, again when Kjell promoted him to steam conductor two years later, and the last time on a warm Wednesday in June 1940.

Gerhard stood in the office's doorway and noticed how tired Kjell looked. The heat and humidity lingered like thick smoke in the small room, and the old man constantly wiped his forehead with a dirty rag.

"You wanted to see me?" *What was this all about?*

"Yes. Right." The two men stood looking at each other, both visibly uncomfortable. "Let's take a walk," Kjell finally suggested. "Tea?"

"*Nej, tack.* No, thanks."

The older man ran his dirty hands up and down the front of his vest, wiping dirt and grease on his chest. Gerhard knew that his employer missed the hard labor of the men beneath him. He wore regret openly on his face. Kjell was never meant to wear a suit. Strangers to the station would never guess he directed it all.

He led Gerhard to the station platform where two young boys sat and waited for the 7:10 to Malmö. Kjell took a deep breath and looked around, lost as to what to say next.

"Let's go look at your Number 7."

When they reached the train, Kjell at last turned to his young worker. A lock of white hair fell loosely onto his forehead.

"Listen, Gerhard, you're one of my best conductors. You're dedicated to what we do here. I've noticed how, for the most part, you keep to yourself."

Gerhard nodded in agreement. Other than speak with Robert, his assistant, Gerhard mostly kept to himself.

"Something's come to Trelleborg, something I've been put in charge of directing. And I'm going to ask you to assist me because I trust you. You're earnest and hardworking, and you don't meddle with the things the other boys do." Kjell spoke slowly and lifted his hand to shield the sun from his eyes. The creases of his forehead and the cracks around his eyes brimmed with dirt. A single drip of sweat ran from his brow to his chin, streaking a line of soot as it rolled. Gerhard said nothing.

"I've been asked to set aside a daily train, a round trip route from here to Kornsjø. We'll transport German troops each week across the Norwegian border. I want you to run it. I want you to run it and I want you to keep your mouth shut about it. Say nothing to no one. If anyone asks, direct him to me. You understand what I'm asking, don't you?"

Gerhard nodded stoically. He'd do anything for Kjell; he'd built his life around following orders.

"Good."

Later that morning, Robert, Gerhard's young apprentice responsible for stoking the coal in the firebox, leaned against their engine car and rolled a cigarette as Gerhard approached.

"Morning, Robert."

"Morning, Gerhard." The young boy lit his cigarette and inhaled. "Nice weather."

Gerhard agreed.

"The switch at mile two is sticking. They've got men out there trying to grease it up," Robert informed him.

"Sounds good." Gerhard began his habitual inspection of the Number 7. He looked for flaws: divots in the wheels, loose screws, obstructions, jams, or rust. As usual, his train looked perfect—the epitome of human ingenuity in raw steel.

"Did you hear about the boat from Germany?"

Gerhard looked up at Robert briefly before turning back to his work. He'd heard nothing.

"It wasn't in the papers, but everyone down at the docks is talking about it. I was down there last night."

Robert was an Artful Dodger: too young to know he was too young to know it all.

"Some Germans tried to forge the 100 kilometers across the border, but their raft sunk. They all drowned. All but one. The only survivor made it to shore around four o'clock this morning, mumbling nonsense. The boys and I couldn't really make out most of it. Said he'd been trying to escape from Sassnitz. Said there had been twelve of them." Robert took one last long drag on his cigarette. "You should have seen this guy. Skin and bones. Couldn't have weighed more than forty-five kilos. Anyway, the old man kept crying the same word: *Vernichtung. Vernichtung.* Do you speak German, Gerhard?"

"Not well enough."

"Me either. So I asked a guy." Robert paused and looked beyond Gerhard to where the distant land met the sky. "It means extermination."

The morning of the first transfer was electric. The sky was a muted, washed-out purple—the color of veins under a pale forearm—and a strangeness hung in the air. White noise? Gerhard arrived at the station early and met Robert on the tracks. His young companion was restless; it was obvious he knew what they were about to do.

Gerhard suspected all the men at the station knew what was going on. How could they not?

It made Gerhard nervous, and he wanted to tell Robert to settle down. The wind whipped the boy's hair back and forth across his forehead as he struggled to lick a cigarette paper. The sun rose slowly in the sky like a white slab of damp clay.

The German train arrived from the shipyard quietly, crawling its way onto the foreign soil as if it knew it wasn't supposed to be there. This train was a sly fox in a chicken coop. Gerhard didn't like it.

He never forgot the first face he saw from behind a little window in one of the cars. It was small and white and round, surrounded by shadows. The soldiers crammed into the cars, standing in the pitch dark. They appeared innocent and naïve. Some looked like children. They certainly didn't resemble the beasts Gerhard had imagined them to be.

There was a thirty-minute pause, and then a shift in energy as the car doors opened and men came stepping out into the muddy rail yard. They stretched their legs, lit cigarettes, and chuckled in low murmurs to each other. He'd been told they were noncombatants, that they were there to provide aid to injured soldiers on the Norwegian border, but Gerhard knew by looking at them that they were military. And the Nazis themselves didn't seem so concerned with maintaining the ruse.

The soldiers were deliberate and calculating in their movements. They worked as a single force, and Gerhard found them stronger and more powerful than any group he had ever seen. There didn't seem to be an individual heartbeat among them; there was only one living, breathing beast.

After the brief respite, the soldiers transferred onto Gerhard's cars while he stood watch. A few young soldiers glanced his way and they locked eyes, questioning each other silently.

Once they'd all boarded, Robert smiled somberly toward Gerhard and held a small flask up in mocking jest. "Heil Hitler," the young fireman whispered, and he lifted the flask to his lips.

XXVI.

In the middle of the night, I woke up in a cold sweat. I had been dreaming of Grandmother. We sat in the slave graveyard Dad had shown Greta and me. Grandmother sat on a beautifully woven blanket in the middle of the grass and I lay with my head in her lap as she read from a book. She was reciting Grandfather's story to me, and as she spoke, the stories were played out like a marionette show in front of my eyes. The characters hung from strings: Gerhard and Lasse, Åsa and Leif, Anna, and Robert. Their movements were jerky and uncoordinated.

And then, all of a sudden, Grandma stopped reading and the puppets fell into a lifeless heap on the floor. "The End." Grandma shut the book, shrugged her shoulders apologetically, and folded her hands.

"But I don't understand." I began to panic. "What happens?" I looked at the stage where the puppets lay still.

"It's what happens, Louisa." Grandmother reached down and stroked my hair, trying to ease my alarm. "It ends."

"But what about me? What about Dad?" I asked anxiously.

"Your dad? What does he know about anything? He ran away, remember?"

"He wants to know!" I shouted at her, but she only stared sympathetically back at me, as if I wouldn't face the truth. And I suddenly realized I didn't know *what* the truth was. "I think he wants to know."

"Then tell him," she whispered.

"Tell him what?"

"The end," she smiled sadly.

And then I awoke. I walked to the hallway bathroom and drank a glass of water from the faucet. It tasted metallic. I stared at my reflection in the mirror. For a split second I could have sworn I saw Grandmother's face staring back at me. She flashed quickly into my eyes—from *behind* my eyes, her face replacing mine—but then she was gone. I splashed water onto my cheeks and rubbed the mirror with a wet hand. Was I chasing her or she me?

The story is coming to an end, I thought. Grandmother had been calling me for two months, and I finally felt closer to discovering the mystery. But I couldn't see the conclusion. I leaned on the sink and ran my fingers through my hair in frustration. *Think, think, think. What am I supposed to do? I have this story that no one seems to know but me, and I don't know what to do with it. Do I tell Dad? Won't it be painful for him to hear? Do I really want to be responsible for that pain?* I stood under the fluorescent lights for five minutes in a sleepy stupor, and then a truly horrific thought came to me: *What happens when the phone calls stop?*

I snaked my way down the hallway to Greta's door, but hesitated before reaching out to open it. How had this happened? How had we become so distant?

I slowly opened the door a crack and peered inside. The comforter rose and fell silently with each breath. The floor was cold beneath my feet so I scurried across the room and crawled in next to my sister's warm body. She stretched and reached out to touch me.

"Louisa?"

"Greta," my tears wet her shoulder as I collapsed against her and let all of my contained helplessness escape in one choked breath. "I'm sorry I never asked if you were okay."

She sat up in bed and placed her hand on my head, letting me surrender all of it. We lay there in silence until my tears and breathing steadied.

"I really feel invisible, Louisa," she finally said, her voice full of emptiness. "I miss her so much. Don't you?"

I turned to look at her and thought her face seemed tired and faded.

Miss Mom? Only every time I hurt, or laugh, or feel something new. Every time Dad says something lame or I ace a pop quiz or Gabe holds my hand.

"All the time," I swallowed. It was the easiest and the hardest phrase I could muster.

"I know Dad always wants to know what's going on with us, but sometimes Mom's absence is suffocating. And I feel like I have to be all grown up because she's not here . . . when all I really want to do is curl up in her lap like I used to. Or tell her how I'm completely, insanely terrified of what's going to happen next year when I'm really on my own. And I turn," Greta removed her hand from my hair to gesture toward an invisible guest, "and no one seems to be there who cares."

"But I—" I began to protest before Greta held up her hand for me to stop.

"No one who cares like Mom would. You feel it, too. I know you do. You must."

"I wish I could tell her about you. I'm scared for you, Greta. I don't know what to do," I grabbed her wrist but she pulled it away defensively.

"You have to keep it a secret," she whispered sternly. "I've ended it. Promise me you'll keep it a secret."

But I couldn't promise. At least, I couldn't promise out loud. I buried my face into her shoulder and nodded, wanting so badly for it to be morning and feeling so tired of my secrets.

Dad didn't notice my puffy eyes the next morning at the breakfast table. Greta had given me some of her moisturizer to ease the swelling. She tried to smile and engage me in conversation so Dad wouldn't catch on to my reticence.

"Louisa, you've been invited to a black-tie event. And you have two boys in your life! I hope at least one of those guys will be on your arm that night," Greta forced a smile across the table. "Which one?"

"It's kind of come down to that, hasn't it? I can't ask both," I replied cynically.

"That doesn't work. Trust me . . . I've tried." Greta laughed encouragingly.

Dad leaned out from behind his paper, raising an eyebrow at Greta. She chuckled innocently, while I tapped my coffee spoon on the tabletop, deliberating. I thought about Gabe's freckles and protruding ears. I thought about how he always said the right thing, how he made me laugh, and how he gave me flowers. An endless supply of flowers. And I thought about Chris: his long hair, his flip-flops, his allure, his mystery. I thought about being a turtle with him.

"I'm inviting Gabe." The words slipped out before I had time to catch them on the back of my teeth. I didn't consciously select them; I just needed to say something. I needed to decide. And I chose Gabe.

"Are you sure?" Greta slowly began peeling an orange, its smell reminding me of Chris.

"Yes, I'm sure."

But as soon as I said it, I knew I had never been so *unsure* about anything in all my life. Gabe was the logical choice for the art exhibition, I reasoned with myself on the ride to school. Above all my feelings for him—the butterflies in my stomach, the kiss on the ski lift—he'd been my biggest source of encouragement throughout the process. We had talked about the project together, and I'd even go so far as to say he inspired some of my entries. So why did I feel like I was forfeiting a good thing?

My stomach ached. I knew that once I officially asked Gabe to the art show, my friendship with Chris would be practically nonexistent. I didn't feel like I'd had enough time with Chris, and I was sad to know there would be no more late-night adventures. No more back-alley surprises. Would Chris understand? Did I?

I decided I just needed to bite the bullet and take action. I wasn't going to change my mind. Somewhere in my subconscious, Gabe came out as the front-runner. And yet, there was Chris waiting for me in our History final. The teacher began handing out exams and immediately announced, "No talking." Chris stretched next to me in his desk, his dark arms reaching over his head. He looked over and smiled at me. I smiled back.

I'm such a jerk.

"Eyes on your own papers. You have ninety minutes. You may begin."

That night, Dad and I went to Weaver's to pick up ingredients for a stuffed cabbage dinner. I was hoping to find Gabe. I needed to ask him to go with me to the gallery event, and I needed him to prove I was making the right choice.

"I'm going to go pick up the cabbage," I hollered to Dad who stood studying the different grades of ground beef behind the deli counter.

"Don't forget the allspice!" Dad shouted over his shoulder.

I found Gabe restocking cans of soup.

"Hey!" He stood up, looking happy to see me. "I finally talked to Jenn. She was crazy angry, but I think she finally gets it. I picked you." He looked relieved, and I inhaled slowly.

I picked you, too, I thought.

"Mr. Franz invited me to showcase my photography essay at a gallery in Philadelphia. There's kind of an opening reception, black-tie thing." I bit my cuticle nervously. He could still say no. "I was wondering—"

"Are you kidding? I'd love to go!"

"Huh?" Here was one of the most popular boys in school, and he was agreeing to be my date to a gala in the city. How did this happen? I couldn't believe I'd had the nerve to have actually asked him in the first place. For a moment, I was quite proud of myself.

"Or were you not asking me?" Gabe blushed and looked back at the cans waiting to be stocked.

"Of course I was asking you!" I exclaimed. "You're sure you want to come?"

Gabe's smile returned full force. "I was born in a tuxedo. We'll have a great time." He winked, flashed a devilish grin, and took me in his arms as if we were waltzing.

"Will there be dancing?" he whispered seductively into my ear.

Every thought of Chris melted into a distant world.

XXVII.

Gerhard didn't know how, but by July everyone in town knew about his weekly transactions. The exchange became a spectator sport for curious children. What did the Nazis look like in the flesh? Some days the transfers took longer than usual. Fifteen minutes. Thirty. An hour. Each new train brought new faces, but they were all the same as the first. Ghost faces in the dark.

One warm morning, Kjell escorted Gerhard back into his office where they were greeted by two men. One was familiar to Gerhard: Lukas Österberg, head of city council. He was the man responsible for Lasse's seeming imprisonment in Trelleborg; he alone stood between Lasse and Lasse's desire to serve in Sweden's military. Gerhard studied Österberg's countenance, a face that stretched downward and bore sunken sockets with lackluster eyes that looked out at the world impassively. In all the years of seeing him at town events, Gerhard had never seen the man smile. The other man next to Österberg was a stranger. He stood erect in a slate, Schutzstaffel uniform with an officer's cap under his arm. His black boots were newly shined.

"*Guten Morgen.* Stefan Litzing," the officer introduced himself before switching to English. "You've been summoned to this meeting on official request from German Foreign Minister Joachim von Ribbentrop."

"Gerhard, I—" Kjell began to interject, but the German threw his hand in the air to silence him. Kjell fell back.

"Gerhard Magnusson, your government appreciates your cooperation for peace between our two nations." He looked at Österberg, who nodded in agreement. "So we are giving you more responsibility.

Your previous charge still applies. You will continue your passages to Kornsjø as normal, but we are adding new cargo to your route."

Gerhard looked to Kjell for more information, but the old man only shrugged his shoulders before looking sheepishly at the floor.

"Listen, I've got work to do. May I get to it?" Kjell asked between his teeth. He seemed desperate to leave.

"You are dismissed." Österberg waved him away and Kjell disappeared.

Gerhard looked at Österberg with disgust. Everything about the man reeked with conceit. Gerhard wanted to escape the meeting and run to Kjell, but he felt compelled to stay. Österberg gestured for him to sit, but Gerhard remained standing. It was one small act of defiance of which he was capable.

"You see, Gerhard, we'll need your continued discretion in this matter. No one can know what we're doing here," Österberg crossed his arms and leaned casually on Kjell's small desk.

Gerhard wanted to laugh. Everyone knew what they were doing.

"You will transport our wagons *to Norway* as you have been for the past months. Continue your good work." Litzing smiled. "But Germany now has new cargo we'd like you to transport *from Norway.* You are not permitted to open these wagons between the Norwegian border and Trelleborg. If they are opened before they reach this destination, there will be consequences." Litzing began putting on his black leather gloves to signal the meeting was coming to a close.

"What's the cargo?" Gerhard asked, surprised with the command he heard in his own voice.

"That's none of your concern, son." Österberg shifted his weight effortlessly. His tone made Gerhard feel insignificant. *How did he do that?*

"You want me to transport trains across my country without me knowing what's in them? I feel I have some right to know—"

"But that's where you're wrong." Litzing ceased putting on his second glove, turned to look Gerhard in the eye, and grinned. "The only right you have left is to obey your country. Am I correct, Herr Österberg?"

"Correct," the councilman nodded in absolute agreement. His bottom lip turned out like a swollen, purple worm.

Gerhard recoiled.

"Keep the cars sealed, hmm?"

The German tapped Gerhard arrogantly on the cheek before exiting. Österberg followed silently.

Out on the waiting platform, the two men spoke quietly to themselves and Gerhard studied them from the entrance of the station. Occasionally, Litzing gestured to the trains and Österberg nodded. There was something in the way Österberg stood; he seemed smaller, weaker than the other man despite being about the same size.

"I didn't believe it," mumbled a voice from behind.

Gerhard turned; he'd been unaware someone was sitting on the bench behind him. He turned to see Pontus, legs wide apart, his gut protruding aggressively from his waist. He stroked his mustache habitually and stared beyond Gerhard to the platform.

"The SS has arrived." Pontus glared steadily at Litzing while Gerhard eyed his uncle suspiciously. *Why was he here?*

Pontus stood laboriously and slowly sauntered toward the men. His wavering gait betrayed his attempts to appear sober. From his pocket, he revealed a small, red object. At first, Gerhard thought it was a Nazi armband like the one Litzing wore, but as he looked closer he saw that Pontus held his ticket to America—the same ticket he had flashed so proudly to the family before. Gerhard trailed his uncle closely; he was beginning to feel uneasy. *What was Pontus doing?*

In broken German, Pontus began to speak in nonsensical phrases.

"Excuse me, sir, but I have this ticket to America. I took it off a dead man, if you'll believe it. I have this ticket . . . I must get out of Sweden. I need to go to America."

Litzing raised an eyebrow and looked down at Pontus with disgust.

"Please, can you help me?" Pontus reached out desperately to touch the captain. "I was supposed to have a second chance! America was my second chance! You can help me. If I can just get out of Sweden—"

Pontus grabbed Litzing's shoulders, but the German turned suddenly. In one swift motion, as if swinging a tennis racket, he produced a small pistol from his hip. The soldier held the handgun to Pontus's head and cocked it. *Click*! Gerhard heard the sound above Pontus's rising sobs. It echoed in his ears, draining out all other noise. The men were at an impasse. Pontus crumpled to the ground while Litzing stood erect, his arm stretched steadily out as if it was made of wax. *Whose move was it?*

"It's fine! It's fine!" Gerhard shouted. "He's just drunk. It's fine!"

"He's not very good target practice!" Litzing shouted across the tracks, laughing violently at Pontus lying in a drunken heap in the dust.

Gerhard swiftly lifted Pontus. He felt his uncle's weight and nearly buckled under the pressure. The stench, the heaviness, the gun. It all left Gerhard feeling nauseous. He needed to get Pontus away from here. He needed to take control. Österberg watched coolly as Gerhard slowly dragged Pontus away from the platform.

Litzing replaced the pistol in his belt. "Too easy. He'd be impossible to miss."

Gerhard dreaded having to tell Lasse what happened when he returned home. The story would put Lasse into a frenzy. His brother was already obsessed with the war, and Litzing's actions would only fuel his fascination.

So Gerhard decided not to tell. Lasse didn't have to know what happened. *The less he knows the better*, Gerhard thought quietly to himself as he stumbled up to the house with his uncle. Still, something in his silence left him feeling guilty, empty. Lasse would want to know what happened; he deserved to know. But it was easier pretending life was still safe, and things were still normal. *It's easier this way*, Gerhard sighed, collapsing on a bench in front of the house. *It's better this way.*

XXVIII.

Like most things, the week of the art exhibition came up faster than I had expected. In the interim, Mr. Franz had me busy reworking my project so it could be better displayed. I had to dissect each page, sometimes transferring all of my photos and text from the back of one page to the front of another. I had to create a mat for each folio and mount them properly. All in all, I had seven frames. Seven pages of matted photos and memories of my mother. I found the end product to be rather spectacular. And when I showed them to Greta and Dad, the three of us had a good nostalgic cry. Dad expressed his ceaseless pride, and Greta gave me butterflies by complimenting my "sincere artistry." I was on cloud nine.

On top of all of that, it was the second half of my sophomore year, bringing a change in schedule. I had enrolled in Photography II, as had Gabe, and my American History class was replaced with a special elective offered on the history of the Brandywine Valley. It seemed Chris had opted out of this class, and as luck would have it I was left sitting next to Jennifer Adams. She sat smugly in her desk, proudly applying a very familiar shade of red lipstick.

"It looked better on my car," I muttered under my breath.

"And you look better on a broom," she smiled coyly into her compact.

We spent the rest of the class purposefully avoiding all interaction. I only saw Chris in the lunchroom, usually sitting at his table of other misfit high schoolers, and more than once our eyes met across the room. He was better at holding the eye contact than I was, and I usually found myself feigning a distraction. My table, too, had rotated in the changing of the semesters, and I traded my seat next to

Allison for one next to Gabe and his friends. They welcomed me happily. Sitting beside Gabe was excitement in itself, but seeing Allison's face when I made the switch was a sweet added layer of icing on the cake. I'd been ignorant of how far jaws could actually drop. Allison's reaction set me straight: four-and-a-half inches.

News quickly spread around the school of Gabe and me being together, though neither of us actually discussed it. I was content with my final decision. Gabe made me unbelievably happy, but I couldn't deny—though I'd never admit it to anyone—a minuscule touch of remorse that I wasn't going to explain things to Chris. Knowing him, I was pretty sure he wouldn't want or care about an explanation. Or did he? Still, there was that unmistakable twinge. Didn't I owe it to him? Didn't he deserve to know?

The Saturday before the exhibition, Rosemary took Greta and me to the King of Prussia Mall—a monstrosity of a shopping center—to seek out an appropriate dress for my big debut. Having never been to this mall, Greta was immediately in shopping heaven. She excused herself from Rosemary and me and took her purse and her debit card on a much-anticipated rampage. Later in the day, she referred to it as her "epic comeback." She hadn't done that type of shopping since we'd left North Carolina, and it was funny to see her back in her element. By the end of the day, Greta struggled to juggle her eleven shopping bags in various sizes and colors. Every time she set them down and picked them back up, she had to count to make sure everything was accounted for, like a shepherd looking after her flock.

But Rosemary and I were on a completely different mission than Greta. We needed to find something for me that was stylish but not too showy. I wanted something a young, urbane artist would wear, and Rosemary was more than eager to help.

I tried on long shirts with leggings, dark skinny-legged denim jeans, black slacks and black vests, silver dresses and purple pumps, red blouses and white minis. I examined patterns that ran the gamut: plaids, stripes, polka dots, and houndstooth in a variety of electric colors, and accessories that would turn heads. But nothing seemed like *me*. As Mr. Franz had explained, many of the exhibit patrons would wear tuxedos and gowns, but it was also quite acceptable—especially for the artists—to wear something a little less formal. Rosemary seemed to agree with my idea of taking liberties and wearing something more unique and stunning. To me, this exhibition was more important than homecoming and prom combined. To me, this event was so much a part of me, and no outfit seemed to be as perfect as I needed it to be.

"What about something of your mom's?" Rosemary at last suggested. Despite being a little jealous I hadn't thought of it myself, the sentiment was so appropriate and wonderful I wanted to hug Rosemary for suggesting it.

I was so eager to raid Mom's old clothes that I insisted we leave for home immediately to comb through the wardrobe bags Dad had never been able to throw away. And why should he? He had two young daughters who would, one day, very much want to know their mother. Apparently, not only had that day arrived, but Dad's salvaging of the clothes provided a goldmine of outfits for me to sort through.

I never thought I'd be okay going through Mom's old belongings with Dad's new girlfriend, but the situation presented itself, and never once did it feel awkward. Rosemary pulled dress after dress out of long plastic clothing bags and eagerly held them up for my approval. We created three piles: the "Yeses," the "Nos," and the "Maybes."

"Your mother had really great taste," Rosemary complimented, pulling out Mom's old pink sequined dress.

This dress, I knew, my mother wore to her thirtieth birthday party before she'd been diagnosed. Dad had arranged the party, specifically stating on every invitation that the party had a "black" theme and every guest should arrive in black dress, only. Wasn't it a surprise then, when Mom pulled up in a black limousine wearing a hot pink sequined dress with the smallest bit of black trim? It was a memory I didn't personally have stored away, but one I cherished just the same.

"She looks like she was a lot of fun." Rosemary held up the dress, and I tried it on immediately.

Twenty minutes later, I stood in front of my bedroom vanity in Mom's birthday dress paired with black Chuck Taylors—my perfect outfit. Then Dad knocked on my bedroom door telling me I had a phone call. It was exactly what I didn't want to hear.

"They say it's walking pneumonia." Gabe coughed into the phone. "I'm on antibiotics for two weeks and I'm not allowed out of the house. I'm grounded by bacteria, Lou." Gabe coughed again.

The gallery event was in three days, and my date—my amazingly wonderful, adorable crush—was bedridden. I should have seen it coming. I was naïve to think this night could go so seamlessly.

"I'm really sorry," he apologized, but there was something strange in the way he said it. Like he wasn't being completely honest with me.

"Is there anything I can do?" I offered, my voice laced with despair.

"I'll let you know," he responded curtly. "Listen, I've got to go."

I thanked him for calling, passing on my wishes for a speedy—though it wouldn't be speedy enough—recovery, and set down the phone. Rosemary, who'd been sitting on my bed listening to the entire conversation, looked at me with compassionate eyes.

"Walking pneumonia," I informed her, and she nodded in understanding. I slowly began taking off the dress, my mood the complete opposite of how I had felt putting it on.

That night as I lay awake staring at the ceiling, I kept replaying Gabe's tone over in my head. Something wasn't right about it, but I couldn't pinpoint what. I thought about how I had ended up here: the conversation with Greta over the breakfast table. What had compelled me to utter Gabe's name? What was it inside me that picked Gabe over Chris? I didn't know.

And then my mind wandered to an alternate universe. What would have happened if I had said Chris's name instead of Gabe's? How would it feel sitting at Chris's lunch table next to him with his arm around me? I closed my eyes and pictured myself tying my sneakers, smoothing down Mom's dress and skipping down the front stairs, two by two, to answer the knock at the door and find Chris waiting to take me to my art show. I imagined Chris's beautiful tan skin, his dark hair pulled back in true debonair fashion. He looked uncomfortable in his tux, but exquisite. In that picture, I saw that he was destined for greatness. He was handsome and tall, and that familiar careless grin and twinkle in his eye let me know that we were going to have an amazing time together, no matter where the road took us.

I sat up in bed and looked around my dark room, eyeing the sequined dress suspended from a hanger on my closet door. *What if I'd made a mistake?* What if this was my chance to choose a different path? Maybe Gabe's sudden illness was a sign that I was meant to be with Chris. The thought was agonizing, and part of me felt like a fool for even considering it. But Rosemary said that she had seen me happy. Perhaps I was destined to be happy with Chris, not Gabe. I was desperate to know.

If I had picked up the telephone and called Chris that instant, he would have answered. But I couldn't pull the trigger. I needed to sleep on the possibility. If my mind was still unsure in the morning, I'd visit Chris at Fat Bottoms and ask him to take me to the art show. And then, maybe, I'd finally be rid of this feeling of uncertainty. Walking pneumonia could quite possibly end up being the fork in the road toward a different happiness.

I woke up the next morning nervous. I hadn't slept well because I wasn't able to stop my mind from fluctuating between Gabe and Chris. I'd thought this part was over. I had finally made up my mind, and then Gabe had to throw a monkey wrench into the entire situation and make me start doubting myself. Was it fair for me to ask Chris to replace Gabe? Absolutely not. I knew what I was formulating in my head was so completely selfish and absurd that I didn't dare ponder what Gabe would think of me if he found out. But I also knew that life presented roadblocks and offered escape routes and second chances. Maybe somewhere, someone was telling me I chose wrong. Maybe I was being given another chance. And I knew where to find that other opportunity: he'd be starting his shift at Fat Bottoms at around four o'clock. And that's where I was going to be, exploring a different path.

XXIX.

For an entire month after his meeting with Litzing, Gerhard barely saw his brother. Lasse's mind seemed to be somewhere else; he seemed distracted. Most nights Lasse finished his dinner and went straight to bed. At first, Gerhard didn't want to bother him. But by the fourth week, Gerhard's concern had grown too great. He didn't like how distant his brother seemed. Something was wrong.

For the first time in his entire life, Gerhard felt disconnected from his twin. Since birth, he and Lasse had sensed each other's pain, known their inner desires, and recognized their deepest fears. But now, Lasse seemed far away in a place he didn't share with anyone. Lasse had also grown quiet; his once boisterous laugh was seldom heard, his smile rarely seen. Somehow, somewhere, Gerhard had lost his best friend.

Lasse was only one of Gerhard's problems. On July 8, 1940, the Swedish public officially learned about the formal agreement between Sweden and Germany: one daily, round-trip train from Trelleborg to Kornsjø and another weekly train from Trelleborg to Narvik. Each train carried approximately five hundred Nazi soldiers and supplies. This agreement, now a legal arrangement, was the result of Swedish Prime Minister Per Albin Hansson's desire to maintain peace. He continued to tout Sweden as a neutral country, but this, of course, was the greatest trick he would ever perform.

In an attempt to remain impartial, Hansson exported relief supplies to Norway, Denmark, and Finland, while also transporting iron ore to Germany. The duplicity and compliance left Gerhard bewildered. *On what side of the war did his country stand?*

Still, his daily routine began to feel second nature. He executed his schedule flawlessly: after arriving in the Trelleborg harbor on one of the railcar ferries—sometimes Lasse's, sometimes not—the German trains continued through Trelleborg's station and connected to Gerhard's own engine. He and Robert smoked cigarettes and watched as new passenger cars appeared in the early morning sun. His train and its travelers arrived at the Norwegian border by one o'clock, completing their seven-hour trip. Gerhard always followed a schedule. He didn't dare deviate from the routine.

But one wet day in late summer, the system altered. That afternoon, as the sun hid behind clouds and the rain fell steady and hard, Gerhard slowly pulled his haul into the Norwegian city, Narvik. The air smelled of manure. This afternoon was different. A huddled crowd of men stood waiting for him on the platform.

The downtrodden group—crippled young boys in faded green—all wore the same vacancy in their eyes. Their clothes, the color of muck on stagnant pools, hung loosely over their weary limbs. They were expressionless zombies. On the far end of the platform stood a handful of armed SS guards, their polished guns pointing menacingly at their prisoners, their pressed khaki shirts contrasting sharply against the dull green. As Gerhard's passengers exited his train, they reacted with the prisoners on the platform like water and oil, one group shuffling aside to avoid mixing with the other. Two incompatible bodies; two contrasting worlds.

"What's this?" Gerhard asked while disembarking his car.

"New cargo," the head German answered.

"Cargo?" Gerhard glanced at the crowd of grave faces. They stared back at him behind dead eyes.

"You're a Swede?" one of the prisoners shouted to him in Norwegian, right before an armed guard knocked him to the ground with the butt of his machine gun.

The young man whimpered in agony and struggled to get back up. None looked his way; none attempted to help. It was as if they wanted him to remain down. As if it were *better* for him to stay down. The prisoners stared submissively at the train, at Gerhard. He clutched his throat where his collar felt tight around his neck. He needed to breathe, but his lungs constricted. Gerhard coughed loudly and looked away, shutting his eyes tightly, trying to squeeze their gaunt faces from his mind. He wanted the prisoners to know he wasn't who they thought he was. But they didn't seem to care.

"You're taking these prisoners of war to Trelleborg where they'll continue to Germany. Officer Litzing will meet them at the Swedish docks. He'll travel with them across the border. You only take them to Trelleborg." The SS soldier nodded to Gerhard before turning back to the group. "Go, now! Go, board!"

Gerhard didn't have time to stop them; they poured over the platform through his car doors. They were eager and fatigued. *How long had they been waiting for him?*

"Wait, wait, wait," Gerhard turned to the German. "I can't take them to Trelleborg."

But the soldier didn't respond; he was busy pulling bandaged, bloodied men from the crowd and pushing them hurriedly into the cars. Gerhard watched helplessly. Robert came to join him up front.

"What are we doing, Gerhard?"

But Gerhard only stared. He had no answer.

Arriving back in Trelleborg, Gerhard met a new group of German soldiers who took over the ride. He watched his train disappear down the tracks toward the docks where, he assumed, Litzing waited to carry out their final leg of the trip. Gerhard couldn't stay at the station. He felt sick and tired and wanted desperately to crawl into bed. As if waiting for his return, Lasse sat on the bench outside their house, eating an apple.

"Good afternoon," he greeted warmly, shielding the sun with the palm of his hand.

"So you decide I'm worthy of you again?" Gerhard patronized.

Lasse looked quizzically at his brother before shrugging and tossing the apple core out into the road.

"Where have you been for the past four weeks?" Gerhard's voice broke, as if his mental stability would crumble at any moment. Beads of sweat rolled down his temples and he held out his hands, holding onto something that wasn't there.

"I've been here," Lasse spoke casually, looking confused.

"You know what I mean," Gerhard slumped beside him.

For a long moment, Lasse said nothing while Gerhard caught his breath.

"What did I do to deserve your silence?" Gerhard shook the fallen bangs out of his eyes and stared at his brother. It was like looking into a mirror.

At once, Lasse began to laugh, uncontrollable, frantic laughter, the likes of which often accompanies exhaustion. Gerhard's shoulders stiffened and he imagined grabbing his brother by the collar. All the agony of the day, all his confusion, all the uncertainty boiled ever so close to the surface that Gerhard trembled with rage. *Why the mockery? Why the jest?*

"Gerhard, you've done nothing!"

"Then tell me what's going on because you can't shut me out," Gerhard pleaded, lowering his voice so no one in the house would hear. "You don't know what I had to do today."

Lasse stopped laughing and his face grew serious.

"What's that, Gerhard? What did you have to do?"

"I transported fifty Norwegians to God knows where, taking them to where only God can help them," Gerhard explained, holding out his hands for Lasse to see his shaking.

Lasse leaned his head back against the house and looked up toward the sky.

"I was under strict orders," Gerhard started to explain, but even he could hear the fear—the uncertainty—in his voice.

"Orders? Come now, Gerhard," Lasse paused and took a deep breath. It seemed a struggle to continue. "For a year, I've watched and listened. I've listened to Father, I've listened to Pontus, I've listened to you. I've heard and seen things on the ferry I never asked to see or hear. Haven't you? Don't you know about the camps and the deaths and the exterminations?"

Lasse raised his eyebrows waiting for a reply, but Gerhard didn't have one.

"Don't you know about their 'final solution'? Have you seen the bodies in the water like I have? Swimmers trying to escape—their bodies so frail that they float like driftwood. From what are they escaping? You know. I know you know." He looked beyond Gerhard, choking on something deeply lodged into his memory.

Gerhard stood up from the bench and crouched down into the dirt. He didn't want to hear what his brother had to say. He didn't want to hear what he'd suspected for so long. He wasn't willing to let go of the fantasy he'd created for his life: a life free of guilt and responsibility.

"And don't act like you're innocent with the rest of them. 'Following orders'?" Lasse's words came spitting out with disgust. "You don't want to think about the blood on your hands. But that's just it, Gerhard. There's blood on all of our hands." Lasse held out his palms for Gerhard to see. "We shouldn't fear the Germans. We should fear ourselves."

Lasse looked down at Gerhard hugging his knees. "The way we've been acting? Our willful blindness? That's not us. It's not Sweden. It's time to *act*, Gerhard."

Gerhard waited a long time before collapsing at his brother's feet. His mouth felt dry, and he didn't think he was capable of speaking. He remembered Österberg's apathy and Kjell's impotence. He was going to be sick.

"So," Lasse sighed. "You ask where I've been? I've been here, watching and waiting. I'm going to act, Gerhard. Trelleborg is going to burn, and you can either be the hero or the coward."

XXX.

When I arrived at Fat Bottoms the next evening, students I recognized from school and other young people crowded the porch and spilled out of the front door. I could hear a steady beat ripple through the air. I'd forgotten that the small coffee shop was hosting an evening of live indie music. I'd built up my courage to confess to Chris I'd made a mistake, and I refused to let my nerves sway me after I'd come all the way downtown. I elbowed my way through the throngs of people and squeezed past the front door. I saw Chris immediately, steaming milk and brewing espresso. He looked like a natural-born barista.

Shouting to him was pointless. The music was too loud, the crowd too dense, and I could tell he was preoccupied with work. I needed to get closer, so I stood behind a thick line of people waiting to put in their orders. Eventually, my foot found the beat.

The music was good. Peeking around the corner, I saw a small makeshift stage and a tall, thin guy with teased black hair crooning into a microphone. Behind him stood a bassist, rhythm guitarist, drummer, and keyboardist. The bass drum had the name "The Ottomans" taped on in black wire tape. Very hip. I immediately liked the band, this scene. I was getting more and more convinced this was where I was supposed to be. Here, with Chris.

The line didn't move once in five minutes, and I was getting anxious. I was so afraid if I had to wait another five minutes, I'd chicken out, throw in the towel, and retreat back to the house. My phone buzzed in my pocket.

Where are you? Greta texted me.

My face lit up. Of course! So easy!

At Fat Bottoms. Greta, you're a genius! I love you! I texted back.

I'd had Chris's number in my phone ever since we worked on the almanac project together. *Hey, I'm here*, I sent to him. *You look busy.*

Within two minutes, I saw Chris hand some girls their frothy mugs and pull his phone out of his jeans, checking his new message. Immediately, he looked up. I waved from my place in line, ten people back.

"Hi," I mouthed silently, smiling broadly.

He looked happy to see me and returned the smile. My heart melted into a molten mess inside my chest. Maybe it was the setting or the music, but he looked the best I'd ever seen him.

"Can we talk?" I hoped he could read lips.

He stared back at me and held up his arms with a "how do I get away from this?" look.

My shoulders slumped. There was no way I'd be able to have this discussion any other day. My bravery was up. Right here, right now. I gestured to the other room, indicating that I'd wait. Chris nodded before getting back to his work. *Take it easy, Louisa*, I reassured myself. *It's just Chris.* So why did I feel like I was falling to pieces?

For another hour, The Ottomans played on. I looked around the coffee shop, people-watching. There were girls with pink hair, ripped tights, and leather jackets. There were peroxide blonds in tight skirts and cowboy boots. There were lots of tattoos and the scent of sweet tobacco—clove cigarettes—hung in the air. There was even a group of intellectuals in Ivy League sweaters and wire-rimmed glasses in the corner. I doubted there was anyone in the coffee shop over the age of thirty. It was quite an amalgamation of people: the hipsters, the college kids, the Ottomaniacs (self-dubbed groupies), and the local misfit high school kids I recognized from Chris's lunch table. Chris's ex, Lacey, delivered coffee from the bar. She never once asked me if I needed anything.

By nine-thirty, three-quarters of the crowd had filtered out of Fat Bottoms's cramped interior. The band started packing up their instruments. Chris wiped down the bar and counted the cash register. He looked exhausted. At ten he finally took a chair at my table, handing me a cappuccino.

"I didn't know you were coming tonight," he smiled, leaning back in the chair and lifting his apron over his head.

"I didn't know I was either." I shifted nervously in my seat.

"What's up? I feel like I haven't seen you in forever." It was good to hear his deep voice again.

"I know. I'm sorry about that." I cocked my head to the side and started playing with a divot in the table. I had to pull myself together.

"So," I began, looking up into his eyes. For a moment, I got lost. Chris lifted his brows for me to continue. "So, last semester, I had this photography project, right? A photography essay. I did mine on my mom, kind of chronicling her life through pictures. Well, mine was the best in class."

Chris chuckled at my arrogant honesty.

"No, it's true!" I laughed, too. I was feeling more relaxed. *It's just Chris.* "Mine was so good I was asked to show it at a gallery in Philadelphia. The opening is this week, actually."

"Well," Chris sounded a little confused why I'd come all the way to Fat Bottoms and waited an hour for his shift to end, only to tell him something seemingly inconsequential. "Congratulations."

"Thanks," I continued running my fingers over the chip in the table. "So, here's the thing," I inhaled, cautiously, "there's kind of a gala tomorrow night. Opening night. I wanted to know if you wanted to come. With me. To the gala . . ." My voice trailed off, sounding hesitant.

Chris folded his arms. He stared at me for a couple seconds as I sat in agony not knowing how he'd respond. The Ottoman drummer dropped his snare drum, and the entire room turned to look in his direction. Everyone but Chris and me. We continued our awkward silent showdown.

"Louisa, I don't really think it's a good idea." He sighed, looking indifferent.

I broke our eye contact, directing my attention to a hangnail. I didn't say anything. I was quietly trying to figure out how to get him to change his mind.

"It's not really my thing, you know? I'm not a "gala" type of person."

There was something in the way Chris said gala that sounded antagonistic, like he was making fun of me for even asking. Suddenly, I wanted to be as far from Fat Bottoms as possible. But Chris didn't stop there.

"Anyway, it's probably going to be a bunch of stuffed shirts. Not my scene."

"Really?" I swallowed, my throat feeling hot. "So you think I'm a stuffed shirt?"

"Well," Chris chuckled, looking around the room. "You're not exactly inconspicuous here, for example."

I couldn't tell if he was purposefully trying to be mean, unjustifiably superior, or just completely unaware. None of the options made me feel very good.

"And what?" Chris continued. "You thought we'd be good together because we both belong to the Maternal Abandonment Club?"

My mouth fell slightly agape, and he diverted his look to something behind me, clearly uncomfortable with his own insult.

"My mom didn't *abandon* me, Chris," I seethed. "She died."

I waited for him to look at me but he refused. Where was all of his hostility coming from? Had I so utterly misjudged him that I'd fooled myself into thinking he had feelings for me? Was all of this humiliation my fault? Or was there more to it?

"Why don't you ask Weaver? I thought the two of you were shacking up?"

Bingo. There it was. He knew. He knew he was my second choice.

I bit my lip, realizing that instead of admitting that he was jealous, admitting I'd hurt him, Chris chose to hurt me back. He was used to impressing people with his daring spontaneity and passionate rhetoric. He was intoxicating with his adventures and his philosophies, but he was incapable of voicing how he truly felt.

How long had I been trying to solve the mystery of Chris Harris, chasing the allure, the deep voice, and the bristly chin? But now I was finally seeing him for what he really was: no more mature than Gabe or me. Nor more exotic. Just an astoundingly good actor, playing the role of the misunderstood outsider. There, he'd found his niche. There, he wasn't afraid of rejection.

But I *had* rejected him, and he wasn't willing to give me a second chance. And I knew I didn't deserve one. I said my adieus to Chris and left Fat Bottoms feeling utterly depressed. Not only was the gallery event tomorrow, but my original date was supposedly bedridden and the torch I'd once carried for Chris felt like it'd been doused in a bucket of cold water. The event I had been so looking forward to was now an obligatory homework assignment.

And to top it all off, I had just discovered that my grandfather had faced far worse choices than I would ever have to make. What was he going to choose? Optimism was the last thing on my mind.

XXXI.

Lasse admitted from the beginning that his plan wasn't comprehensive—he knew there were holes. He had been trying to work through these snags for the past four weeks. They were the reason he'd been aloof. He had never intended to include Gerhard. The plan was too dangerous to make it a two-man operation, but then he saw that Gerhard was ready.

"I surrender," Gerhard told his brother when faced with the choice. "I cannot bend to them anymore. They've destroyed me."

"Good." Lasse placed his hand on his brother's shoulder. "That's how you need to feel. That's how it should feel. Now," he smiled wickedly, "let's start a militia."

Gerhard agreed that a guerrilla army would send a clear message to Germany and the Axis Powers. Sweden could finally answer the Norwegian and Danish calls for assistance with boots on the ground. But there were problems. Could it be done? Did they have it in them? Who to trust? How to mobilize? Neither brother knew where to begin.

Gerhard lay awake, deliberating the flaws in Lasse's plan. Everything about it seemed to put people's lives in danger. Every road seemed to lead to failure, and failing was something neither man was prepared to do.

When the solution came to Gerhard, he couldn't believe he hadn't thought of it earlier. Everything seemed so much clearer, the plan so much more possible. The answer came from the heart of the problem; the solution lay on the rails.

Gerhard knew his train: the ride, the route, the risk. He knew how to crash, or, at least how to derail. The rest could be left to fate.

Gerhard shook Lasse awake at three o'clock in the morning.

"I can do it!" he whispered to his groggy brother. "The switch at Mile Marker Two hasn't been working for over two months. They've had to send a man out there to manually shift the track for us. If a train hits that switch going the right speed and the switch hasn't been shifted . . . no one would walk away from a crash like that alive. That's how we'll do it." Gerhard felt proud. He'd found a way, but he soon was overcome with apprehension. *If this works, it's a suicide mission,* said a frightened voice inside him.

"That's how *I'll* do it," Lasse corrected.

"But—" Gerhard began, "it's my train." He'd come up with the plan. He'd thought of it first. And yet, he wondered, was he willing to die for it?

"Gerhard, I'm not going to argue with you. I've spent a month coming to peace with my decision."

"My plan," Gerhard whispered defensively.

For a moment, he wondered if he would vomit. Were they actually arguing about who would die? Lasse rolled over and propped himself up to stare his brother in the eye.

"I can do it," Lasse challenged.

The statement was so familiar. How many times had Lasse volunteered to do something first? Something better? And now, it had come down to the ultimate offering. His final sacrifice.

"I won't let you." Gerhard clung tightly to his ownership of the plan. He wasn't going to let his brother do this. He stared back at his brother, his eyes stern.

"Then we'll do what's only fair." Lasse sat up and reached for something on the bedside table. He held up a coin suggestively. It glimmered in the twilight shining from the window. "Call it. *Krona eller klave*? Crown or hoof?"

"*Krona*," Gerhard muttered, annoyed.

He watched as Lasse tossed the coin into the air, caught it, and flipped in onto the back of his hand. Without hesitation, Lasse lifted his palm and exposed the twenty kronor coin. Crown side up.

"So it will be you," Lasse swallowed, staring at the coin in disbelief, looking ill.

Gerhard felt more than a little queasy himself. "We'll plan more in the morning," he whispered, his throat tight in his chest as he crawled back to his own bed, feeling faint.

The twins spent their Saturday morning walking to town. They told their mother they were going to buy her flowers.

Leif and Pontus were down by the shore playing a game of *boule*. The boys sat a distance from the lawn game and watched to see who would toss his balls closest to the *lillen*, the smaller target ball. Leif won the first round.

At first, Leif didn't notice his sons. But after some time he looked up and saw his boys sitting alone on a rock in the distance. Immediately, he knew something was wrong. Something in the boys' rigid stances, or in their vacant stares. Leif couldn't put his finger on what it was; he only concluded that a father knew when his sons were troubled. He lifted his hand to wave, but only Gerhard returned the gesture. *Very strange.* The second round began and, by the time he looked up again, the boys were gone.

The twins walked the streets of Trelleborg, stopping occasionally to look in a storefront window or to greet a colleague on the footpath. At last, they settled on the grounds of the *Sankt Nicolai kyrka*. In the summertime, the open grasses surrounding the church were dotted with picnickers, and only occasionally did someone enter or leave the church. Lasse and Gerhard were two of a handful of people around. They were glad of that.

"When?" Lasse asked, his tone hostile. He was still sore about losing the coin toss.

What a grotesque thing to be jealous of, Gerhard thought to himself. He addressed Lasse delicately. He wanted no ill will between them in their final days together.

"The route is the same every day. Same times. You will, of course, need time to escape Trelleborg. I imagine they will come looking for you," Gerhard said evenly.

"Thursday, then? They won't be able to get up here until at least Monday."

"Sounds fine. Robert will know about the plan only minutes before it's executed. He will need to stoke the fire, and jump from the train as I accelerate while approaching the switch. You will need to get to the marker before I do and turn the track. Don't wait to see what happens. Just go. Have your bags already packed. Once you leave, you won't be able to come back," Gerhard had rehearsed this speech all morning. Everything had to be perfect; any flaws in the plan could mean death for both of them.

"And what happens if something goes wrong?" Lasse asked.

"What do you mean?"

"You need an out. If something happens, someone discovers us, you can't go through with it, anything. Anything to make the crash impossible to carry out. You'll need an out," Lasse, apparently, had been doing some strategizing of his own.

"What do you suggest?"

"The train whistle. I'll be able to hear it from the switch, right?"

"Yes, you should be able to hear it from five kilometers, at least," Gerhard stated proudly. All his studying of train mechanics had suddenly become the essential bones of their entire operation.

"As you approach the mile marker, blow it twice to let me know to switch the rails. Blow it once, and the plan is off. Blow it once, and we meet back at the house. Okay?"

"Don't hesitate after I sound it twice," Gerhard warned.

"*If* you sound it twice."

They paused. Finally, Gerhard concluded their preparations, "Thursday, then."

"Thursday," Lasse agreed.

The plan was set. For the rest of the afternoon, the boys went their separate ways to deliberate their fates in solitude. Neither son remembered to bring Åsa her promised flowers.

Since the beginning of the Swedish rail, there had been only a handful of train wrecks. In 1875, two trains collided head-on in the city of Östergötland resulting in nine fatalities. Then, in 1912, a Swedish train in Malmslätt crashed full speed into an idling passenger train. Twenty-two people died and twelve were severely injured. In 1917, a Swedish train carrying invalid Russian soldiers created a pileup near Soderhamn. Eleven casualties. But nothing compared to what happened in Getå.

On October 1, 1918, in the small town of Getå, near Norrköping, a mudslide covering the train tracks hurled ten passenger cars off the tracks. The cars caught fire instantly. Forty-two passengers and train workers died: some instantly in the crash, others burned alive, trapped inside the fiery cars. The crash reverberated throughout Europe and newspapers the continent over featured the tragedy.

Since entering the profession, Gerhard was well versed in the crash's history. Workers mentioned the Getå crash on a regular basis, warning against rail-driver delinquency. Gerhard wondered how the Number 7 would compare to Getå. Would newspapers report the crash at Mile Marker Two?

Gerhard woke up Thursday morning and sat on the side of his bed. *It's just another day*, he silently convinced himself. *For my sanity, it's just another day.* His bones popping and breaking the silence, he reached for his pocket watch on his bedside table. *I can't deviate from my normal routine.* He began winding his watch, a habit he'd had for three years: wind the watch first thing, and then briefly again at the station. He felt the weight of the mechanism in his palm, that familiar heaviness he loved. Lasse's bed was unmade and cold. His brother had kept his role in the plan: wake up, go to the ferries with Leif as usual, and then fake sudden illness and request afternoon leave. From the harbor, Lasse would ride his bicycle to the switch and wait for the train whistle.

The watch clicked into place. Gerhard closed the face and set it back on the table. He stretched, stood, and began going through his morning routine, trying to think about anything but the day's plan.

He walked downstairs to the kitchen; the oven was still warm from Åsa's preparation of the family's breakfast. Åsa rarely made pancakes for breakfast, usually saving them for dinner. But today there was a warm plate waiting for Gerhard on the stove. Why had she decided to make them this morning?

When he was a boy, Gerhard used to love watching his mother when she made pancakes. She'd take a pat of butter and let it sizzle before pouring the thin, eggy batter into the pan. She'd swirl the skillet in the air, letting the batter coat the bottom. Åsa was born to make pancakes.

The first try was always a throwaway. It never came out right, as the pan took time to properly heat. Åsa called it "Loki's share," referring to the old Norse trickster. She'd roll the sacrificial morsel and throw it out the front door to a stray dog.

This plate represented everything Gerhard loved most about his mother. It was his favorite meal. How fitting for it to also be his last.

He smiled forlornly at the dish. He'd wanted to say goodbye to his mother. But there was no time to go find her. Gerhard had to get to the station. He looked at his watch to check the schedule before grabbing a rolled pancake. The smell reminded him of what he was leaving, and he soon felt suffocated. He needed to get out of the house. The air was getting too thick, the temptation to surrender too great. Gerhard closed the door to his house for the last time. How would Åsa feel when she realized he wasn't coming back? Would Leif stare at the door waiting for him to walk in? He wrapped his jacket tightly around him. The July breeze was chilling and unusually cold. No doubt there was an approaching gale off the coast.

It took him ten minutes to bicycle to the train station. He stood on the platform, looking at the sky, committed to his daily routine. The cloud cover was extensive. Which direction was the sun? Gerhard took out his pocket watch: 6:55 in the morning. He was right on schedule. The day's new batch of German railcars would arrive at the station from the harbor in ten minutes, and he'd pull the Number 7 out of Trelleborg by eight o'clock sharp. For the last time.

He watched the little hands of his watch move ever so slowly around the center wheel. *I love this machine.* What was it Leif had told him so long ago? *Wind it every day and it will never fail you.*

Casually, Gerhard glanced up at the tall, black clock standing erect on the platform. The timepiece was iconic to the Trelleborg station, towering four meters tall with a face as large as a serving platter. Looking at the clock was the first thing Gerhard did that day that strayed from his normal routine. He had never referenced any other clock but his pocket watch. What made him look up to see its ghostly white face that day? Gerhard never knew. As he stared, he felt his body go numb, felt his heart stop beating, and he held his breath until he felt dizzy.

8:13.

The platform clock read 8:13. Gerhard quickly held his pocket watch up in the air to compare the two clock faces side by side.

6:58.

8:13.

The gears and wheels of Gerhard's brain revolved, creaking into place. He slowly saw how all the pieces fit together. He closed his eyes and watched his twin brother standing at the washbasin, shaving his identifiable beard. He watched as Lasse sat discreetly on his side of the bedroom, staring each morning as Gerhard wound his pocket watch religiously.

Gerhard's mind imagined Lasse lying awake, waiting for the perfect moment to crawl out of bed and softly lift the pocket watch from his brother's bedside table. Lasse quietly opened the crown. Behind closed eyes, Gerhard watched his brother arrive at the station on schedule. He could see him now, on the track, manning the lever, approaching Mile Marker Two. And Gerhard suddenly realized his own role in this new plan: he had to get to the switch before the Number 7 did.

He sprinted off the platform toward his bicycle. He knew he could get to the mile marker in twenty-five minutes via a shortcut through the woods. The Number 7 would cross over Mile Marker Two in thirty minutes. There wasn't time to think. Gerhard had to get to the switch.

From the sky, the Skåne woods looked like an extensive chart of ant tunnels and animal burrows. Swedish locals visited the woods regularly and had developed a comprehensive map of dirt paths. Since they were young, Gerhard and Lasse had explored these woods with a tireless conviction. Gerhard felt as familiar in these woods as he did on the railroad or on the streets of Trelleborg. He knew exactly how to reach Mile Marker Two.

Gerhard wondered if Lasse knew he was on his way. He wondered if Lasse had planned it, knowing Gerhard would have just the right amount of time to reach the predestined spot on the rail to successfully execute the plan. How long had his brother planned this?

Gerhard had adequately prepared himself for his own demise. He had found his peace. But Lasse changed the rules. He cheated. And Gerhard was overcome with rage. Did Lasse think this was another competition?

Mile Marker Two lay in the bald side of a small knoll. It was the only clearing in the dense woods between the cities of Trelleborg and Vellinge. The Swedish railroad planners had created the switch as a way for trains to pass each other on the track coming in and out of Malmö. One train was able to pull itself onto a small stretch of track that lay parallel to the main route to allow an oncoming train to pass. It usually resulted in a ten- to fifteen-minute wait, but the conductors were happy to be patient if it meant avoiding a collision. The waiting track ran the length of a standard, full train—about ten car lengths—before turning back onto the main line. There were no barricades at the bend to prevent derailment; drivers would enter the alternate track cautiously. Never had there been any train malfunctions at Mile Marker Two, not until it had begun sticking. It provided the perfect opportunity for Lasse to derail the train, plunging it full speed into the thick Swedish forest.

At the spot where the two rails diverged, Gerhard jumped from his bike, discarded it at the base of a tree, and pulled out his watch: 8:41. He had four minutes to think before he'd see the black locomotive barreling around the bend, traveling full speed toward the end of the line.

Gerhard ran his hands through his hair, pushing his fingertips hard against his skull. *Think, think, think.* He knew he had the option of doing nothing and letting the train continue on its path all the way to Kornsjø. He didn't have to switch the lever, he didn't have to act. He walked over to the switch. It felt cold and hard, and he felt impotent.

It would take two seconds to make the decision.

He was a fool to have believed Lasse's coin toss. He should have expected his brother to take his place at the conductor's seat. Everything Lasse had ever said or done, everything leading up to this moment should have warned Gerhard what would happen.

And then Gerhard stopped.

Indeed, he was a fool.

This was Lasse's plan. The choice of sacrifice was never up to Gerhard. No coin should ever have been tossed. This decision to act had been Lasse's from the very beginning, and Gerhard had no right to insert himself and steal his brother's glory. But that didn't keep him, standing in the small clearing at Mile Marker Two, from hoping to hear his brother's change of heart. Just one whistle.

At 8:44 Gerhard saw his Number 7 round the south bend in the tracks, the same bend Gerhard had traveled countless times. Despite the cold wind, he held his hair in place, his two palms smoothing over his forehead. He looked at the front of the train from a distance, trying to see through the front window to glimpse his brother's face. What had Lasse decided? Where did he stand? But Gerhard saw only a reflection of the sky in the glass. He bent over as if to retch and screamed out in frustration. It wasn't supposed to be this way. He couldn't do it.

The train whistle blew, penetrating the woods. Its screech was loud and high-pitched. His ears pricked up, hoping—praying—to hear nothing more. He wanted to let the train continue its journey to Norway. He wanted his brother to live. And if that meant the war would last forever or if it meant that German forces would occupy Sweden, so be it. Gerhard was ready to walk away; he was satisfied with pretending that things weren't as bad as they seemed.

The train continued forward at an alarming rate. If Lasse jumped now, he'd surely meet his death. Still, the train came faster. Gerhard thought about what he'd told his brother the night before, "The faster the train, the bigger the crash." Then the second whistle blew.

Gerhard felt as if he would collapse. How had this happened? How could Lasse have let this happen? And then he caught a glimpse of his brother through the window. A shadow crept across the glass and Gerhard saw him seventy meters away—beautifully handsome, standing tall at the front of the train. Lasse smiled peacefully and nodded, staring lovingly and intently in Gerhard's direction.

Time stopped.

Gerhard remembered their purpose. It wasn't about them, the Magnusson twins from Trelleborg. It wasn't about Sweden or its compliance. This was about seeing the world for what it was. This was about staring into hell while realizing heaven still exists. Gerhard knew what he had to do.

Slowly and with resolve, Gerhard reached out and felt the lever next to the track. Methodically, he twisted the handle and watched the track shift into place. He made the decision. The train was going to crash. Lasse was going to die.

XXXII.

I lay in bed that night, my cheeks rough with dried tears. I hadn't slept at all. I was devastated at the horror of Grandpa's sacrifice and the guilt from which he suffered. He'd labeled himself a murderer; he'd hauled that title from Sweden to America. Was he ever able to fully release himself of it?

I alternated emotions, switching from sorrow to anger to sorrow. I mourned the loss of a family member I'd only recently come to know and love. Lasse was as much a part of me now as Grandma and Grandpa were. Their triumphs and losses equaled those in my own life. And I was exhausted from the heartache.

I felt an animosity—justified or not—toward my dad for never knowing this tale himself. He'd never asked. Or had he? Grandpa never got the chance to tell his only son his story. Was it because he never found the right words? Was the pain too great? Was it because Dad reminded him too much of Lasse? Or did Dad remind him too much of himself?

Dad really didn't know much about his father. He'd run away from home, and with his departure, Grandpa's narrative was lost forever. Lost, until my phone rang that first night in my grandparents' house. For whatever reason, I'd been chosen to hear the tale. And lying in bed, I didn't know if I should feel gratitude or disgust. The only thing I knew—and this I finally understood with certainty—was that I had to tell Dad. He deserved to know, whether knowing would hurt him or not. Isn't that why we were here? So that he could find peace with the one wrong decision he made years ago? Whether he knew it or not, he'd decided to look back. He made that decision when he returned home.

After the phone call, my current boy troubles seemed so woefully insignificant that I was ashamed at even remembering my own problems. What did I know about grief? And then I thought about Mom. I did know real heartbreak. I understood what it felt like to lose the person closest to me.

Though it didn't come naturally, I decided I needed to be excited about the gallery event. I had become too wrapped up in the logistics of my date—Gabe's sudden illness and the possibility of Chris being my unrealized soulmate had sidetracked me. Looking back on my behavior over the past week, I was utterly embarrassed. How had I so completely lost my way?

The gallery event was the very thing I needed: a celebration of my mother. I was tired of distractions. Grandma's story made me realize just that: the gallery event wasn't about me, wasn't about my dress or my date. The night was dedicated to my mom and her life. This is what I was grateful to remember and I felt indebted to my grandparents for reminding me. Dad, my amazing father who deserved more than the brunt of my anger, dressed to the nines for my gallery event. He pulled out his old tuxedo—still in immaculate condition due to little wear—and pressed it for an entire hour to remove every wrinkle. He'd gone to Weaver's and asked the florist—disoriented in Gabe's absence—to create a corsage for me. How the florist had found chrysanthemums in February, I'll never know. Greta, usually the focus of any room, came out of her bedroom in an understated black dress. Her hair was pulled into a plain, unassuming up-do, and she wore one of Mom's emerald-encrusted brooches in her hair. She was beautiful because she was Greta, but she was the plainest I'd ever seen her. My wonderful older sister was giving me my night. She really had grown up since we had moved to Pennsylvania. And in her black cocktail dress, wearing Mom's jewelry, she looked like our mother's daughter. She was so graceful. That night I was—and I suppose I always will be—in awe of her.

I fumbled with Mom's dress and felt a little awkward pulling the pink sequined cloth over my head. Greta, in her older-sister omnipotent way, helped zip me up and whispered, "Louisa, you look beautiful. You know Mom would be so proud of you." She looked me up and down in my vanity mirror. "Even if you are wearing those sneakers."

I grinned. Mom would be proud of me for staying true to myself. Dad came in and pinned the purple mums to my dress. He looked rather smitten with his two daughters.

"You're sure you're okay with Rosemary coming, Louisa?" he asked as he closed the clasp on the corsage.

It was the tenth time he'd asked me. There were obvious reasons he would think I, or Greta, would have reservations about Rosemary coming to an art exhibit focusing on our mom. But the truth was, Rosemary's absence would now be noticed. She'd become part of our family. And I wanted her there, too. In our few months of living on October Hill Road, Rosemary had become a close confidante and a great source of support for some of my biggest secrets. She was a friend, not a parent. I was grateful to Rosemary for bringing my dad the happiness he was missing.

"I'd love for her to come," I assured my dad with a smile, smoothing my dress in the mirror. I was ready. "Let's go get her."

Other than the spotlights highlighting the artwork on the walls, the gallery was dimly lit. It made my eyes fuzzy when I focused on any one piece of work and then turned back into the room. An acoustic guitarist played Fats Waller tunes softly in one of the corners, and patrons slowly swayed back and forth, unconscious of their own movements. There was a bar in the adjacent corner serving plastic cups of wine to anyone who asked. Greta and I looked like the only people underage in the gallery. At one point, Mr. Franz pulled me aside and introduced me to a crowd of people as his "new star pupil." I shook hands with the gallery owner and made small talk with an older gentleman from South Jersey. He told me he was an art collector and a "chaser of shadows." All of his collection, he explained, contained some oddity or playfulness with light and dark. He told me he believed Mr. Franz was a serious photographer.

"Well, for my sake, I hope he doesn't leave Wyeth," I joked with the man before excusing myself to see my own display.

My photo essay took up a four-foot-long space of well-lit wall. Though I'd looked at the pages a countless number of times—editing and arranging, cutting and matting—the photos looked different tacked onto the wall under the bright lights. I walked the length of my display, starting at Mom's earliest pictures and finishing at the clip I'd inserted of her obituary. I'd titled my work "The Unsung Dancer" and I liked the way my name looked in the small frame on the wall.

Louisa Eloise Magnusson.

"It's a beautiful collection of art, Louisa," Rosemary complimented, as she found a spot next to me staring at the photographs.

"Thanks."

"Your mom appears to have been quite the woman." She leaned in closer to the wall to examine the shots.

The first in the series included old black-and-white headshots from when Mom thought she wanted to be an actress—a career that was over practically by the time the headshots were developed. I'd also decided to include a playful print from a trip to the zoo, where Mom licked hungrily at a chocolate ice cream cone while an Asian elephant watched her longingly. Next, I'd mounted colorful portraits of Mom's wedding day at the courthouse, where she and Dad looked too beautiful, too happy to be in the small, sterile confines of an industrial office building.

"I like this one the best." Rosemary pointed to the one of Mom and me in our leotards.

"Me, too." I smiled.

"How's it going? You haven't come to visit in a while," Rosemary said. It was the first time we'd been alone all night.

I shrugged and took a sip of my ginger ale. "I know what I'm supposed to do now."

"Oh?" Rosemary looked to me inquisitively, crossing her arms.

"I think she wants me to appreciate the life I have. Or celebrate the life I've been given. Or something like that."

"Sounds about right," Rosemary agreed. "I really loved your grandparents, as I think I've told you. Your grandpa always used to bring me a pint of strawberries from the market every weekend in the spring. He didn't say anything, of course, but he and Eloise would stop by and deliver the berries, even if I wasn't around. They were wonderful neighbors and wonderful friends. I hope you'll share their story with me someday."

"I will."

"So is it over?" she asked, turning back to my art.

"I don't know." My voice sounded very sad, and I knew Rosemary could hear it, too. "I hope not, but it will have to be, eventually, I suppose."

She turned to me and gave me a hug. She smelled like primrose and powder.

"You're an incredible girl, Louisa. Stop by sometime soon, okay? Even if it's just for a cup of coffee."

I returned the hug and nodded. And then Rosemary turned around to go and find Dad. I stood at one of the bar tables positioned around the room, ripping my napkin into tiny little pieces. Dad came over to congratulate me and to express his unending pride in the person I had become. Standard Dad stuff. Then, Greta floated over with a middle-aged woman who was interested in talking to me about my work and my interests. At the end of our conversation, the woman handed me her card.

> Jannelle Davenport, MFA
> Pennsylvania Academy of Fine Arts
> 118–128 N. Broad St.
> Philadelphia, PA 19102
> 215-972-7600 ext. 090

"It's never too soon to start looking at schools," the woman said with a wink. She was outfitted in a '60s mod dress, black cloche hat, and orange heels. She leaned in toward Greta. "Good luck with everything." Then she was gone.

"Wasn't *she* a little Mary Tyler Moore? So cute!" Greta giggled.

I smiled, looking down at her card. It was nice to know that someone other than my dad, my sister, and my teacher saw some talent in my work. This essay project—and this exhibit—opened up my eyes to new possibilities. I decided to start taking my Film Photography II class more seriously. Mr. Franz would demand it of me, and besides, I wanted to grow as an artist.

"Want something from the bar?" Greta asked. "The crab cakes are pretty good."

"No, thanks, I'm okay. You go; I'll wait here."

She disappeared into the crowd, and I was alone again.

Then suddenly, I heard a voice behind me. "I've been growing those mums in my greenhouse for the past four years. They've never looked better."

I spun around, caught off guard, and found myself face to face with Gabe. He grabbed my hand and adjusted my corsage. He was dressed in black and white from head to toe, a classic tuxedo with black bowtie. He looked amazing.

"Gabe!" I gasped, and he laughed at my surprise. "How are you here?" I wanted to throw my arms around him and nuzzle his neck, but I was too afraid.

"We need to talk." He glanced around the room for a quiet corner before spying my collection. "But first, why don't you introduce me to your mom?" Gabe gestured to the wall where my project hung in the lights. He grasped my hand, intertwining his fingers with mine, and led me over to the spot.

"She's beautiful," Gabe observed, making his way down the line of pictures. "And she looks . . . really kind."

"She was." I squeezed his hand, letting him continue studying the images.

He leaned over and kissed me on the cheek. I smiled to myself. I didn't care who was watching us: Dad or Greta or Mr. Franz. This was my moment. And as Gabe pulled me eagerly toward the exit, I was happy to let the rest of the room disappear.

Outside, in front of the gallery, Gabe hopped up, taking a seat on a brick wall. "You know, Jenn called me and told me you were cheating on me with Chris Harris," he admitted, staring at his hands folded in his lap.

I didn't say anything. I couldn't say anything.

"I'm sorry I lied about the walking pneumonia," he continued, "but I needed to buy some time to figure things out."

"And have you?" I croaked, trying to mask the lump in my throat.

"Well, I talked to Chris." He finally looked up and stared deeply into me.

"And?" I managed to whisper.

"And he said that whatever you guys had was lost. 'Disappeared in history' was his phrase." Gabe ran his hand through his hair and then casually untied his bowtie, letting it hang loosely around his neck. "Lou, you know I think you're kind of spectacular." He grabbed my hand, and his words rushed out with an uncontrollable force. "I finally told Jenn that she and I were never, ever going to happen. I want to be with *you*. I want to be with you on Valentine's Day, I want to take you to the prom, I want to spend our summer together. I don't want there to be any more doubt about whether we are or we aren't together. But I can't tell whether you think we are . . . or we're not."

"Gabe," I tried to explain, "everything about you is different. And I like your different. It takes me a while to figure things out, but I always find my path. I'm kind of like my mom that way." When I uttered those last words, one vivid, once-lost memory came flooding back to me. My indecisive mom used to agonize over which color was her favorite. But then, after tirelessly going back and forth between muted earth tones and bright primaries, she'd always find her answer. "Yellow," Mom would proudly declare. "It's always been yellow. And I've always known it was yellow."

"Yellow. Memory 523," I grinned. It was a lost memory now returned. The first memory to add to my list in two years.

"What?" Gabe squeezed my hand.

I took his hand and pulled him close.

"We definitely, definitely are together," I smiled.

We kissed like two people first in love. This was the beginning of everything. On the way home, in the safety of Greta and Rosemary in the car, I made the announcement.

"Dad, I have a boyfriend." I braced myself for the worst.

"That's great, kiddo. I have a girlfriend." Dad grinned.

Rosemary turned in the passenger's seat to face my father. "You do?" She looked shocked.

Dad took his hand off the steering wheel to affectionately squeeze Rosemary's knee. She smiled and sat back in her seat, before Dad added quickly, "Well, you are, aren't you?"

"Oh, yes, I am," she agreed assertively, looking pleased.

Sitting side by side in the Subaru, the two of them looked completely at home with one another. Greta only rolled her eyes at us all.

XXXIII.

Gerhard traveled for forty-eight straight hours through wood and bog, keeping off the main roads and steering clear of people until he finally collapsed near a farm south of Växjö. He had nothing but the clothes on his back.

He'd fallen from his bicycle when its tire blew two towns back, so he'd abandoned it and continued his journey on foot. His beloved pocket watch's face had cracked in his tumble, and it lay lifeless in his pocket. He spent the night in a barn next to a warm heifer in a pile of hay. When he awoke, he wasn't alone. A small boy stood watching him.

Guardedly, Gerhard rubbed his eyes and stretched. His body was stiff and ached.

"Are you him?" the small boy asked, taking a seat on the barn floor. He picked up a piece of straw and placed it in his mouth, chewing thoughtfully. The cow shifted her weight.

"Who?" Gerhard sat up slowly, staring at the boy with both interest and confusion.

The youngster reached behind him, grabbed the daily news, and tossed it to Gerhard's feet. Gerhard lifted the paper up to a stream of light breaking through a crack in the wooden wall behind him. The front page contained a large picture of the train wreckage at Mile Marker Two between Trelleborg and Kornsjø. The headline read, "Local Vigilante Brothers Sabotage Nazi Route."

Gerhard read the article, which vaguely described the events leading up to the accident. It reported that Gerhard Magnusson, conductor of Trelleborg's Number 7 train, died either in the crash or in the fire that ensued afterwards. His brother, Lars "Lyckliga Lasse"

Magnusson, hadn't reported home that evening; he had disappeared from Trelleborg and was assumed an accomplice in the crime. Reading further, Gerhard wasn't surprised to see that the Nazi party had announced a full-scale investigation and search for the missing brother. Swedish Prime Minister Hansson, in agreement with Lukas Österberg, was quoted as saying that Sweden did not condone, support, or encourage acts of rebellion of any kind. Österberg continued to say that Swedes were a peaceful and neutral people. The only portion of the article Gerhard found shocking was that the order for the search party came directly from the Führer himself.

Herr Hitler's official statement was, "This act of brutal injustice, including the murder of 479 innocent German soldiers, will not go unpunished."

Gerhard smiled to himself, realizing how big a disruption the Trelleborg sabotage must have triggered in Germany for Hitler himself to make such a statement. Lasse had been right: the two brothers *could* influence the war.

"So, are you him? Are you Lars "Lyckliga Lasse" Magnusson?" The boy pointed at the front page.

Gerhard smiled tenderly at his brother's childhood name, Lucky Lasse. But Gerhard didn't deserve the glory. He also realized, however, that this moment, sitting in this barn, a wanted fugitive, was not the time to expose himself. He needed to be a ghost.

"*Nej*, it's not me," Gerhard winced as he stood. His muscles felt tightly wrapped over his bones. "Thank you for the shelter."

"My father is gone for the day. He told me to give this to you, if you were him," the boy held up a small aluminum pail. "But I'll give it to you anyway."

Inside the pail, Gerhard discovered two loaves of rye bread, a small wheel of cheese, and a liter of fresh milk. He thanked the boy for the charity before he consumed one of the loaves with a few bites of the cheese, and continued his journey without destination.

The following week, after making his way through most of Småland and taking up lodging in the occasional vacant summer house or farm stable, Gerhard felt brave enough to travel through Jönköping, a middle-class town situated at the base of Lake Vättern. He took a seat on a stone bench in the center of town, facing the water. It was late in the day, and the sun was setting slowly on the west shore. Seagulls skipped across the waves, scavenging for small fish. A fat man with thick fingers slumped down next to him on the bench. He was panting heavily. Immediately, Gerhard inhaled the pleasant smell of boiled sausage. He turned and saw that his companion was a sausage cart salesman. Gerhard had no money to purchase a sausage, but his growing hunger didn't care.

"*Hejsan*," the man greeted, continuing to gaze out at the water.

"Hey to you," Gerhard smiled, hoping to work an angle.

"Crap for a day, huh?" The man laughed heartily and winked at Gerhard.

"Oh, I'm just passing through. It's a nice town," Gerhard attempted to flatter the man.

"It's a crap town," the man gurgled, taking out a small flask from his jacket pocket and taking a swig before offering Gerhard some.

"No, that's okay," Gerhard held up his hand in refusal. "But if you have any sausages left that you'd like to throw away . . . "

"Sure, friend!" The man smiled, gesturing for Gerhard to help himself.

Gerhard eagerly stood at the cart and fished out a long sausage from the steaming water, dropping it into a roll. He didn't ask for mustard; he was happy just to have something to eat. After finishing, Gerhard produced his small tobacco tin and began rolling his final two cigarettes. He was sad to see the last of his tobacco go, but was pleased to share it with the generous man. The two sat smoking for a while, watching the sun linger in the sky.

At last, the man spoke. "You hear the damned Nazis caught the Magnusson boy?"

"Oh?" Gerhard's ears perked up. He feigned as little interest as possible, not wanting to attract attention to himself.

"The papers released a German report that they had found him dead in Skåne. Apparent suicide, if you believe that." The man took another sip from his flask. "It's a shame. Those boys were the closest thing this country had to heroes."

Gerhard sat a moment, digesting the fabricated Nazi ruse.

"Do you have a paper and pencil, friend?" Gerhard leaned toward the fat man, putting out his cigarette on the bench.

One week later, every daily and evening newspaper in all of Sweden, Norway, Denmark, and Finland published the following letter under the headline "The Number 7 Phantom Sends Message Beyond Grave."

Dear Editors and Staff,

I have recently been informed of a printed report, obtained from German sources (no doubt members of the Third Reich) regarding my apparent suicide. I regret to inform you and all members of the Nazi party that your article is grossly, factually, and completely inaccurate. Indeed, I am not dead. I am very much alive and well, living in the heart of Sweden, my homeland. Let it be known to all of Sweden, Germany, and the rest of Europe that the recent events at Trelleborg Mile Marker Two have also been falsely reported. It is true that my brother and I successfully sabotaged German transport between Trelleborg and Kornsjø and caused the death of 479 Nazi soldiers. It must be corrected, however, that it was not I but my fearless brother, Lars "Lyckliga Lasse" Magnusson, who sacrificed his life. It doesn't take much

> for one to understand why the Third Reich would hope I am dead. I am now not only a threat but also a reminder of German weakness. It would be wrong to proclaim the train crash as a statement for all of Sweden, but I am proud to declare our actions as a statement from two Swedish brothers. Brothers who, having once chosen to turn a blind eye to both German and Swedish monstrosities, turned instead to look horror in the face. We could no longer deny the existence of unremitting German crimes against all of mankind. I cannot—nor would Lasse have wanted me to—apologize on behalf of our country. We are tired of making excuses for Sweden. Brothers and sisters, aren't you tired of looking away? Lasse would want you to open your eyes.
>
> Sincerely, Gerhard Magnusson

After the letter's publication, eyewitnesses—some credible, others not—reported sightings of "The Number 7 Phantom" all over Sweden. His newfound notoriety caught Gerhard off guard. He insisted on sleeping in barns instead of domestic lodgings. No one ever asked Gerhard if he was who they believed him to be. After the publication of his letter, which never made its way over the German border, the Nazi party spent a significant amount of time and resources trying to find the fugitive brother. Until 1945, Gerhard was ceaselessly on the move.

At times, he missed his family desperately. He missed Anna and her bright eyes, and he missed his loving parents who, he was concerned, worried about their son constantly. Often, he thought about writing a letter to explain Lasse's final wish and to apologize that he hadn't been wise enough to foresee his brother's plan. But he never sent a note for fear he'd put his life and his family's lives in danger. He hoped the letter in the newspapers was enough proof for them that he was alive.

Two weeks after his own letter, Gerhard read an editorial in the newspapers of Robert's account of that fateful day's events. He read how Lasse had gone to Robert three kilometers before Mile Marker Two and demanded the fireman jump from the moving train. Robert suffered a broken arm but was also given recognition for his bravery. Gerhard regretted that he would never see the boy again.

At the war's conclusion, Gerhard considered returning back to Trelleborg. But after six years of being a nomad, his life had changed. It was impossible to return to Trelleborg without Lasse. He would never be at peace there.

So on May 2, 1946, the "Number 7 Phantom" boarded a ship for Boston, Massachusetts, with a red White Star Line ticket stolen from a dead man. Gerhard had found it in his jacket pocket the day of the train crash. Somehow, Lasse must have convinced Pontus there was a way for him to have his second chance by giving it away. A note written in Pontus's scribbled hand accompanied the ticket. It read, "A chance to begin again."

Somewhere over the Atlantic, Gerhard shed the skin of his old life. He told his story only once, but he carried it around with him as if he were *Atlas Telamon* holding the entire world on his shoulders. Gerhard wanted so badly for his son to know him—he wanted Christian to understand, but he never got the chance to explain it all to him. It was too hard for him to talk about it. And he was too scared that Christian would see him as a coward. He loved his son more than anything. He wanted so badly to protect him from the truth.

When Gerhard died, I took up his burden. I dragged the story around the house with me like old luggage. Eventually, I locked it away in the attic where I wouldn't have to see it, where I wouldn't have to hear it. There it stayed until you found it. It was easier for me to keep the secret to myself, but that's not what we're supposed to do. You're stronger than I was, Louisa. You remind me so much of him, his spirit. And now you must be his voice. It's time now.

XXXIV.

The week after my last phone call was difficult for me when my grandmother finally called me by my name. Since I'd arrived at October Hill Road, I'd come to rely on routine: wake up, go to school, come back to the house and do homework, wait for Grandma. Now, the longing I felt for people whom I had never known—lives that never truly coexisted with my own—was paralyzing. Some days I'd lie in bed and do nothing. I stared at the ceiling for hours and thought of Gerhard and Lasse. Two brothers surrounded by confusion. Two brothers who had been just a little older than I was.

That week was insipid. I tasted nothing. Felt nothing. Wanted nothing. It hurt to know my life—on the outside—was the same. Nothing had changed but me. I was different, but I wasn't able share it with anyone. Not yet. For a month, I climbed the attic steps and waited every night by the phone, waiting for a call I knew would never come. Grandma had finished her narrative—what more was there to tell? Sure, I wanted to know about what happened after—about Dad and his childhood—but that wasn't the story she needed me to know. She left me panicked about my own role in the tale. What did she expect me to do? I was torn. Part of me wanted so much to sit Dad down and tell him everything I knew, but I wasn't ready to become the storyteller. I didn't know if he was ready to hear it. What if he ran?

Gabe knew I was distracted by something, and the only thing I could tell him was that I was struggling with my past. Somehow that seemed to be both completely sufficient and entirely inadequate at the same time. And then one day he surprised me with bus tickets into Philadelphia.

"There's a history museum there. I thought you might like it. You might find some answers." He suggested gently. He was trying so hard while also giving me my space.

I wanted to collapse. How could it be this whole month, this suffocating month of mourning, and I hadn't thought about it? The American Swedish Historical Museum. The old man with the stories and the *fika*. I needed to revisit that large, dark building and go talk to the man. *Somehow he could help me.*

The bus was running late and we arrived at the museum near closing. The parking lot was as deserted as it had been the first time, but I knew better. In my memory, I could see the old man sitting up in his stuffy library with his shoes to the side and his socked feet rubbing themselves against the carpeted floor. I saw him leafing through old photo albums and carefully fingering the cracked spines of dusty books.

"I'll wait here." Gabe zipped up his ski jacket and shoved his hands in his pockets.

"But I—"

"You need to find it on your own. Whatever *it* is. I'll be here when you get out." Gabe nodded toward the door. "You better hurry—it closes in ten minutes."

I stood conflicted but turned to go. Gabe was right. I needed to hurry. I clenched my own fists together to keep warm while sprinting up the cement steps to the museum entrance.

I rang the bell three times to make sure the front desk heard me. The door slowly opened.

"We're closing." The same unfriendly woman wrapped her cardigan tightly around her shoulders as she squinted down at me.

"I know," I bounced my knees nervously. "But there's someone I need to look for."

I tried to peer behind her beyond the lobby and up the staircase. She watched my eyes, and I saw a hint of recognition as her face softened. She stepped aside to let me pass through the doorway.

I waited at the front reception, never once taking my eyes off the staircase, waiting to see the old man materialize. The woman bolted the door against the winter wind and slowly shuffled her way behind the desk. I hurriedly dug through my shoulder bag to produce the entrance fee, but the woman held up her hand to stop me.

"He's not here."

"The old man?"

My question seeped with disappointment. I met her gaze and immediately regretted it. Standing in the cold lobby, I found myself staring at a woman whose red-rimmed eyes expressed unquestionable bereavement.

"He passed away last week." She inhaled deeply and shut her eyes as she composed herself. Her palms pressed firmly down on the desk as she managed a tender smile, "He suspected you might come back."

I couldn't find the words to say anything. A growing ball lodged itself inside my throat.

The woman bent beneath the desk and reappeared, producing a large manila envelope. "He gave us explicit instructions to leave this for you. In case you came back." She held out the paper envelope for me to take. For a moment I just stared at it, unsure what to do. Finally, she pushed it further toward me.

"I'm going to go turn off the lights, and then you'll have to go."

I stood alone in the lobby wondering what I might find inside the parcel. It wasn't completely sealed, and one of the metal brackets had broken off. I bent the remaining clasp up and released the flap. Inside was a newspaper clipping and a note written from a shaking hand; the script barely legible.

> Flicka: After our conversation, I could not help but recall an old myth from my youth. At first I did not believe the chances of your relation to my childhood hero, but as I combed over the books I kept as a boy, I found the proof for which I had searched. Now, you have it. I hope you

> know what your grandfather did for his country during sadder days long ago. Find a Swedish friend and have him read this article to you during fika. I think this may answer some of your questions. Vi syns, Henrik Malmström

The newspaper clipping was yellowed, with fragile, torn edges, and had multiple creases where it had once been tenderly folded. Big block letters read,

> "FANTOMEN PÅ SJUAN SLÅR TYSKARNA!"
> The Number 7 Phantom Takes Germans!

XXXV.

I decided I needed to write my grandfather's story out while everything was still fresh in my memory. It took me two weeks and forty pages to get it right. Gabe constantly asked me about my new, important project. It was difficult for me to keep him out, but I promised that he'd be there for the final reveal. I made sure Dad didn't suspect anything. I needed to tell the story on my own terms; I needed to tell it how it was told to me. But I kept postponing the retelling. It never seemed like the right time. And then, something happened that made it impossible for me to put it off any longer. Greta and I had pulled into our driveway in The Thing one Friday in early April. We were alone; Dad was still at work. Greta turned the ignition off, but she didn't move to open the door. She stared straight toward the house before holding up her arm.

"This," she pulled up her sleeve and offered her wrist to me so I was forced to look. "This was a mistake. It was stupid. I did it once and I'll never do it again. I know that. And I won't just disappear again. I've said my goodbyes to Mom now. But damn it, Louisa, we have to stop pretending. All of us. I can't be invisible anymore. We need to see each other again; we have to open our eyes and stop turning away from each other. We're all we've got, Lou."

I sat rigidly still until she reached out and tenderly placed her hand on my leg.

"I miss her, Lou. So unbelievably much. But I changed when she died. So did you, and so did Dad. We're all going to have to move on, I get that now, but we have to do it *together*."

"No matter what you believe, Greta," I swallowed, staring at her across the armrest, "you've never been invisible to me. I love you, but I can't keep your secret any longer."

"I know. I'm going to talk to Dad. He and I have a lot of catching up to do, I guess." She smiled softly, and then she reached for the door. "I love you, too, Louisa."

Dad wasn't supposed to get back for another hour. I fetched the mail out of the mailbox, but the box's lid came unhinged. An old, rusted screw fell to the ground into the pansy bed Gabe had recently planted for us. Purple and yellow petals fluttered in the light spring breeze. Summer was coming. Soon, we'd be barefoot. I reached down to grab the loose screw from the moist dirt. I needed a screwdriver, and I knew just where to find one. How hard could it be to fix a mailbox?

The cellar doors were heavy. The smell of damp earth overtook me as I slowly stepped down into the humid cavity. Grandpa's workbench was still covered with cobwebs and sawdust. The cellar was a giant catacomb for various parts, miscellaneous pieces, and scrap metal. His model trains were strewn in pieces, some unfinished, some unpainted. I looked under the table for his toolbox but found none. Old coffee cans housed loose nuts, bolts, screws, and nails. A hammer and a socket wrench sat in an old wire crate, but no screwdriver. I reached for a coffee can high up on a crowded shelf. More loose parts. *Where was the screwdriver?* And then I spotted a wooden toolbox under some used paint cans. I lugged the box to the top of the workbench, got it under the light, and blew off a thick layer of dusty grime. The top lifted easily.

In the top tray of the box lay a handful of rusty nails. I picked up the tray and placed it aside. I finally found the screwdriver underneath an oily rag, but my hand knocked against something else when I moved to pick up the screwdriver. I slowly pulled the object out of the ancient toolbox: an old tin container for Cherrydale Farms Peanut Crunch.

I shook the tin and the contents that rattled inside. The lid was rusted onto the base, but I tried working it, and it popped off without much trouble. Inside the container, I found Dad's boyhood treasures—the ones he'd described to me in the woods on Thanksgiving morning.

I dumped the contents onto the workbench: a pinecone, a chestnut, stones of various shapes, sizes, and colors, an old harmonica, a few wooden spools of thread, a snakeskin, a small, whittled, wooden horse, and one long mallard feather. But there was something else inside, wrapped in an old handkerchief.

I slowly unfolded the cloth. There, gleaming dully under the faint cellar light was Grandfather's pocket watch. I recognized it at once. Its face was cracked, just as Grandma had said it would be. I lifted the timepiece out of its temporary casket and turned it over in my hands in disbelief. I wound the stem, hoping to hear it run, but it remained silent. Maybe it was too old. Maybe it'd been too long. I polished the gold case on the end of my shirt and held it up to the light. I read the faint inscription:

Till min son med hjältens själ.

Grandpa had added to Leif's inscription. What message had he left behind? What did he want us to know?

In my bedroom, I held the timepiece closed in my palm as I leafed through the Swedish-English dictionary I'd bought at the used bookstore with Chris. The first part of the inscription I knew. *Till min son*, to my son. But what was *med hjältens själ*? I looked up each word and scratched them down in pencil on a loose scrap of paper. And then I saw it—the translation complete. Of course.

To my son with the hero's soul.

I held the watch near my ear. *Silence.*

I had to try it again. Just once more. I hesitantly popped the winding stem, and twisted it between my thumb and forefinger. It spun to the right, and I wound it until it clicked into place. Incredibly, the watch started to tick. The sound was so beautiful, so simple. It was both soft and deafening. It reminded me of Grandma's phone. Whispers of sounds of lives long gone. *Tick, tick, tick, tick.* This was my grandfather's voice, his spirit echoing from the folds of time, that space between earth and the grave. He was telling me he needed his son to know the truth. He was telling me to finish the story.

I sat alone on our front steps with the watch, staring blankly into the yard until Dad pulled into the driveway. He whistled as he unloaded his briefcase from the car.

He took a seat next to me on the stoop, moving the watch to make room and handing it to me without a second glance. He had no idea what he'd just held.

"Those buckets—" Dad pointed across the street to the galvanized containers clinging to the sugar maples. "We need to tap them again. My dad taught me how to do it once, but I thought maybe you and I could get them going again. I think he would like that."

"Dad, I—" My face felt flushed.

"Hey, you okay?" He finally looked at me. Really looked at me. He wrapped his arm around me and pulled me close to him.

"I need to tell you something," my voice trembled.

I was stalling. This was harder than I thought. I felt guilty for keeping Grandma's calls from him. It had already been too long. It wasn't my gift to keep. Since we'd arrived, Dad had tried catching up with the life he'd once had when he lived with his parents on October Hill Road. With my help, he was about to meet the Gerhard Magnusson he never knew, to know *his* story, to know his heart. I was going to introduce him to the Gerhard who loved and laughed and lived; the Gerhard who died with his brother. I was finally able to give Dad what he never had: the truth about his father, the hero *and* the coward. This wasn't only Gerhard's story. This was Dad's story. This was my story.

I took my seat at the head of the table and gently placed the old man's newspaper clipping and Grandpa's stopwatch on the surface next to Grandma's antique telephone. Its rotary and letters were no longer foreign to me. I knew its weight and the way it felt against my ear. I knew its shape on the attic desk, the shadows it sent against the wall, and the sound it made when it rang. This phone was the direct line to my grandmother and grandfather. In it, I'd heard of all the events that led me here.

I looked around the table at the faces of my family: Dad, Greta, Rosemary, and Gabe. Somewhere near—I could feel them close—Mom and Grandma watched over us. They stood as anxiously as the rest, each wanting to hear this, too. It felt good to have them there. The narrative was complete, and yet it was just starting.

I took a deep breath and let the story begin: "The problem with hiding secrets is they run a lot faster than we do. They're bound to catch up with us sometime or another."

ABOUT THE AUTHOR

Jessica Lidh pulls inspiration from her Swedish heritage and experiences as a high-school teacher in suburban Maryland. In encouraging young minds to suck the marrow out of life, Jessica often uncovers the fascinating and hilariously horrifying insights of the twenty-first century teenager. When Jessica isn't fervently teaching or writing, she loves to watch old musicals, bake Swedish cinnamon buns, and go on imaginary bear hunts with her daughter, Elsa.

P9-CQP-965
T 42982

Overnight

Overnight

Overnight

ADELE GRIFFIN

G. P. PUTNAM'S SONS

NEW YORK

a division of Penguin Putnam Books for Young Readers, 345 Hudson Street, New York, NY 10014. G. P. Putnam's Sons, Reg. U.S. Pat. & Tm. Off.
Published simultaneously in Canada. Printed in the United States of America.
Book designed by Gunta Alexander. Text set in Photina.
Library of Congress Cataloging-in-Publication Data
Griffin, Adele. Overnight / Adele Griffin. p. cm.
Summary: Gray hopes that going to a slumber party with the "Lucky Seven" at her private school will take her mind off her mother's cancer, but when she is taken from the party by a deranged woman, both she and the other girls discover things about themselves and each other.
[1. Cliques (Sociology)—Fiction. 2. Interpersonal relations—Fiction. 3. Kidnapping—Fiction. 4. Sleepovers—Fiction.] I. Title. PZ7.G881325 Ov 2003
[Fic]—dc21 2002069778 ISBN 0-399-23782-8
1 3 5 7 9 10 8 6 4 2
First Impression

For Charlotte

Overnight

Gray

Gray forgot her sleeping bag for Caitlin Donnelley's birthday party. She did not see that it was missing until her mother pulled up to the front doors of Fielding Academy. When she reached for her overnight things piled in the backseat, it was not there.

"My sleeping bag!" she exclaimed. "I left it at home!"

"Oh, for goodness' sakes, Gray." Her mother sighed. "How could you be so forgetful?"

"Please, Mom, go back!"

"If I go back, you'll both be late for school."

"Mom, it's important!"

In the backseat, Gray's younger brother, Robby, began to whimper. He was seven, four years younger than Gray, and he copied whatever she did.

Mrs. Rosenfeld rested her forehead on the steering wheel, practicing her yoga breathing to keep calm. When she lifted her head, she said, "Gray, get out of the car this instant so that I can drop off Robby at school. Then I will go home and collect your sleeping bag and I will bring it to Fielding later this morning."

"You know which one! The pink one with the fairies on it!" Gray insisted as her mother drove away. Her breath, damp and fast, made icy puffs in the February cold. "Not any of the other ones! The pink one!" Her voice was lost to the car, but she continued shouting through her fingertips as it disappeared. The last thing she saw was Robby mouthing teary good-byes from the rearview window.

Later that morning, one of the school secretaries delivered Gray's sleeping bag to the sixth-grade classroom. It was not her fairy-folk bag. It was the navy blue bag that her father took on fishing trips.

When Caitlin Donnelley and Kristy Sonenshine saw it, they exchanged google eyes and stuck out their tongues at each other. Gray saw them do this and it made her feel dizzy, as if she might throw up. Worse, she would have to sleep without her fairy folk. Gray liked to believe that at night, while she fit snug inside the bag, the fairies came alive.

Alive like real people but better joining together hand in hand in an enchanted circle protecting me from all bad things.

Gray knew it was a babyish thought. She even knew it was a babyish bag. Plain pastels or wildflower prints were the only acceptable sleeping bag styles this year. Part of her, though, especially her nighttime, lights-off part, needed the fairies.

The navy bag looked twice the size of the other girls' bags. It smelled like the woods and was dark as a midnight ocean.

Who would protect her now?

Mrs. Donnelley was waiting to catch the girls as they spilled out of Fielding Academy's front doors at the school day's end.

"Hello there, Miss Gray! How's your mom? I meant to call her yesterday."

"Oh. She's fine."

Mrs. Donnelley nodded hard, as if her head were being jerked by puppet strings. Yes yes yes—casting a spell that would make the cancer leave. In that way, Gray's mother and Mrs. Donnelley were alike. They both put Safety first. Safety first and no mistakes, which was why Gray's mother and Caitlin's mother were friends. Gray had slept over at Caitlin Donnelley's house lots of times, and she had watched Mrs. Donnelley's struggle to make each detail of her home perfect, indoors and out. Each dead leaf picked quickly off the yard and every slice of toast crisped tan.

The way my mom used to be but not anymore.

As girls trundled outside, lugging their sleeping bags, Mrs. Donnelley gave instructions. "I can take four, so that means three of you girls must go with Topher in his car. I don't have enough seat belts to buckle up everybody!"

She pointed across the parking lot to where Topher was leaning against the side of his battered Volkswagen. Topher was Caitlin's half brother. He was in college and home for mid-winter break. He had a goatee. When he laughed, he crossed his arms and tipped back his head like a genie. Gray had known Topher since she was five years old, and she still did not like to talk much when he was around.

Quickly, Gray jumped into the minivan so that she could sit right behind Mrs. Donnelley. The three girls who clambered in after her were Leticia Watkins, Serena Hodgson, and Zoë Atacropolis. Zoë sat up front so that she could talk Mrs. Donnelley's ear off. Topher would be taking Caitlin and Kristy and Martha Van Riet. Already they were crossing the parking lot, Kristy springing next to Caitlin like a puppy and Martha snaking up behind them.

Seven girls in all. Of the fifty-one sixth-graders enrolled at Fielding Academy for Girls, they were the "Lucky Seven." That's what they called themselves. Other girls called them the "cool group." Or the "in crowd." Or the "snobby girls." Or "Martha's group." Or "*those* girls."

Gray looked out the window to where some of the uninvited girls were standing, plumped in wool coats, waiting for buses and carpools. The uninvited girls, eyes lowered, watched as Mrs. Donnelley's minivan and Topher's Volkswagen circled the parking lot, and their faces pretended indifference. After all, it was Friday! The weekend! Who cared about Caitlin Donnelley? Oh, they weren't missing anything much!

Gray knew what they were thinking behind their faces. This

past fall, when she had been nearly expelled from the Lucky Seven and Martha had not invited her to her roller-skating party, Gray had thought those same kinds of thoughts.

Annie Dearborne, slumped on the bus bench, raised her hand to wave good-bye. Annie was Gray's writing comprehension partner. When Gray was having problems with the Lucky Seven, Annie Dearborne almost had become Gray's new best friend. Almost.

Before anyone else saw, Gray flicked her fingers good-bye at Annie. Then she turned away. She pushed her seat forward so that she could smell the perfume at the back of Mrs. Donnelley's neck. She used the tips of her shoes to pedal her wrong sleeping bag deeper under the driver's-side seat and she clicked on her seat belt very loud so that Mrs. Donnelley would hear and appreciate Gray's carefulness.

"It's all a mistake. How could this be?" Gray's mother had asked this question in the hospital last spring, Robby tucked on one side of her and Gray curled up on the other, though the bed was too narrow and one of Gray's legs was getting cold, pressed-jammed hard into the bed's metal side rails.

Gray had thought her mother meant how could this be that she was lying in this bed, in this hospital. A mistake, because she wasn't sick after all!

Later, Gray understood what her mother really meant. That no matter how Safe a person tried to be, cancer was a mistake forced on a few unlucky people.

"We're having pizza!" exclaimed Mrs. Donnelley.

"And cake and ice cream?" asked Leticia.

"And are there goody bags?" asked Serena.

"And do we get to watch movies?" asked Zoë.

"Of course!" Mrs. Donnelley's voice trilled, filling the car with promises.

"Yes!"

"Yes!"

"Yes!"

Gray adored Caitlin's room. The furniture was quaint, like *Little House on the Prairie* if Ma and Pa Ingalls had been rich. Mrs. Donnelley had decorated it herself and kept the room pin-straight, the curtains and canopy bed freshly fluffed and vacuum marks on the carpet. There was a Victorian dollhouse in one corner and a pigeonhole desk in another corner. Neither of these pieces was used, since both were antiques. Besides, Caitlin had hated her dolls since she was nine—had hated everything about her room, in fact, since she was ten—and she did all her homework on the computer at her built-in study unit.

What Gray loved most about Caitlin's room were Caitlin's fairy paintings. There were four paintings altogether, one for every wall and season. These were not silly cartoon pictures, either, but framed portraits of ravishing enchantresses with dewy eyes, veined wings, and the tingling of the outdoors in their cheeks.

The winter fairy, dressed in cobwebby white, lounged like a fashion model along the branch of an icicle-spiked tree.

Two spring fairies chased each other in a daisy field under an azure sky.

The summer fairy kneeled on a lily pad, absorbed in her watery reflection.

The autumn fairies were gathered around the stump of a tree, some leaning against cushions, their faces serious, as if they were at a Seder.

Autumn was Gray's least favorite picture and the one she stared at most. But the autumn fairies did not fit with the other paintings. For one thing, the painting was overcrowded, and not just with fairies, but spindly-legged frogs and hunchbacked gnomes and pop-eyed hobgoblins and even one leering, rickety cricket.

For years, ever since Gray had first started staying overnight at Caitlin's house, she had put herself to sleep wondering about those ugly autumn wood creatures. Why had the fairies invited them to their Seder? Why? Why? She would stare and stare until her eyes lidded over.

"Come on, Gray! Drop your bags! We're going down to play Enchanted Castle." Caitlin nudged Gray from her trance. "Stop looking at that picture. Did I tell you I get to redo my room any way I want for a birthday present? Dad and Mom said okay, even for humongous posters and a futon, if I want."

"That's cool," said Martha. " 'Cause your room sucks."

"Duh! I know!" Caitlin laughed shrilly. "Whatever, though! It's changing in, like, a week!"

The other girls tossed down their bags and changed quickly from their uniforms into jeans and sweaters. Giggling and pushing, they herded out the door. Then down the hall, down the stairs, and down the stairs again to the family room in the basement.

Gray listened to them go. Alone in Caitlin's room, she changed clothes and sighed. The other girls' sleeping bags were so pretty, so *right.* Pale rainbow colors or tiny sprigs of flowers. Gray dropped her stupid, ugly sleeping bag and kicked it hard as a soccer ball under Caitlin's bed, hiding it from sight. She despised the idea of sliding into it tonight, trapped inside a giant's stinky sock while everyone else was tucked into butterfly cocoons.

Hot, easy tears welled up in her eyes. It wasn't fair. It wasn't fair that this new version of her mother made so many mistakes. Mistakes on account of her sickness, mistakes that might seem silly or thoughtless but also were careless enough to hurt.

The others already had set up the Enchanted Castle board by the time Gray joined them in the family room. Gray frowned as she slid into her chair. Enchanted Castle was dull. The object of the game was either to capture the Evil Queen or to find her three treasures—her crystal ball, her golden nightingale, and her jeweled crown, all of which were hidden somewhere in her kingdom. But if the Evil Queen managed to lock up three princesses in the dungeon, then she won.

The Evil Queen had the best time of anyone. This afternoon, the Queen was Caitlin, obviously. Gray was surprised that Caitlin wanted to play Enchanted Castle at all, especially with Martha rolling her eyes and saying, "Ugh, Caitlin, it's so spanky, so loserish, this game."

Caitlin insisted, though. Maybe just to be stubborn, or maybe since it was her birthday. Or maybe because she really liked Enchanted Castle and she knew that today was one of the few times she could get away with making everyone participate.

On her third turn, Gray began to feel sleepy, the same stupor that sometimes overcame her during afternoon classes. She could hardly keep her eyes open.

"I don't really want to play Enchanted Castle anymore," she said. "If that's all right with you, Caitlin?" She figured it would be. If she quit, Caitlin had a better chance of winning.

Caitlin shrugged. "Okay."

But Martha sang, "Rainy Gray, go away, come again some other day—*not!*"

Gray took her princess off the board and stood. She ignored Martha. To say something back meant trouble. Martha always shot the dart that started a fight. And Martha never let go. Last year, Martha had been so nasty to Beth Terrene that by March, Beth had transferred from Fielding Academy to Saint

Carmela's. She said it was because her grades were bad. Which was probably true. How could Beth have concentrated on school with Martha Van Riet making every second of her life more miserable than the last?

Most of the time, the girls brushed aside Martha's jabs and stabs, otherwise she'd be at them all day long.

On the couch, Caitlin's younger brother, Ty, was watching race-car driving, clenching his hands and whispering, "Go go go! Turbocharge it! Pedal to the metal!"

Gray flopped onto the couch and Ty scooted over obligingly. "It's the Daytona Five Hundred," he told her. He seemed so spellbound that Gray did not have the heart to ask him to switch the channel to see what else was on.

Around and around went the cars, the same thing again and again. Gray wondered what else there was to do. Everything seemed dumb and boring, she was hungry and she itched to wander. Maybe she would sneak up to Caitlin's room and look through her bookshelf.

"Would you like something to drink?" she asked Ty. "I'm going to the kitchen."

Ty looked up, startled from his sports trance. "Uh. Grape juice," he said. "No. Cranapple."

"Be right back." She stood, undecided whether to ask if anyone else wanted a drink. "Does anyone want, like, a snack or something from the kitchen?" But the other girls seemed too absorbed in Enchanted Castle to answer. Or they were being rude on purpose. Ignoring Gray was a game the group sometimes ganged up to play against her. "Save my seat," she said, to nobody.

Gray walked upstairs to the empty kitchen. The polished glass sliding doors that looked out over the Donnelleys' backyard and swimming pool were now solidly dark, creating a mirror effect, doubling the image of the kitchen's gleaming chrome. She flipped on a light and flipped it off again.

Upstairs, Gray heard Mrs. Donnelley and Topher talking and laughing. That was nice. Gray knew that Mrs. Donnelley was not Topher's real mom. Topher's real mom was some lady who had been married to Mr. Donnelley a long time ago, who lived somewhere else now and was not part of this Donnelley family.

Abruptly, Gray wondered what kind of lady her dad would choose if her mother died and he got remarried. What were the chances that she and Robby would have a stepmother as nice as Mrs. Donnelley? Even as Gray tried to picture different mothers—all her friends' mothers came to mind—she felt awful, like a traitor, a cheat, jinxing her own mother's chances to get all the way better.

Gray pushed aside the vision of the other mothers.

Would she be in trouble if she helped herself and Ty to some juice? Would Mrs. Donnelley mind? She opened a cupboard and was confronted with rows and rows of sparkly clean glasses. Mrs. Donnelley's house had so many rules! There was probably a special glass for each type of drink.

She closed the cupboard and noticed the phone on the wall next to the refrigerator. Maybe she would call home and tell her mother to come by with her fairy-folk bag. Although her dad would be angry if he found out. Gray and Robby weren't supposed to bother their mother with extra errands and requests and lists of "I need."

Well, so what? So what if he was angry? It was her mother's mistake, after all. Gray picked up the phone and punched in her home number.

Four rings and then the answering machine. She left a message.

"Mom, it's me at Caitlin's. Will you please bring me my right sleeping bag? You brought the wrong one to school. I need *my* one, my pink one. You know which, with fairies on it." She was trying not to whine and her voice sounded clogged at the base. She hung up the phone. From behind, she felt the prickling tug of being watched, although when she glanced around, nobody was in sight. The kitchen was quiet, gleaming, humming. Like a shut-down space station, Gray thought.

She opened the refrigerator. All this food! Cartons and bottles and tubs and containers of it, neatly wrapped and normal looking. No dark spinach and organic glop like what her mother ate now, for her health. The only problem was that none of the Donnelleys' food looked easy to get to. Even the bottle of Cranapple juice Ty wanted was unopened, sealed around its lip with a thin, clear, childproof band.

A crisper filled with fruit seemed most promising. Gray slid open the drawer and pinched a bunch of fat purple grapes. They tasted okay, but coming from such a perfect refrigerator, she felt a brief flicker of disappointment that they should have been fruitier, cleaner, better.

She closed the refrigerator door.

A tattered apparition stood outside, behind the sliding doors. A woman. Gray's heart jumped and her throat closed and she started to choke on her grape. As she coughed, the woman's eyes rounded and her mouth dropped into an *O* that looked too big for her shocked face.

Gray stopped coughing and the woman's mouth shut. She had sad eyes and long, ropy brown hair tied back in a handkerchief. Underneath her layers of clothing—a baggy dress and a rust-orange-colored coat with a feathery trim—she was knife-thin. Gray could see the bones of her neck and wrists, the shadows scooped into her cheeks and temples.

Now the woman rapped her knuckles on the glass and motioned for Gray to let her inside. Gray stared. She did not recognize the woman as a friend of Mrs. Donnelley's. She did not recognize the woman as a mother from school, either—although she was about the same age as a mother. Perhaps she was one of the Donnelleys' next-door neighbors? Like Mrs.

Nuñez, who lived across the street from the Rosenfelds? Mrs. Nuñez wore safety-pinned bath towels as skirts and she never turned off her radio and she strung Christmas lights in her holly bushes all year long. Gray's parents called Mrs. Nuñez "a real piece of work" and always wished she would move away.

Maybe this woman also was "a real piece of work"?

Gray paused another moment, then crossed the kitchen, unlocked and slid open the door. The woman did not move. "Hello, you!" she exclaimed in a soft, curious voice. "Am I late? I saw the balloons."

"Oh, those are for Caitlin. It's her birthday party."

"I've been driving around and around, looking for the party. When I saw the balloons, I guessed I was at the right place." The woman stared at Gray expectantly.

"Do you want to come inside?" Gray wondered if this was the right thing to ask. She was not stupid. She knew all the rules about not talking to strangers.

The woman seemed harmless, though. She stepped delicately into the kitchen as if it were stuffed with people, not just herself and Gray. She kept her back pressed against the glass wall. Her eyes darted from counter to counter. "Oh, I don't like it here. It's different on the inside. I like more lights, maybe a radio. This isn't my party, after all."

"Are you a neighbor?" Gray asked.

"Yes," said the woman. "Do you live here?"

"No. And I need to go home," Gray blurted out. Tears souped her eyes. "I have to pick up my sleeping bag."

"Of course." The woman agreed as if she knew that already. "I think we'd better go now." She held out her hand for Gray to take. "All set?"

"Oh!" Gray smiled. "Are you here for me? Are you from Helping Hands?"

"Yes, that's right."

No. That couldn't be right. This woman did not look like a Helping Hands person, and Gray had met quite a few of them. Last year, when her mother had been very sick, Helping Hands people had been around a lot of the time. Mostly women, but there had been one man, Brett. They all were nice, especially Ann Lee and Moira, although Moira could get impatient if Gray didn't know the directions to soccer practice or kept her waiting too long in the Fielding parking lot.

This woman could not be a Helping Hands lady. Also, Gray's parents did not use the Helping Hands service anymore, now that her mother was recovering.

Or do we use it but only sometimes because maybe Mom picked up my message and called in for a Helping Hands person for just this once this one important errand?

"We're going to get my sleeping bag and come right back?" Gray asked.

"Yes," said the woman. She snapped her fingers. "We need to hurry. I have a lot of other things to do."

Zoë

Zoë was going to win. She was the best. She knew that. Besides, the other girls did not care as much about winning. Their hearts did not flutter when the Enchanted Castle game board was opened. Their mouths did not dry up when the scorecards were laid out, neat as buttons, all in a row. Their fingers did not sweat with each roll of the dice.

I'll win this game, Zoë thought. Yes, yes! Because I always win this game.

From the start, though, Zoë sensed that Kristy was trying to tip off the table to let Caitlin win. Kristy Kiss-up, that's what Martha called Kristy behind her back because of how she acted toward Caitlin. Sure enough, when Caitlin got up to go to the bathroom, Kristy leaned forward.

"You guys, it's Caitlin's birthday," Kristy whispered, "and she never wins. Let's let her beat us this once."

No, no! thought Zoë. Not fair! Caitlin had too much luck already. Caitlin was a girl who always had the right sneakers, the right hair bands and clips, even the right day—Valentine's Day!—for her birthday. The right mother, too, because Mrs. Donnelley was perfect. Mrs. Donnelley, who wore thigh-length tennis dresses, whose legs were shiny, moisturized, and tan—even in winter—and who picked up Caitlin at school on time every afternoon. And who, glamorous as she was, never was doing anything so important that she couldn't interrupt herself to perform even the silliest, smallest errand for Caitlin.

Caitlin didn't need to win! No fair!

"Gosh, I think letting Caitlin beat us is a sweet idea, Kristy," said Martha in a honeyed voice. She winked at Zoë and pursed her lips into a kiss. Zoë swallowed and clenched her fists and was silent.

"That's cheating," countered Leticia, "and I won't play if the game is *fixed!*"

Serena sighed prettily and shook back her thick ginger hair. "I agree."

"Me, too," said Zoë, relaxing her hands. Ha, ha, you lose, Martha.

"Oh, you're all such morons," said Martha. "Like it matters who wins! Like it means anything!"

"Yeah, have it your own dumb way," said Kristy. "Here comes Caitlin back, so shut up about it."

On Kristy's next turn, Zoë watched as she picked up a card and rubbed her nose. She must have found one of the Queen's treasures. Kristy was easy to read. She had so many tics and twitchy habits.

Yawning, Kristy replaced the card in the Throne Room. Zoë, her own face blank, made a mental note of it.

When Gray quit the game, Zoë's victory was assured. Gray was good at Enchanted Castle. She paid attention and followed the rules.

Zoë watched as Gray mumbled some excuse and retreated to the couch. She looked worn and sunk.

What was wrong with Gray these days? Her mom was supposed to be cured, or at least close to cured. So it couldn't be that.

Zoë would not be the one to bring it up. She had learned her lesson this past fall when she had found Gray crying in the bathroom. Concerned, she had made the mistake of telling the others in the group. As a friend! As a friend was why she told!

"Poor Gray! She was crying in the stall next to mine. What do you think's the matter? Do you think it's about her mom?"

"Gray's such a lick," Martha had answered. "I bet I could make her cry just by staring at her."

Then Martha had stared at Gray all through lunch, unsmiling, unspeaking, until Gray had collapsed in tears. "Why are you doing that, Martha? Stop watching me!"

That was how the game started. Stare-at-Gray-till-she-cried. Ignore-Gray-till-she-cried. It was sort of funny but not really. Then Martha didn't invite Gray to her skating party. Eventually, Gray was pretty much nudged out of the Lucky Seven, but last month she had drifted back in. Probably on account of Caitlin's influence, Zoë figured. Caitlin's and Gray's moms had been friends forever, so Caitlin and Gray used to be best friends when they were little.

Zoë bet next year would be different. These days, Caitlin and Kristy were stuck together like peanut butter and jelly. And Gray sometimes acted like a *lick*, she was too *spanky*, she could be *unc;* all Lucky Seven words that Zoë herself had made up. It was Martha who loved to use the words Zoë had invented for the group. Zoë didn't. Not on Gray, anyway. Gray's feelings got hurt too easy.

After Gray went upstairs, Martha turned to Zoë and said, "I bet she's pigging down the cake."

Zoë laughed, though it made her feel guilty. Gray was small and underweight, but she was always hungry, always eating in the same rabbity, bad-habit way that Zoë bit her nails. But Zoë laughed because there was something magnetic about Martha when she was joking and friendly. Her eyes sparkled like gold firecrackers, a change that warmed her hard, flat face.

"Gray can eat the whole entire cake and she'll never gain a pound," Caitlin said. "My mom always makes stuff low-fat, so that I can watch my figure."

Zoë thought it was cool that Mrs. Donnelley was already thinking about Caitlin's figure. It made Caitlin seem mature.

"I have a really good metabolism, so I can eat whatever I want," Zoë said.

"Ugh, Zoë, you get High Honors every single report card. Isn't that enough? Why does everything have to be a competition with you?" snapped Martha. She began talking in an announcer's voice. "And now, Fielding Academy's prize for Best Metabolism this year goes to—Zoë Atacropolis! Again, folks! Amazing!"

Everyone laughed. Zoë smiled, but only to show she was a good sport.

Sometimes, secretly, Zoë wanted out of the Lucky Seven. Even if it was the best, the most popular group, sometimes the group did not seem fun enough for the effort it took to stay in it. The problem was that if she dropped out, then she would be a quitter. Maybe even a loser. Two things her older brother, Shelton, would never let himself be.

Martha was talking into her microphone fist, still acting like a broadcaster. "This is Miss Atacropolis's sixth straight year of winning Best Meta—"

“Hey, would you shut up, Martha?” Leticia interrupted. “I can’t concentrate.”

The others stopped laughing.

Martha stopped talking. She looked surprised.

Nobody spoke. Everyone watched as Leticia drew a card and finished her turn.

“Go, Kristy,” she said, pushing the dice.

And so the game continued.

Martha

Martha noticed that Gray had been gone for a while.

"Where is Mouse?" she asked. Mouse was Martha's special behind-her-back name for Gray, because she was so small and squeaky.

Caitlin smirked. "Who cares? The fun is here, and the Evil Queen shall win all."

Martha rolled her eyes. Caitlin was getting on her nerves, using too much time on her turn and cackling, "I'll get you, my pretty!" when it was anyone else's. Enchanted Castle sucked for anyone who wasn't the Evil Queen, and it looked as if Zoë was going to win. Zoë, as usual.

"Gray!" Martha shouted so loud that Serena, sitting next to her, had to cover her ears.

"Gray went upstairs to get me some juice," called Ty from the couch. "But that was a long time ago. Like half an hour ago."

"Shut up!" yelled Caitlin. "You're breaking the rule! You butt in and say one single more thing and I'll make Mom send you out of here to watch TV in your room forever!"

Zoë pointed to Martha. "Your turn, Mar."

Martha rolled doubles and moved her princess into the Hall of Mirrors.

"I'll get you, my pretty!" screeched Caitlin for the thousandth time. "And your little dog, too!"

"Caitlin, do you know how goddamn annoying that is?" asked Martha.

The table hushed. Martha smiled. Bad words were plentiful as rocks and just as easy to throw; they hardly took any nerve at all and she didn't know why people found them so startling.

But they did.

All the noise left in the room was the sound of the television, of race cars roaring around the track.

"Girls! Ty!" shouted Mrs. Donnelley. "Pizza!"

"I'm gonna eat all you girls' pizza!" Ty stretched his arms. "Chomp chomp chomp! I could eat sixty gazillion slices right now!"

"That's it, Ty!" Caitlin sprang from her chair, knocking it over, and rushed her brother. She flung herself over the back of the couch to cuff Ty hard from behind with the flat of her hand. "Shut up, shut up, dumb third-grader vomit face!"

"Caitlin, come back," implored Zoë.

Zoë was two turns away from winning, and Martha could tell Caitlin was glad for any interruption.

"I hate you, Ty!" screamed Caitlin at the top of her lungs.

"Ha ha ha ha ha! You're not s'posed to say *hate!* I'm telling!" Ty jounced up from the couch to yank a fistful of his sister's hair so hard that he came away with loose strands like shucked corn. "Painful, ainnit? Painful, ainnit?" he yelled, lunging for more.

As Caitlin started screeching loud as an ambulance siren, Ty changed his mind and jumped off the couch and up the stairs. Martha watched him leap out of reach before Caitlin could bite or scratch him. She gave chase anyway.

"I guess the game is over?" asked Zoë. "I guess I won?"

"Nuh-uh, nobody won, stupid." Martha despised how Zoë sort-of pretended how she didn't care about winning when really she wanted it more than anything.

Mrs. Donnelley and Topher were in the dining room, working on the table's finishing touches. Topher was a hottie, Martha thought. He had not been noticing her nearly as much as she wished. She half closed her eyes and tilted her head and put her hands on her hips, but still he didn't notice.

Mrs. Donnelley had prepared the room with a pink paper tablecloth and pink napkins. There were pink paper plates and cups and pink plastic forks and spoons. Seven pink crepe-paper streamers tied from the chandelier looped a path to a goody bag at each place setting. Pink, pink, pink, because Caitlin was born on Valentine's Day, which would be tomorrow.

Mrs. Donnelley began ticking off names as the girls settled into their seats. "Serena, Zoë, Martha, Leticia, Kristy, and Caitlin, my birthday girl!" She pointed to the empty place setting and asked, "Who is missing?"

"Gray," Martha answered promptly.

"Oh, yes!" Mrs. Donnelley smiled. "Where is Gray?"

"She's in the kitchen, getting me some juice," said Ty. He was standing at the sideboard, scooping Valentine red hots into his mouth and pockets.

"No one's in the kitchen," said Topher as he plowed through the swinging door with a soda bottle in each hand. Diet grape and diet orange.

"I'm not allowed to drink anything carbonated," said Leticia.

"I'm not allowed to drink anything diet," said Martha. This was not true, but she liked to see the anxiety pulse in Mrs. Donnelley's face.

"That's why there's lemonade on the table. *My pretty!*" squealed Caitlin, protected by her mother's presence and staring Martha down.

"I'm allergic to peanuts," said Zoë. She reminded people of this constantly.

"Ty, go find Gray," ordered Mrs. Donnelley. "Hurry, hurry! And don't eat those!"

Ty shook one more handful of red hots into his mouth and galloped out of the dining room. Mrs. Donnelley turned a proud eye on the table.

"Doesn't this look wonderful? As soon as Gray is here, we'll be perfect."

Martha smiled a tiny closed-lips smile, and her heart flipped pleasantly. She had a feeling that something was going wrong. Gray really should have come back by now.

In a few minutes, everyone was shouting for Gray.

Everyone except Martha.

She stayed in her seat as the room emptied.

As soon as she was alone, Martha switched her goody bag for Serena's bag, which was stuffed fat as a pincushion with the most candy. To make sure Serena didn't trade back, Martha opened the bag, selected a heart-shaped chocolate, and dropped it into her mouth. The chocolate smeared on her fingers because the Donnelleys' house was too warm.

The heart tasted plasticky but was liquid on the inside. Martha let the chocolate muddle over her tongue and bleed down her throat, warm and thin and sweet.

Nice, nice enough.

Mr. Donnelley came home.

"I'm home!" he shouted. He kicked the front door shut with

his heel, twisting the corner of the carpet runner as he did so, a rude guest in his own house.

Martha, nauseated from having eaten three more chocolate hearts, had slid out of her chair when she heard his car in the driveway. Now she leaned against the dining room door, half hidden by it, watching.

The family rushed Mr. Donnelley from all sides as if he'd just caught the pass in a football game. Nobody saw Martha.

"Daddy, my friend Gray is missing!" yelled Caitlin.

"Daddy, Topher says we should call the cops!" yelled Ty.

"I've been trying the car! I've been trying your cell phone!" Mrs. Donnelley nearly tripped and fell as she rushed down the stairs. "Go, go on, Caitlin, Ty. Leave me to talk to Daddy alone."

Martha hardly dared a breath. She made her eyes stony and unblinking. On their mother's push, Caitlin and Ty slipped away into the kitchen and then could be heard outside, shouting for Gray again.

Now it was just the three of them.

Mr. Donnelley's arms were weighted with his overcoat and his briefcase, so Mrs. Donnelley could not touch him. Her hands twisted together and she spoke in a jabber.

"One of the girls has wandered off. You know Gray. Into thin air. I was up in the attic, cobwebs all over me, on any chance she might have—"

“Maybe she’s asleep somewhere in the house. By the way, we lost the appeal.”

“Honey, I’m so sorry.”

Mr. Donnelley handed over his overcoat with a grunt. “Do you mind? I’m dead on my feet.”

“Yes, you look exhausted.” Mrs. Donnelley took the coat and opened the hall closet. “I’ve searched the house top to bottom, the attic, everywhere. Topher is trying to keep the girls from running down the street. It’s chaos. And I can’t get hold of the Rosenfelds.” She selected a heavy wooden hanger from its bar and hung the coat, smoothing it carefully into place with the others. “Should we call the police? What should we do?”

“Let me shower and change. Then I’ll decide.”

Martha thought Mr. Donnelley resembled an old professional wrestler. He was big and ruddy and balding, with the same wide clown mouth as Caitlin. Bad luck for Caitlin.

After Mr. Donnelley went upstairs, Mrs. Donnelley spied Martha. A wisp of frown crossed her face, though her tone was pleasant as she asked, “Martha, sweetie, do you have any idea where Miss Gray might have wandered off to?”

Martha pretended to think. “Maybe she walked home? She seemed . . . depressed. She didn’t want to play Enchanted Castle with us. Gosh, I hope she didn’t try to walk along the highway!”

She watched this bright new fear touch down in Mrs.

Donnelley's eyes. Martha enjoyed the game of digging to the secret fears inside people.

In fact, today had been a great day for secrets. Today, Martha had caught hold of her best secret yet. And it had been Mrs. Donnelley's fault, sort of. Mrs. Donnelley, who, earlier this afternoon, after directing all the girls out of the minivan and Topher's car and instructing them to put their overnight and sleeping bags in Caitlin's room, had exclaimed, "Oh, gosh! The mail! Darn! Could someone run down and get the mail?" She had pointed to Martha. "Sweetie? Do you mind?"

Martha did not mind. She had run outside again, all the way down to the edge of the lawn, to the mailbox tied with bobbing pink balloons, and collected the mail.

The lady had been standing right at the bottom of the driveway. She had long thick hair like yarn and her face and lips were sparkly and she was wearing a feathery orange coat. She waved at Martha.

"Hello, you!" said the lady. "Am I late to the party?"

There was something about that lady. She looked messy, like a wild animal, Martha had thought. An animal turned into a human by an enchanted spell but who still had something of the forest clinging to her. Her eyes looked glazed and she was too skinny, and her smile pulled back fierce, revealing long teeth.

"Party?" Martha repeated.

"Isn't there a party? Balloons mean a party!"

Martha shook her head and ran. Ran as fast as she could. Ran up the lawn and into the house through the garage, and even when she was safe inside the Donnelleys' house, she had locked the door.

Her breath had burst forward, and she had stood there for a long time, panting, until she had collected herself enough to drop the mail in the living room and rejoin the other girls upstairs.

Now Martha closed her eyes and the knowledge sang in the back of her throat.

The lady is my secret, she thought. Mine to tell it when the time is right, and not a second before.

Leticia

Leticia couldn't help thinking that it was not all bad that Gray had disappeared. As long as nothing terrible had happened to her. As long as she came back soon. But right now it meant a break from the pink party. Topher was excited about it, too. After he rounded everyone back inside and into the kitchen, he handed out flashlights and spare batteries and ordered the girls to pair up.

"Each of you grab an official buddy, and stay together," he instructed. "Nobody else is getting lost on my watch."

"Guess I'll look with you," Martha whispered. When Topher had called her out of the dining room, she had slid up on Leticia's side.

Leticia did not answer. She switched her flashlight from its high to low beam. *Click, click.*

"If I can't look with you, I won't look at all," Martha said into Leticia's silence. Then: "I don't know what makes you think you can act like such a snot. You were being a jerk during Enchanted Castle, too. If you're mad at me, you should come out and say."

"Why would I be mad, Miss A-plus?" asked Leticia in a soft voice that sounded friendly.

She watched Martha's face go blank. "What are you talking about?"

"You know." *Click, click.* High, low. "That A plus you got on the earth science test. That grade is a lie, you cheater. After I told you that you couldn't copy me, you just switched seats and looked off Zoë's paper. I saw you do it. Now the proof is written next to your name in Ms. Calvillo's grade book. A plus."

"That test was a cinch." Martha covered her mouth as if to stifle a yawn, but her eyes were flinty. "It was stupid easy."

"Not *that* easy, considering." Leticia took a deep breath. "Considering I only got a B plus."

"Sucks to be you," Martha recited. She smirked. Then shrugged. Then she turned away from Leticia, sneaking back into the dining room.

Leticia unhooked her jacket from the pantry peg. Her throat was dry and her fingers were cold. Going up against Martha was hard. It was easier to be friends. Only three weekends ago, she had spent the night at Martha's house. It had been fun. Martha had filched her older sister Jane's diary to read to Leticia. Later that night, they'd phoned Ralph Dewey, a shy boy from Martha's church, and in spooky voices they had chanted,

"You are the son of the devil, Ralph Dewey! You are the son of the devil and you are going to hell!" while he squealed, "Who is this? What do you want from me?"

Then they had hung up and laughed until their stomachs hurt.

Later that night, Leticia had felt bad. The echo of Ralph Dewey's lonely voice would not leave her ear. And she was upset about Jane's diary, too, about knowing strange, private things personal to Martha's older sister.

Not that Martha cared, and Leticia was used to being on guard against Martha's tricks and pranks. Nobody was spared, not even Leticia herself. "Mar, do Leticia giving her oral report!" Caitlin had commanded the other day at lunch. The other girls had turned to Martha, their eyes gleaming expectantly. Obviously, they had heard this imitation before, Leticia realized, when she was not around. "Now, Teesh, don't be mad, it's *funny!*" Caitlin had coaxed. "Come on, do it for her, Mar!"

Martha had not needed to be asked twice. She had launched into a savage impression of Leticia presenting her social studies oral report. "There are, uh, ma-ny In-can sites through-out Per-u, uh, that have not yet been, uh, ex-ca-va-ted." Martha had it all down—the clogged, wobbling vowels, the gulped breaths, even the way Leticia fixed her eyes on the wall clock—as the other girls exploded with fits of giggling.

Of course, Leticia had to laugh along, pushing past the bead of anger that had lodged in her chest. Too harsh, Martha! she had wanted to protest. Public speaking took guts, even if she wasn't great at it. Now she had to be mocked for it, too?

But nobody was safe from Martha.

Leticia zipped up her jacket and stepped outside. The night spun a shiver through her. When she looked up, the stars twinkled and the moon looked full and soft as a cushion in the sky. Through the dining room window, Leticia watched Martha return to her seat and reach across the table for somebody else's goody bag. The back of her head looked small and lonely as an unpicked flower.

Leticia looked away. "Serena!" she called. She twirled her flashlight, which caught Serena's gingery hair like a sunlit wave in the light's beam. "Hey, come be my pair! Let's find Gray together, you and me!"

The search stopped being fun almost as soon as it started. For one thing, the temperature seemed to drop every minute. Also, anytime a pair of flashlights moved too far down the street, Topher called them back. Leticia stayed close to the pack. She watched as Mrs. Donnelley, Ty's hand gripped in hers, flitted from door to door, knocking, ringing bells, alerting everyone. Her phony voice: *"Hello! Sorry to bother you, but we're looking for a little girl. . . ."*

Soon a few of the neighbors had joined in to help. Over and over, in answer to their questions, Leticia described Gray.

Brown hair, chin length. Brown eyes. Wearing jeans with a navy and white snowflake sweater.

Nobody had seen her.

"Maybe she got stolen by a pack of wild dogs," Leticia joked.

"Woof! Woof! Pftew! This girl is too bony!" barked Caitlin.

"Don't say that," chided Mrs. Donnelley, overhearing them. She turned. "That's a terrible thing to say." Her features, normally pulled into this or that agreeable expression, all fell together into a hard glare. A glare aimed not at Caitlin, but Leticia.

Right there, that's Mrs. Donnelley's real face, Leticia thought. Uncertain, panicked.

What a phony.

Oh, sure, on the surface Mrs. Donnelley was nice enough. Usually her expression was a nearly perfect mask, pale eyes shiny and her smile stretched wide, right from the start. "Leticia, honey, what can I get you to *drink?*" "Leticia, honey, Caitlin says both of your parents are *lawyers!*" "Leticia, honey, I understand you were at *Rotterdam* last year?"

Always so extra-polite. Always with the *honey, honey.*

Phony, phony.

Last spring, Leticia had left Rotterdam Elementary as one of the most popular kids in her class. She had stood out as the girl with the quick jokes and throaty laugh, as the girl who could kick a soccer ball past any goalie, as the girl who could think up a million fads—like wearing gel stickers on the bottoms of her sneakers or gold Magic Markering her fingernails.

This past fall, when Leticia had started Fielding Academy, she'd stood out only as the black girl. Actually, the other black girl. But Daria Moore was ignored to the point where she seemed invisible. That was what Fielding girls did, Leticia's sister, Celeste, had told her. Fielding girls ignored. Ignoring was their specialty. Celeste had graduated from Fielding last year, and she knew everything.

Right away, Leticia had spotted the cool group. Martha Van Riet's group. As a whole, they were bigger than their parts. They joked the most. They laughed the hardest. They had the best time. They rubbed shoulders in an enchanted circle.

Martha was their leader, and the way in. Martha had a wide flat face like a freckled toad, and at first she did not smile at Leticia's jokes or care when Leticia laughed at hers. Martha did not seem to care about anything except being noticed. She was always sassing back at teachers or running in the hall or wearing nonregulation clothes with her uniform. Martha seemed fearless, and everyone was in awe of her.

It was during language arts class that Leticia made her move. She turned around in her chair, flipped Martha a Post-It note with a squiggly face drawn on it, and, with all the other girls listening, said, "Dare you to stick this note on Miss Bruce's butt."

Martha received the dare coldly. But she did it. Slapped on the note quick and perfect when Miss Bruce walked down the aisle, handing back homework.

That same day, right before the bell rang for history, Martha came back at her.

"Hey. Uh, Leticia. Dare you to pull down Mr. Wolferson's map of North America."

Mr. Wolferson was not in the classroom yet. Leticia acted fast, jumping up from her chair to rip it down with both hands and all her strength. Her stomach churned. The class chortled nervously. When Mr. Wolferson came in and demanded a culprit, nobody told because it was Martha Van Riet's dare.

They teamed up, Leticia and Martha. Dares were more fun to do together.

They made animal noises during chorus practice. They started a Tater Tots food fight during lunch. They faked injuries, limps, and spasms to annoy the gym teachers. They got detentions together.

Leticia slipped inside the loop of Martha's group. Soon after, Zoë nicknamed them the Lucky Seven. Inside the loop was everything in the world. Leticia felt home safe.

Only nothing is ever really safe, Leticia thought as she swept her flashlight back and forth like a lighthouse beam. She watched as Mrs. Donnelley and Ty crossed the street to ring another doorbell. Mrs. Donnelley was not really safe. She was too phony, and her home was hot and pink and bright and strange and slightly unwelcoming, no matter how many times Leticia had stayed over.

And Martha was not safe, either. Martha would do anything to get her way.

Suddenly, Serena squeezed her elbow. "Teesh, I'm scared!" she said. "It sounds weird. Listen."

Ty and Mrs. Donnelley and Topher and some of the neighbors were calling Gray's name. Gray's name was a single sound that did not stop.

Graaaaaaaaaaaaaaaaaaaaaaaaaaaaaaaaaaaaaaaaaaaay!

A lost, lonely sound, thought Leticia.

She hoped Gray was safe, wherever she was.

Leticia tucked Serena's hand more firmly into the crook of her elbow. "Nothing to be scared of," she said, though her thoughts skittered nervously as she took a long breath and then added her voice to the night.

Gray

All of Gray's favorite characters were brave and not like her. Brave Alice in Wonderland and Anne of Green Gables and Buffy the Vampire Slayer and Jo March and Heidi and Pippi and Nancy Drew and Becky Thatcher and Dorothy in and out of Oz. Brave, all of them. None of those girls would have liked Gray much. She was not the kind of girl Tom Sawyer or a stray dog would follow home. She was not the kind of girl who could summon that scrap of bravery that raised her just a tiny bit above the other girls. The feisty girl in the bittersweet adventure who was an inspiration, who made everybody clap and who gave everybody a bit of hope to cling to at the end.

No, Gray was not that kind of girl. Gray was a too-scared girl, and she knew it. Too scared of too many things. Of boys and stray dogs and the dark and bringing the wrong sleeping bag. She was scared of bigger things, too, of the smell of hospitals and of her mother maybe dying. She hoped that one day she would outgrow her fears, but so far, fear seemed to be sticking with her.

So when the strange lady who might be from Helping Hands offered her hand and ordered Gray to hurry up, and when she clamped her fingers around Gray's wrist and did not let go, Gray did not do anything brave. She decided to trust the lady because it was easier. If the lady had asked Gray to close her eyes and fall backward into her arms, Gray might have done that, too.

She tripped along at the lady's side. Out the sliding glass door into the freezing air and down the driveway and a left at the end of it, to where the lady's car was parked. An old car, too dark to see the color it truly was.

In the back of Gray's jumbled thoughts, one idea burned bright and kept her from turning and running. The lady did not look like someone from Helping Hands, but she did look like someone her mother might have met at the hospital.

She tested it. "You know Mom from the hospital?"

"Well," said the lady, "I don't like when people call it that."

"Are you sick?"

"The door's unlocked," the lady answered.

Gray touched the car door handle and looked around, hoping for a glimpse of a neighbor. But it was cold, too cold to be comfortably outside, and all of the brick or stone fortress-thick houses on Caitlin's street were set back from the road, for privacy. There was nobody to see or to be seen by. Gray did spy

Bumpo standing at the edge of the property because his electric collar did not permit him to escape his generous run of lawn. His head was cocked and quizzical.

"Can the dog come?" Gray asked. *Yes! Bumpo! It would be easy for me to take off his electric collar and say come on come on Bumpo come in the car for a ride! Just in case maybe things don't turn out all right maybe Bumpo saves the day! Because dogs do that yes sometimes on TV. Sometimes they do.*

"Don't be silly!" said the lady.

Oh, of course she was being silly. Gray opened the door and slid into the backseat of the car, and she buckled her seat belt, for Safety.

She would be gone and back before anyone noticed. She would get her sleeping bag and her mother would not have had to do all that driving, because she had sent in her place this odd lady, this "piece of work" who might be a friend or might not, who might be from Helping Hands or maybe not.

And even if her mother had not sent this lady, it would turn out okay, because the lady did not seem dangerous, in her glossy lipstick and feathery coat. She just looked a little bit confused. She would be happy to take Gray home and return her to the Donnelleys' before cake time.

Bumpo whined, then turned and trotted back to the house.

The car was rattling and noisy, as if it had swallowed a handful of coins. The lady took roads that Gray knew. But the ride was uncomfortable, unheated, and the tires slipped loose on the road. The lady drove as if she had only just learned, hunkered forward and her lower lip caught hard in her top teeth.

Out of the corner of her eye, Gray stared at the lady. Her face in the light-by-light reflection of the streetlamps was made up with eye shadow and rouge and a papery, sparkling powder smoothed over like a glittering fish skin to hold everything in place.

Maybe the lady was not one hundred percent real? Maybe she was a fairy, or an angel-ghost, and she was taking Gray on an adventure that would turn out to be a dream.

Gray touched a finger to the lady's feather-tufted coat collar.

"Don't do that!" the lady snapped. "Don't frighten me when I'm driving!"

Gray winced. That did not seem to be a very angel-y thing to say. "There's a price tag hanging off your coat sleeve," Gray said as she noticed it.

The lady shook her sleeve to see for herself, then bit it off, snapping the tag and little plastic tail in exactly the way Gray's mother told her not to because it damaged the fabric. The lady spit the tag and tail at the door. "Thanks," she said.

"What's your name?" asked Gray.

"Katrina." The woman thought for a moment, then added, "Just Katrina."

"I don't mind how fast you're driving," Gray said. "Since we have to get back to the Donnelleys' house soon. It's almost time for pizza and cake."

"I haven't driven a car in a while," said Katrina. "I liked driving, but it's not coming back easy. And I've been on the road so much today. All the way into town and around and around. When we get back, I'm going to take a nap."

"Back to my house, right?" When Katrina did not answer, Gray said, "I thought we were going to my house? If you want to take a nap on my bed, you can."

"My house first."

"Okay." Gray wished she didn't sound so scared. By now Nancy Drew would have found the important clue about Katrina, a clue to solve the mystery, and her story would have been called *The Clue in the Rattletrap Car.* Alice in Wonderland would have said "Curiouser and curiouser" without a trace of worry in her voice.

Driving down a dark road in a dark car with a strange lady seemed worse than curious. Gray decided she would try to imagine it in a friendlier and safer way, as an adventure.

Yes, that was how she would see it.

As an adventure!

Katrina lived at a turnoff at the end of a back road that Gray had never been down, but it was close to the same road that turned onto Knightworthy Avenue, which led to Fielding Academy. Gray had marked all these points in her mind.

Memory pebbles, she thought, which will lead my way back to Safety.

The house was small and paint-chipped, surrounded by shaggy pine trees peaked at the top like witch hats. One amber lightbulb burned above the stoop. Moths flew out of nowhere to fall against it.

Katrina got out of the car and slammed the door behind her. She seemed to have forgotten about Gray, who trotted behind. Gray was hungry. She made a plan. As soon as she was inside, she would use the phone first to call home, then the Donnelley house. She could give pretty good directions to this area, and people might be worried by now.

And after the phone calls, she would find something to eat.

She joined Katrina, who stood on the stoop, fumbling with her keys. They both stamped their feet to keep warm as Katrina drove key after key into the lock and jiggled the doorknob. The last key let them in.

Katrina clicked the lights and plowed ahead of Gray into a room that was small and cluttered with the kind of lightweight furniture most people used on their lawns or patios. It was even messy like a patio, littered with soda cans and magazines and ashtrays and clear plastic glasses and stacks of fast-food napkins.

"I need to make a phone call," Gray said. "Everyone is allowed a phone call. Isn't that some kind of rule of the law?"

"The phone is turned off, I guess the bill wasn't paid," said Katrina. "Do you want to watch television?" She pointed to a television positioned on a table against the far wall. It was square and old-fashioned, with bunny-eared antennae tips padded in aluminum foil.

"No," Gray answered. She looked around for a telephone. Maybe Katrina was lying? When she did not see a telephone anywhere, a new, raw nervousness hummed in her throat and ears. Her eyes pricked with the tears that never were too far away. "I made a mistake," she admitted out loud, "and I want to go home. You said you would take me home."

"Oh. But I don't know where you live."

"Well, *I* do," said Gray. "And you know where Caitlin lives. We just came from there. Actually, I want to go back to Caitlin's birthday party. I'm missing all the fun. I'm missing . . . things."

Katrina seemed to think about it. Under the stark overhead light, Gray noticed that her eyes looked feverish, a thin border of dark blue nearly drowned by animal-black pupils. "Let's wait until Drew comes home," Katrina said. "I'm low on gas, and I'm not feeling good enough to drive anyone anywhere."

"You have to bring me home or back to the Donnelleys' house. Now," Gray insisted. "Please, I mean. I have twenty-eight dollars in my savings account. I'll write you a note giving it all to you. You can buy a lot of gas with that money. As long as you take me away."

"Well, listen to you, thinking you can order me around!" Katrina's laugh was harsh. "I already took you away! Now I'm spent. I should lie down." She pulled at the handkerchief. The ropy brown hair had been attached to it, and now it all came off in a heap, revealing Katrina's real hair, which was extremely short and prickly pale as a spring peach.

So it was true, after all! Katrina was sick. She had been in the hospital. Gray softened. "Are you having chemotherapy?" she asked politely.

Absently, Katrina dabbed a finger at her scalp. "A little nap," she said. "A night nap."

Gray continued, "My mother is sick. She got a wig last year, when she was having chemotherapy, but she's better now. Her real hair has grown back in. My brother wore the wig for Halloween. He sprayed it with glitter and was a rock star."

"I'm better, too," said Katrina. "That's what Drew said. That's why he took me away before I could have my party. But he said we'd have another party." She smiled. When she smiled, she appeared childlike, younger even than Robby. "Don't worry. Drew will come back soon."

"You don't understand, they'll be wondering . . ." But Katrina was finished with Gray. She turned and slipped down the short hall and disappeared behind a door.

Then Gray searched the front room inch by inch until she discovered a telephone under the couch. There was no dial tone. She plugged the phone into another outlet, double-checking, before she gave up and slid the phone back under the couch where she'd found it.

There was not a lot to the rest of the house. Gray walked through it carefully, looking for clues. Through the cracked-open bedroom door, she saw Katrina sprawled facedown and motionless on a bare twin frame. Aside from the bed, there was a blowup chair, the type used in a swimming pool, with a palm tree design and a drink holder sunk into its arm. The chair was half deflated, sagging sideways as if it, too, were asleep. The door next to the bedroom revealed a bathroom. In the back of the house was a skinny wedge of kitchen.

Retracing her steps, Gray opened the door to the hall closet to find it filled with winter coats and boots and, in the corner, a tiny dead brown mouse that had been long caught and crushed in a spring trap. Gray gasped—she had never seen a dead mouse before, and she would not brave inspecting this one. *Little lump his neck is squished oh so mean those mean traps little paw poor poor mousey.* She slammed the door. Shivering, she ran back to the couch, where she sat, pulling at the blanket draped over its back, and then wrapping it around her shoulders.

She was cold. She had left the Donnelley house without her coat.

They would probably be calling her name, searching for her inside and outside. It had been a while since she left. Caitlin would be angry. Mrs. Donnelley might be upset, too. She did not like for things to go wrong and to interfere with her perfect plans.

Gray hated to think of Mrs. Donnelley being upset, and knowing that she was the reason for it. Dumb, oh, this was so dumb, to have convinced herself that Katrina was from Helping Hands! When in the back of her mind, she had known all along. . . . And it was her mother's fault! If her mother hadn't gotten sick, there wouldn't be such a thing as Helping Hands. If her mother wasn't sick, she would not make mistakes about which sleeping bag.

Now here I am stuck here in this little lonely bad house without my sleeping bag and probably I missed the cake too.

She tried to find something cheerful in her mind to tug on to, a festive thought, like one of Caitlin's pink balloons, but a blur of new fears batted at her. She wanted to scream. A scream began thickly in her stomach and expanded, filling her lungs, her toes and fingertips. She pressed her knuckles against her mouth. Jumped up from the couch and walked outside in case she had to release it.

The night was huge and black, but no worse than the dark thoughts that swept in and out of her as she tried to imagine everything that might be lurking. Gray hopped off the stoop and took a few faltering steps. As far as she could see—which was not far, because of the trees—was nothing. Without sight of the road, the house seemed sunk too deep in the woods, like the gingerbread house in "Hansel and Gretel" or the lone cottage of the Seven Dwarfs.

An adventure might be even better than Caitlin's party. After all, it was an escape from the Donnelleys' loud, warm house and boring Enchanted Castle. It was an escape from food that looked better than it tasted. Best, Gray escaped faking happiness when Caitlin opened Gray's present, a *Make It Yourself!* beadwork kit that Gray herself desired so badly, she had considered keeping it and giving Caitlin an unopened package of bath salts. One of those "get well soon" gifts people were always foisting on her mother.

Caitlin already had everything, anyway. She'd bead one necklace and shove the kit on the top shelf space of her closet on top of her *Material Girl* fabric-patching kit and *Jamboree Gems* glass-polishing kit.

"I am not in any danger." Gray spoke out loud. "I can always run off into the woods and then follow the road to Fielding. Even if it took me until morning, by then maybe the police will be looking for me. So. I know where I am. I know where I am."

The sound of her voice and the truth of her words eased her mind. She went back into the house. The next plan would be to keep calm, to watch television, and to wait for Katrina's friend Drew, whoever he was.

Whoever he is he will know what to do.

Another quick check in the bedroom showed that Katrina must have moved a bit, because now her pretty coat was crumpled in a heap on the floor.

"Katrina?" called Gray softly.

Katrina's breathing was deeper, heavier than regular napping. It reminded Gray of the way her mother slept, and seemed stronger proof that Katrina and her mother were linked. Yes, Katrina was sick, and the medication was affecting her abilities.

"Katrina?" she called again.

No answer. Gray retreated into the living room and turned on the television.

The remote control was touchy, none of the channels came in well, and there was no cable. Her hunger was beginning to make her feel light-headed. She wished she had taken some more grapes. She pressed her head against the dark window glass.

What would Heidi do? What would Gretel do? What would Pippi do? They understood the outdoors and how to navigate it using their own wits.

Think. Think.

Although her heartbeat ticked too quickly, Gray was surprised by her calm. She could feel the flame of fear inside her, yes, but it was not a wildfire, she was not burning up, she had not been engulfed. Not yet, anyway.

Zoë

Zoë would find Gray. She would find her and her picture would be in the newspaper. She would be the hero. She would be the winner.

Zoë's picture had been in the local paper twice before.

Once for the Fielding Academy Science Fair, where she had won second prize for a pinball machine she had constructed using thin pipes that played a tune depending on how you hit the ball. Only it didn't work exactly because no tune played, just haphazard ping—ping—ping notes. So stupid! Why hadn't she done an important project about arthritis, like Natalie Brady, who won first prize?

The second picture was for the Maple Creek Water Club Intermediate Swimming Championships. Zoë had won first place for breaststroke, that was good, but the photograph taken was of Zoë in her bathing suit. Horrible! Her face and her name, paired with the word *breast*, pinned up in the school's front lobby on the "Regional News and Events" bulletin board.

When the others saw that picture, they'd made fun of her. "Yoo-hoo! Look at you, Zoë!" Serena had teased. "What's next? The *Sports Illustrated* calendar?"

"Zoë should swim breastless stroke," added Caitlin.

Martha had looked and said, simply, "Dork."

Zoë had never thought about how she actually *looked* as a swimmer until that picture. Her parents had always told Zoë that she was "attractive," with her dark, curly Atacropolis hair and her square chin, and she had blindly believed it. Stupid! She had ripped down the newspaper clipping to stare at it in the privacy of her own room, a blood-rush of shame in her cheeks, wondering if her bangs fell crooked or if there was something funny about her chin. And of course hating her non-breasts, squashed flatter under her swimming suit.

If Zoë found Gray tonight, she would get another chance, and a better photo in the paper. This time, it would be perfect. "Local Girl Saves School Pal." Her bangs styled just right and her chin tucked, with her arm hooked confidently around Gray's shoulder. No stupid breastless bathing suit. No second place.

Just last week, Zoë's brother, Shelton, had been quoted in *The Wall Street Journal* because he knew every single thing there was to know about business technology. "Your son, Shelton, is a genius," people often said to her parents.

"Zoë's no lightweight," her father would answer.

"Zoë's quite bright herself," her mother would refrain.

They never said she was a genius, though.

If she found Gray, then Zoë figured she would be better than a genius. She would be a psychic. Because in the interview next to the picture of them, Zoë would be quoted explaining how a shivery feeling came over her, how an electric black-and-white picture *of exactly where Gray was* had zapped into her head and she knew.

"I'll find you, Gray," whispered Zoë to the night.

She tore down the street. They were supposed to stay in groups, but the others were no help because they didn't care enough about winning.

The night was cold, too cold to be out for the fun of it.

Why would Gray have left the nice, safe house?

Zoë inhaled deep into the bottom of her lungs and called Gray's name. The sound went on and on like a bell.

I am superhuman, Zoë thought. My powers are greater than the others. I will get a supernatural picture of Gray in my head. It will direct me to the pothole where Gray tripped and broke her leg. It will direct me right to the side of the road where Gray got hit—but not too bad—by a car.

Please let me be the one to find you, Gray.

She hoped Gray was okay, wherever she was. Maybe she had run away on purpose. Maybe she was sick of Caitlin and the Lucky Seven and having to hide in the bathroom when she was sad. Maybe she was tired of pretending that she was the same sweet, easygoing, no-problems-here Gray from back in fifth grade, before her mother got sick. Maybe, if Zoë found her first, Gray would confess all these things and Zoë would not tell the others like last time.

Because this time, she would protect Gray against Martha's mean jokes and Caitlin's bored face. Yes, yes, she could do that.

Zoë widened her eyes until they hurt. She thought she might be able to see in the dark. Tonight her hearing seemed animal-sharp. She had watched plenty of TV shows about mystics and psychics and fortune-tellers. The senses were everything.

"I found Gray because people in my family have the Sight," she would tell everyone at lunch on Monday. "I guess I do, too. It's no big deal. I was born to it."

She would become a local legend. Wouldn't her parents be proud! And wouldn't Shelton, Mr. Business Technology, be jealous! Though of course not to her face. To her face Shelton would have to praise her.

Zoë ran on and on, her mind open and waiting to receive the Sight.

"I'll find you, Gray," she whispered. "I promise."

Martha

The grandfather clock in the front hall chimed seven times.

Martha had settled on the bottom step of the staircase. She sat very still and listened to the endless shouting for Gray across and up and down the street.

She wondered if Gray was safe or in danger.

In danger, she bet, with a tug of envy. Wherever Gray was and whatever she was doing, Martha bet that it was more exciting than anything happening in this house.

Occasionally someone came inside, up or down the stairs, past Martha. Once, as Mrs. Donnelley swept by, the cold of the outdoors on her body, she said, "That's right, you stay there, Martha. In case Gray comes through the front door. You call for me right away. I'm just outside. Tell Mr. Donnelley, too, when he comes down. I'm just outside."

Mrs. Donnelley did not want to think that Martha simply had decided not to look for Gray. Which she had. Frankly, she did not feel like looking for anything, and her stomach ached from chocolate. Besides, it only would have been fun to search for Gray with Leticia, and Leticia was acting strange tonight. Martha wished she would snap out of it. Since when did Leticia care so much about stupid school stuff?

As the sound of chiming fell away, the Donnelleys' dog, Bumpo, began to bark outside.

"Bumpo! Quiet, Bumpo!"

"Does he see anything?"

"I think he's barking at a squirrel."

"Are you sure?"

Bumpo kept barking. *Wolf wolf wolf! Rough rough rough!*

Too late, Bumpo, thought Martha. You think you're such a good watchdog! Why weren't you watching Mouse?

Martha listened to the distant rush of water through the pipes as Mr. Donnelley showered. A long shower, considering that Gray was missing and Mr. Donnelley said he would be the one to take charge. Maybe he was taking his time on purpose, Martha thought, to scare Mrs. Donnelley. To show her that he was the one making the decisions, however slow or fast he needed. To show her that she had messed up bad.

She watched the clock tick past eleven more minutes before Mr. Donnelley thudded downstairs. Damp, red-faced, and changed into an ugly tan-striped tracksuit. He plodded past Martha and into the dining room, his cell phone in hand, talking to himself.

"The mail, the mail. What the . . . ? Did we not get mail today?" He was peering into an empty basket on the console. He was standing so close to Martha that she could have stepped on his slippered foot.

"There." From her perch on the first step, Martha leaned forward and pointed across the hall to the coffee table in the darkened living room.

That's where the mail got dropped in her house.

Mr. Donnelley frowned as he noticed Martha. He lumbered into the living room. Martha watched him snatch up the stack of mail, cross the hall back into the dining room, and drop the whole bundle in the console's mail basket. Then he took all the mail out again to read, proving his point to nobody.

Picky, picky, thought Martha. That's the Donnelleys. Him *and* her. Maybe that's what made them marry each other. Or maybe one turned picky to copycat the other.

Mr. Donnelley ripped open envelopes and hardly read their contents. Soon, he had discarded the whole mess in the mail basket.

"Yes, I'm here!" he barked into the phone. "I've been holding for over three minutes. Hope this doesn't indicate how you guys handle emergencies!" There was grit in his voice. Mr. Donnelley was used to getting things done. Martha bet he was a mean dad or boss when he got angry. "I'd like to report a child who might be missing. Description? Um, stay right there. Let me put my wife on the line."

When the two police arrived in their squad car, the Donnelley house became a public place of banging doors, of heavy footsteps, of deep adult voices asking questions, of walkie-talkie static and blue lights swirling.

The police, Officer Mustache and Officer Bird Eyes, ordered the girls to come inside—"Too dangerous!"—and they asked them all the same things.

Who had seen Gray last?

Approximately when was Gray seen last?

What was the last thing Gray said?

Where did Gray say she was going?

Zoë talked the most, but Ty had the most answers. He said Gray had left the family room to get some juice the same minute the car Fiori Dulce passed Renata in the Daytona 500.

"It's a rerun, but we can still pinpoint that time," said Officer Bird Eyes, making a note in her book.

Martha's own secret squeezed her stomach. Should she tell the police about that lady by the mailbox? No, no, not now. The right moment would come. Besides, it was fun to have a secret. It was fun to hold her secret like a chocolate heart melting in her mouth.

"Look, guns!" said Leticia, pointing to the holsters as the officers went upstairs to talk to Mr. and Mrs. Donnelley privately, in the den.

"My dad owns a gun," Serena admitted softly.

"Mine, too," lied Martha, trying to imagine her bookworm father with a gun dangling from his soft hand.

"Rugrats, listen up," said Topher. "Cops say you have to stay put and all together. So we're gonna camp out here in the dining room. You leave only with special permission, and only for, like, the bathroom. Got it? 'Cause we don't know if there's, y'know, someone . . ." His eyes darted to the window, to the parked police car alive with light and scratchy sound.

"Gray is ruining my party!" Caitlin burst out. "I'm sick of looking for her and thinking about her!"

"Me, too," added Kristy.

"Wow. If your friend got, like, *hit* by a *bus* and is lying in some, like, *hospital* room, *unconscious* and *bleeding,*" Topher answered, "then I personally will go sit beside her bed and wait for her to wake up. So that I can be the first one to tell her how *you guys* said she, like, *ruined* your party. Some friends *you* are. *Brats,* more like. Now who wants pizza? Plain or pepperoni?" He pointed to Leticia. "Plain or pepperoni? Let's go!"

"I'm lactose intolerant," said Leticia. She had not looked at Martha once since she had come inside. Not once. Leticia was being a pain. A real fun-wrecker, and all over such a tiny thing as cheating.

"The pizza's cold," said Serena.

"I'm not hungry," added Zoë.

Martha said, "Lemonade and pepperoni."

Topher snapped his fingers and pointed at her in a way that

made Martha blush. "Take an example from this kid. One lemonade, one slice of pepperoni, coming up. If it's too cold, give it to me and I'll stick in it the microwave."

Girls glanced uncertainly at Martha and then began to sit down, spreading their laps with pink napkins as Topher opened the pizza boxes on the sideboard. He used a spatula to carry and slide the first piece onto Martha's plate. He poured her lemonade. Martha said thank you and took a huge bite to show the rest of them how easy it was.

One by one, the other girls asked for orange, grape, or lemonade. For plain or pepperoni. Leticia peeled cheese off her slice without a word. Nobody said that the pizza was too cold, although it was.

Topher moved around them like a hasty waiter, the type Martha's parents would complain about. He removed Gray's place setting, slapping the paper cup and plate on the sideboard.

When Mrs. Donnelley returned to the dining room, Martha could tell she had been crying. Her eyes had that salted look. With a wobbling arm, she picked up the grape soda bottle, found an empty pink cup, and aimed.

"The police say that Gray has probably wandered off on her own adventure and will be back soon," said Mrs. Donnelley, rocking the bottle up and down so that the liquid tipped out in small spurts. "The one officer said it happens all the time! It's only been maybe two hours at the most. Silly girl! I don't know what I'll do when I see her again. Hug her very tight, I guess!

Very tight! Who wanted this cup of grape soda? Oops, maybe I poured it for myself!"

She laughed and took a sip. Mrs. Donnelley thought she had them fooled, but she didn't fool Martha, even as she forced the birthday party to continue.

"Cake time!" she sang.

She carried out Caitlin's candlelit pink cake and started the girls singing "Happy Birthday" and she didn't let Caitlin blow out the candles because Caitlin was just getting over a cold and nobody wanted germs, right, girls? Then she returned the cake to the pantry for Topher to cut and serve, and she set the tray of presents from the sideboard in front of Caitlin.

"Open mine! Open mine!" the other girls begged.

Martha did not want Caitlin to open hers. She squeezed out of her seat and trailed Mrs. Donnelley back into the pantry.

"Stan Rosenfeld works in the city, I just got hold of him and he's on his way," Martha overheard Mrs. Donnelley say in a low voice to Topher. "He thinks Lenora took Robby to an early movie and dinner, so nobody's at the Rosenfelds' house right now. He's going to get a neighbor over in the event Gray shows up there. Oh, dear lord, if something happened to that child, nobody will ever forgive . . ."

Mrs. Donnelley bumped against Martha as she swung around the corner, a pink plate of pink cake in each hand. She blinked. "Martha, what are you doing in here? Go sit down," she chided. "It's almost time for presents."

Martha scowled. Her mother had bought Caitlin's birthday present, and it was sort of stupid. A green velvet beret and matching mittens. But her mother preferred practical gifts to toys, and she had said it was either the beret-and-mittens set or a giant leather-bound *Complete Works of Shakespeare.*

"Mom! That's, like, a present that a teacher would give!" Martha had protested.

"Oh, Martha. If your sister Jane were as critical as you, I'd be at my wit's end." Her mother had flopped her pocketbook on the counter. "Let's take the hat set, then. It's absolutely adorable and it's on sale. End of story."

At the time, Martha had been relieved that her mother had not tried to push the Shakespeare book. But the hat-and-mittens set was not a good present, either.

Right this very moment, it seemed especially bad. Totally *unc.* And with Leticia acting all nasty tonight, Martha knew there was a chance she might get teased for it. Martha preferred to be the tease-r, not the other way around.

She waited until Mrs. Donnelley went upstairs to join Mr. Donnelley and the police. Caitlin had just opened Kristy Kiss-up's gift, three CDs and a bottle of SPF 30 glitter sunscreen.

The other girls ooohed, how expensive, how nice!

Topher's cell phone rang and he stepped into the kitchen to take the call in private.

Martha slipped out of her seat and followed him.

I have to go to the bathroom, she mouthed.

Topher put his hand on the mouthpiece. "Use the one down here."

She nodded, then left swiftly through the pantry and raced upstairs. She sneaked past the den, pausing a moment to listen in on what was being said behind the closed door. In voices soft and overlapping, the police and Mr. and Mrs. Donnelley were talking about assembling a search party, about who else to notify, about what to do and what not to do.

". . . keep the little girls together until their parents come for them," said one of the officers.

"Yes, yes. Topher has it under control," squeaked Mrs. Donnelley.

They were being sent home? Tonight? Ha ha ha. Some party. Oh, this would be a good one to hold over Caitlin. How her birthday party was the worst one of the year. Martha smiled to herself and took a lively hop hop hop down the hall.

The Donnelley house was boring for exploring. It did not have secrets. The lights burned too high for shadows and the wastepaper baskets were empty. Inside every closet that Martha opened, the hangers faced the same way and the clothes hung straight and unwrinkled.

In the master bedroom, Martha discovered that Mrs. Donnelley's closet was sorted by color. Pale to dark, then prints, with hatboxes on top and a partitioned shelf to house each pair of shoes. Martha rearranged a few pairs with their wrong mates.

Mr. Donnelley's closet had plenty more ugly tracksuits. Maybe he thought tracksuits made him look young and athletic, and disguised the fact that he was too old for Mrs. Donnelley? Nice try, thought Martha. He looked especially old in their wedding picture, compared with Mrs. Donnelley, whose hair was like black silk while he had about three strands left. Gross. Why had Mrs. Donnelley picked him?

She placed the wedding picture facedown on the nightstand.

It was inside the cedar chest at the foot of the Donnelleys' bed, underneath the neatly folded squares of sweaters, that Martha found her treasure. A cellophane package of mothballs, delicate as spun sugar candies.

Aha!

She knew mothballs were seriously poisonous. One of Martha's first memories was of her mother uncurling her fingers to pry out a mothball like a pearl from its shell. Then cuffing both Martha's hands under the running faucet.

"Never, ever! Where is your sense, Martha?"

Martha ripped out a Kleenex from Mrs. Donnelley's bedside table, then she opened the package. The sweet, acrid smell burst into the air. Making pincers of her fingers, she pronged and dropped a single mothball into the Kleenex, then folded it neatly. Stole down the hall into Caitlin's room, where she tucked the packet in the zip pocket of her carryall bag.

She smiled as she zipped her bag. It was fun to sneak around, mess with things, claim tiny souvenirs. She liked to think of the dopey Donnelleys puzzling over the turned-over wedding picture, the mismatched shoes, and the ripped cellophane package.

Where is your sense, Martha?

Her parents both liked sense, and so did her big sister, Jane. All they did was read, read, read. They never did anything. It was always up to Martha to do the fun things, to shake things up and flip them upside down, even if it meant getting into trouble. Martha was usually willing to risk trouble over sense. That's why she was the head of the Lucky Seven.

In Caitlin's bathroom, Martha scrubbed the smell of stinky mothballs from her hands. Then she sat on the bath mat and waited until she was sure that her present was unwrapped and done with.

Leticia

"Martha's not here because she got you a lick present."

Leticia was guessing, but she bet it was true. Mrs. Van Riet was a mom who purchased practical gifts. Mrs. Van Riet was practical to a fault, and completely preoccupied with health. Whenever Leticia stayed over at Martha's, there was always a salad plus a vegetable and boring juice Popsicles for dessert. Mrs. Van Riet was also the only mother Leticia knew who had taped little *x*es on the rug to show how far away you were supposed to sit from the television. Mr. Van Riet was no better, either, always layering Martha against the cold and telling her about how scientific studies proved that sunlight and dyed food were potentially deadly.

"Quick, open it!" Leticia said. She thumped her fist on the table.

"Open it!"

"Open it!"

"Open it!"

Caitlin clawed at the wrapping paper.

"What is it? What did she give you?" Leticia craned forward.

With the tips of her fingers, Caitlin held up a green velvet beret and a pair of matching mittens attached by a string.

"Mittens!" Exaggeratedly, Leticia slapped a hand over her mouth.

Serena laughed. "Who wears mittens, right?" she asked softly, looking over at Leticia and shaking back her hair.

"God, that is so cheap," whispered Kristy, sliding her eyes at Caitlin. "That must have cost the least amount of any of our presents."

"No kidding." Zoë's voice was quiet, too. Leticia knew that it was because nobody wanted to risk the chance of Martha overhearing.

The dare rushed through her and made her talk loud. "Hey, you guys, let's call Martha *Meow,*" she suggested. "You know, like, because of the three little kittens who lost their mittens?"

The others looked at Leticia and giggled and then looked around at one another. Rarely did they gang up on Martha. Usually they spent their time trying not to land on the wrong end of one of Martha's jokes.

"All of us have to call her that, or it won't work," coaxed Leticia. "C'mon. It'll be funny."

Kristy picked up the mittens. "Meow, meow, meow," she said. "I can do a good meow, I don't even move my lips and I sound just like a cat, listen."

Through tensed, slightly parted lips, she made tiny mewing noises, and the others agreed she sounded exactly, completely like a cat.

"You should do that when Martha's around," said Leticia. "You're so good at it. Nobody can even tell it's you. I *dare* you."

Kristy looked nervous.

"I double-dare you," said Caitlin.

That did it. Kristy agreed with a nod.

Martha came back into the dining room.

"Hey, where've you been, *Meow?*" quipped Leticia. Stifled laughter sounded around the table.

Martha gave Leticia a look. Leticia returned it, dead-on, although her heart tripped fast and frightened. She had never played a trick on Martha before.

Until now. Waves of angry thought chopped at her. How could Ms. Calvillo be so blind? Martha never, ever put effort into science class. An A plus was such obvious cheating! Leticia set her chin and tried not to let her face betray her. She wondered why she cared so much. Maybe it was because she had studied so hard and only got a B plus. Or maybe she was just sick of Martha, sick of her traitor's jokes, sick of laughing along.

"Kiddos!" barked Topher, clapping his hands as he reentered through the kitchen. "Clear your plates. Grown-ups are taking over the main floor, and we're going downstairs to watch movies. But first, everyone into the kitchen to help Caitlin's mom call your parents."

"Why are we calling parents?" asked Caitlin. "Is my party ending? Gray is coming back soon, I know it. My party shouldn't end just because Gray left for a little while!"

"My party shouldn't end!" Ty mimicked in a squeaky voice.

"You're dead!" Caitlin grabbed him from behind and they both crashed to the floor, scratching and yanking at each other. Leticia watched. She was glad she had an older sister instead of a little brother.

"Kitchen, kitchen," Topher ordered. Then he began pulling at Caitlin and Ty. "Can't we call peace between you two for one lousy second?" he growled as he heaved them apart.

Leticia jumped up from her seat and herded through the door into the kitchen with the others. She took care to keep away from Martha.

The kitchen was crowded with the unfamiliar faces of the Donnelleys' neighbors. From outside came voices, people joining forces to organize in small search parties. Scouting, shouting, talking on phones, counting off into car caravans, sounding off opinions that rattled in Leticia's ears—"What could have happened to her?" "Oh, please! Nothing, *nothing* bad ever happens in this neighborhood." "She could have gone . . .

where would she have gone?" "And we're sure they've checked the whole house?" "The basement? Everywhere? Everywhere?"

Most parents were not available. Mrs. Donnelley kept leaving messages.

Leticia's mom and dad were in Key West at a conference until Sunday. Leticia listened to Mrs. Donnelley explain the situation to her family's housekeeper, Mrs. Grange. "Leticia is perfectly welcome to stay until tomorrow, and then I'll take her home," said Mrs. Donnelley in her best phony hostess voice. "But we want to notify everyone of the . . . situation."

Leticia knew she was staying because Mrs. Grange did not know how to drive.

Kristy's mom was out to dinner with her boyfriend.

Martha's parents were out of state, at a bed-and-breakfast. Leticia heard Martha tell Mrs. Donnelley that she did not know the name of it. Leticia had a hunch this was a lie, but Mrs. Donnelley was too upset and distracted to question her.

Zoë's mom was playing violin with the city orchestra tonight. Her dad was in the audience with his cell phone turned off.

Serena's parents were home. They said they would be right over.

Topher counted heads like duck-duck-goose. Then he led the girls and Ty from the kitchen back downstairs to the family room.

"It's still my birthday party, and I still pick *Titanic,*" squawked Caitlin, spreading her arms across the television screen as if to protect it from another choice of movie. "Topher, it's in the rack. Will you put it on?"

Ty made two thumbs down and started to boo. Topher swatted him. "Yo, it's still your sister's night tonight, Ty, so cool your jets."

Topher stood in front of them, spinning the *Titanic* disk on his finger. He had a way of doing things in a careless, college-ish way. All at once, Leticia was overwhelmed with a sharp, aching wish to see her sister. A desire to run as fast as she could out of the Donnelleys' house, across three states, straight to Celeste's campus and dormitory and into the security of her arms. Too much about tonight was out of place. Celeste would know how to make things right again.

"Here's the rules," Topher said. "Pay attention 'cause it's just three words. Everybody Stay Put." Topher's eyes moved to Ty. "And the men are gonna watch this movie and like it. It's that or bed."

"Aww . . ." Ty rolled onto the floor and propped his chin in his elbows.

Titanic was so boring, especially since Leticia had seen it a thousand times. She suppressed a sigh as she curled up in the armchair and opened her goody bag. Other girls dropped onto the couch or carpet. Bumpo's eyes followed Leticia's fingers as she poked a chocolate into her mouth. She took out another chocolate and stealthily dropped it to the rug. Bumpo gulped it down happily.

"*Titanic* is crap," Martha muttered, lifting her head from where she was stretched under the coffee table.

Leticia leaned forward. "Wow, I can't believe you said that!" she exclaimed. "Criticizing Caitlin's favorite movie on her birthday. Sheez!"

"Yeah, Mar," Serena agreed, flipping her hair. "What's your problem?"

Martha scowled. "Sor-ry. But at least I'm not trying to make my friend's dog sick by feeding him chocolate. You might as well give him poison, Leticia. Don't you know anything about dogs? Chocolate is potentially deadly to canines." She sounded just like her father, Leticia thought.

But Caitlin turned and shot Leticia a look of exasperation. "Yeah, Martha's right. Don't feed Bumpo chocolate," she said, while Ty jumped up and began to pry open Bumpo's jaws.

"He already ate it," Ty announced.

"Nice going, Leticia," said Martha.

"I didn't mean to," Leticia mumbled, careful to avoid Martha's eyes and the tiny gleam of triumph she knew would be shining in them.

Topher's cell phone rang. He picked it up and edged to the back of the room, sliding into the beanbag chair. Leticia listened.

"Yo, dude! Uh-uh. Not a trace, and we're going on, like, three hours. Aw, dude, I can't come *out*. We got cops here!" Topher's whisper cracked with excitement.

The movie's sound was turned up loud, but voices made a constant static above. Leticia could hear that Mrs. Rosenfeld had arrived with Gray's little brother, Robby. Then she thought she heard Mr. Rosenfeld's voice, too, along with the more distant scratch of police shortwaves.

We are like the Enchanted Castle princesses, thought Leticia. We are trapped here in the dungeon while real things in the real world are spinning all around us.

A few minutes later, Serena's parents arrived, chattering, jostling down the stairs behind Mrs. Donnelley, and making so much fuss that Caitlin had to press PAUSE.

Serena stumbled to her feet, reluctant. "I don't wanna . . ." she began. But Mr. Hodgson pulled her up in his arms while Mrs. Hodgson touched Serena's nose, her cheeks, her hair, to reassure herself that all the princess pieces of lovely Serena were here.

They were overprotective, those Hodgsons, half-crazy with parent love. Like that time when Serena fell in gymnastics competition, Leticia remembered, how they swept in from the audience and scooped her up and away like she was made out of stars and glass.

Her own mom and dad were different. They had raised Celeste and Leticia to be independent. They weighed and balanced and related everything back to The Law, to Ethics and Conduct and Responsibility. "Figure it out," Leticia's mom liked to say. "It's your life. You live with your decisions, and you should be prepared to defend them."

The Hodgsons held a parent net to catch Serena every time. Now Leticia watched them cling to her. Then Mrs. Hodgson turned to Mrs. Donnelley. "It's *late.* Shouldn't the girls be in bed? Some are staying the night, isn't that correct?"

"Yes, yes, yes." Mrs. Donnelley sounded defeated. Her mother power was gone since she had lost Gray. She was not being who she liked to be—a show-off perfect mother. A mother who said, "Caitlin, you really need a hair trim!" or "Caitlin, let's get you some new sneakers because your other ones are absolutely, positively *shot.*"

Ha, ha, thought Leticia.

After Mrs. Donnelley and the Hodgsons went upstairs, Zoë said, "Maybe the Hodgsons came because they want to take Serena far away and safe from the kidnapper. Like what happened to that other girl. Remember that story in the newspapers?"

"There's no kidnapper! Shut up!" Caitlin threw a pillow at Zoë's head.

"I was only thinking out loud," said Zoë.

"Yeah, but don't say stuff like that, Zoë. Just because Gray is missing *temporarily* doesn't mean that poor Caitlin's birthday party should be ruined." Kristy's voice was stern. "She'll probably be back any minute."

"Thanks, Kristy," said Caitlin in a sad little voice.

"That kidnapper was a man, though," said Martha. "Right, Zoë?" Leticia thought she detected worry or something like it in Martha's voice.

"Yeah, yeah, that's right. Remember?" Zoë sat up. "It was all over the news a while back, every channel, my mom was talking about it all the time, that horrible scary story about that girl—"

"Stop, Zoë, I swear, or I'll get nightmares!" yelled Caitlin.

"Hey, kids, lower your voices, how about?" called Topher from where he was, on another phone call.

"C'mon, everyone stop talking and play the movie." Leticia did not want to think about kidnappers, or worse. She thumped her fist like a gavel. "It's just getting good. It's about to start sinking."

The room hushed. Caitlin pressed PLAY and raised the volume.

From somewhere in the room came the sound of a cat meow.

"Did you hear that?" asked Martha after a moment.

Nobody answered.

"It sounds like a cat!"

Nobody said a word.

"Gee, you're all so funny, I forgot to laugh," said Martha with a yawn.

Kristy raised her mouth and eyebrows and looked over at Leticia, who smiled.

It was working. It was really working.

They were following Leticia. They were playing her game. Ignore-Martha-till-she-cries.

Only Martha never cried, did she?

Gray

The voice woke her.

"Kathy!" he said. "Kat. Get out here! Who is that kid?"

Gray opened her eyes to see a man standing in the middle of the room. From outside, she heard the rumble of a car driving away too fast.

Kathy, Kat. That was Katrina.

The man, who must be Drew, was not much older than Topher. He was small, heavy-boned, and fattish around his middle. Not as nice-looking as Topher. No, not at all, with that bumpy pink skin and those gluey, oyster-blue eyes. His hair straggled over his ears and a plum-colored tattoo of a swan marked the upper half of one of his arms. Then Gray saw it was a birthmark.

In a fairy tale, Drew would not have been the handsome prince, but he might have been the tailor's apprentice or the cook's apprentice. The jolly, foolish man who somewhere along the way has helped the unlucky princess. Who, as a reward at the end of the story, gets to work at the palace.

Drew did not look very jolly right now. He looked angry and confused.

Katrina shuffled from the bedroom as Gray sat up and wiped some drool from her cheek.

Drew turned. “Kat?” he drawled. “Who’s the girl, Kat?”

“My name is Gray Rosenfeld,” said Gray. “It’s time for me to go home.”

“Who? Who is this? You know this kid?” Drew kept steering his questions in Katrina’s direction.

“She’s from my party,” Katrina answered primly. “Which, as it turned out, wasn’t my party after all. I couldn’t find my party.”

“Party? Kat, we’ve been through this. I’ll have a party for you when we’re more settled. Next week, maybe.”

Katrina clenched her fists in her lap. “You told me whenever I wanted it. You promised . . . and I thought you were tricking me when you left this afternoon! I thought I was supposed to come find you!”

“Find me? I said a thousand times I was going out with Tony for a while. I had some errands, I said. I *told* you.” Drew’s drawl was dropping into a low grumble.

Katrina did not say anything. So Gray recited her address and her phone number and her mother’s car phone number and her mother’s cell phone number and her father’s work number and her father's cell phone number. She was halfway through Caitlin's address when Drew interrupted her.

"Okay, okay." He held up a hand for Gray to stop. "I'll take you home. My girlfriend, Kat, she's a little, you know . . ." He pulled his hand through his greasy hair. His feet were restless on the floor. They carried him a little bit here and then there. He turned to Katrina again. "You took the car and went out? Where to?"

"Oh, around. The store, and then some roads with houses. I thought I was supposed to find you."

Drew spun in a clumsy half circle and made a frustrated growling noise. "You said you'd stay here and wait for those guys to drop by. Did they come by while you were out?"

"How do I know if they came by while I was out? I was out! Why are you yelling at me? I hate it when you yell!" Although it was Katrina's voice that blared. She cupped her hands over her face and began to wag her head back and forth.

"And where'd you find her, this kid?"

"I stopped by the party and she came out with me. She wants to leave, but I don't know if I can drive any more."

Gray edged herself forward on the couch. She allowed herself to suck both ends of her thumbs, which she had been long trained against doing. She needed food. She needed to use the bathroom. She could feel panic crawling like invisible bugs on her skin, and she wished she knew her mother's yoga breathing tricks.

All her life, Gray had obeyed the rules of grown-ups. The rules were work hard, finish homework, be polite, volunteer, and play fair, and all the future rewards—happiness, safety, and a nice college—would be hers to enjoy.

Under these rules, Gray's entire life until her mother got sick had made sense. And even after the sickness, there were rules. New rules, some not as easy, but they existed just the same. They existed along with old rules, these new rules such as don't upset Mom and don't cry and be brave for Robby and keep it down and please no more crying and we all have to pull our weight around here, Gray! were harder to follow.

She did try, even though she wanted her old mom back. The livelier, more fun mom that she used to have. The mom who took Gray and Robby to SpaceRollers restaurant on Sunday nights, the mom who turned raking leaves in the backyard into a family game. That mom always wanted Gray and Robby to experience things. Taste this soup, Gray. More pepper, do you think? Listen, Gray. That's a jaybird. Look, look, Gray, up at the skywriter! Oh, Gray, can you smell that awful factory smoke? Peee-yew!

Before she got sick, she had been more radiant with life than any mom. Always she had led the way, waltzing ahead and doubling back, circling and coaxing Gray and Robby into the enchantment of what she saw and heard and knew.

Gray missed her old mom, but she respected the new rules.

Not one single rule in her life had prepared her for this night.

Gray looked from Drew to Katrina and back again. The two of them seemed to shine with a jittery energy. Gray could not see if these people had RIGHT or WRONG stamped across them. They were mixed-up and smeary. They blurred.

If a real grown-up were here, the grown-up would know what kind of danger might flood this house. Gray could not tell. She tried but she could not grasp it.

"I have to go to the bathroom," she said.

Drew pointed to the bathroom door. His eyes remained on Katrina.

"I can't believe you went out," he said. "I can't believe you took the car and went out. After what I told you. Did you run into anybody? Anyone you know?"

"No, nobody. I'm sorry I went out," Kat answered. "I didn't think you'd be mad." She did not sound very sorry. She sounded as if she were speaking to finish up the conversation.

Gray looked from Drew to Kat and back again. Searching for clues and rules.

Would they take her home? Would they hurt her?

She didn't know. She escaped to the bathroom and locked the door.

She stayed in the bathroom for a while, searching. There was nothing to find. In the medicine cabinet was a bottle of mouthwash, dental tape, a bottle of pills to stop burping. On the windowsill was an abandoned spiderweb in which was trapped a husk that might once have been a small fly. On the toilet tank was an air deodorizer in the shape of a sleeping unicorn. In the shower was a piece of soap worn thin as a tongue.

These people no they are not bad no because if these people were bad shouldn't there be more dangerous clues lying around?

She could lock the door and stay in this bathroom all night. She could sleep in the tub. Shut her eyes and wait for her parents to find her. Maybe they were already on her trail!

She climbed in the tub and hugged her arms around her knees. Closed her eyes and tried to transport herself to somewhere else.

Right at this moment, she bet Martha Van Riet was saying awful things about her. That's what Martha did whenever one of the group was not around. Last week, it had been Zoë who was absent, and Martha spent the whole day slamming her.

All those terrible things she said! Like, "I could put a leash on Zoë's eyebrows and walk them as pets, ha ha ha!" And, "Have you ever noticed how know-it-all Zoë talks like she's got a stick up her butt, ha ha ha!" And, "You know, once I heard a rumor that Zoë French-kissed a dog on a truth-or-dare last year at camp!"

Ha ha ha! Ha ha ha!

Everyone laughed and said no way and that's so gross, Mar, and everyone sort of came to Zoë's defense, but not really.

Now Martha was probably slamming her. Caitlin would be

over-ready to laugh about Gray, too, since Gray had wrecked her birthday party.

The bathroom was beginning to feel cramped and suffocating. From behind the door was silence. Had Drew and Katrina left the house? Left her behind? Was it safer that way, to be here in this house without them? Alone?

Gray emerged from the bathroom. She saw Katrina lying on the couch, the remote control in her hand. Drew was standing behind her, staring sulkily out the window and biting the edge of his thumb.

"I'm hungry," said Gray.

Katrina nodded. "Me, too."

"No, I mean, I'm really hungry."

"Me, too. I'd like some chickpeas and feta cheese."

"You don't understand. If I don't eat something, I might faint," said Gray.

Although she had never fainted in her life, not even when she stepped on a glass bottle on the beach and was taken to the hospital, where she got five stitches. That afternoon was scary. She'd thought she might faint plenty of times. When she saw flies land on her blood that spattered dark across the sand. When the doctor, meaning to be helpful, showed her the black stitching thread. When she caught sight of the metal butterfly clip that pinched the skin back into place.

But she had not fainted. Not once.

She was not about to faint now, either. But if Drew and Katrina refused to give her something to eat, then she might deduce some clues about them. That they were criminals or something.

"There's no food here," said Katrina.

Drew was making a slow lap of the room, peering out each frost-smudged window. "If they came by and didn't see the car, I guess they'll be back," he said.

"Do you have a cell phone?" Gray asked Drew politely. She tried to imagine what was happening at the Donnelley house. It was cake time, maybe. Or presents. She wished she had put on her watch this morning.

"Why, who do you want to talk to? You can't call anyone right now. I don't need to add you to my problems." Drew dismissed Gray with an impatient glare. "What are you saying, there's no food left, huh, Kat? There's gotta be something."

"Nope." Katrina shifted. "I looked already. Hand me that blanket?" She pointed to the blanket Gray had left on the floor by the front door.

Drew picked up the blanket and walked over to Katrina and dropped it on her in a heap. "What's that junk all over your face?"

Katrina touched her cheek and spoke in her baby-girl way. "The ladies made me up at the department store. They did it for free, for my party. They gave me a free lipstick, too. Mango Tango, it's called."

"Kat, for crying out loud! There is *no party!*"

"Well, I think that's a shame." Katrina pulled her arms over her head and yawned. "You know what? I'm going back to bed." She shook off the blanket, stood up from the couch, stretched, and touched her toes.

"I could go see if there's some food in the kitchen," Gray offered.

It was as if she had not spoken at all.

It was just like that mean game Martha and the others played against her.

Drew returned to looking out the window, and Katrina shuffled away to the bedroom.

Gray slipped into the kitchen and snapped on a light that popped and blew. Now the trickle from the living room was the kitchen's only illumination. She opened the rust-edged refrigerator and inside found a sandwich furry with mold, a sandwich bag filled with carrots and celery sticks, and a couple of cans of beer.

"Whatcha got?"

Gray jumped. Drew had crept up behind her.

"Nothing."

He reached past her and hefted a beer. "Kat wasn't joking," he said. He swiped the sandwich bag, too. "This'll do us."

Gray nodded. Together, they sat down at a table-and-chairs set that looked better suited to ornament a pool or patio area.

The chairs were padded with spongy cushions, and the plastic-topped table was thin and frail enough that Gray might have picked it up and moved it anywhere else.

"Check the cupboard." Drew cracked open the beer. "This is my, uh, buddy's place and they're out of town for the week. Which is why it's lean on supplies."

Gray thought Drew might be lying to her. Aside from the spiderweb and dead mouse in the trap, she had noticed a lot of dust around the house, too, in places where people who lived here would have wiped clean. Also, the rooms all had a mushroom smell. An odor of things that have sat too long in closed air.

She did not contradict, though. She did not want to make Drew angry. She stood on her toes to open the cupboard. She saw baking powder and chili powder, salt and pepper, vinegar, and a dented box of crackers. She pulled down the salt and vinegar and crackers. Maybe she could use the crackers to make a version of salt-and-vinegar potato chips? That might taste good. In another cupboard was a saucer that looked useful for dipping. She returned to sit at the table and she unscrewed the top to the vinegar.

"You want some crackers and dip?"

"Ymm," Drew said as he sipped his beer. He set the can on the table and studied her. "Gray Rosenfeld, right? Rosenfeld. That's Jewish. I got a couple of Jewish friends. But you don't look like any Rosenfeld I met."

"I was adopted," Gray answered promptly. She had been told and had told others that she was adopted ever since she could remember. "Jewish people come in all shapes and colors," she added. Someone had said this to her once. She pooled the vinegar into the saucer's center and floated a cracker like a small white raft on swamp water.

"Yeah, and you don't look like any Gray I know, either." Drew put a hand over one eye, then the other, studying Gray as if she were an eye chart. "Nah. I never met anyone named Gray. But if I did, she wouldn't look like you. Nope, no sirree."

"What do I look like, then?" she asked, although she was not sure if she was ready to know. Besides, she did not like Drew's tone.

"I dunno. Maybe like a half Chinese? Or Mongol? It's your eyelids, see. How they bend funny."

"They do not!" She could not resist touching her fingers to the outer corners of her eyelids, which felt the same as always.

"You're small, too. Like maybe you're stunted, huh? Where were you adopted from?" Drew leaned in on his elbows. "Some malnourished country?"

Gray used her pinkie to flip over the cracker. It was soaked with vinegar and its shape bloated. She could tell that it was not going to taste very good. "I don't know. Not from very far away. Not from another continent or anything. I'm American."

"You sure?" Drew took another sip. Gray wondered if he was trying to provoke her on purpose. "You were adopted in

America," he continued, pointing his finger at her. "That's all you know for certain. Right? But you could have come from anyplace else. Originally."

"My birth mother lives in America, in the Southwest. I'm allowed to contact her when I turn eighteen," Gray explained. "And, for your information, practically everyone in the United States comes from someplace else, *originally*."

"Everyone comes from someplace, sure. But *you* could come from *any*place." Drew sat back and winked. "Chew on that."

"I know who I am," said Gray. She was not upset, not really—Drew was being a bully, like how Topher sometimes acted to Caitlin and Ty—but she felt her eyes sting a little, as if to remind her that she could be sad if she wanted. "What about you? What's your last name?"

"Doe." Drew smiled as if this were a joke. "Brothers, sisters?"

"I've got a younger brother. He's seven."

"He's adopted?"

"No."

"Yep. That happens all the time."

"What? What happens?"

"You know, folks try to have a kid and they can't and so they adopt and then they're relaxed and that's when they end up having the kid they want. Their real kid."

"I'm their real kid."

"Okeydoke."

"I am!"

"Whatever you say. Whatever you say, whoever you are, Gray Rosenfeld." Drew smiled. His teeth looked mean. They were too square, each one identical to the next one over, like teeth soldiers at attention against her.

Gray decided she did not want to talk to Drew Doe anymore. He was sort of a jerk. Also, he was a stranger. She shouldn't be talking to him at all as a rule.

She lifted the dripping cracker and balanced it on the flat of her hand. Then she shook a little bit of salt on top. The cracker dissolved on her tongue. When she swallowed, it was as if it had never been there.

"How is your snack, by the way?" Drew asked. "Looks retarded." After a second, he said, "Oh, you're ignoring me now?" He sounded annoyed.

Maybe it wasn't a good idea to anger Drew.

"No. It tastes okay." She would be nice, but calm. Drew did not need to know that she was too-scared of him. "What's wrong with Kat?" she asked.

The question startled Drew more than she thought it would. "What did she tell you?"

"I've been around lots of sick people since my mom got cancer," said Gray honestly.

"Sorry to hear."

"You don't have to be sorry." Gray disliked when people said they were sorry and made pitying eyes at her. "She's getting well. She's in remission."

Drew opened his mouth to say something. Then he seemed to decide against it. He took a carrot stick and twirled it like a pen in his fingers.

"Kat's been my girlfriend so long that I can't remember when things were different with her, or even if they were. She's a nice girl, a normal girl, you know? I'm tired of everyone telling me what's wrong with her. Everyone's a critic. Let me tell you—there's a million things right with her! The situation is never black or white. I'm good for Kat. I take care of her."

"Has she been in the hospital? Is that why her hair's so short?"

"Naw, she's not sick that way. She tangles it when it's longer. Twists it in her fingers and before you know, she's got a knot in there the size of a rat. I bought her that wig for fun, see. To show it doesn't matter to me. 'Cause long or short, she's always my girl."

Drew eased back in his chair. He was speaking to Gray and yet he seemed to have forgotten she was there. "When I visited her last time, we put on the radio and danced. She loves music. That's when it hit me, how right we are, us. She's always better when she's with me." Drew pointed a finger on Gray. "I got what we need for a fresh start. Away from the critics." His hand winged the air. "From now on it's me and Kat and nobody standing in our path. We're taking off."

"Okay." Gray squared her shoulders. "As long as you drop me home before you go. I live less than half an hour from here.

But I could walk partways, if you're in a hurry. I really want to go home, see. I need to. Please."

Drew smiled wide, a wolf smile, and shook his head. "Little Gray Rosenfeld, you're the last thing I need to slow me down." He stood up, tipped back his head to finish the beer, and then shook free a carrot stick from the bag.

"Maybe you could drop me home now?" she asked. "People are wondering, I think."

"Don't worry your little head about it. You let me do the planning. I'm gonna check up on Kat," said Drew. "Meantime, sit tight. Those are orders. Do not wander off."

She would not wander off. Where was she supposed to go?

Drew was intimidating, though, the way he liked being the boss so much, showing off.

Saying those are orders holding rules over me for the fun of it just to be nasty to be a bully.

Martha

Topher seemed restless. He had finished his phone calls and he wanted to go up where the action was. Martha could tell. She was restless, too.

"Rugrats!" he said finally. "I'll be right back. You know the drill. The three magic words are . . . ?"

Nobody answered him. Everyone was absorbed in the end of the movie. Topher frowned and muttered, "Everybody stay put." Then he took the stairs, two at a time.

Martha waited a few minutes, then stood.

"Drink of water," she murmured with a yawn. "Does anyone want anything?"

Nobody answered. Were they playing a game on her? Martha's pulse quickened. Everyone was acting weird tonight. Probably it didn't mean anything. Probably it was because of Gray.

Martha crept quietly up the stairs, across the hall and into the pantry, her spy nook. Through a chink of opened door, she had a view of the kitchen. Still crowded. Some neighbors. Officer Bird Eyes and Officer Mustache. The Donnelleys. Mr. and Mrs. Rosenfeld were sitting at the table. Gray's little brother, Robby, was flopped like a sack of potatoes on Mr. Rosenfeld's lap.

"She might have needed some time to be by herself," Mrs. Rosenfeld was saying. "Gray does that. This past year has been a challenge for us, but Gray, poor thing, she's taken it very hard. I could understand if she wandered off. Gray isn't irresponsible. Emotional, but not irresponsible. But truly, Officer, I don't think forgetting her coat means—no, no, I don't think it means anything."

Mrs. Rosenfeld's sickness had stretched lines across her forehead and pressed folds into the sides of her mouth. Her eyes were sunken into fleshy skin flaps. If people had not known Mrs. Rosenfeld before she got sick, thought Martha, they might have thought she was a grouch.

Mrs. Rosenfeld did not look like Gray, but Gray had inherited other things from her, Martha decided. Gray possessed her mother's tame manners; the same way of sitting with her hands cupped over her knees, the same way of lifting the end of a sentence so that it sounded like a question. Anyone could see that Mouse and Mrs. Rosenfeld belonged to the same family.

"Listen," Officer Mustache answered. "We've got a search

on, but we can't do as much as we want until daybreak Tomorrow's weather is forecast for clear, and by then we'll have an aerial watch, the best dogs. We've got precincts eleven through fifteen combining forces. If she's run off, we'll find her. . . ."

"For God's sakes, where were you, Patsy?" asked Mr Donnelley, turning on Mrs. Donnelley as if she had invented this problem all on her own. "When she left. Where were *you?*"

"I was . . . I was upstairs." Mrs. Donnelley cleared her throat

"Upstairs? For how long? Did it ever cross your mind to go *downstairs?* Any one of those girls might have—"

"Whoawhoa. No need to get into that." Now Officer Bird Eyes stood. She was walking straight toward Martha. "Coffee-pot is out here, right, ma'am? Mind if I help myself?"

The coffeepot was in the pantry.

Quickly, Martha ducked and fled on tiptoes into the living room. Hiding by the front window, concealed behind a curtain she pressed her palms, nose, and forehead against the cold glass. She looked over the smooth lawn, at the pink balloons bobbing from the mailbox like baby-doll heads, at the strong alarm-coded, motion-sensored stone columns at the base of the driveway.

Right there, that was where she had seen the lady. That was where her secret happened.

She could walk into the kitchen and tell them about the lady right now.

No, not now. It's my secret, she told herself. Another thing had started to bother her, though, ever since Zoë had brought up kidnappers. Maybe the secret was too big? Maybe she had held on to it too long? What if she got in trouble? That was no good. Martha did not want to be trapped shamefully in the Donnelleys' kitchen, making excuses to police and parents, while Leticia led the party without her.

She would wait until the other girls had gone to sleep. Then she would let the police in on her secret and deal with all those questions. Yes, that's what she would do.

Martha moved from behind the curtain and tipped her head back to gaze at her own reflection in the window. In the darkened glass, her freckles did not show. Her face appeared to float in mist, ghostly, like a drowned girl.

What if something bad already was happening to Gray?

"You!"

Martha turned. Topher was standing at the door, pointing at her. "Get yourself downstairs, runaway rugrat. Everybody stay put, remember? You gotta understand, kid, this isn't a game."

Zoë

"Where is she? No kidding, I mean. Where do you think Gray went?" asked Zoë as they hopped around Caitlin's bathroom and bedroom, taking turns brushing their teeth and changing into their pajamas. The question had begun to bother Zoë. She had been so sure she would find Gray. She had been so sure that Gray would be there in the night, waiting for Zoë to scoop her up like another prize.

Now it was too late. The movie was finished and it was bedtime. And with Serena gone, they were down to a Lucky Five.

"Hmm, I bet she went for a long walk and got lost," said Caitlin airily. "I really hope nothing, y'know, *happened* to her. But if it turns out she went for a walk, I guess we're going to be pretty mad at her on Monday at school."

"Maybe she got taken by some*thing,*" said Zoë. She chewed on her pinkie, her last nail left. Her parents would be upset to see her nail nubs tomorrow. Tonight she had undone two full weeks of not biting them. "A friendly something. Like a space alien. Or a shape-shifter. A friendly shape-shifter, though."

"Or maybe she went outside and she met somebody interesting in the neighborhood, and she's watching a movie over at her—over at that person's house," said Martha. "Gray has body odor, anyhow. Did anyone ever notice that?"

Kristy started to giggle.

"Oh, that's a super-cool thing for you to say, Martha, if something terrible happened to her. If she's *dead* or something," said Leticia.

Kristy stopped giggling.

Zoë looked at Leticia, whose eyes sparked with outrage. But Leticia knew how nasty Martha could be, Zoë thought. Everyone did. Why did Leticia seem ready to pounce on Martha for every little thing tonight? The others could feel it, too. Zoë was sure. Leticia's thrusts against Martha had thrown an uncertain voltage into the air.

"She's not dead," said Martha. "Don't be an idiot."

"Listen. Caitlin's right. Gray went for a long walk is all," said Kristy smoothly.

"Everybody better quit talking about it or I won't be able to fall asleep," Caitlin added. "I'm too wide-awake as it is. I know! Let's listen to one of my new CDs. We'll put it on quiet so people don't hear."

"And I'll be the judge," said Martha. "I'll rate the best dancing."

Zoë liked that idea. It was time for a new game.

Caitlin tore open with her front teeth one of her vacuum-packed birthday CDs and dropped it into her sound system. Soon the music had everyone dancing. All around the bedroom and in and out of the bathroom. Crowding and pushing and twirling and laughing and shoving and bumping and toppling against one another, leaving footprints on the fluffy pink carpet.

"Pretend you're at their concert!" cried Kristy. "Pretend you're at their concert and you're in the front row where they can see you!"

Like butterflies, they bounced and flapped their hands and watched themselves in Caitlin's large dressing-table mirror and her floor-length closet mirror and her bathroom mirror, pretending.

Zoë used her first-place breaststroke movements and kicked her legs. She was strong, she would dance with the most energy even if she wasn't the best. Endurance was how she won against Shelton—holding her breath the longest or staying in the pool the longest, right up until the moment he said how stupid this was, how it was just an immature kid game, which was his way of giving up. Shelton was a sore loser. Zoë guessed she was, too, but she couldn't help it. Winning got all the attention.

Martha sat cross-legged on Caitlin's bed and watched and judged.

"What are you girls *doing?*" Mrs. Donnelley's voice was so low that she hardly sounded like herself.

Zoë froze, startled. She watched as Mrs. Donnelley dashed across the room and snapped off the music.

"Mom! Don't! Every time my party starts to get fun, it's ruined!" Caitlin wailed. "Gray wouldn't want my party spoiled just because she's not here to enjoy it!"

"No, no. No, no." Mrs. Donnelley shook her head. She went to Caitlin and hugged her. "Now is not the right time for fun, not while Gray is missing. Everyone must cooperate. Let's get you girls in your sleeping bags. Kristy and Zoë, your parents will come for you tonight, but I don't know what time exactly. Until then, I think that the best thing to do is to settle down."

Something in Mrs. Donnelley's eyes scared Zoë, and the truth hit her hard, the way it always did. Gray had disappeared outside of people's reach, outside of rescue. This was not a game to give up when everyone got tired of looking. Gray was gone, really gone, and she might be in real trouble.

Zoë counted back. Five hours was too long a time to be lost. "I guess I *am* tired," she said suddenly. It seemed like a helpful thing to say.

"That's right, Zoë, thank you, yes." Mrs. Donnelley looked grateful. She tucked Caitlin into her bed as the others followed Zoë's lead and zipped themselves up into their sleeping bags.

"Good night and sleep tight, girls," said Mrs. Donnelley, giving Caitlin's bed a final pat. She went to the door and put her hand on the light switch. "Of course I'm certain that Gray is perfectly safe and fine, but she is . . . *misplaced* right now, and she might be scared. Why don't each of you say a loving prayer for her? Asking her to find her way home. I know it would mean a lot to Mr. and Mrs. Rosenfeld and Robby."

She clicked off the light and left the room, closing the door behind her. After a few seconds, Caitlin slid out of her bed onto the floor.

"I've got my flashlight right here." She snapped it on. The others sat up. Their shadows pulled up like dark flames against the wall.

"Arrr-oooh!" howled Kristy softly. She used her hand to make a shadow-puppet wolf. "Hey, Martha. Who won the dancing?"

There was a moment of silence. "Leticia did," said Martha.

Zoë scowled. Unfair! Martha only said that to get on Leticia's good side. Which was strange, actually, considering how Leticia had been acting awful to her tonight.

Was Martha scared of Leticia or something?

"No, I didn't. *Kristy* won. For real," said Leticia as if it were obvious. "She's the best dancer of us by a million. I mean, Kristy's been taking ballet since she was, like, five years old!"

Kristy coughed. "Since I was three," she said.

"If I won, that would be called *cheating*," said Leticia. "Right, Martha?"

"Cheating, like how Kristy wanted to cheat so Caitlin would win Enchanted Castle?" countered Martha.

"What are you talking about, Martha?" asked Caitlin.

"Yeah, what are you talking about?" echoed Kristy.

"Nothing. Forget it," said Martha. Leticia shrugged.

Zoë stayed quiet, but her mind whirled.

Leticia against Martha. Martha against Leticia.

The Lucky Seven was breaking up.

If it's Leticia against Martha, thought Zoë in a sudden pull of panic, which side am I on?

"This is bad for Gray, I guess," said Kristy, turning to Caitlin and changing the subject, "if your mom wants us to pray for her."

Caitlin nodded. "Yeah, my mom's not really into praying except at Thanksgiving and stuff."

"Can a not-Jewish person say a prayer for a Jewish person?" asked Leticia.

"I think you can say a prayer for anyone as long as they're American," answered Kristy.

"And Gray isn't really Jewish, stupid," said Martha. "She was adopted."

"Don't say Leticia's stupid," Caitlin reprimanded. "Besides, everyone knows Jewish parents only adopt Jewish babies."

"Yeah, I'm not stupid, *Meow,*" said Leticia.

"Leticia, why are you calling me *Meow?*" asked Martha, her voice casual but cold.

"Because you're the little kitten who lost her mittens!" Leticia answered gleefully. Kristy and Caitlin burst into shrill peals of quickly smothered laughter.

Zoë chewed her pinkie nail nub and glanced at Leticia. Why? Why was she doing this?

In daylight, Leticia was so dark that Zoë could always spot her first. In the cafeteria, in the gym wearing her white-and-gold Fielding Athletic uniform, tall Leticia's black skin seemed to make anybody who stood next to her appear that much paler.

By flashlight, though, Leticia's eyes jumped out of the darkness, the black pupil defined against the orchid-petal whites.

Leticia, the shape-shifter. Black-and-white eyes staring Martha down.

Would the group split down the middle? And if it did, how would everyone team up, and which half would be better?

Who was Luckier? Martha or Leticia?

Right now Zoë felt too tired, too perplexed. She would have to wait and see. She would rely on her special, extrasensory perception, because it was important to get this answer right.

"Maybe we should do a séance," she suggested. "Maybe that's how we figure out what happened to Gray."

"A séance. What's that again?" asked Kristy.

"That's when you hold hands and try to raise the spirit of

the departed. But first we need to make a shrine using things that belong to that person," Zoë explained. "To provide a way for Gray to communicate."

"You can only do a séance if a person is dead," said Martha flatly. "Which Gray isn't."

"No, but if, like, if she's in trouble, or got abducted even, then we could be the first to know," said Zoë.

"Abducted," Martha scoffed.

"Is a séance like playing Ouija board?" asked Caitlin.

"Except there's no board. You have to channel the person through your own powers. Like them." Martha grabbed the flashlight from Caitlin and pointed it on the wall at Caitlin's picture of the fairies and monsters. Zoë shivered. She never liked that picture. It did not fit with the other pretty things in Caitlin's room.

"No, that's not . . . they're only . . . come on, stop it!" Caitlin exclaimed. "We don't know for a fact that anything's happened to Gray. We shouldn't, like, hex her! I vote no séance!"

"Me, too!" said Kristy. "No séance, no way!"

"I vote yes to the séance," said Martha. She smirked at Zoë, as if she knew something that Zoë didn't.

"I'm tiebreaker," said Leticia. "And I vote no. A séance is creepy."

"Three against two. Sorry, Zoë. Sorry, *Meow!* I've had enough." Caitlin snapped off her flashlight and jumped up to go back to her bed. "Ouch! I just tripped on something." The flashlight snapped on again. "What is that?"

The other girls looked.

It was Gray's sleeping bag.

"If I were you, I'd take it as a sign," said Zoë. "Gray wants us to contact her. Please, let me try. Just for a minute, please? Please?"

Gray

Today was Friday the thirteenth, Gray remembered. Tomorrow would be Valentine's Day. What did that mean, to have a day of bad luck right before a day of hearts and candy?

She dipped a celery stick into the saucer of vinegar. She had stayed in the kitchen after Drew left. He had said don't go anywhere and so she didn't, even though she had been alone here for a long, long time. She felt the tears in her eyes but she did not spill them. She must keep hold of whatever bravery she had. That was always a good rule, although it seemed impossible, a joke, as if she'd slipped Robby's toy pirate knife into her pocket.

Even with the vinegar, the food tasted like nothing. Hardly any taste at all. It was like dipping food into the sea. She leaned back in her chair and chewed up the celery into its watery, stringy fibers and she tried to believe that everything was going to be fine. She swallowed the tasteless celery mash and took another stick.

Why is this night different from other nights? The question seeped into Gray's mind and made her ache in memory of last Passover.

Last Passover, when she had to give up her participation in the Seder.

Last Passover, when Robby had been allowed to ask the Four Questions at the table.

"Robby is seven. He's a big boy, Gray." Her father bent and hugged her. "I know it's hard to give up something you love," he said quietly. "But that's what gives your gesture meaning."

She had nodded her head in agreement, although her mouth set in a stubborn line. The Four Questions of the Haggadah was her favorite part of Passover. Already that night had been too different from other nights. Her mother had been at her most feeble, hardly able to stay awake, and the whole house looked and smelled funny. That was because earlier, Mrs. Caplan and her daughter, Jennifer, had come over to scour and scrub down the kitchen.

Gray had overheard them talking, complaining lightly.

"What a lot of work!" Mrs. Caplan harrumphed.

"Too much," agreed Jennifer. "We'll have to scrape it clean."

"Well, she can't be blamed. So sick."

They had attacked the kitchen, using bleach and ammonia they had brought, even going over the stove and windowsills with Q-Tips. All for the worst Passover ever. Gray's mother had not even been awake for most of the reading obligations. Her chin sank into her neck or pitched wildly from side to side like a boat at sea, her sleep trance a not-death that scared them.

Gray had watched her mother in silence. She had sat with the bitter taste of her own private questions filling her mouth.

Aren't you ever going to get better, Mom?

Why don't you just try harder, Mom?

Why did this mistake have to happen to you, Mom?

What are the rules if you die, Mom?

Robby had not messed up the Questions. His childish voice was slow and brave. When he finished, Gray squeezed his knee under the table and smiled at him. She did not feel toward Robby what Caitlin felt toward Ty. Gray loved her younger brother intensely. Loved him right from the moment she'd seen his squashed, angry newborn face and her father had said, "Gray, say hello to the newest member of our family!"

She set the example, and Robby loved her back. It was always with disbelief that Gray witnessed Caitlin and Ty's nonstop fighting. There was no place in Gray's house for bites or scratches or hair-pulling or tattle-telling or wet willies or Indian burns or elbow slaps or dead legs or, afterward, forced, fake apologizing with crossed fingers while Mrs. Donnelley said, "See? If you didn't fight, you wouldn't have to make up!"

Drew had tried to hurt her by saying that she was adopted. He tried to hurt her by saying that she was not really Gray Rosenfeld, not really Jewish, not really meant to be part of her own family.

He tried to hurt me with his mean wolf smile but my mom and dad told me about people like Drew Doe and I was Chosen not once but twice.

Gray knew who she was when she stood in her family.

With her friends, it was a different story.

"The popular group has two leaders and all the rest are followers," Annie Dearborne had proclaimed during that time when she and Gray were friends. "Martha is the first leader, Leticia is the second leader, and whoever they pick is who gets to be cool."

"No," Gray disagreed. "It's not like that. Different people are leaders at different times."

"Leaders are always leaders," said Annie matter-of-factly, "and followers are always followers."

Gray had shaken her head. No no no.

Deep inside, though, Gray knew Martha was the leader of a group Gray was hanging on to by the fraying thread of her friendship with Caitlin. A friendship worn bare of what it used to be, now that Kristy took up all of Caitlin's attention, now that anything Gray and Caitlin had shared in common had slipped away long ago. Gray suspected that Caitlin stayed nice to her only because of their moms, or because of what had happened to Gray's mom, but it wasn't enough. Pity would not keep her in the Lucky Seven. She knew that.

Being friends with Annie Dearborne was almost as good as being in the Seven. Annie was loyal. Annie was a girl who whispered if your zipper was down instead of pointing and yelling it out like Martha. Annie was a girl who wouldn't blab to others if she caught you crying in the bathroom, the way Zoë had. Annie would not make faces if your sleeping bag looked wrong. Gray valued loyalty, too, but that quality never seemed very important to her other friends.

The moon broke through a cloud and shone into the kitchen. Gray stood up and moved to the sink. Sometimes the moon had a blue cast and other nights it was tinged orange, as if its core burned with lava. Tonight it was creamy yellow white, like a cheesecake that was the tiniest bit lopsided. Ms. Calvillo had told them in science class today that by Saturday night, the moon would be full.

"So remember to look up at the sky," Ms. Calvillo had said.

Gray thought she remembered having read a story about how a moon, if looked into directly, made people go crazy. She made herself look into the moon's single open eye. She might need to be a little bit crazy tonight. A good kind of crazy. A brave kind.

From another part of the house, voices rose. Drew and Katrina were arguing about something. Gray could not make sense of the words. Her heart began to beat quickly again. She did not feel brave.

She continued to chew her celery and stare into the moon, one wise yellowish eye in the darkness, until the voices grew too loud to ignore.

Gray found them both in the bedroom. Katrina sat in the inflatable chair. Drew was standing over her. In one hand, he held Katrina's coat bunched at the collar like a garbage bag. When he heard Gray at the door, he turned.

"You see what she did?" Drew asked. His face was angry, purpling. He shook the coat at Gray. "You see what she did? Ask her what she did! Ask her what she did!"

Gray caught Katrina's eye. Katrina did not appear to be frightened. She made a dazed half-grab for the coat. Drew stepped back and held it away from her.

"Katrina, what did you do?" Gray asked obediently.

"She took all the money. Our money!" Drew burst out before Kat could answer. "She took it and she used it to buy this ridiculous—coat!"

"It's a pretty coat," said Kat in her foggy, girly way. "It was for my party."

"Ask her how are we gonna get out of here with no money, no identification?"

Gray thought she did not need to ask that. "Katrina, can't you return the coat?" she asked instead. "And get the money back?"

"She can't prance back into that store!" Drew spat. "They'll be waiting for her!"

Waiting for her. Did that mean Katrina was missing? Did that mean people were searching for her? If so, it was good news, Gray thought. If people were searching for Katrina, then they would find Gray, too. Gray would be a bonus person.

"I said I was sorry. I wish you wouldn't shout." Katrina made another reach. Drew dropped the coat on the floor and kicked it across to her. "*You* told me you were going to have a party for me," Katrina pleaded. "*You* were the one who changed the rules."

"They're gonna come by looking for the money, and then what do we do? Then what do we do?"

Neither Drew nor Katrina was paying attention to Gray anymore. They were hardly paying attention to each other. There was no use talking to them. They were locked up in the enchanted spell of their own strange world.

She left them there. Light-footed, she walked down the hall and through the front door, into the icy night.

Whatever was going on between Drew and Kat, one thing was for certain. Gray was not in the middle of their problems. She was an extra. She was a tacked-on, last-minute problem.

The night filled the outline of her and colored her over. It wrapped and disguised everything, the shapes of the trees and the house and the distance. Gray stared at the cheesecake moon. It was late. Bedtime.

When she got back home, the first person she would call would be Annie Dearborne. Maybe she would invite Annie to her house for a sleepover. Annie would not care that Gray wrecked Caitlin's party. Annie would listen to Gray's story and ask, "Weren't you scared?" And Gray would answer, "Yes! Yes! I was terrified! I thought they were killers!"

How scared was she, honestly? On a scale of one to ten? Strength seemed to be draining out of her. Her legs felt jellied and boneless, not solid enough to keep her upright. Everything was too confusing. Noise was filling her from the inside.

On a scale of one to ten, maybe a seven.

If she screamed, if anything bad happened, nobody would hear her. Nobody would know.

Maybe an eight.

From inside the house, voices continued. Drew and Katrina had moved into the living room. ". . . have to pick up that little kid," Drew was saying.

Gray opened her mouth and made the scream happen. She screamed so loud and long that soon it stopped being a scream and bloomed and blossomed into something else that might carry on forever. And then it seemed to her as if the scream never had been inside her, after all, but was always outside. She made the noise go on and on, expanding outward, taking up all the air and space until it was as big as the night itself.

Leticia

"Gray, are you out there? Gray, speak to us!"

They had all joined hands in a chain around Gray's sleeping bag, which sat in the middle of them like an upright log. The flashlight was balanced on top, pooling a spotlight onto the ceiling. Leticia linked herself between Kristy and Caitlin so that she would not have to touch Martha's hands.

Martha glared hard at Leticia. No matter how fiercely Leticia stared back, she could not mirror the meanness in Martha's eyes. Double-mean now, since Leticia had crumpled up Martha's last friendship valentine—that dumb lie-cheat that Leticia had won the dance contest.

I can do this, Leticia told herself. I can go up against Martha. People will side with me. Everyone resents Martha for one thing or another.

"Gray, do you hear me?" intoned Zoë. "Gray! Speak through one of us if you can."

Zoë was too much, sometimes. Always pushing for everyone to believe in her. She was doing a good job, though. She was scary. Involuntarily, a shudder rippled across Leticia's shoulders, and she noticed that Caitlin's hand was clammy in her own.

"Good acting, Zoë," said Martha.

"Shh! Let her concentrate," said Caitlin.

"Oh, tell us!" Zoë implored. "Tell us where you are, Gray!"

"Tomorrow morning," said Martha in a regular speaking voice as if there were no séance happening, "when the police find Gray walking down some road, lost, whatever, and then she hears that we were doing these things, I bet she'll tell on us to our par—"

"Gray, I-I-I hear y-you!" Zoë's voice was stuttering and unnatural.

Kristy gasped.

"Do you really?" whispered Caitlin. "Honest?"

Zoë's head listed and lolled and drooped over her neck. "Shhh. She is t-t-telling me." Her mouth fell slack, listening. "She's telling me that she's l-locked in a very small space," Zoë whispered. "Like a c-cave."

"A coffin, maybe?" breathed Kristy.

Zoë's eyes blinked and rolled. "She says she is s-safe here? She wants us not to w-worry about her?"

"Oooh, where is it?" asked Martha sarcastically. "Get directions, if you know so much."

Leticia could sense that Caitlin and Kristy were rapt, listening. "She is saying do not be fr-frightened for her," Zoë continued. " 'Do not fear me! Have no f-fear!' is what she says. Oh!" Zoë dropped Caitlin's and Martha's hands to shade her eyes.

"What is it?" Caitlin leaned toward Zoë and cupped her shoulder. "Are you okay?"

"I'm okay. It's just—" Zoë exhaled raggedly. "Well, if you want to know, but you have to promise not to tell? Lots of people in my family have ESP. I grew up around it. It wasn't till now that I was sure, but I guess I have the Sight, too!" She pledged her hand to her heart and seemed to collapse against it.

"Oh, brother," said Martha. "I wonder if Fielding gives out a Best Psychic prize."

Leticia held back the laughter that burbled in her throat. Any other time, Leticia thought, either she or Martha would have caught the other's eye with a sly wink, and they would have burst out laughing over Zoë and her dramatics.

I'm going to miss being friends with Martha, she realized. In spite of everything. I'll miss laughing with her.

"My ESP is a secret, Martha," said Zoë stiffly. "So don't spread it around."

"Zoë, you should tell the police about this cave vision of yours," said Martha. "If you don't, I think someone else should. Unless, of course, you're making it all up."

Now Leticia caught Martha's eye in a different way. "Why

would Zoë make up having ESP, and why would you go blab about it, if it's a secret?" she asked lightly. "Why are you always going against people who are supposed to be your friends?"

Martha lifted her chin into another stare-off. "Actually, Luh-tee-sha," she answered, biting off each syllable of Leticia's name as if it were some bitter food, "I know for a *fact* that Zoë is faking."

Leticia rolled her eyes. "Really? And what makes you so smart?" But she could sense all eyes on Martha now.

"Because I've got some real information about what might have happened to Gray. Information that, unlike Zoë's, is one hundred percent true. If I tell it, though, you all have to promise not to inform anybody outside the group. Because it's confidential." Martha looked around the circle. "Promise?"

"Promise," said Caitlin and Kristy in unison.

"Promise," mumbled Zoë.

"Promise," said Leticia. Inside she fumed. All the attention had turned to Martha as if she were a magic lantern. Just the way she liked it.

"Okay. When I went to get the mail for Caitlin's mom this afternoon," Martha began, speaking slowly so that nobody missed a word, "I saw a lady at the end of the driveway. Her hair was long and tied back with a scarf, and she was wearing a dress and this ugly coat with feathers hanging off it. And she was standing near a dark green or blue car that I think was hers. She came up to me and she asked me who was having a party. She talked like a preschooler. She was weird."

"Oh my gosh." Kristy giggled nervously.

"You didn't give out my name, did you?" asked Caitlin. "You didn't say who lived here or anything, right?"

"Of course not," said Martha. "I didn't say anything to her. I'm not stupid."

Leticia shook her head. "If that's true you saw a stranger lurking around here," she said, "you should have told the police. Not us."

Martha breathed a patient sigh. "Obviously," she said, "I already told the police. In private, while you all were watching the movie. And they said don't tell the other girls because it's confidential. Pluswise, they thought you-all might get scared. See, I was trying to protect you." She turned to Zoë, cold-eyed and disdainful. "That's why I think it's funny that you *conveniently* decide to have ESP, but you *unfortunately* can't recall that lady." She yawned. "But whatever. Now you know. The real truth."

In the silence that followed, Leticia could feel Zoë's embarrassment.

"Yeah, Zoë. You were faking your ESP, weren't you?" Caitlin sniffed. "Faker."

"Yeah, faker," whispered Kristy. "Faker faker, credit taker."

"ESP is for real!" Zoë hissed. "It's not something to wish for. The Sight is a curse."

"A fake curse," said Martha.

"Enough, you guys." Leticia moved toward her sleeping bag. "If the police have a suspect, then they're probably close to finding Gray. By the time we wake up tomorrow morning, she'll be back with us. Anyhow, my cousin Bethany is psychic, and she can predict if it's a girl or boy on any pregnant lady. So *I* believe you, Zoë. Since you always figure out a lot of stuff before anyone else."

Leticia's eyes held Zoë's a moment.

"Thanks, Leticia," said Zoë.

Alone, staring at the ceiling, listening to the others settle down around her, frustration surged in Leticia's brain. Somehow, Martha had turned the séance to her own advantage. Somehow, she had pulled ahead of the rest of them and shown herself to be the leader again.

Was that story about the lady even true?

Martha's a quick thinker, thought Leticia. But so am I. And Martha shouldn't have been mean to Zoë, mocking her like that. Just because Gray isn't around to pick on tonight doesn't mean Martha should transfer her bullying to the next easiest target.

Leticia thought through her plan. Because it was a plan,

yes, it was. She saw that now. She was making a plan to split apart from Martha, and to split up the Lucky Seven, permanently.

She also realized that no matter how she sliced the group, she needed Zoë. Although Zoë was not a leader, she was always a winner. Zoë would always be Fielding's class president, Student Government president, swim team captain, and the girl most likely to win Fielding's end-of-year Gold Blazer. Best Everything of Everything, that was Zoë on record.

Off record, Zoë pushed too hard, she was too know-it-all. But if Leticia and Zoë were a team, Leticia could guide her. They would be the right combination of finesse and brains, and everyone else would follow them into a new and improved, cooler Lucky Seven. Only it would be another lucky number.

What she needed to do was to talk to Zoë. She would say the right things. She would win Zoë over.

I can do this, Leticia reassured herself. I had what it took to get in this group. That means I have what it takes to become the leader of it. I can turn the Lucky Seven into whatever I want it to be.

She yawned. She was sleepy. Stressed-out, Celeste would say. But if anything good already had happened tonight, it was that Leticia had proven to the others that Martha Van Riet was not as strong as everyone thought she was. That in fact, Martha could be teased, ganged up on, made fun of, and ignored just like everybody else.

She, Leticia, had been the one to show the others. She had torn down some of Martha's supposed strength. That had to count for something.

Didn't it?

Martha

Martha was in a fog, twitching inside thoughts that were almost like dreams. She knew she had to stay awake the longest so that she could sneak out and report her secret to the police for real. Dread constricted her stomach. She had held on to this stupid secret too long, and it had turned big and ugly and was squeezing her from the inside. Telling the others had been right for the moment, but had not shrunk it. In fact, now the secret was bigger. Now she had to let it go. Every minute she waited only made everything worse. She wished she had never seen that lady.

Why couldn't the secret just disappear?

She heard the clock chime and chime and chime. It must be midnight, she thought. She heard voices from the study, and the crackle of the police transistor radios, but Gray's disappearance and all of its chaos seemed far away.

If only she could put off telling until tomorrow. Uneasily, she drifted.

Light cut Martha's eyes and startled her. Had she dozed off? She shielded an arm.

"Ouch!" she hissed. "Turn that off!"

"Shh!"

Who was it? Martha propped up on her elbows, reached out, and knocked the hand that held the flashlight, jumping the light away.

"Whossat?" she whispered. She squinted. Leticia? Yes! A trickle of hope ran through her. Was this a friendly visit? She kept her voice neutral. "Teesh. What do you want?"

"I want to tell you what Celeste said."

"Celeste?" Martha's pulse jumped against reason. Was Leticia inviting her to come along on her visit to Celeste's college this spring? Martha knew a trip had been planned. "What about Celeste? What did she say?"

"It's a joke she told me." Leticia aimed the light, vicious and bright, into Martha's eyes again.

No, this was not a friendly visit.

"Well, it better be funny," said Martha, shifting herself into shadow. "Funny enough to wake me up for."

"Celeste said your freckles show up on the outside of you to let other people know how you're rotten inside. Like spots on bad fruit, like on apples and bananas."

Under the sleeping bag, Martha clamped her hands together, forcing herself not to touch her face. She could feel the sizzle of each freckle on her skin. She never should have told

Leticia how much she hated her freckles. She never should have told Leticia a lot of things.

"Like worms ate through you!" Leticia was laughing softly, hee hee.

She's trying to scare me, Martha thought, wide-awake now and fully alert. Like when we crank-called Ralph Dewey that time. "If this is really about the science test, Leticia, you need to get over it," she said. "If you'd been smart enough to get an A plus, too, I bet you wouldn't be so bent out of shape."

In the pause that followed, Martha sensed that Leticia was considering this. "Cheating on tests is only one of the ways you don't play fair," said Leticia.

"Speaking of unfair." Martha's hand snapped out like a jackknife. It caught and wrenched the flashlight out of Leticia's grip and turned it off. "I've got a joke for you. Maybe you won't think it's so funny, but here it is. I'm dropping you out of my group." She laughed, too, hee hee, parroting Leticia. "I see what you've been doing tonight. But I've gone to Fielding since kindergarten and I know every single girl better than you do. Everyone has been way better and longer friends with me than they have with you."

"Longer doesn't mean better."

"I could get anyone to go against you."

"You can't do anything. It's not *your* group."

Martha was silent. Was that true? She could hardly imagine the Lucky Seven without herself at its center.

"But you're right about one thing," said Leticia. "Which is that I don't want to be part of any group that you're in."

No no no, thought Martha, confused. Leticia was joking, right? She didn't really want out, did she? What kind of group would the Lucky Seven be without Leticia? Martha scrambled for the right words, the words to pull Leticia back on her side without actually having to admit that she was worried or scared or sorry for what she had done. Which she was, but the only thing worse than the pain of these feelings would be to acknowledge them.

"Teesh, we used to be friends." Martha despised herself for the yearning that curled up in her voice. "I wouldn't mind going back to being friends with you if you admitted how much of a jerk you've been tonight."

Please, Martha thought wildly in the silence that followed. Please stay friends with me. She'd never had a real best friend before Leticia, and she couldn't believe it was already over. It had been so fun! As if parts of them had disintegrated and recombined into a single, perfect person. It was a better best-friendship than Caitlin and Kristy's. It was a better best-friendship than anyone else's. And now it was over. Now Leticia had knifed herself apart from Martha, and she had turned into somebody completely different, a stranger Martha hardly knew.

"Good night," said Leticia. In the darkness, the quiet expanded between them, forcing their distance.

"You're such a loser," said Martha finally. "I was only joking

I'm bored of you, anyway, if you want to know the honest truth."

"Good night," said Leticia again.

Martha listened to the rustling as Leticia crawled back to her sleeping bag.

Alone, she waited. Waited for Leticia to come back for the flashlight. Waited for Leticia to come back and tell her she was playing a game. She was so hot, burning up. Her breath sounded loud, as if she were alone in a tunnel. She smelled the scrubbed flower scent of her nightshirt and the soapy heat of her skin underneath. Everything seemed extra-real. She tried to pretend that she was made out of stone. Unmoving, unfeeling. But her eyes watered anyway, and when she closed them, she saw hot pink and yellow jagged lights.

Leticia was not coming back.

It felt bad now, but it wouldn't tomorrow, Martha promised herself. Tomorrow, she would start to hatch some plans against Leticia. Good plans that would show once and for all who was the real leader. Only she wished she could do something mean against Leticia right this minute. Some kind of revenge that would get the others on her side by morning.

She had to go to the police now, she had to tell, and yet the weight of the secret kept her pinned in place, helpless.

How had this night slipped so far out of her grasp?

Gray

Drew's hand smelled bad, like underneath a car, like gasoline. The hand had stopped her voice. Gray writhed and wriggled to get free.

"What are you doing?" With the force of his fingers, Drew squeezed and shook her head back and forth. "What's the big idea, screaming your head off like that?"

"*Mrrmmmp!*" Gray swatted and pried at Drew's fingers, sealed heavy as a guard bar in a carnival ride. Dizzying, sickening. Nothing budged. She jumped up and down.

"Look, kid, I'll take my hand away if you promise not to scream again!"

She nodded her head yes, yes, yes. Drew took off his hand and Gray did not scream. She was finished with screaming, for now.

"Okay," said Drew. He was too close, intimidating her with his chunky self. "You, Kat, me. We all gotta leave. My friends are coming back any minute, and they'll want money for this stuff they're delivering. But *poof!* The money magically turned into a coat, right?" His laugh was tight with displeasure. He seemed nervous. His feet shuffled back and forth like a boxer. "So, for my next trick, I will make myself disappear. And you're coming with us."

Gray quaked. "Can't I stay here? In the house?"

"Yeah, right. Last thing I want is some blabbermouth little girl putting the whole state force on Kat's tail."

"I won't talk. Promise, cross my heart." Gray crossed her heart. Her teeth were chattering from the cold. It would be safer to be inside the house than in the car. She'd hide in the tub, or under the couch maybe. If she got too hungry, she would eat the moldy sandwich and wait for the sun to come up. In the daytime, the answers would come clear.

"Sorry, Gray Rosenfeld. I can't take chances. Look," Drew continued, "it's not like I'll drive you the whole way. I'll drop you somewhere. But you can't be *here.* I can't risk it. Okay?"

Gray nodded.

"I'm going back inside to pull my stuff together. You jump in the car and wait. Kat'll be out in a minute."

"And you'll drop me off at a gas station or something?"

"Yeah yeah yeah."

She moved to the car slowly. Her arms wrapped around her shoulders. It was too cold to be outside with no coat. Was now when she should break for it? But break for where? She was too far away from everything.

Gray opened the car door and slid into the backseat. Of course Drew would drop her off somewhere safe. He had to.

Eventually, Katrina appeared. She was wearing her feather coat and her wig. She waved at Gray and settled into the front passenger seat.

"Katrina, do you remember where you picked me up?" Gray asked. "Do you think you could tell Drew to drop me off close to there?"

Katrina stared straight ahead as if under a hypnotist's trance. "What I like best about cars is the radio. I close my eyes and I listen to the music and imagine I'm in these exotic places, like Fiji."

Gray leaned back in the seat and fumbled with her seat belt. Katrina was so infuriating, like the Mad Hatter at the Wonderland tea party. Only, unlike Gray, Alice never turned into a crybaby. Alice treated the Mad Hatter as if he were a small, silly child. Katrina was like a silly child, too, but in real life, a grown-up acting like a child was scary.

Gray wondered what the other girls were doing now. They were in their sleeping bags. Maybe playing truth or dare, or would you rather?

Would you rather eat five live caterpillars or would you rather ride the school bus naked? Would you rather live in a sewer or would you rather be blind in one eye? Would you rather have warts or pimples? Would you rather have one missing finger or two missing toes?

The Lucky Seven would play this game until their stomachs were sore from laughing. But it was so funny to imagine even a single terrible thing actually happening to them. As if anybody would really go blind! Or get warts! Ridiculous!

Would you rather be kidnapped by strangers, or would you rather have your mother die from cancer?

But Gray wasn't really being kidnapped. Her mother wasn't dying, either. She was in remission. And in real life, there was no choice about what bad luck or what mistake you would rather have happen to you. It just happened, and then you would survive it or you would not.

"I think it's really unfair," said Gray, speaking up to Katrina in her most authentic adult voice, "that you picked me up from the Donnelleys' house and you didn't even have a plan to get me back."

"I think it's really unfair that you came along," said Katrina, Mad Hatterishly.

It was no use talking to her. Gray slumped back in her seat and waited.

After another ten minutes, or maybe longer, Drew emerged from the house. He was holding a fresh beer and a paper bag that he tossed in the backseat next to Gray. She peered into it. It was full of clothes.

"Ready for our road trip?" he asked.

Neither of them answered. Drew put the key in the ignition. The car leaped to life.

Gray hooked her thumbs beneath her fastened seat belt and looked out the window, trying to memorize the house, the road, and the trees. As soon as she was dropped off, or got away, or something, she would be able to give good descriptions to her parents and to Mrs. Donnelley.

Poor Mrs. Donnelley. She might be mad at Gray for a long time, for ruining her daughter's party. Maybe Gray could take Mrs. Donnelley one of her mother's "get well soon" gifts as an apology. Some soap or a scented candle or slippers. Mrs. Donnelley would probably appreciate a thoughtful present.

Katrina was asleep. Her seat was cranked back all the way and her seat belt was unfastened. Gray waited for Drew to tell Katrina to buckle up, but he didn't. He switched to his high beams. The lights shone onto a wall of woods.

Katrina yawned and turned her cheek. Reflected light caught the sparkle in her face. With her arm thrown in a long arc over her head, she looked like one of Caitlin's fairy paintings.

Maybe that's why I followed Katrina in the first place that's how bad I want something magical—something better to believe in?

Watching Katrina sleep, Gray remembered how she used to watch her mother as she slept in her hospital bed. The veins of her mother's eyelids were webbed dark in her pale skin, like the mold swirls in blue cheese. Gray would stare at her mother and wonder if she would ever wake up.

Drew belched, interrupting her thoughts. Gray leaned up toward the driver's side. "Drew? Drew? You're not supposed to drink and drive." Her voice was just above a whisper.

"Stuff it, Gray Rosenfeld. It's only a beer."

Gray sat back.

"A beer is hardly even alcohol," said Drew after another slurp.

Gray knew that was not true. She was too nervous to argue more.

Tears flooded her eyes again.

She should argue more. Here was the place where she should draw on any strength that might be buried inside her. Here was the place where the brave girl escaped from the car, got on the bike, the plane, the train, put out the fire, saved the school, the town, the dog, the land, yelled at the Bad Person, pointed to the Good Person, explained why the rules were wrong, and forced the tiny change that always made Gray wonder, *Could I do that? Is there enough bravery inside me to do this one small strong thing that makes a difference?*

And always Gray wanted to believe *Yes! Yes! Yes!*

Even though she doubted it.

Zoë

Before she fell asleep, Zoë said a prayer, since Mrs. Donnelley had told them to.

She prayed: Please, God, let me fall into a psychic sleep and in my dream I will be the one to see where Gray is and then I can rescue her.

Maybe it was God who was supposed to help her win. Zoë figured God was on her side for most things. Like today, He helped her spell *ancillary* right on the English test, and yesterday He helped her find her green notebook. God granted Zoë plenty of luck when she asked for it, although He helped Shelton more.

If her dream gave her some clues to find Gray, then Zoë would get more attention than Shelton, more attention than anyone at Fielding, and maybe even in the whole town.

Now she had pushed herself into a dream that was not quite

going her way. Swimming through murk, she had found Gray, who was stuck underwater in a dark cave, so it was lucky that Zoë could breathe underwater. The problem was that Gray was screaming and ruining Zoë's rescue.

"I've got you! I've got you!" Too late, Zoë realized the dream had turned nightmarish, because she didn't have Gray. No, in fact, it was just the opposite—Gray was trying to drag Zoë down into the cave.

Zoë's eyes snapped open. Her heart was beating fast. Sweat was sticking to the back of her T-shirt. What time was it? How long had she been sleeping? She listened to the room. Caitlin was snoring, but otherwise the room was quiet. Outside Caitlin's room, down the hall, the house was awake with muffled goings-on, but none of the noise suggested that Gray had returned.

"Hey," Leticia, on her side, whispered so quietly, Zoë could hardly hear her. "Are you okay?"

"I was having a nightmare," Zoë whispered back. She was still breathing hard. She flattened a hand to her heart.

"You were talking in your sleep. You seemed mad."

"I was?" Zoë yawned. Had Leticia been sleeping next to her before, or had she moved places?

"Yeah, and I wondered if it was because of the science test."

The science test? What was Leticia talking about? "Well, I think I got an A plus," said Zoë, trying to keep her voice nonchalant. It was unc to brag about grades.

"Well, guess what? Martha got an A plus, too," whispered Leticia.

"Nuh-uh. Martha never gets A's."

"Not on her own. When she asked to copy off me. I said no, so she went and sat behind you. To cheat off *you.* I thought you knew about it."

Zoë frowned. She hadn't known. It irritated her to think of Martha copying her test. Without cheat permission, even. But she did not want Leticia to think she cared more than she did. "It's no big deal, I guess. We're friends."

"Oh. I thought you two were in a fight about it. But I guess it must be about something else."

"No, no—we're not fighting, Martha and me. Why would you think that?"

"It's just . . ." Leticia turned on her side to face Zoë. Her breath smelled like bubble-gum toothpaste. "Just that Martha's been especially on your case tonight. Right from saying you didn't win Enchanted Castle when we all knew you did. Then telling you that you don't have ESP. She makes you out to be such a loser."

"You think? Do other people think that?"

"Oh, I don't know. . . . Listen, I'm sorry," said Leticia. "I guess I shouldn't have said anything."

"No," said Zoë. "I'm glad you did." Her mind wound back through the night. Now that she thought about it, Martha had been pretty mean. Worse than usual? And was Leticia only saying this because she and Martha were in a fight?

"You're sure she got an A plus?"

"Positive."

"And it was from cheating off me?"

"Positive."

"Huh." Zoë gnawed the edge of skin around what was left of her thumbnail. "Um, Teesh? Do you also think Martha made that stuff up, about the lady? Because I really do believe my ESP was right. About the caves."

"I don't know. I was thinking, though. Probably we should go to the police and tell them what Martha told us." Leticia's voice was the barest whisper. "Just to double-check. Don't you think?"

"Except that it might get Martha in trouble," said Zoë. "I mean, what if she really made it all up? As a prank or whatever."

"See, that's how we'd find out for sure," said Leticia. "If she was telling the truth or not. Because she couldn't lie to the police."

"It seems kind of a big deal, going to the police."

"So what? C'mon. It'd be like a dare."

Zoë rolled on her back. So what? "Maybe. In a few minutes," she said. "Let's make sure everyone is asleep."

"Hey, I wanted to ask you something." Leticia's whisper

lifted, lightened. “In a couple of weeks, my parents and I are going to visit Celeste at her college. They said I could bring one friend, anyone I wanted. But just one, you know.” She paused. “Maybe you’d want to come?”

“Yeah, that’d be cool.” In the dark, Zoë smiled and nodded. She knew, all right.

Martha

Martha had strained to hear what Leticia and Zoë were whispering about. Now it seemed that they had fallen asleep. Martha could predict what was going to happen, though, and it infuriated her. Tomorrow morning, there would be two pairs. Caitlin and Kristy, Leticia and Zoë.

Martha despised the image of herself at breakfast the next morning, being called *Meow,* being laughed at or frozen out, plus in trouble with the Rosenfelds and Donnelleys and the police.

She shouldn't have been so hard on Zoë.

She tried to put her secret out of her mind. Maybe she had just imagined it. She wished something else would happen. Something to distract everyone. Something to shake things up.

The idea opened her eyes. A hush of balanced breathing, like a soft ocean, washed in and out around her, its calm broken by the hovercraft of Caitlin snoring in her bed above.

All clear.

She slithered out of her sleeping bag, then groped in the dark for her overnight bag. Fumblingly, she retrieved her Kleenex-wrapped mothball and her other bag of candy and chocolate hearts. She tiptoed into the bathroom, shut and locked the door, and snapped on the light, which made her squint. After she stopped squinting, she looked at herself in the mirror and touched her face gently.

"My freckles are where I'm bulletproofed," Martha whispered to her face. It was a silly thing she used to tell kids back in kindergarten if any of them dared to make fun of her freckles. Only tonight she didn't feel bulletproofed. Tonight, she felt as if she had been shot with a thousand darts.

She dropped, cross-legged, on the bath mat. Carefully, she used the edge of her fingernail to push into the chocolate heart. She made a small dent that slowly cleaved into two perfect halves. She licked out liquid chocolate. Then she fit the mothball into the heart, neat as a toy surprise, and she closed it up.

She tiptoed out of the bathroom, out of Caitlin's room, closing the bedroom door quietly behind her. She tiptoed past the den that rumbled with voices of the grown-ups.

A fresh pot of coffee had been brewed in the pantry and the lights were on in the kitchen. She would have to be quick and careful.

Bumpo was in his basket bed. He raised his head to watch her. She paused.

Maybe this was not such a good idea after all.

But if she could make Bumpo sick, Martha reasoned, then she could rescue him. She would call for help from Topher. Best of all, they would blame Leticia, for feeding Bumpo chocolate earlier. And when she finally told about the lady, there would be potentially two people in trouble tonight instead of just herself.

A perfect plan. She dared herself to try. She was good at dares.

"Here, boy," Martha coaxed. She slid to her knees on the floor next to the dog basket. She scratched Bumpo's ears and under his collar, the way he liked it. "I've got a treat for you."

One single mothball would not really hurt him, Martha figured. Her parents were always cautioning about the dangers of this and that, but experience had taught her that nothing was ever as bad as they warned. The mothball would only make him sick. Sick enough to help her.

She held the chocolate heart to Bumpo's mouth. At first, she thought he wouldn't eat it. His pink tongue lolled and licked the chocolate heart absently.

"Come on, boy! Please!"

Bumpo sighed, licked the candy again, then took it between his teeth as if to please her. The mothball crunched in his teeth. He gulped it down and immediately started to cough. An awful hacking sound from deep in his throat.

Martha stood. "It's okay, boy," she told him.

She spun on her heel and ran downstairs to the family room.

“What are you doing down here?” asked Topher.

“I went down to get some juice, and I found Bumpo. I think he’s sick.”

Topher used the remote to snap off the television. He stood and followed Martha up the stairs.

“Dude! What happened?” He pointed to the puddle. “What did he barf up?”

Together, they inspected it. “I think that’s chocolate,” said Martha. “One of our friends was feeding him chocolate hearts earlier tonight. Leticia Watkins.”

Bumpo stared at Topher and whined slightly. Then gave a giant, shuddering, teeth-baring yawn. Topher dropped on all fours to check Bumpo.

“It smells like something else,” he said. He sat up on his heels and propped open Bumpo’s eye to inspect, as if he were a veterinarian. “Poor ole guy. Poor ole Bumpo. Getting long in the tooth, as they say.” Topher scratched and rubbed Bumpo, who whined and panted. “You want some water, boy?”

“And I want something to drink, too.” She could stretch out her time with Topher a little longer. And maybe if she explained about the lady to him first, he would be so excited to break this news to the police that she would not get in as much trouble.

“Let me take care of the dog first.” Topher filled the water bowl and set it in front of Bumpo, who began to slurp it down greedily.

"Poor Bumpo," she said. "Probably Leticia didn't know any better."

"There's lemonade and Cranapple and diet sodas. Or I'll microwave you some Ovaltine, if you want. That's what I'm gonna have," said Topher, moving to open a cupboard. "I should have known you'd be bopping around—Martha, right? Little Grasshopper! You've been jumping out of my sight all night. All the other kids are sleeping?"

"Yeah. The other kids." She leaned against the counter. When Topher said kids, did he think Martha was a kid, too? She wondered if Topher thought she was cute. She wondered if she could get him to believe she was, even if he didn't think so now.

"I'd like Ovaltine, too," she said, since it would take the longest to make.

"Coming up." Topher pulled down two mugs and the Ovaltine. He dropped three spoonfuls into each mug and filled them both with milk and placed them in the microwave. While he set the timer, Martha looked at Bumpo's throw-up. She could not tell if the mothball was in it, so maybe it was still in Bumpo. Would he still be sick tomorrow? He didn't look too bad. Definitely not bad enough to get Leticia in trouble.

She cleared her throat. "I've been trying to get a reading on Gray," she told Topher. "In my family, a lot of us have ESP."

"Is that right?"

Martha thought she saw Topher smirk. It made her feel

extra small and freckly. Quickly, she added, "Some people don't believe in it. I don't even know if I do, either, but I guess I'm getting worried about Gray."

Topher's face turned serious. "At school, we're studying all that stuff in the class I'm taking. Psychology. Pretty strange. I wish I didn't know as much as I do. About human nature and all."

"Wow. You must be really smart," said Martha.

"No, not . . . I mean, I get by." Topher rubbed his eyes. "My grades would be way better if I studied, put some effort in."

"Me, too," Martha agreed.

"Tell you a secret," Topher said. "You look like the type who can handle a secret, and it'll be news by tomorrow, anyway."

"What?"

"They think Gray got picked up. Abducted, you know?"

"Abducted." Martha took a breath. The shame of the secret flooded through her.

"Mmm-hmm." Topher nodded. "No signs of forced entry or struggle. But there's no sign of her, either. A kid who runs off gets sighted along the way. Cops have got nothing. So far, at least."

"Gosh," she said. "That's scary."

"She might have even let him in, is what they're thinking."

"Into the house?"

"Yep." Suddenly, Topher jogged a couple of steps to the

back door and checked the lock. He returned, grinning sheepishly. "Sorry. Paranoid. But it's wild to think, how you can buy a nice house in a nice neighborhood, and you can lock the doors, set the alarms, buy the big dog, everything, and still some kind of evil might find its way into your house. You're never safe enough, you know? It's never zero risk. Freaks me out."

Martha suddenly felt dizzy. She slid onto one of the counter stools. "Me, too."

The timer binged. Topher took the mugs out of the microwave and handed one to Martha. "Careful. Hot."

She took the mug. "Thanks."

"Sure." Topher yawned. "Not much sleep going on in this house tonight. There's a night patrol, but the real deal starts at the crack of dawn. Then they're gonna start a helicopter search."

"Helicopters!" Nobody ever paid this much attention to Mouse before.

"But know what? I have this hunch a phone call will come in, and it'll be somebody who saw something and then we'll sniff out a clue. There's always a clue. There's always one person who remembers something. I mean, if she was taken. Somebody sees something, right? A car, a creepy dude . . . well, not to scare you."

Martha raised her mug to hide her face. "I'm not scared." In her mind, she saw the lady again, her glittering eyes and yanked-back smile, wrapped in that feather coat.

She would tell the secret as soon as she was finished with her drink. Even though she was definitely getting in trouble for it. Helicopters were serious. She took another tiny sip of Ovaltine.

Bumpo shuddered and whined. His tail thumped the floor and his eyebrows knit as he looked at Martha and then Topher reproachfully.

Martha shook her head. "I told Leticia a million times not to give Bumpo chocolate."

Upstairs, something was going on. Was that Zoë's voice? And now footsteps were running up and down the hall, and people were speaking, moving with new energy. Mrs. Donnelley suddenly called down, loud and demanding. "Topher? Is Martha Van Riet downstairs? We need her upstairs. Now!"

"Yeah, yeah. She's down here. We'll be right up." Topher made a face. "Guess they discovered your escape hatch, prisoner. Back to the pen, huh?"

Martha shrugged her shoulders. She could not seem to find enough air to breathe. Her secret was out. Zoë had beaten her to it. Zoë, of course, who always had to win everything.

"Now!" Mrs. Donnelley's voice cried. "In the study!"

Martha was sick from the secret, anyway. Relieved, even,

that it no longer belonged to her. She set her mug on the counter.

"I'm ready," she said. "I'm finished."

"Yep." Topher knelt down to give Bumpo one last pat. "All right, doggy, okay, ole boy," he said. "You're gonna be okay. Jeez, Bumpo. I wonder what got into you?"

Gray

She pressed her head against the car window and watched the broken white lines on the road. They moved so fast, white black white black white black. Sometimes she saw the white and the black separated and sometimes she saw the blur, depending on how she watched.

She wondered where they were going.

What was out in the movable dark? Past her house and her friends' houses on the roads close by and past Knightworthy Avenue and past Fielding Academy.

"You can drop me off here," she said.

Now they were getting onto a ramp. Now they were on the highway.

"You can drop me off here," she said again.

Gray felt too-scared again. She was crying softly, hoping that something better would happen to her. Hoping that her parents would pull up out of nowhere or that the car would get a flat tire or that she would wake up from this terrible dream.

She wondered what happened to girls when they got kidnapped by kidnappers who hadn't planned on taking them.

Because wasn't she getting kidnapped, even if it was an accident?

Katrina was singing a soft song along with the radio. Drew was talking to himself under his breath. They were not real grown-ups, Gray thought. They had the bodies of grown-ups but inside they were fragile and see-through to their strange kid selves. None of their rules were right or fixed or understandable.

"Are you going to drop me off anywhere?" she asked again.

"Just calm down and let me think," Drew snapped.

She was not going to get the answer she needed. Maybe she was asking the wrong question. She wished she could think of something wise and calm that would lead the way to a wise, calm decision. All she was good at, though, was crying.

Crying was the best that she could do.

She started to cry. Loud. Her hands pounded on the window. Her breath and fingers marked the glass. "Let me out! Let me out!"

"Shut up! Shut up!" Drew barked. He glanced up at her through the rearview. His eyes drilled into her. "Stop being such a girl!"

Now she was really crying, and it was too hard to stop. Crying might be the best that she could do, and she could cry pretty well. She could cry great.

In the front seat, Katrina started to whimper, copycatting Gray, the way Robby had this morning.

"Shut up, both of you!" Drew yelled. The heel of his hand hit the steering wheel. "I can't concentrate!"

Katrina sniffled and hid her face.

"I can't help it!" Gray screamed. "I can't help it!"

In the next moment, the wheels screeched and the car skidded to the side, guttering into the shoulder of the road, nearly hitting the guardrail, and stopped. Drew slammed open the door.

"Get out!" he yelled.

"Here?" she choked.

"Right here. Here is where you're getting dropped."

"But there's nothing out here."

"It's the end of the road for you," said Drew.

With numb, icy fingers, Gray unhooked her seat belt buckle. Drew hunched over, shoving himself and the seat forward so that Gray could climb out of the car. "But where am I?" she gasped as she stood in the highway. Her breath was convulsing, tearing through her.

"Figure it out yourself, Gray Rosenfeld. I've had enough of dealing with you!" She had to jump out of the way to avoid Drew slamming the car door shut on her.

Outside, stunned, she blinked at her own reflection in the window glass.

There I am same old me.

"Gray!" Katrina yelled. She had unrolled her window and was leaning up and out of it. The wind spiked up the hair around her head like an angry cat. "Get back in the car, Gray! It's too dangerous! Please!" Saying Gray's name out loud seemed to have jolted Katrina from her usual dream state.

Now Katrina held out her hand. "We'll take you to a gas station. It's not safe to be out on the side of the road."

Not safe in the car, not safe on the road. It was a choice between bad ideas. Gray's feet chose for her. Stumbling, she backed off, then turned away from the car and ran headlong into the night.

Behind her, Katrina was yelling Gray's name, on and on, like a siren.

Gray did not turn around. She listened to the sound of her name but still she did not turn. Not even once. She ran until she knew she was far away enough that even if she had looked, she would not be able to see Drew and Katrina again.

Cars whizzed past her and she kept running. Nobody slowed down. Maybe nobody saw her. Her arms and legs chopped and swung, her lungs were fiery with pain, and she could not feel her face from cold. But she trusted herself, and from out of nowhere a wild joy burst through her. Health joy and life joy and escaping joy and running joy and rescuing herself joy.

"Little girl! Little girl! What are you doing?" The car had come out of nowhere to slow down next to her, its automatic window rolling down in one smooth swipe to reveal an older man, maybe around the same age as her dad, who was leaning halfway across the front passenger seat to talk to her. She glanced at him without breaking pace.

"Kid, are you crazy? Do you want to get yourself killed?"

He looks nice too but I don't know this man he might be Safe or not I don't know.

She looked away, waved him on. Too dangerous.

The man muttered something, and then sped ahead of her. She kept running. She could feel herself smile from deep inside, although her face was sore and hurt from crying, although she was freezing, and she wondered if this was her chip-scrap of hope, of bravery, the place inside her that knew maybe things were not going to turn out as bad as they had started.

What was Safety anyhow, but trust in the road she was running on? What was Safety anyhow, but trust in herself? She would run until she saw an exit for a gas station. She would not stop until it was okay to stop.

I know where I am even if I don't right this second I know where I am I'm right here.

On the other side of the guardrail, the woods lay thick and deep. If she had to, she could always jump over the rail, off the road, away from cars, if cars meant danger. She listened to her breath and the slap of her sneakers. She listened to the Safety that had come alive inside her, doing its best to figure things out.

Everything was going to turn out okay. She was making sure of it, she was watching out for herself, she was under her own protection. Even before the noise of the police siren grew deafening and the blunt blue light parted her from the darkness. Even before the squad car pulled close and stopped when she stopped and opened its door to fish her out of the night. Even before, Gray knew that the worst horror of the night was over, the worst of the night lived only in her memory now. And she had escaped it, she had survived it, she was on her way home.